CW01209637

DECRYPTED

FORGOTTEN AGES BOOK TWO

LINDSAY BUROKER

Decrypted

by Lindsay Buroker

Copyright @ Lindsay Buroker 2013
Illustration: Merilliza Chan
Formatting: Deranged Doctor Design

No part of this book may be reproduced, scanned, or distributed in any printed or electronic form without permission. Please do not participate in or encourage piracy of copyrighted materials in violation of the author's rights. Thank you for respecting the hard work of this author.

This is a work of fiction. Names, characters, places, and incidents either are the product of the author's imagination or are used fictitiously, and any resemblance to locales, events, business establishments, or actual persons—living or dead—is entirely coincidental.

Foreword

Thank you, good reader, for picking up another adventure with Rias and Tikaya. They've been up to... Well, you'll find out. Before you jump in, please give me a moment to thank Kendra Highley and Becca Andre, my tireless beta readers. Also, high fives to Glendon Haddix for the cool cover design and Shelley Hollow for the editing (her edits are also cool). Lastly, thank *you* for coming back to Turgonia (and now the Kyatt Islands) again and again with me, giving life to characters that otherwise would have existed only in my mind. (Trust me, they would have been terribly bored with just me to entertain.)

PART I

CHAPTER 1

TIKAYA CROSSED OUT ANOTHER OPENING line. A letter should not be so hard to write. True, the conditions were not ideal: the ship's wooden railing made a poor desk, the salty wind tugged at the paper, and something redolent of seagull poop adorned the side of her pencil. But it was the topic that made the message a challenge. And the fact that she didn't know the names of the people to whom the letter would be mailed. Nor was she certain they existed.

She glowered at the page.

"Linguistics troubles?" a familiar baritone asked.

Tikaya turned and spotted Rias. A *clean* Rias, the first time he'd appeared so in more days than she could remember. She flung herself into his arms with enthusiasm that would have knocked over most of the men on her island; he caught her with ease. His six-and-a-half feet complemented her annoyingly tall six-foot frame nicely. But that height, along with those broad shoulders and the dense armoring of muscle beneath his shirt, reminded her how unmistakably Turgonian he was. For the eight- or nine-thousandth time, she worried that none of her ideas for inspiring her people—her *family*—to accept him would work. Even getting him past the port authorities could prove challenging.

The basalt cliffs rising from the eastern side of the island told her they had a few more minutes before the ship reached the harbor. She could worry then. For now...

Tikaya rose on her tiptoes, kissed Rias, and wriggled deeper into his embrace.

Catcalls and whistles floated down from the ratlines.

Someone yelled, "Ain't pass'gers s'posed to have cabins for that?"

"Give 'em a blanket, so's we got a show to watch!"

Most of the sailors' comments were easily ignored—especially considering how little of Rias she had seen during the three-week voyage—but the surly mutter of "traitor" from a passing man stole her ardor.

Tikaya broke off the kiss. "Sorry."

The sailor had spoken in Kyattese, and she wasn't sure if it was one of the words Rias knew, but he had to have guessed the nature of the comment. He merely raised his eyebrows. "I hope that apology is for stabbing me in the neck with your pencil—"

She blushed and adjusted her hands.

"—and not for kissing me," he finished. "Because if you've forgotten how much I enjoy the latter, I've been spending far too much time in that stokehold."

His brown eyes twinkled, but she winced at the reminder that he had paid their fare with his labor. Granted, he was the fittest forty-three-year-old man she had ever met, but neither that nor the fact that women were not allowed in the stokehold assuaged her guilt. She had strolled the deck or sat in their cabin and studied pages full of symbols and runes, while he shoveled coal into the furnaces twelve hours a day. He had already given up a world to be with her, and she feared the sacrifices would only increase. What if he came to regret his decision?

"No," Tikaya said when his brow furrowed at her silence. "I just wasn't sure if it was appropriate for a woman to fling herself into the arms of a naval admiral on the deck of a ship."

"It's not my ship, and these days I'm rather retired..." Exiled. "So, unless it's unseemly for a dignified philology professor to be seen tongue wrangling with a man in a public venue, it doesn't bother me."

"You *have* been down in the stokehold too long if you think I'm dignified."

Rias offered his familiar half smile, caught her hand and started to lift it to his lips, but paused at the paper crinkled in her grip.

"I'm trying to write a letter." Tikaya realized she had not answered his original question. "To Corporal Agarik's family. They'll probably hate me on principle, but I want them to know that he was a good man, that he saved my..." She swallowed. "What he did for us... I want them to know."

"Ah." Rias unbuttoned a shirt pocket and withdrew an envelope smudged with coal dust. He handed it to her. "I wrote to my parents to let them know I'm alive. I was going to ask you to mail it. If you tuck your message inside with a note for my father, he'll get your letter to the family. Include Agarik's name, rank, and that Bocrest was his commander."

Tikaya eyed the envelope, daunted at the idea of asking for a favor from his—from Fleet Admiral Sashka Federias Starcrest's—parents, especially when she was every bit the enemy to his people that he was to hers. "How about I give you the letter and *you* mail it with a note for your father?"

"I don't know where the post office is on your island." Rias smiled, but his eyes remained serious as he pressed the envelope into her hand. "And if something happens to me, I'll be comforted, knowing you'll be able to mail it."

"Rias, my people are peaceful. We don't have capital punishment, even for enemies of the nation. They're not going to—"

A cleared throat nearby made her pause. It was the captain, a steely-haired man with a scar on his cheek almost as long as the pipe dangling from his chapped lips. He nodded to Rias. "You sure you want to get off here?"

The captain ignored Tikaya. The couple of times he had exchanged words with her, they had been in Kyattese, her language. He spoke in Turgonian now.

"Yes, sir," Rias said.

The honorific surprised Tikaya. Though Rias had only a few gray hairs sprinkled about his temples, he had been as highly ranked in the Turgonian military as an officer could be, so the "sir" sounded strange coming from him. But, then, he had told no one who he was, and, as far as she knew, no one amongst the multiracial crew had identified him. With his short black hair and clean-shaven face, he probably had not changed in the two years since his last command, but most of the world thought him dead, thanks to the story his emperor had circulated. This was a merchant vessel, too, and the captain hadn't mentioned anything about being a part of the war.

The captain's gaze flicked toward Tikaya. "Because of her?"

"Yes." A wary note crept into Rias's tone.

"Had a talk with my chief engineer this morning." The captain removed his pipe and tamped it. "Seems you two have had a few dialogues."

"We've spoken," Rias said.

Tikaya leaned against the railing, waiting for the captain to make his point.

"Seems you know the machinery," the captain said.

"I've sailed on something similar."

Tikaya almost laughed. She wondered what the captain and the engineer would think if they knew Rias had been designing a vessel of his own while he had been shoveling that coal. He had sketches in their cabin, and even though he'd been a military strategist rather than an engineer, she had little doubt he could build a craft from scratch.

"The chief isn't usually blunt," the captain said, "but he was this morning. He says I was an idiot for putting you in the stokehold."

"The exercise suited me." Rias lifted a hand. "Besides, the trip's over now."

"It needn't be. Chief's planning on retiring in the next year. He seems to think you'd be a better replacement than any of his junior officers."

The offer sent a flutter of nerves through Tikaya's belly. It *shouldn't* appeal to Rias—even if they didn't have plans to put his mathematical inclinations to work decoding ancient mysteries, it would be a pedestrian job after the challenges he had once encountered daily—but it reminded her that, imperial exile or not, he could find a place in the world just fine without her or the hospitality of the Kyatt Islands.

"I thank you for your consideration, sir," Rias said, "but I'm not looking to stay on."

The captain inhaled deeply, puffed out a ring of smoke, and sized up Tikaya. Her cheeks warmed as his scrutiny drifted from her spectacles above her freckled cheeks to the baggy military uniform that hid her curves—it was all she had for clothing until she got home.

"We visit Saltarr twice a year. The women there have teats like this—" the captain demonstrated lofty proportions with his hands, "—and they'll do *anything*." He jerked his pipe at Tikaya. "She doesn't look like anything worth risking your life over."

Rias's jaw tightened. "She's worth it."

Tikaya pushed away from the railing and lifted her chin. "And *she* speaks Turgonian and understands what you're saying."

The captain shrugged and took another puff. "Just used to watching out for my crew. Men do stupid things for some skirt. It's not safe for a Turgonian to step foot on Kyatt right now, not after the war. They might not shoot you," he told Rias, "but they've got wizards and telepaths, and they'll lock you up and brainwash you until you don't know your own name."

"That's not true," Tikaya said, though the fact that one of her people had inflicted a telepathic interrogation on her a few weeks earlier stole some of her certainty. That had been a relic raider, a woman who gave up the oath she swore before the Ministry of Science to pursue riches. "In my nation, it's illegal for telepaths to pry without consent. As for brainwashing, I'm sure you Turgonians, with your manuals on torture methods, would know more about that than my people."

For the first time, the captain stiffened, and his dark eyes narrowed. Tikaya tensed. Before she had been kidnapped by Turgonians, she would not have expected a man to strike her, but her captors had not appreciated hearing her opinions.

Rias chuckled, stealing the tension from the air. He gave her a fond smile. "I thought you only read the chapter on alchemical interrogation techniques."

"I did," she said. "The brainwashing comment was just a guess."

"Chapter Seven," Rias said.

The captain snorted, whether with humor or disgust Tikaya couldn't tell, but at least he no longer looked like he meant to punch her. When a midshipman scurried up to report, he returned to his work.

Tikaya turned her back to the ship and resolved to push the captain's comments from her mind. Worse insults would come, for both of them. She sighed and propped her forearms on the damp railing. Spray misted her cheeks.

Rias wrapped his arms around her from behind and rested his cheek against her temple. "You're worth the world."

The sentiment warmed her more than the sun glittering on the sea, but it didn't alleviate her doubts. "I hope you still feel that way after you've met my family."

He chuckled, his breath stirring goosebumps as it tickled her ear. Not for the first time, she lamented his indenture below decks. The stokers received few baths, and he had been unwilling to share a bunk with her when he was caked in coal dust and dried sweat. Now he was clean, but they were about to dock. Maybe the reception would go more smoothly than she anticipated and they could spend the evening somewhere pleasant.

"So, is Saltarr a port you're familiar with?" Tikaya smirked as she turned her head to eye him. Though it had no archaeological significance and was not the type of place to attract her interest, she had heard of the vices plied there.

"After more than twenty years at sea," Rias said, "I've been to most major ports in the world."

A yes. Her smirk widened. A *careful* yes. "And did you meet any of the women there?"

"That would have been unwise."

"Because you were married then?"

"That and because..." His eyes drifted up and to the side in his making-a-calculation expression. "One in three."

She twitched an eyebrow. "And that is the solution to what equation?"

"Given what the sawbones told me, that's about the odds of a man returning from shore leave in Saltarr without... ah, I'm not sure what the Kyattese term is, but we call it pizzle rot."

"You Turgonians are a blunt people."

"Indeed we are."

Tikaya leaned back into his embrace, trying to relax and enjoy the last peaceful moment, but a landmark above a beach caught her eye. The lighthouse. Snakes tangled in her belly. They were entering the harbor.

Though the merchant ship had Turgonians in the crew, none of them walked down the gangplank with Tikaya and Rias. More police than she had ever seen strode along the piers and the quay. In their sandals, shorts, and yellow button-down hemp shirts, they were far less intimidating than Turgonian marines, but the fit men and women all carried cudgels or crossbows. Much had changed since Tikaya last visited the harbor.

Only two months had passed since her kidnapping, but she had secluded herself on her parents' plantation during the previous year, mourning the fiancé she had thought dead. Now she wished she had paid more attention to the goings on in the capital.

Tikaya and Rias mingled with the crowd as people wound their way down the busy pier toward the streets of Yikyo, but their height made them stick out. The departing passengers and crew represented a number of nationalities, but Rias's size, bronze skin, and black hair left little doubt to his origins. Merchants at vendor carts selling everything from chilled coconut milk to sarongs and sandals to dictionaries for foreigners eyed Rias as he passed. Despite her dubious outfit, no one glanced twice at Tikaya.

The first policeman they passed frowned deeply. His eyes grew distant, the expression of a practitioner calling upon his science—or a telepath communicating with someone.

"Trouble?" Rias murmured.

"Likely."

"A lot or a little?"

Rias carried a rucksack but no major weaponry—Tikaya had convinced him to trade their rifle and longbow for coin, figuring it'd be best to walk onto the island unarmed—so that shouldn't bother the police. But he would stand out here no matter what he wore. Also, he'd kept a short blade that hung in a belt sheath. She would have called it a dagger, finding it plenty long and sharp enough to slit throats, but he'd balked at the idea of classifying it as a weapon. The Frontier Toothpick, as he called it, was a mere utility knife by imperial standards.

"It depends on whether they recognize your face or they're just reporting that there's a militant-looking Turgonian strolling the docks." Tikaya picked up her pace. She planned to report to the capitol building straight away—better to tell the president she wanted to bring a war criminal to visit than being caught trying to sneak him onto the island—and thought it'd be best to arrive *with* the news, rather than after it. Besides, the president had once said he owed her a favor for her pivotal role in ending the war. This was his chance to redeem it. He owed *Rias* a favor as well—when he'd still been fleet admiral, he'd stopped the Turgonian emperor's deadly young henchman from assassinating the Kyattese leader—but Tikaya feared the president might never have received the warning note or otherwise learned of the incident.

"*You* didn't recognize my face," Rias said.

Yes, and he had been careful to withhold his identity during the first couple of weeks they'd been dodging assassins, decrypting deadly alien technology, and otherwise getting to know each other. She'd forgiven him for that subterfuge, but she did wonder how their relationship would have developed if she had known who he was from the beginning.

"*I* spent the war with my nose buried in your military's encrypted communications. And I've spent the rest of my life with my nose buried in philology and archaeology books. My family members are lucky I recognize *them*."

Rias bumped her shoulder and smiled. "Sounds like you need more field work. More adventures. Wait until you see what I'm planning for—"

"Halt!" a male voice cried.

The crowd parted in front of Rias and Tikaya. A row of policemen stood at the head of the pier, blocking the quay and access to Harbor Avenue and the city beyond it. The squad aimed crossbows and muskets at Rias.

Though she didn't expect them to shoot, Tikaya moved to step in front of him with her arms spread.

A firm grip on her elbow halted her, and Rias stepped in front of her instead. She snorted. There was probably some Turgonian regulation against hiding behind a woman.

Tikaya leaned around him and told the policemen, "I'm a citizen. This is my guest. Is there a problem?"

She had never seen a whole squad of men and women drop their jaws in a synchronized stunned gape before. A seagull landed on a pier and squawked. The sound stirred some of the policemen into shutting their mouths.

"Your *guest* is Fleet Admiral Federias Starcrest?" the squad leader asked. "The slaughtering bloodthirsty tyrant who decimated our ships during the war? The nonpareil war criminal of the high seas? The heinous Turgonian emperor's most dangerous lackey?"

Rias looked over his shoulder, his eyebrows raised in a question.

"They recognize you," Tikaya said. "And, uhm, they don't like you."

"Yes, I gathered that. There were a lot of words in there you haven't taught me yet though."

Curse him, he sounded amused. But then, she'd seen him grin maniacally in the middle of battle, despite being surrounded by people attempting to kill him—no, *because* he'd been surrounded by people attempting to kill him.

"My people like vocabulary words," Tikaya said, trying not to sound worried.

The police advanced with wariness despite Rias's easy humor—they likely had no trouble understanding him, as most Kyattese learned Turgonian and Nurian in school, and those working around the docks would have had practice speaking with visiting foreigners. Four policemen kept their weapons trained on him while two edged forward, one clenching a baton, the other gripping handcuffs.

Rias let them shackle his hands behind his back. His eyebrow twitched when a policewoman took his knife, but he didn't try to stop her.

A third man stepped toward Tikaya. "You said you're a citizen, ma'am?"

His words elicited a faint sting. She had never sought glory or recognition, but it was disappointing that the common man had no idea about her and what she'd done to help her people during the war. Of course, the president had deliberately kept her identity secret, hoping the Turgonians wouldn't figure out who the Kyattese code breaker was—and punish her. He'd underestimated their fact-finding abilities.

"Tikaya Komitopis," she said.

Her ancestors had been among the original refugees who colonized the islands, so at least the policeman nodded in recognition at the family name.

"You'll need to come with us for questioning, ma'am."

"Me? Why?"

Rias lifted an eyebrow. "You were planning to leave me to be tortured alone?"

"I thought we might expedite the process if I could go straight to the president," she said.

"Expedited torture. Oh, good."

"*No* torture. I told you, we don't do that anyway, but he owes me a favor." Tikaya smiled, though she feared it did not reach her eyes. Rias would not face the sort of torture with which he was familiar, but she had no doubt he would be in for an ordeal—an image of sugarcanes being smashed in her family's press came to mind—if she couldn't get an appointment to see the president promptly.

One of the policewomen cleared her throat. At first, Tikaya thought she'd issue a warning that they should speak in Kyattese instead of

Turgonian. But, "President Mokkos is on Akatoo this week," was what she said, naming the smallest of the Kyattese Islands, and the most distant. "He and his team are assessing the ongoing damage in Ititio Harbor due to the season's increased lava flows."

Tikaya grimaced. "Do you know when he'll be back?"

Before the woman could answer, the squad leader lifted a hand and said, "It's irrelevant. It takes months to get an appointment to see him, and I doubt your family name will hasten that process. You'll deal with the magistrate. Come."

Tikaya wanted to state that her surname had nothing to do with anything, that it was her deeds that had earned her the right to see the president in a timely manner, but the police didn't care to converse further. The squad swarmed around Rias, leading him away, and a pair of men stepped to either side of Tikaya, gesturing for her to follow. They did not otherwise restrain her, but that only made her feel guilty as she walked behind Rias, observing the handcuffs trapping his wrists behind his back.

CHAPTER 2

A BREEZE WHISPERED DOWN AN ALLEY outside the window, rustling fallen palm fronds and other debris, but failing to stir the air inside the muggy interrogation room. Strange to think that Tikaya should need to become readapted to the climate in which she'd been born, but she found herself noticing the heat and humidity. Long hours had passed since the police had deposited her in the room with nothing more interesting than a single bamboo chair and a pitcher of water to keep her occupied. She guessed the delay was a result of searches of her and Rias's rucksacks. The black alien sphere that had helped her with translations was tucked inside hers, and his held a dagger that was, though simple, made of the same strange black alloy. Those finds had to have the police scratching their heads and wondering where she and Rias had been.

Tired of pacing, Tikaya sat on the hard chair and attempted to work on language puzzles in her head. Her mind kept bringing up thoughts of Rias and what they might be doing to him. She wished the police hadn't separated them.

Finally, the door creaked open. The police chief entered, accompanied by a blonde-haired woman in a nondescript hemp dress. Perhaps thirty years old, she seemed familiar, and Tikaya tried to place her. She decided they'd studied at the Polytechnic at the same time.

The woman flexed her fingers and a further realization came: she was a mental sciences practitioner. Tikaya had never been detained by the police—alas, she had been too busy studying in her youth to rebel against authority, professors, or even her parents—so she had no idea if it was normal for a telepath to attend a questioning. She *did* know there were laws against intruding upon citizen's thoughts. However, strong telepaths could often sense emotions without actually delving into a person's head.

A young assistant brought in a second chair, and the chief settled in opposite of Tikaya. *His* chair had padding.

"Ms. Komitopis." The chief propped his elbows on the armrests and steepled his fingers. His green eyes regarded her solemnly from beneath thinning red hair and brows, the latter separated by deep worry lines. "We have a file on your kidnapping. It's good that you've made your way home. Your parents will be relieved."

His tone was friendly. Why didn't that reassure her?

"Thank you. I'll need to see them as soon as possible, of course, but it's more urgent that I communicate with the president, in regard to my... guest. Will that be possible?"

"We'll see."

"He knows me," Tikaya said. "I helped in the intelligence department during the war."

The chief's lined face, pale despite the sunny clime, gave away little, and she couldn't tell if he believed her or not. "The president isn't on the big island currently."

"I know," Tikaya said. "But surely I can send him a message?"

"Let's see how things progress here first, shall we?"

Tikaya felt her fingers curl into fists and forced herself to unclench them. She almost missed the bluntly honest Turgonians. Captain Bocrest would have smashed her against a wall by now, but at least she would have known where she stood with him.

Abruptly, she remembered the telepath, and alarm flared inside her chest. The woman had taken up an unobtrusive position near the door, mostly blocked from sight by the chief's chair. Deliberate placement? Either way, Tikaya had best not let kindly thoughts about her former captors seep out. When she'd run into Parkonis, her ex-fiancé had been certain she'd been suffering from captive complex.

"Why is she here?" Tikaya nodded toward the woman. "I haven't signed a consent form."

"It's her job to ascertain your emotional stability through sensing feelings." The chief spoke pleasantly, even enthusiastically, as if they were discussing the promise of a plentiful coconut crop this season.

"While strong thoughts may reach her net, your defenses won't be violated. Not during this preliminary investigation."

Tikaya stared at him. What did *that* mean? Later violation was a possibility?

Sweat trickled down the inside of her arm. She forced herself to sit back and take a deep breath. If they wanted to read her thoughts, that could be a good thing. It could clear Rias of whatever suspicions they must have over his appearance.

Maybe.

She thought of Gali, the woman who had torn through her mind back in the tunnels and reached the wrong conclusion about Tikaya's relationship with Rias. Having access to another's thoughts did not make a telepath omniscient. People sometimes saw what they wanted to see and interpreted memories in such a way as to support their beliefs.

"Why don't you tell me what's happened since you disappeared?" the chief asked.

Tikaya would have preferred to save the story for the president, but he wasn't there, and she wanted to clear up whatever she could so she could go home. It stung to be so close, after having been so far, only to be denied a trip of a few miles to her family's plantation. She wouldn't go without Rias though. She had to make these people understand that he wasn't a threat. So Tikaya spent the next hour telling the story. She didn't go into many details about the ancient technology, as dangerous weapons remained in those tunnels, and she wanted to consult with her Polytechnic colleagues before revealing much—if anything—to the world in general. She also rushed through the announcement that she and Rias were... close. Before long everyone on the island would know, but the judging eyes of the chief and the telepath made her uncomfortable. She felt like a child caught doing something forbidden, and now she squirmed on the chair, awaiting her punishment.

If the artifacts his people must have found intrigued the chief, one would never know. He didn't ask any questions during that part of her story. In fact, he asked nothing at all until the end of the hour. The sole question, when it came, was, "What's Admiral Starcrest's purpose here?"

"Me," Tikaya said.

"You." The chief exchanged looks with the telepath.

"Yes, *me*. We wish to..." Get married, Tikaya thought, though Rias hadn't mentioned the idea since their night in Wolfhump, where they'd struggled to decode the alien artifact amidst a grisly pile of frozen bodies. And he'd been speaking hypothetically then. Perhaps he wasn't ready for a commitment of that magnitude or perhaps he had doubts whether a permanent association could work out. She hoped that wasn't the case, because she'd already started wondering what their children might look like. "We wish to be together," Tikaya said. "I brought him here so I can introduce him to my family."

"Ms. Komitopis." The chief pinched the bridge of his nose. "Surely you must have considered that he's using you as a cover and is truly here for nefarious purposes?"

Tikaya shook her head. "He was stripped of everything and exiled two years ago. He has no loyalty to the Turgonian emperor any more. He wants a new career and a new life. With me. We're going to work on archaeological puzzles together. He's very smart."

"Oh, nobody's doubting *that*."

No, they were just doubting *her* intelligence. "He's an honorable man. Why don't you talk to him for a while? You might change your opinion."

"I don't speak more than a few words of Turgonian."

"He knows some Kyattese."

The chief's eyes narrowed. "Does he, now?"

Uh oh. Was Rias pretending otherwise to see what her people said when they thought he couldn't understand? She could hardly blame him for such subterfuge. She wouldn't open her mouth around potential enemies either. Unless—she snorted to herself—they intrigued her first with a puzzle. That was all it had taken for Captain Bocrest to convince her to speak.

The chief withdrew a piece of paper from a pocket and unfolded it. He held it before Tikaya's spectacles. "What do you know about this?"

The drawing was familiar. Precise pen strokes delineated the cross-sections of an engine while neatly written equations lined the margins. Rias had been working on his blueprints whenever he had spare time.

"He wants to build us a ship so we can launch our own expeditions, something with enough space to house a team of—"

"It's not a ship," the chief said. "We had an engineer look over his drawings. It's a vessel designed to travel underwater. Turgonian steam power alone wouldn't suffice—the fire would eat up the limited oxygen—but if he had access to the energy orbs our mental scientists craft, he could make this a reality. Can you imagine the advantage that would give the Turgonians? They could drop anchor in our harbor, spying on us from beneath the surface, and we'd never know they were there."

"The war has been over for more than a year, sir," Tikaya said. "If Rias wants to build a—" there was no Kyattese word, so she used the Turgonian one for the concept, "—submarine, it's because he likes a challenge. He said it's something his people haven't managed for the very reasons you stated."

"You *did* know about it." The chief's eyes widened, and he glanced at the telepath again.

"He doesn't have any diabolical reasons for building it. I imagine being able to travel beneath the waves would be an advantage during storms."

"During storms." The chief's jaw tightened. "I understand you're a linguistics professor, so I must assume you possess intelligence of some sort, but I question your wisdom. Perhaps being sheltered in academia has left you naive to the workings of the world."

Now it was Tikaya's jaw that tightened. So much so that it ached.

"Or," the chief went on, "perhaps you're in collusion with the Turgonians."

She forced herself to unclench her jaw. "Philologist," she said calmly.

"What?"

"I'm a philologist, not a linguist. While I do speak numerous tongues, my specialty is dead languages."

The chief took several deep breaths. "I see. You don't wish to cooperate. I'll be forced to put collusion on my report."

"Cooperate, how?" Tikaya asked. "You haven't asked me to do anything."

"Tell me why Admiral Starcrest is *really* here."

Tikaya sighed. "I can only tell you the truth, not what you want to hear."

"I see," he said again. "Your family will be informed, and a plan will be discussed in regard to treatment for you."

"Treatment?" Tikaya mouthed, but he was already stalking out of the room.

The door slammed shut. Outside the window, the debris in the alley rustled as a breeze stirred. The air also carried the faint sound of voices. The chief and someone else. No doubt, they were discussing Tikaya. She could not pick out many of the words, but thought she heard, "parents." Would the police send a message, instructing them to come to the station? After all she had been through, Tikaya should have relished the thought, but dread curdled in her stomach, not just because of the threat of "treatment" that had been mentioned. Listening to the chief's condescending accusations had been bad enough; hearing them on her mother and father's tongues would hurt.

"It's not your fault," the telepath said.

Tikaya twitched. She had forgotten the woman was still in the room.

"The Turgonians are masters of interrogation and brainwashing." The woman strolled over to stand beside Tikaya. "Though they favor violence, it doesn't surprise me that Admiral Starcrest would use charm to win a woman over. He's a handsome man, after all."

True, though he had been a mess, buried beneath two years' of hair and grime, when Tikaya first met him.

The woman put a hand on Tikaya's shoulder. Though Tikaya was not trained in the mental sciences, she sensed when someone was applying them nearby, and the hairs on her arms rose now.

"It's not your fault," the telepath said, a soothing sensation accompanying her words. "You're the victim here. We'll have a therapist work with you, and you'll come to realize—"

Tikaya lunged to her feet, breaking the contact. She whirled to face the woman. "Don't touch me."

"Of course." The telepath clasped her hands behind her back and bowed her head. "Too soon. I understand. You'll need to be separated from him for a while before you return to your senses. With time, his influence over you will wane."

Tikaya tried the door. It was locked. She backed to the wall, folded her arms over her chest, and eyed the window again. She briefly toyed with the idea of kicking the woman's legs out from beneath her, searching her for a key, and escaping if she had one. Except this was an island and it was home. Where would Tikaya go if not here?

"You don't need to stay with me," she said. "I promise I won't get lonely if you go."

The woman only smiled.

"I'm surprised you aren't busy sifting through Rias's thoughts," Tikaya muttered.

"He didn't consent to that. We asked."

No, he wouldn't. She remembered a comment he'd made that he'd been tortured by Nurians that way once.

"You gave him an option?" Tikaya asked.

"We don't force people."

Tikaya snorted. "Unless it's for therapy?"

The door opened, and she tensed.

The chief strode in and glowered at her. "You're free to go."

Tikaya dropped her arms and gawked. It couldn't be that easy. "I'm not leaving without Rias."

"He can go too."

The telepath inhaled a startled breath.

"What?" Tikaya asked.

"There are provisos," the chief said. "War criminals can't be permitted to stroll the island unsupervised, but, yes, he can leave with you."

Too easy. This was too easy. "Who were you talking to outside the window?" Tikaya asked. "The president hasn't returned, has he?"

"High Minister Jikaymar," the chief said in a clipped tone.

The man Tikaya's supervisor had reported to during the war and who had overseen the guerrilla efforts against the Turgonians. Yes, he would know who Tikaya was and how she'd helped the nation, but they had not spoken more than once or twice, and she had never received the impression he liked her or would go out of his way to do her a favor.

"What sort of provisos?" Tikaya asked.

"Come." The chief waved her into the hall.

Tikaya glanced at the telepath as she left. A bewildered expression furrowed the woman's brow.

As Tikaya followed the chief, she noticed her heavy Turgonian boots thudding on the bamboo floor. Sweat dampened the wool socks inside. A flutter of anticipation stirred in her breast. If the chief spoke truly, by that evening, she could be at home, wearing sandals and a light dress again, and enjoying a meal with her family.

The chief pushed open a door at the end of the hall. Rias stood inside, surrounded by men in white robes, the hems and sleeves adorned with gold stitching. Tikaya hesitated. At the least, they were science professors from the Polytechnic, but given the number of gray-haired heads, they might be members of the Council of Science Policies and Affairs.

Someone had taken Rias's rucksack, jacket, and even his boots and belt. A seashell bracelet with a glowing red stone strapped his wrist. Beyond a brief meeting of her eyes, he did not react to Tikaya's entrance.

She frowned at the chief and pointed at Rias's wrist. "Is that a lizard tracking device?"

It was one of the professors who responded, a slight wiry man with gray hair. "It's true the zoology department uses them for keeping track of rehabilitated predators to ensure they don't attack people again, yes. This one has been modified for human use."

"So Rias can be killed with a thought if some fallible controller thinks his behavior is questionable?" She searched Rias's eyes, an apology in her own. Bringing him home had been a mistake. Had she truly thought it wouldn't be misery—or worse—for him?

"Nobody's going to kill anybody," the professor said. "It's to be used to render him insensate if he becomes violent." His tone grew chillier. "And I'll be the 'fallible' controller accompanying and observing you. Professor Yosis." He turned a cool look of warning upon Rias. "My colleagues will serve as backup, in case something should happen to me. A death command could be given in response to such an event."

Tikaya balled her hands into fists. "This is inhumane and unacceptable."

"It's the only way we're letting him walk around the island," the chief said.

"And he agreed to it," Yosis added.

"You did?" Tikaya asked Rias, switching to Turgonian.

He nodded once.

She waited, expecting him to say more, to explain his thoughts, but he remained tightlipped. Like a prisoner of war not wanting to give anything away to the enemies holding him captive. And why shouldn't he feel that way? Essentially, that's what he was. She would have to get him alone to have an open conversation. But if Yosis was accompanying them, that might not be possible for a while. A long while.

CHAPTER 3

HUMIDITY SMOTHERED FIELDS GREEN WITH new growth, but a pleasant breeze brought relief as it rustled through the coconut trees lining the road. A beach stretched along one side with gulls swooping and squawking over the waves.

The six-mile bicycle ride from the city to the plantation would have been pleasant if not for Professor Yosis pedaling behind Tikaya and Rias. Though more gray than blond marked his thinning hair, he wasn't considerate enough to grow weary and fall behind.

"I'm sorry about the tracker," Tikaya told Rias, feeling the need to apologize before they met her family—and she had more reasons to express regret to him.

"You needn't be," he said.

They spoke in his tongue, but the professor doubtlessly understood it.

Tikaya gave Rias a sad smile. "You won't say that after you've felt the bite of... Ah, just don't give our monitor back there a reason to use it."

"I've felt its bite."

Her hands tightened on the handlebars. "They used it on you?" She glared back at the professor.

"It is necessary for the subject to feel the pain that misrule elicits so as to fully realize the need to avoid it," Yosis said, thus verifying he understood Turgonian. "Also, it is necessary for us to test the subject's pain threshold in order to calibrate the device."

"They used it on you a lot," Tikaya whispered, horrified. She braked and dropped her boots to the ground. She wanted to kick the old man off his bicycle. "What gives you that right? He's a human being. That's torture."

Yosis stopped beside her, while Rias waited a few paces ahead.

"Really, Ms. Komitopis." Yosis regarded her mildly. "Do you believe he hasn't done far worse to far more human beings?"

"I thought our people prided themselves on being more civilized than the Turgonians—than any of the more warlike cultures in the world." Sweat dripped down Tikaya's arms and splashed on the gravel. "Knowledge. Wisdom. *Peace.* Aren't those words still engraved above the entrance to the Polytechnic?"

"Our way is more humane than theirs," Yosis said. "Do you know how many of our people were maimed and disfigured, mentally and physically, when they returned after the treaty signings? Those who returned at all, that is. As you know, many were lost to us forever."

Rias gazed at the sea. If the professor's highhanded logic disturbed him, one would never know. His thoughts remained locked in his head. Tikaya wondered if he'd yet decided he'd made a mistake in coming here.

She returned to pedaling.

Before they had gone far, Rias nodded at a ridge across the field. Verdant ground sloped upward toward the top of the volcano that one could see from anywhere on the island.

"What's up there?" he asked.

"Not much," Tikaya said. "A few hunting cabins and campsites. The majority of our agriculture and settlements are down here in the flatlands."

"I saw a reflection, like light striking glass. A spyglass, perhaps."

Tikaya adjusted her spectacles, though she doubted she would see anything. It was miles to the base of the hills, and lush trees and foliage carpeted the slopes.

"Could be someone hiking or working," she said. "I can ask later. It's my family's property, so only my kin or perhaps the neighbors would be wandering around up there."

Rias cocked his head. "How much land does your family have?"

"I'm not sure exactly. It takes about a day to walk across it."

He blinked. "So, forty miles? That's huge on an island this size."

"Probably closer to twenty," Tikaya said. "My people have shorter legs than yours, and we rest a lot more often on a hike."

Yosis snorted.

"Still, if that's twenty on all sides," Rias said, "you've more than two-hundred-and-fifty-thousand acres."

"If you're trying to impress me with your math skills," Tikaya said, smiling, "it'll take more than a simple square-miles-to-acres conversion."

"Oh?" The corners of his eyes crinkled. "Perhaps you can show me the plat map later, and there'll be ragged borders that require more sophisticated calculations."

"Why do you care how much land her family has?" Professor Yosis asked, his tone cold.

Tikaya lost her smile. "I'm sure he's only curious."

"Doubtful," Yosis said.

Rias returned his attention to scanning their surroundings. He would have stuck up for her, she had no doubt, but he seemed resigned to whatever fate her people had in mind for him. Well, *she* would stick up for him, even if he wouldn't fight for himself.

"How much land did *you* walk away from," Tikaya asked him, "when you chose to help me destroy those weapons and escape instead of turning them over to your emperor?"

"Not much," he said. "I'm my father's third son, so I wouldn't have stood to inherit the family properties. I just had what my grandfather left me."

"More or less than twenty square miles?" Tikaya said.

"Well, more, but Turgonia is huge, so proportionally, far less."

"Uh huh. So, your family controls how many millions of acres?"

"A few million. But it's largely undeveloped. Mostly mountains and trees."

"Ore and timber?" Tikaya asked.

"That follows, I suppose."

Tikaya gave their spy a frank look. "And to think, he could marry me and walk into a fiftieth share of our taro farm and poi factory."

"Poi?" Rias's lip twitched into a half smile. "Didn't you promise me rum?"

"You are naive for your age, Ms. Komitopis," Yosis said.

"Yes, I'm hearing that a lot today. I believe the consensus is that my years ensconced at the Polytechnic left me unwise to the workings of the world." She titled her head toward Rias as they coasted down a slope. "Have you found me to be flawed in that manner, as well?"

"I'd call that trait more endearing than flawed. I've dealt with enough worldly and jaded people to have grown weary of them." Rias didn't glance back at Yosis—he didn't have to.

"We're almost to the main house," Tikaya said to edge out any comment that might spring to the professor's lips. "That building over there is—"

An explosion boomed, and an orange blaze erupted from the earth. Stunned, Tikaya almost fell off the bicycle.

"What was that?" Yosis asked.

"The pumping house," Tikaya whispered.

Without thinking to tell them to follow, she veered off the road. She cut through the stubbled field, the bicycle bumping over the uneven earth. Though it jarred her to the bones, she pedaled faster, angling toward the source of the explosion. Rias appeared at her side, matching her pace.

"An attack?" he asked.

"Attack, no. An accident, must be. There's a boiler in there. It might have exploded. Anyone nearby could be hurt or..." She drove her legs faster, not bothering to glance back to check if Yosis followed.

Sweat streamed down her face by the time they drew near the pumping house. The top of the earthen dome had been blown off. Brush fires burned in the nearby grass.

Her father lay by the door, blood soaking his gray hair.

Tikaya jumped off the bicycle. "Father!"

She sprinted to his side, barely noticing that Rias jogged into the structure. A clatter came from inside.

"Father?" Tikaya rested a hand on his chest.

He was breathing, but his eyes were closed. She removed the uniform jacket tied around her waist, wadded it up, and pressed it against the gash on his head. She patted him, checking for other wounds.

His blue eyes fluttered open, wide and dazed at first. Then they squinted shut as he grimaced in pain. His hand went to his head, and he bumped her arm. He opened his eyes again, focusing on her this time.

"Tikaya?" he whispered.

She gripped his bloody hand. "Yes, Father."

He lifted his head, concentration on his face, as if he couldn't understand her. The explosion must have stunned his ears.

"Dead?" he mouthed.

Not sure whether he had thought she was dead or maybe feared that *he* had died, Tikaya spoke again, more loudly this time. "Nobody's dead. It's me. I'm home. What happened? Are you all right?"

"Yes... That's right. They said you... were coming."

They who? The police? It didn't matter, Tikaya told herself. When Father put a hand on the ground, she helped him sit up. Blood ran down the side of his round face and spattered his sweat-stained shirt. His gaze landed on Yosis, and his brow crinkled in confusion.

The professor straddled his bicycle a few meters away, fresh dust gathered on the hem of his white robe. He'd taken out a notepad and pencil—maybe that was his idea of being useful.

Father opened his mouth, but a shadow fell across him, and he said nothing, only gaped up at the source.

Rias had come out of the pumping house, sans shirt. "There are two more injured inside. I made makeshift bandages—" he gestured at his bare chest, "—but they need medical attention."

Father didn't seem to hear him. He lunged to his feet, staggering before catching his balance, and, instead of heading inside to check on the others, he stomped over to Rias and glared. His eyes didn't even come to Rias's collarbone, but that didn't keep his shoulders from tensing, his eyes from turning icy, and his hands from curling into fists. His chest rose and fell in fast, deep breaths, as he ignored the blood dribbling into his eyes. This wasn't how Tikaya had imagined Rias's first meeting with her family going.

"Father." She rested her hand on his forearm. "This is Rias. He's—"

"One of those bloodthirsty barbarians who kidnapped you. What're you doing here, Turg? Come to steal my grandchildren this time?"

"He brought me back," Tikaya said. "He saved my life several times."

Father shook her hand off his arm. "You can't trust him. You can't trust any of them. They're godless heathens, girl."

Rias clasped his hands behind his back. "You may want to attend to your workers, sir. And perhaps search your property for intruders. The failure originated in the feed water pump, a malfunctioning float switch. It may have been an accident, due to aged equipment, but it may have been sabotage as well."

Father looked like he wanted to fight, not analyze the incident, but he pushed past Rias and stomped inside. Tikaya tried not to feel stung that she had been gone months, months when her parents must have wondered if she was even alive, and he hadn't even given her a hug. She shook the thought away. It was more important to tend to the injured and find out what had happened to the pumping house.

She headed for the door and, though conscious of Yosis's watching eyes, leaned her shoulder against Rias for a moment. He surprised her by slipping a folded piece of paper into her hand. She pocketed it and continued past him.

Inside, the air was cooler, though afternoon sun slanted through a gaping hole in the domed ceiling, the jagged edges smoldering. Warped machinery steamed, and the entire boiler was missing. The energy orb that heated the water lay cracked and dormant on the earthen floor amongst shattered bamboo pipes and ceramic shards. Father knelt beside two hired workers. Rias's jacket, which bandaged one man's leg, was already saturated with blood.

"Is this common here?" Rias touched a bamboo pipe running vertically into the ground. "Modiglar's equations of state, and Fargot's thermodynamics studies suggest this material isn't viable. Copper, wrought iron, or sometimes steel are—"

"Turg barbarian," Father growled over his shoulder. "Men are hurt, and you're worried about our steam technology?"

Rias dropped his hand and winced. "My apologies, sir."

Tikaya shared his wince. She understood getting caught up in musings related to one's passion. Her father never would. He'd always been the practical sort, someone more flustered by than interested in his children's fancies.

"Iron or steel has to be shipped in from Nuria or Turgonia," Tikaya told Rias quietly. "It's costly. For centuries, our people have been using the mental sciences to reinforce everything from bamboo to coconut husks."

"I see," Rias said. "Regardless, structural materials don't seem to have caused the incident. The feed water pump dried up, which kept water from entering the boiler."

"I doubt it was sabotage," Tikaya said. "Who would bother out here?"

"What's this place for? Irrigation of the fields?"

"That and supplying fresh water to the house and outbuildings. The well—"

"Tikaya," Father growled, "stop sharing the workings of everything with him."

Tikaya sighed. "Father, he's not... He's my..."

She studied the packed earth floor. By age thirty, it should be a simple thing to admit to one's father that one had a lover, shouldn't it?

He didn't look at her, but tension hunched his shoulders. "Go to the house. Tell Telanae we need her healing skills."

"Yes, Father."

Tikaya almost crashed into the professor on the way out. Yosis stood in the doorway, scribbling in his notepad.

"Can you do anything useful," she barked, "except stand back like an observer in a science experiment?"

"I have no medical training, if that's your inquiry."

"So, the answer is no." Tikaya brushed past him and strode to the bicycle.

Yosis bent his head and wrote something else. Rias followed Tikaya out, pausing to frown down at the professor. Unfortunately, Yosis did not notice. Even more unfortunately, his writing did not delay him from hopping astride his bicycle and keeping up as Tikaya led the way home. She wished she hadn't snapped at him—he was doubtlessly there to observe *her* as much as Rias—but it was too late to do anything about it.

A bumpy dirt road led from the pumping station to the main house. Rias kept glancing toward the ridge as they pedaled down the slope.

"I'm sure it was an accident," Tikaya said. "Maybe one of the hired hands removed something for maintenance and didn't get it refastened properly."

"An accident that happened as your father happened to be in the vicinity? And as we happened to be riding to your home?"

"You Turgonians are a suspicious folk."

"One of my commanding officers used to say, 'The paranoid survive.'"

"Pithy," Tikaya said. "I wonder why Turgonia isn't known for its poets."

"It's hard to compose poetry when you're sharing the gun deck with two hundred rowdy, unwashed men."

"Did you ever try?"

"That's one of those questions a wise man doesn't answer," Rias said. "If I say yes, you'll expect me to write you poetry. If I say no, you'll think me an uncouth illiterate."

"Maybe you could just compose me a nice math theorem sometime."

Rias bit his bottom lip and gave her a shy-hopeful expression. "I've actually been working on something for you. My men used to call it Starcrestian Search Theory—I used Groatian Statistics to narrow possibilities in the search for missing vessels. I thought I could adapt it so we could hunt for historic wrecks, sunken ships, or maybe even thus-far mythical ruins with archaeological significance. Surely, the bottoms of the ocean hold all sorts of secrets, maybe even—"

Rias's head jerked back. He gasped and tumbled backward off the bicycle.

Tikaya skidded to a stop amidst a cloud of dust. She lunged to Rias's side. On his knees in the dirt, he clutched his head with both hands, his face to the earth.

"Rias?" She rested her hand on his back.

He managed nothing more than short, pained gasps.

Suspicion lifted her gaze. The professor had stopped and he watched, his eyes cold. Tikaya jumped to her feet, ready to flatten the man with a punch.

He lifted a hand, and she crashed into an invisible wall.

"Stop," Tikaya demanded.

A finger on Yosis's other hand twitched. Rias sucked in a deep breath and knelt back. He closed his eyes for a long moment and collected himself.

"You will refrain from discussing such topics, foreigner," Yosis told Rias.

"Such *topics*?" Tikaya said. "Archaeology and math? By Akahe's Eternal Spirit, what's befuddling your mind?"

The professor's cool gaze rotated toward her. "Ms. Komitopis, after so long amongst the Turgonians, you are not above suspicion. Do not incriminate yourself by meddling."

She curled her lip and swore at him, though she couldn't quite bring herself to do it in a language he would understand.

Rias got to his feet, picked up the bicycle, and nodded for Tikaya to lead on. All traces of his humor—his personality—were gone, hidden behind a face that might have been carved from stone.

CHAPTER 4

THE HOMESTEAD CAME INTO VIEW, the buildings nestled beneath ancient palm trees near a bluff overlooking the sea. Made from cob and tigerwood, the main house rose two stories with several cottages around it. Wood lanais wrapped each building, and breezeways ran between the structures. Smoke rose from the kitchen chimney, bringing the scent of cinnamon-vanilla yams along with the tantalizing aroma of pork slow cooking in the earth oven.

"That smells fantastic, doesn't it?" Tikaya smiled at Rias, though it was strained. Guilt over the professor's attack rode the bicycle with her.

"Yes," he said.

"My mother's a good cook."

Rias glanced back at Yosis, probably wondering what other topics would result in punishment. "Are you?" he asked her quietly, lips quirking up in a brief smile.

The question served as a reminder of how little they knew about each other in a domestic sense. Without a life-or-death adventure to bond them, would he remain interested?

"Didn't you say you were impressed with the raccoon kabobs I made on our trek down from the mountains?" Tikaya asked.

"Hm. Impressed with the creativity, I think I said."

"Not the flavor? I'm better when seasonings are available."

A small figure darted across the path in front of them. Tikaya braked, skidded, and hit a rock. She pitched sideways into the grass, landing in an ungainly heap.

Rias was at her side before she sat up.

"Apologies," he said.

"For what?" Tikaya asked. "You're not the one who ran across the path in front of me."

"Isn't it my duty to catch you when you trip or otherwise try to hurl yourself to the ground?" Rias had caught her stumbling quite a few times on their frozen trek in the Turgonian frontier lands. "The bicycle slowed me down."

Accepting his hand, Tikaya rose to her feet. "I was hoping I'd be less likely to do that back in my homeland." She raised her voice. "Lonaeo, was that you?"

Movement stirred the tall grass on one side of the road. A slight curly-haired boy slipped out from the cover. He carried a jar and a butterfly net. His green eyes bulged when they locked onto Rias. Lonaeo stumbled backward, tripped on his bare feet, and landed on his rump, his gear flying free.

"Must be a relative of yours," Rias said.

"Because we look similar, or because he tripped like I always do?" Tikaya asked.

"Indeed so." Rias's eyes glinted.

"Tikaya!" Lonaeo climbed to his feet and hurled himself at her for a hug. "You're alive!"

The boy's momentum almost propelled her onto her own rump, but Rias steadied her with a hand to her back. Yosis had stopped a few yards away, and he waited with his notepad on his thigh.

"I'm alive," Tikaya managed around a lump in her throat. Finally, someone was greeting her as if she'd actually been missed. "Rias, this is one of my nephews, Lonaeo. He'd rather hunt insects than do chores."

"Lon-a-e-o?" Rias asked, his tongue awkward around the extra vowels. "As to the rest, who wouldn't?"

Lonaeo sneaked a peek at Rias beneath Tikaya's armpit. "Are you a joratt?"

Tikaya winced at the racial slur, one derived from the particularly thickheaded gorillas of the southern steppes, primates noted amongst ethologists as being particularly brutal in the way they mated and defended their territory. "Don't use that term, please."

"Grandpa does."

"Grandpa's mouth is even uglier than his hammertoes."

"I'm Turgonian, yes," Rias told the boy without any hint that the term bothered him.

"Is it true that you kill babies that are born weak or deformed?" Lonaeo asked. "Because they're not strong enough to be warriors?"

Lonaeo had been born prematurely and was still small for his age. Tikaya glanced at Rias, wondering if the boy would have been sacrificed if he'd been born in Turgonia.

"Not so much any more," Rias said. "That's an old custom from a harsher time."

"Are you going to kill me?" Lonaeo asked. "Or Tikaya? Or Grandma?"

Rias crouched so his eyes were level with the boy's. "No."

"Then why are you here? Joratts, I mean Turgs only come here to kill people."

"Sorry, Rias," Tikaya said, releasing Lonaeo, "he's only seven. With four years of war, he didn't know a time when your people were just traders who passed through."

"I'm here to visit," Rias told Lonaeo. "That's all."

"Oh. Want to see my red-wing speckled butterfly?" Lonaeo darted to the jar he'd dropped.

Professor Yosis sighed, a bored expression on his face. Tikaya was tempted to take a good long time examining her nephew's find, but her father would be waiting for Telanae.

"A fine specimen." Rias nodded at the jar as Lonaeo displayed the butterfly.

"The red-wing speckled is a skipper," Lonaeo explained. "A small butterfly that skips from flower to flower. You can tell by the big eyes, see, and how its wings fold up when it's at rest." He opened his mouth, probably readying himself to launch into a long lecture.

"Does your mama know you're drilling air holes into the lids of her good canning jars?" Tikaya asked.

Lonaeo blushed. "Maybe."

"I won't tell her if you help us find Telanae. Father needs her healing skills up at the pumping house. Did you hear the explosion?"

"Explosion?" Lonaeo scratched his head. "Maybe. I dunno. I was busy chasing my butterfly." He brightened. "I know where Telanae is though. The tide's out, and she's clamming at the beach. I'll get her!"

"Tell her to go to the pumping house!" Tikaya called after him.

Lonaeo acknowledged her with a wave.

"He'll talk about bugs for hours if you let him," she told Rias.

"Burble on about his passion, you mean? Sounds like another sure sign he's a relative of yours."

"I guess I can't deny that."

Tikaya walked her bicycle toward the main house's lanai, with Rias matching her pace. Several exterior walls housed floor-to-ceiling wooden shutters, many standing open to invite in the breeze. Inside the house, dishes clanked and cabinet doors thumped.

Tikaya took a deep breath and headed for the front stairs.

Before they reached the door, a woman walked out wearing a sleeveless floral dress that showed more leg than most bathing suits. Cousin Aeli. Tikaya's reaction was halfway between a smile and a wince. She was, of course, glad to see all her relatives, but Aeli did grate at times, perhaps more so because she'd been a promising anthropology student before deciding to become the town floozy.

"Tikaya." Aeli flung her arms wide and hopped down the stairs, bosom bouncing, to hug her. "They said you'd be here tonight. How wonderful. You look good too. Lost a few pounds, did you? Haven't I always told you an adventure would do you good? And this is the Turgonian who brought you home?" Her eyes lit with interest.

Standing shirtless, Rias did make for an interest-inspiring spectacle. When Tikaya had first met him, he'd been half-starved and more bone than muscle, but he had filled out in the last couple of months, and his weeks shoveling coal on the steamer had left him more fit than ever.

Knowing Aeli couldn't breathe without flirting, and wouldn't be cowed by the grisly reputation of Turgonians, Tikaya was tempted to step in front of Rias and growl, "Mine." She kept her response to, "He's Turgonian, yes."

"Is it true what the police said? That he's the Black Scourge of the Seas himself?" Aeli released Tikaya and faced Rias, eyeing him up and down like a particularly delectable morsel on the dinner table.

"I just call him Rias," Tikaya said. "It's easier on the tongue."

"Oh, I'm sure he is. Easy on the tongue that is." Aeli winked.

Tikaya could have kissed Rias for the fact that he was watching her instead of Aeli, despite the fact that she was going out of her way to thrust her breasts out and flip her blonde locks. He wore an am-I-supposed-to-humor-this-woman-because-she's-related-to-you-or-can-I-ignore-her expression.

Aeli didn't notice—or perhaps she noticed but wasn't deterred by—his lack of interest. She strolled up to Rias and leaned against his arm. "Handsome fellow, isn't he? Does he know any Kyattese?"

"Yes, he does," Rias said.

Surprise flickered across Aeli's face, but she recovered quickly and smiled. "Wonderful." She clasped his bare forearm. "Are you coming to dinner?"

Rias lifted his brows in Tikaya's direction.

"Yes." Tikaya removed Aeli's hand so Rias could back away a step. "He is."

"Excellent. If my uncle won't let you stay here after dinner, you can come see me tonight. My place is just up the beach." Aeli pointed past Tikaya without seeing her.

"Wouldn't it be crowded there?" Tikaya asked. "What with the three or four field hands you've usually got warming your bed?"

Aeli, gazing up at Rias, apparently did not hear.

"Thank you. *We* will remember your offer." Rias stepped closer to Tikaya.

"Tikaya?" A blank expression formed on Aeli's face. "And you?" She looked back and forth between the two of them, then shook her head. "Are you sure?"

"You needn't sound so shocked," Tikaya said drily.

"What happened to Parkonis?" Aeli asked. "I heard he's alive and back on the island."

So, the assassin had kept his word and let Parkonis go free. The news was a relief, but at the same time, the potential for complications made Tikaya groan. Yosis, standing silently by the lanai railing, withdrew his notebook again and wrote in it.

"Not that I wouldn't choose this fellow over Parkonis too." Aeli patted Rias on the arm—somehow she'd made the space between them disappear again. "If you get bored with Tikaya, come see me. She's not very experienced or imaginative. Or fun. You know what her problem is? She—"

"Really needs to introduce Rias to Mother now," Tikaya said, hoping to head Aeli off before she could start listing character deficiencies. "But this chat has been lovely. We're all caught up already, and it's as if I never left. Bye now."

"When you spoke fondly of your family, I was expecting people who love and support you," Rias said as they moved toward the front door.

"Aeli does, in her own condescending way," Tikaya said.

"Truly? She seems like someone who would have stolen all your boyfriends in school."

"No, my boyfriends—the scant number that there were—weren't up to her standards. Maybe I should be flattered she's ogling you."

Rias paused to admire carvings sprawled across the house's double front doors. The intricate engravings showed Tikaya's ancestors arriving in the harbor, rowing away from a colony ship and toward the beach. She pushed open one door. A great room opened up with enough rattan chairs and couches to seat the extended family and guests. Two ceiling fans swirled the air overhead. Clatters echoed from a hallway at the back of the spacious room.

"Mother?" Tikaya called.

The clatters stilled. "Tikaya?"

The sound of sandals slapping the hardwood floor came first, then Mother appeared and raced across the great room at full speed.

A plump woman, she jiggled as she ran, and though Tikaya stood a half foot taller, she braced herself for the impact. The hug was welcome, though, and Tikaya buried her face in her mother's shoulder. Tears dampened her cheek, and she wasn't sure if they were hers or Mother's. They held each other for a long moment.

"Honey," Mother murmured, "we've been so scared. We didn't hear anything for weeks and weeks, and we thought..." She swallowed and took a deep breath. "Then last night, we got a message from Parkonis—dear Akahe, his mother is going to carve him like scrimshaw for letting everyone believe he was dead—and he said..." Her head rotated toward Rias. "Yes," she said quietly, "that's what he said."

Tikaya braced herself again, this time mentally. "Mother, this is Rias. Rias, my mother, Mela. That fellow lurking in the doorway is Rias's new keeper, Professor Yosis."

"Ma'am." Rias bowed, not a truncated bending but a full arm-sweeping-away-from-where-a-sword-usually-hung warrior-caste bow.

"Rias?" Mother said. "That's not the name we got."

"Formerly Admiral Sashka Federias Starcrest," Rias said, leaving out the "Lord" that went with the official title. Maybe he thought the

Kyattese would find the notion of lords pretentious. "My exile means I've had my right to the last name taken. I never cared much for the first on account of, ah, boyhood teasing. I started using Federias in school, and friends shortened it to Rias."

Tikaya smiled slightly at the mention of teasing. While he had his share of Turgonian arrogance, and he had no missing confidence when it came to battle and barking orders at men, he had a shy, almost awkward side which she found endearing. She hoped her mother would too.

"And do former admirals not wear shirts?" Mother finally asked.

Rias offered a sheepish shrug.

To distract her from his unkempt state, Tikaya explained the situation in the pumping house.

"I'll check on your father shortly," Mother said. "Come, I want to look at you." She held Tikaya at arm's length and hm'ed and ahem'ed while surveying. "You're well? You've lost weight. All skin and bones. We'll have to put some extra pork on the spit. For both of you. Come, big man, we'll see if we can find a shirt that fits you. Or at least that you won't rip trying to put on."

"Yes, ma'am," Rias said.

Tikaya wondered when the last time was Fleet Admiral Starcrest had been mothered by someone. It didn't sound like he minded.

"At least he's polite," Mother said. "But dear..." She bent her head close to Tikaya's as they headed toward the hallway. "What are you *doing* with him? Is it just that he's bringing you home? Or... Well, Parkonis said you two are... that he might have..."

"I love him," Tikaya said.

"Oh." Mother stopped at the entrance of the hallway. "Oh, dear. Are you sure?" She smiled at Rias, who had stopped a few paces back, then whispered to Tikaya, "He doesn't seem your kind of fellow, honey. Parkonis—"

"He is, Mother. My kind of fellow. You'll see. You just have to talk to him. Give him a chance."

At least her mother was more concerned about Rias's suitability as a match rather than his reputation.

A thump came from the end of the hallway, the sound of a screen door closing. Two men with bows walked inside. The first was her cousin, Elloil, but the second she did not recognize. He had the small build, brown skin, and almond eyes of a Nurian, and Tikaya tensed immediately.

The stranger spotted Rias and jerked his bow up. He shouted a battle cry.

Rias dove to the floor, taking Tikaya and Mother with him. An arrow loosed, whizzing over their heads.

A startled shout came from the great room. Yosis.

Rias leaped to his feet and launched himself at the Nurian. He ripped the bow free and flung it down the hall. The Nurian whipped out a knife. The two men hit the floor in a tangle of limbs.

A shoulder rammed Elloil, and he stumbled, going down with a surprised grunt. The knife flew several feet, skidding on the floor and striking the baseboard. After a flurry of limbs Tikaya struggled to follow, Rias found the upper hand and straddled the Nurian, pinning him.

"Don't hurt him," Tikaya called, not sure who the Nurian was but figuring he was on friendly terms with the family.

Rias clutched his head and pitched sideways.

"Not again." Tikaya spun on Yosis. "Let him defend himself."

"I'll not watch him kill a man," Yosis barked.

The meaty thud of a fist striking flesh drew Tikaya's attention back to the battling men. The Nurian was taking advantage of Rias's incapacitation. He picked up the knife and lifted it above his head.

Tikaya bowled into the stranger. Hard sinewy muscles lay beneath his loose island shirt, but her momentum and greater height helped, and she ripped him off Rias. Her elbow clunked the wall hard enough to send a painful jolt through her, but she batted the knife away. It clattered to the floor.

"Stop!" Mother yelled and rang a bell.

It might have only been the dinner bell, but it startled everyone to stillness. The Nurian glowered at Rias, but Tikaya was halfway sitting on the man and did not help as he tried to squirm free.

"Find peace." Mom crossed her arms over her bosom.

Rias sat up, the pain apparently removed, though he groaned and closed his eyes as he let his head thump back against the wall.

"Are you all right?" Tikaya whispered.

"You'd think a man my *age* would dislike being shot at and wrestling on the floor, but you know by now that's not true. Though the... interruption was less pleasant." Rias opened his eyes and found

Tikaya's gaze. She wondered at the emphasis on the word age, but her more pressing concern was Yosis and his twitchy trigger finger. And perhaps this Nurian as well.

She shifted to let him up. "Who are you?"

"That's Mee Nar," Elloil said, "our new neighbor. We were out hunting snapping turtles, and I invited him to dinner."

"You didn't say that godless dog Admiral Starcrest would be at dinner," the Nurian said, chest heaving, his accented words coming in sputters. "He's killed thousands of my people. He's worse than the devil-spawned Turgonian emperor himself."

Tikaya rubbed her elbow. Dinner was going to be interesting.

* * *

The room made Tikaya feel silly. There weren't any dolls or stuffed animals nestled on the shelves, nor did a pink patchwork blanket cover the bed, but the academic awards and achievement medals peppering the walls created the aura of a student's domicile rather than that of a professor. She had been too busy moping to redecorate during the year she'd spent home after the war. She blushed at the idea of Rias seeing her silly childhood mementos—or sharing the small bed with her. Not that *that* would happen with her parents—and Yosis—in the house.

Tikaya changed out of the stuffy military uniform and into a calf-length calico dress more suitable for the climate. When she folded the Turgonian garb, the pocket crinkled, and she remembered the paper Rias had slipped her outside of the pumping house. She pulled out the folded note and checked the door to make sure it was shut. Rias was with Mother and Yosis, searching for suitable attire, so she had her first moment alone.

A series of gibberish letters adorned the page. Tikaya grinned. Only Rias would pass her encrypted notes.

Periods outlined sentences, and the nonsense letter combinations looked like words, albeit longer than average ones. The addition of nulls would account for that. Rias wouldn't have had time to compose much, so it was probably a simple substitution cipher. It wouldn't take long to break, though she probably couldn't do so by dinner, unless he had given her the key.

She thought back over their day's conversations. With Yosis watching on, Rias certainly hadn't said anything obvious. Even writing and passing the note had been a risk, especially if it contained more than terms of endearment.

His last words after the hallway scramble came to mind. Age. He'd emphasized that, hadn't he?

Rias was forty-three. She mentally shifted the Turgonian alphabet forty-three slots to the right and replaced the letters on the note with the new ones. She resisted the urge to get a pencil and leave written evidence of her deciphering.

Tikaya, the first word said. She'd guessed correctly.

A knock sounded at the door. Tikaya jumped and stuffed the note into her pocket. Before she could invite the knocker to enter, the door opened.

"Ho, Coz," Elloil said.

He strolled into the room, his hands in his pockets. His straight blond hair hung to his chin and had a tendency to flop into his eyes. He didn't seem to mind viewing the world through a curtain. Beneath his tan, Elloil had the family freckles and more than his fair share of the family looks, though his oversized yellow and pink floral shirt distracted one from said looks. One of his pockets bulged with a tin that was usually full of materials for making mood-altering concoctions to smoke.

"Hello, Ell." Tikaya checked the hallway, half-expecting the new Nurian neighbor to stride in on his heels. The sounds of arguing voices floated up from downstairs. Father had returned.

"Just wanted to apologize for that little tiff downstairs," Elloil said. "I didn't figure on there being Turgonian company already invited for dinner when I extended my own invitation. Who is that bloke?"

"You didn't get the message everyone else did about Tikaya's Turgonian?" she asked.

"I've been busy carving wood the last few days, and this morning the waves were breaking oh-so-fine at Black Cliff Point so naturally I spent the day on my board."

"Naturally." Tikaya waited for him to leave; she wanted to get back to the note.

Elloil ambled over, lay on the bed, and pillowed his hands behind his head. "Mee Nar thinks he's some great war criminal, and your father's hollering about you getting sheet-tangly with the Scourge of... something. I forget."

"Did you ever read a newspaper during the war?"

"Nah, but I guess I should have. This is good stuff. For once I'm not the biggest disappointment in the family."

"I'm glad my distressing situation is pleasing you." Tikaya turned her eyes toward the door, implying that he could go anytime.

"Your Turgonian seems all right to me though. Gave me a friendly nod and asked where he could get a shirt like mine. And he asked it like he meant it, not like he was being sarcastic and thought I was too dim to catch on—you know, like how most of the family talks to me."

"Ah." Tikaya eyed the horrible shirt again. Maybe Rias thought something like that would make him appear unthreatening. "You didn't tell him, did you?"

"And give up my sartorial secrets? Of course not. But I did tell him I'd get him one."

"Oh, dear."

"Yes, I'll have him looking like a native right soon, though you'd better get him to grow out that short hair a bit. Makes him look military."

"Imagine that." Tikaya held open the door. "I appreciate your help, Elloil."

"Aren't you curious about the new neighbors?" Before Tikaya could answer, he continued on. "Mee Nar decided to settle here after the war, seems to have fallen in love with a native. They bought a little piece of land off the Kaudelkas, and they're expecting their first baby." Elloil snapped his fingers. "That's probably why he's so upset about a Turgonian nearby. They kill babies, I've heard. To demoralize the enemy."

"Kill them and eat them, no doubt." Tikaya leaned against the door, giving up on her cousin taking a hint. She'd have to get him to leave some other way.... "How's the business going? Sell any surfboards lately?"

"A couple. I have a few orders for custom paint jobs too. Before long, I won't need to mooch meals anymore."

"You should have Rias look at your board designs," she said, silently apologizing for sending her cousin Rias's way. "He's an engineer. He might have some ideas for improvements."

"Oh? A Turgonian engineer." Elloil sat up, clanking his head on the shelf above the bed. "They say the Turgonians are almost as good at engineering as they are at killing."

"I've been in one of their ironclads, and it was impressive."

"Excellent, excellent. I'll talk to him." Elloil slid off the bed and tapped the tin in his pocket. "Join me for a pre-dinner smoke?"

"No, thank you. I need to finish changing." She waved at her bare feet.

"Sure, Tikaya." Elloil paused in the doorway and put a hand on her shoulder. "Good to have you back safe. You're one of the few family members who doesn't look down upon me."

Tikaya squirmed under the display of gratitude, given that she had been trying her hardest to get rid of him. "That's only because you're one the few family members tall enough to look me level in the eyes," she said lightly.

He chuckled and left.

Tikaya pressed her back against the door, yanked Rias's note from her pocket, and deciphered the rest.

Tikaya,

Something untoward is going on, more than animosity for the role I played in the war. Your police chief was initially suspicious of my intentions when he discovered the submarine design, but I can understand that. Such a vessel would *make the ideal spy craft. What's odd is that your high minister walked in, saw the designs, and grew agitated. He covered it quickly, but I read the concern— no, it was fear—in his eyes. When he announced his intention to release me, the police were shocked. Tikaya, animals released into the wild make easier targets for poachers than those kept secure in zoos. I think I'm being set up. I'll worry about that, but I need you to find out if there's any other reason a submarine would be cause for alarm here.*

I love you.
Rias

Tikaya leaned her head back, feeling the knobbiness of her thick braid against the door. More Turgonian paranoia, or was Rias right? She wanted to dismiss it, to think her people had only the best of intentions, despite questionable means, and were observing Rias out of fear for the safety of the islands, but it was hard to dismiss his suspicions. She wagered a lot of his hunches had proved right over the years. Surely one didn't become the empire's youngest admiral and highest-ranking naval officer by guessing wrong often.

She penned a quick, "I'll check into it," using his key, then grabbed a pair of sandals. As she tightened the straps, the dinner bell rang.

CHAPTER 5

"NO, NO, NO, *NO!*" GRANDPA said from the front door, pointing at Rias. Though nearly eighty, the wiry old grump stood with his chest stuck out, his legs spread, and his ropy muscles flexed, as if he intended to charge over and start a fight. "No joratt gorilla is going to sit at my dinner table or sleep in my house, and he sure as spit isn't going to bone my granddaughter."

Tikaya, who was stepping off the last tread on the staircase, froze with her hand on the bannister knob. Two-dozen sets of eyes swiveled toward her, including those of nieces and nephews too young to understand what was going on. Yosis stood behind Rias, a pleased smirk on his lips. Rias wore his hard-to-read face.

"Father." Mother had come out of the kitchen in time to hear the tirade. "Please curb your language in front of the children. And Akahe knows *I* don't want to hear such words either." She placed baskets of fried taro chips on the massive split-log table in the dining area at the end of the great hall.

"*Language?*" Grandpa roared. "That gorilla is swinging from the ceiling fans, and you're worried about words?"

"A man is here for dinner, and he's not made any trouble so far." As she spoke, Mother directed youngsters, using gestures, to set plates and silverware. "There's no reason to yell."

Rias stood on the threshold between the two rooms, holding a tray of glasses and utensils for Mother. She'd found him a creamy, V-neck shirt that left his wrists bare. He filled out the shoulders, but the torso hung limply—the shirt had been designed for someone rotund rather than muscular and wasn't particularly flattering. Perhaps one of Ell's shirts would be an improvement after all.

On the opposite side of the great hall, beyond several sofas and chairs full of relatives, Mee Nar stood in a corner with a woman Tikaya didn't know—his wife presumably. He was as far from Rias as one could be without going outside, and he was watching Rias like the chicken eyeing the fox stalking about outside the coop. He wasn't the only one. Nobody seemed to care that the "fox" was doing nothing more hostile than helping set the table. Kytaer, Tikaya's brother, had come in at some point, and now sat on a sofa with his wife and children, toddlers Tikaya had last seen the night of her abduction. She was glad they were well, though currently they were squirming about, hanging off the edge of the sofa. Their mother was insisting they stay seated instead of playing. No doubt, she worried that the visiting Turgonian would eat them if they wandered too close.

Ky gave Tikaya a relieved smile when he noticed her, but tension edged his eyes.

With great reluctance, Tikaya left the shelter of the stairway and walked into the room. At the same time Father and Cousin Telanae entered through a back doorway, escorting the pair of workers from the pumping house. Rias's makeshift bandages had been replaced with real ones, though the men all appeared much haler. Father met Tikaya's eyes, and his arm lifted, as if to invite her to a hug, but he noticed Rias, and his face hardened and his hand dropped.

"Are they truly going to tolerate Admiral Starcrest at their dinner table?" the Nurian's wife asked, whispering to her husband loudly enough for most people in the room to hear. "And are we truly going to *dine* with him? Do you know how many of your people he's killed? And how many of *our* people died because of his commands? How can they consider extending their food and hospitality?"

"Of *course* I know," Mee Nar whispered back through a clenched jaw.

"*Are* we extending our food and hospitality?" Kytaer asked Father.

Grandpa's eyes nearly bulged out of his face. "No!"

"Yes," Mother said as she laid the last of twenty-odd place settings. "He's Tikaya's guest. And I'll remind you all that Tikaya is back, and she's healthy and well. It wouldn't hurt you all to let her know you're happy to see her, and thankful to Akahe that she's returned safely. I, for one, cannot wait to hear the details of what's happened. Parkonis's accounting was terribly brief and a touch confusing."

Mother's speech inspired numerous hangdog expressions. Kytaer and a few of Tikaya's cousins stood, and started toward her, arms outstretched for hugs as they offered humble apologies. The moment had the makings of being pleasant, but Grandpa's cranky voice shattered it.

"*Details*," he spat. "His people kidnapped her, used her in devil sprites only know what perverted manner, brainwashed her into sympathizing with them, and now he's here to spy on our islands for that beast of an emperor of his. The war didn't end the way those joratts wanted, thanks in large part to *us*—" he thumped his chest as if he'd been out there on the guerrilla ships himself, "—and now they're here to figure out how to get our island in another way. You're all blind if you don't see that, and I'm embarrassed to call you my kin." He stomped out the door, shutting it with a bang.

Tikaya looked past her family members, whose greetings and endearments were faltering in the wake of Grandpa's tirade, and caught Rias's eye. "Sorry," she mouthed, apologizing for the fourth or fifth time that day.

He twitched his fingers as if to say it didn't bother him in the least. That was hard to believe.

Behind him, Yosis bent and scribbled something in his notebook. When Mother took the last of the dinner utensils from Rias, he surprised Tikaya by joining Yosis. There were too many people talking in between her and him, so she couldn't hear what he asked, but Yosis mumbled some response. She wondered if Rias hoped to humanize himself in his watchdog's eyes. She'd seen him do it before, pick the one person he knew he needed on his side and win his loyalty. She couldn't see Yosis developing a fondness for him though.

"Enough dallying about." Mother gestured to the table. "Isn't anybody hungry?"

A flock of people, spearheaded by the children—cousins, nieces, and nephews ranging from three to sixteen in age—descended upon the table. Mother recruited a couple of the older girls to help her carry platters out from the kitchen.

Tikaya received a few hugs and back pats on the way, though Grandpa's words had draped a pall over the house. Even her closest kin peered into her eyes, as if to search for the mind that they were sure had gone missing. Her brother stopped her before she reached the dining area.

"Good to see you, 'Kaya, but this isn't how I imagined you returning home. When I told you Mother was planning to give you a lecture on settling down with a new fellow and making babies, I didn't think you'd do something drastic, like arranging to have yourself kidnapped to find a man."

Tikaya knew he was trying to make her feel better by making jokes, but his grin seemed forced, and his attempt at humor earned a scowl from Father as he strode past.

"It proved a more effective way to meet men than moping by myself in the cane fields," Tikaya said.

"Anything would be more effective than that. Tikaya..." Ky lowered his voice and eased her to the side, putting his back to Rias and blocking her view of him. "Is he... Did he coerce you into bringing him here for some reason?"

"No." Tikaya fought down a grimace. She might as well get used to the question, as variations of it seemed to be on everyone's minds. "I coerced *him* into coming. Which, given the reception he's receiving, was probably a mistake."

Ky blinked slowly a few times. "Oh. But... he's... He'll never be welcome here. Everyone on the island lost someone during the war or had a loved one return maimed. Or tortured. Or neglected for months in their prisoner-of-war camps. The Turgonians are monsters, Tikaya. They don't respect humanity the way we do."

"They're not monsters; they're people, the same as us. From a different culture with different values, yes, but the world is full of differences. It'd be a tedious place to live in if that weren't the case. I know it'll be hard for him to find acceptance here, and we're not planning on staying long. I just had to come home and let everyone know I was all right."

"Not planning on staying? But what about your dream of researching at the Polytechnic and having children and raising them near the beach and all that?"

Tikaya had already reconciled herself to the idea that in choosing Rias she was ensuring that vision wouldn't come to pass, but the reminder did stir a pang of regret in her. Still, she lifted her chin and said, "Some people are worth changing one's dreams for."

Ky stared at her. "Not him. He's—"

"A good man. Yes, he was on the other side during the war, but that doesn't make him a monster. Talk to him. You'll see."

Ky looked like he'd swallowed something bitter. "What about... Oh, what about Parkonis?" he asked, eyes lighting as if he'd experienced an epiphany on how to turn the argument in his favor.

"I thought he was dead for a year. No, he *let* me think that. He let us all think that."

"There's a story behind that, I'm sure."

"Nothing that shines a flattering light upon him," Tikaya said.

"But, still, you were engaged. You made a promise to each other. Shouldn't you...?"

"No. Rias is a bigger man than Parkonis." Despite the seriousness of the conversation, the naughty part of her mind couldn't help but smirk and think, *in every sense of the word*... "And he treats me like I matter. More than anything."

This time, Ky didn't say, "Oh," but his mouth did form the syllable.

"Are you two going to join us for dinner?" Mother asked.

Everyone else had found a seat around the long table. Rias was stuck between Yosis and little Lonaeo whose gestures suggested he'd already started in on stories of his butterfly collection. He definitely wasn't one of those children who was shy around adults. At least Rias would have someone to talk to who wasn't employing frosty glares.

The closest available seat was four chairs down. Tikaya headed toward it, but Mother caught her and veered her in another direction, toward the head of the table. She patted the empty chair there.

"Erp?" Tikaya asked.

Elloil, sitting a few chairs down, pushed his bangs out of his eyes and smirked at her. "Those are the sorts of eloquent utterings that must make Mother and Father proud of the coin they invested in your years of linguistics education."

Before Tikaya could do more than flush with embarrassment—for some reason, all the conversations had stopped, and the whole family was watching her—Mother smacked Elloil on the back of the head. "Hush, dear. We are very proud of Tikaya. And concerned for her too. That's why she's going to sit right there and tell us what's been going on for the last couple of months."

Tikaya met Rias's gaze—my, he was *way* down at the far end of the table—and he gave her a supportive smile. Something in his eyes made her meet them longer than she might have otherwise. Wariness? He was probably wondering how much of the story she would reveal. Everything they had done was top secret, at least insofar as the Turgonians were concerned. Tikaya nodded once at Rias—she didn't intend to bring up the power or the re-write-the-history-books nature of the ancient artifacts. A few people exchanged concerned glances. Because she'd looked to him before settling in? She sighed. An hour with her family, and she was already longing for the secluded library archives at the Polytechnic.

"I imagine you're all wondering where I've been." Tikaya forced a smile, pulled out her chair, and tried to sit down without feeling awkward beneath all those stares. It didn't work. Her rump caught the edge of the seat instead of the middle, and it slipped off. She plopped to the floor, head dropping below the table, chair toppling onto the bamboo floor.

Blushing furiously, Tikaya scrambled to her feet. The good-natured laughter of the children reached her ears. That wasn't so bad. The adults offered a mix of sighs, exchanged glances, and questions of, "Are you all right, Tikaya?"

"Fine." She planted her rump firmly on the seat with her second try. She kept herself from looking at Rias, since people seemed to be concerned every time their eyes met.

"It's good to see that some things never change," Elloil said.

"That's the truth," Ky said. "And that's why I said your theory wouldn't prove true."

"Theory?" Tikaya asked.

"Ell thought the Turgonians kidnapped you for your height and archery skills," Ky said, "and that they were going to put you on some sort of baby-making farm to breed tall, strong warriors. But I pointed out that your clumsiness might be passed down to your children and that the empire would be disappointed in the result."

Before she caught herself, Tikaya threw Rias an exasperated do-you-see-what-my-family-is-like look. She didn't know how much of the conversation he was following—her kin had a tendency to speak often and rapidly—but the corners of his eyes were crinkled in amusement. So long as he felt entertained instead of bored—or endangered.

Mother, walking around the table with a giant bowl of poi, clucked her tongue and shook her head. "Nobody thought that, dear. We knew it was related to your work during the war. But, please, do explain before we burst from pent-up wonder."

Tikaya eyed the table's steaming platters of oysters, seared fish and limu, yams, chicken, and pork, and reluctantly acknowledged that her meal would wait. As the rest of the family heaped food onto their plates, she launched into her story. She took them from the day Agarik had first found her harvesting cane in the fields, to the kidnapping, to the journey across the sea, and the strange prisoner who'd been locked up across from her in the brig.

"I don't see how you failed to recognize him," Father said, interrupting her several minutes after she'd mentioned Rias and had gone on to explain the symbols the marines had given her to translate. Mother gave him a quelling glare. He said, "What? There was a tintype of him in the conference room during the war room."

Dear Akahe, was that right? Tikaya vaguely remembered pictures of Turgonian leaders posted on an "enemies of the islands" wall. Intent on the cryptanalyst work, she'd rarely paid attention to the decor.

"Of me?" Rias asked. "That's flattering."

It was the first thing he'd said to the table. Tikaya had a feeling he was trying to fill the silence that had blossomed after her father's words. Or maybe Rias meant to distract Father from casting judgment upon her.

Father only scowled at him instead. "The high minister enjoyed throwing darts at it while receiving vexing news."

"Ah," Rias said. "I hear the Nurian chiefs had a similar practice." He spoke slowly and took care with his pronunciation, perhaps not wishing to appear unschooled before Tikaya's family. As if he needed to worry about establishing his education credentials.

"You're a popular fellow," Elloil said with a wink, apparently unfazed by Rias's former occupation. Of course, not much ever fazed Ell.

"At the time we met, I wasn't," Rias said. "I'd spent two years in exile on Krychek Island, a—" He looked at Tikaya and asked, "Barren?" in Turgonian. She supplied the Kyattese word, and he continued. "A barren rock in the middle of the ocean. I was living off what... fishes the tides brought in..." He grimaced, fishes apparently not being the exact word he wanted. Doubtlessly he'd had to scrape seaweed and algae off the rocks and scavenge all sorts of dubious foods to make his meals. "And," he went on, "I was also busy wishing not to be eaten by the more... man-eating—" another glance at Tikaya, and she supplied, "cannibalistic." "Yes, cannibalistic residents," Rias said. "I looked like... There weren't any mirrors, but my own mother would have found it hard to identify me."

"Cannibals?" Cousin Aeli asked, touching a hand to her always-on-display cleavage. "That must have been dreadful for you."

"It was an unpleasant experience, yes," Rias said. "But Tikaya's story will interest you more, I'm certain." He nodded toward Tikaya, inviting her to go on.

"Oh, I don't know about that," Aeli purred.

Mother, still walking about and making sure people's plates were full—even though everyone could reach platters and ladle foods themselves—accidentally smacked Aeli's hand with her ladle. "Sorry, dear. More poi?" The shrewd squint that accompanied the question suggested the smack hadn't been so accidental.

At least Mother seemed to be on Tikaya's side. After nibbling on a couple bites of yam, she continued with the adventure. From the point where she started talking of the corpse-filled outpost of Wolfhump, the craziness that descended upon the marines, and the strange device causing the trouble, the family grew silent. Even the toddlers watched her with wide eyes. Rias listened intently as well, perhaps curious how the whole adventure had played out from her point of view, though she did catch him observing the Nurian guest from time to time too. Was he wondering if these details would make it back to the Nurian government? Tikaya trusted that he wouldn't attempt to make the foreign neighbor disappear, but she brushed lightly over information on how powerful the ancient technology was, and she said nothing of how it'd come into existence in the first place. She also didn't go into the details of the language deciphering—as she'd long ago learned, few people in her family shared her philology passion—or of her and Rias's moments of... relationship advancement, as she decided to think of them. But, seeing the interest from the youngsters, she did her best to relay the monster attacks in a lively manner. Knowing that people might condemn her for turning her back on Parkonis, she explained exactly what had happened with him and what he'd confessed to.

"Iweue will smack that boy on the nose with her fattest book," Mother said. "She'll be relieved to have her youngest son back, but, goodness, how could he let his family mourn him? *All* of us, for that matter. We had his funeral, by Akahe."

"Just be glad we didn't have to hold a funeral for Tikaya," Father said. It was almost a warming sentiment until he added, "Joratt Turgonians."

Tikaya might correct her little nephew's use of the derogatory term, but she doubted her father would appreciate chastisements from his daughter. She let Mother scowl at him for her, then went on with her story. Tikaya made sure to mention Gali and her telepathic intrusion. She didn't know if the woman would dare return to the islands after the oaths she'd stomped all over, but Tikaya did fear that the tide would bring other versions of the adventure up to the beach, and she wanted to lay down the facts first.

She finished by explaining how she and Rias had defeated the emperor's assassin and the Turgonian plans for withdrawing the weapons, emphasizing how crucial he'd been in her safe return home. She never could have made her way across those frozen mountains on her own.

"Hm," Father said when she finished. That was all he said.

Tikaya swallowed. She wasn't sure what she had expected, but that wasn't it. She had the impression he didn't believe her, or at least only partially believed her. It was, she admitted, a fanciful and unlikely story, but why would she make things up for them? Especially in front of Rias? Or was it because of Rias's presence that they thought she was making things up? Did they think he was coercing her into telling this story? Why? It hardly slanted the Turgonians at a favorable angle. Though perhaps people were thinking that everything was a ruse to provide a cover story for Rias's supposed spy mission. Surely, they would have thought up a less imaginative story if they were making something up.

Tikaya removed her spectacles and rubbed her eyes.

"It's good that you've made it back to us, dear," Mother said. Sometime during the narrative, she'd finally sat down. "Why don't you eat before you faint and fall off your chair again? It doesn't look like those brutes fed you."

"I will, Mother." Tikaya blinked when she noticed how full her plate had grown. How many passes had Mother made, shoveling food on with each round? Some things never changed.

"That was a good story," Lonaeo said, his green eyes bright. He plucked at Rias's sleeve. "Do *you* know any stories?"

"Nobody wants to hear his stories of blood-thirsty conquering," Father growled.

Lonaeo sank low in his chair.

"Father," Tikaya said, "he's not like that." How could Father truly think that after she'd explained everything? "Talk to him. He's—"

"We've talked enough." Father pushed his chair back and rose so quickly he almost upended it. "I've had enough of being cordial. That man is responsible for many of our cousins' deaths, and his cursed marines raped and tortured half the men and women who fought to defend our islands. That he has the gall to come here, and that he's done Akahe knows what to my daughter, is, is— I can't even find words for this vileness." Face redder than a sunset, Father stalked out of the house, slamming the front door behind him.

"Who wants rum?" Mother asked into the silence. "Or coffee? We make both here on our land, Mister Rias. Is it all right if I call you that or are you a lord or sir or some such? I do find Turgonia's rule by aristocracy terribly impractical, but I suppose all peoples must find enlightenment in their own time."

Tikaya cringed. Only her mother could offer someone a drink and call him a savage in the same breath.

"Just Rias is fine, ma'am," he said, neglecting to comment on the rest.

"Very good. Everyone, if you'll have a seat in the living room, I'll bring drinks and desserts. We have grilled pineapple and caramelized plantains. Jea and Oalaia, come help me serve, please."

Though Tikaya had not eaten more than a few bites, she was more than ready to escape from the table. Rias was rising as well, and she tried to veer toward him, but she found herself waylaid by a handful of nieces and nephews—nephews in particular—wanting more details on the monsters they'd fought in the tunnels. While she was trying to answer questions and simultaneously extricate herself, Elloil led Rias toward a courtyard door. Ell carried a bottle of spiced rum in one hand, and Tikaya worried about what he might have in mind. Getting Rias drunk? Or getting drunk himself? Neither sounded like intelligent propositions.

Before he walked out with Ell, Rias met her eyes across the room, giving her a head tilt that she guessed meant, "I'll be out here when you can get away."

Yosis trailed dutifully after him, so Tikaya doubted they'd find a chance for a private chat. The atmosphere in the great room lightened as soon as he left, with voices growing louder and more animated, and laughter punctuating conversations for the first time that evening. It stung Tikaya that Rias's absence should be so welcomed, but she knew it'd take time before anyone could grow accustomed to him. Nobody had spat in his food or knocked his dish in his lap. Maybe that was a start. Or maybe they just hadn't dared.

The Nurian and his wife said goodnights to Mother and left, both receiving smiles and nods from her family members. Tikaya would have wagered a lot that if the Turgonians hadn't tried to take over the Kyatt Islands, the Nurians would have attempted the same move sooner or later. It didn't seem fair that Rias should receive nothing but hatred while this Mee Nar wandered about on friendly terms with everyone.

Mother shooed the children away, but more people came up to welcome Tikaya home, so several minutes passed before she could escape to the courtyard lanai. She gripped the railing and searched for Rias by the dim lighting of whale oil torches dotting the paths.

The wooden lanai overlooked a garden sheltered on three sides by the wings of the house. The ocean roared in the distance, but not so loudly as to mask the gurgling of a large stone fountain in the center of the courtyard. Tikaya's eyes adjusted to the darkness, and she picked out two figures standing near the water feature. No, three. The third lurked in the shadows of a candle bush a few feet from the others, his white robes standing out against the darkness.

"Rias?" Tikaya asked, picking her way down the flagstone steps and along the path.

"You didn't tell me he doesn't drink, 'Kaya," Ell said, his voice drowning out Rias's quiet, "Yes?"

She joined the two men, pointedly putting her back to Yosis. She hoped the dim lighting would make it hard for him to record notes in his journal. It'd be a shame if someone accidentally kicked the thing into the fountain.

"He's a wholesome fellow," Tikaya said, though Rias had shared an apple liquor with her one night during their adventure, so he was no teetotaler. His reluctance to imbibe here was probably due to not wanting to dampen his wits in "enemy territory." How depressing that he considered her family's home more of a danger than that frozen fort full of dead people where they'd spent the night.

"Wholesome?" Ell asked. "That's a word better reserved for vegetables than men. Drink?" He offered Tikaya the bottle. The air smelled of vanilla and the spices in the rum.

"Maybe later. Rias, uhm..." She wasn't sure what to say. Her apologies were starting to feel painfully redundant to her, but her father and grandfather's behavior needed some explanation, she felt.

His hand found hers, warm and dry. And reassuring. Until he spoke. "I'm going to head into town shortly. Your cousin has offered suggestions on affordable lodgings."

"You're leaving?" Tikaya blurted in Kyattese, then repeated it in Turgonian, realizing he'd spoken in his own tongue.

"It'll be for the best."

She could hardly blame him, after the reception he'd received, but if he disappeared, her family wouldn't have a chance to get to know him. She wouldn't be able to show them that he *wasn't* a monster, that he was a good man. And she wouldn't be able to slip away for a tryst during the night, to discuss plans or engage in less... vocabulary-driven activities. She rolled her eyes, telling herself that sex was the least important thing to worry about just then. She'd been chaste for nearly a year before meeting him. A few nights alone wouldn't be that devastating. Except that it'd already been more than a few nights, due to his long shifts in the boiler room...

"I'll come with you," Tikaya said, even as she admitted that her brain wasn't entirely responsible for the words. An image of sharing a rented bungalow on the beach with Rias sounded lovely, though a guilty twinge ran through her at the idea of leaving Mother, in particular, after only a couple of hours back. "Family reunions are more palatable in small doses, after all," she said by way of justification.

"You should stay with your family. They've missed you and would doubtlessly be upset if you chose to leave shortly after arriving."

"I know, but—"

Rias squeezed her hand. "Also, it hasn't eluded my notice that people think I'm coercing you somehow and have ulterior reasons for being here."

"Oh." Tikaya prodded the base of the fountain with her toe. It shouldn't surprise her that Rias, despite not being a native speaker, had picked up on the nuances of the conversations going on around him, but it meant she knew what he'd say next.

"It'll be better if we're separated for a while, so your family can see that I'm not manipulating you. Others as well." Rias tilted his head toward Yosis, who hadn't moved or spoken since she came out. No doubt he hoped they'd forget he was there and let some devious Turgonian secrets slip out.

"Given what my people believe about imperial brainwashing methods, they'll probably think you can sway me all you like from miles away."

Rias chuckled softly, though she picked out a sadness underlying it. "Your family, at least, should know you're too smart for something like that," he said.

"You'd hope so, but..." Tikaya thought of Parkonis and how quickly he'd accused her of having captive complex. Of course, he'd been hurt that she was choosing Rias over him and had been looking for a justification. That was the problem. In the aftermath of the war, everyone on the island would seek similar justifications. They'd want to believe that all Turgonians were evil. Though a decade or two would dull the wounds, it might be too early to ask anyone to accept Rias as anything other than a savage. "Mother did seem to think you were acceptable," Tikaya finally said, feeling the silence had grown too long. "At least she made pleased grunts every time she circled the table and saw that you'd cleared your plate and were ready for another serving."

From his, "Hm," Tikaya couldn't tell if he was dismissing Mother as an ally worth having or considering the ways she might help his cause. Since they were observed, she dared not ask about any strategies he might plan to employ. If he was strategizing at all. Maybe he just hoped to bide his time until he could escape.

"Can you understand what they're talking about?" Ell asked.

It took Tikaya a moment to realize he was addressing Yosis. The professor ignored him. It didn't seem to bother Ell.

"Because all they've done so far is hold hands. Chastely. I'm beginning to fear The Black Scourge of the Seas *is* wholesome. How disappointing for someone with such a fierce name."

Since Yosis was facing Ell for the moment, Tikaya took the opportunity to slip her response to Rias's earlier note into his hand. "Not everyone wants an audience for... intimate activities, Ell. Perhaps you could take the professor out front and give us a moment to say goodbye."

Ell eyed Yosis, who returned his consideration in a baleful touching-me-would-be-bad-for-your-health way. "I never had much luck getting professors to listen to me," Ell said and dug his tobacco tin out of his pocket.

"Where are you going to stay?" Tikaya asked Rias as her cousin rolled and lit a cigarette. "I need to visit the Polytechnic tomorrow and get some advice from colleagues on the artifacts, chiefly whether we should make them disappear for all eternity or put together a team to study them." She remembered the request Rias had made in his note, that she figure out why someone might be alarmed at the notion of his submarine, and added, "It's a good place to do research," while squeezing his hand.

Rias nodded. "Though I can understand your fascination with the language—and the puzzles intrigued me as well—my vote would be for burying those secrets somewhere. The world isn't ready for them."

Yosis moved a couple of steps closer to a torch and tilted his notepad in that direction so he could write. Tikaya curled a lip at him.

"As to my lodgings, your cousin here says the Pragmatic Mate is affordable."

"And you can get all manner of poki there," Ell added in Kyattese, making Tikaya wonder how much of their conversation he understood. As far as she knew, he'd failed most of his linguistics classes—*all* of his classes, in truth—but more from a lack of interest than aptitude, she'd always thought.

"Poki?" Rias asked dubiously.

"Hallucinogenic compounds," Tikaya said. "But, really, Rias, the Pragmatic Mate? The locals call it the Pernicious Miasma, with good reason, I'm given to understand. The place makes your igloo seem palatial. You must not want me to visit."

"I'm certain I've stayed in worse accommodations. Though it would be a shame if you didn't visit."

"You're lucky I've discovered a new adventurous streak. Also, we don't have to *stay* there if I visit. Kyatt offers many scenic and private destinations." Which she'd dearly love to share with him, if they could get rid of—

"Put out that dreadful thing," Yosis growled, speaking for the first time all evening.

"Dreadful?" Ell lifted his cigarette. "My proprietary blend of vanilla-spiced tobacco is most certainly *not* dreadful. It's—" He crinkled his nose. An acrid, smoky scent had drifted into the courtyard. "That's not me."

"Fire?" Rias released Tikaya's hand and snapped into an alert posture.

"It smells worse than a wood fire," Tikaya said.

A surprised yell came from inside the house, or perhaps the lanai on the far side. Rias must have thought it originated outside, for he ran to the back of the courtyard and raced around the corner of the house.

Yosis cursed and fumbled to snap his journal shut.

Tikaya gripped his arm before he could think of stopping Rias with that ghastly device. "I'm sure he's going to help."

But the rest of her family might not appreciate his "help." Tikaya released Yosis and ran after Rias.

Since she'd changed back into sandals, her footwear slapped against the flagstones as she raced around the house. As much as she'd loathed that Turgonian uniform, the boots had been more practical for active pursuits. She didn't need to run far before a startling sight brought her to a halt so quickly she almost tripped.

The front lawn was on fire.

It wasn't some random bonfire, but three lines of... Tikaya squinted. Letters? Words? From her angle, she couldn't read them.

Her kin were pouring out of the house to stand on the lanai and gape. Tikaya searched about for Rias. When she didn't see him on the lanai or lawn, a hunch drew her gaze upward. He stood on the roof, looking down at the flames, his face grim. She thought about shouting up to him, asking for a translation, but decided to climb up instead.

Using the corner lanai post for support, she clambered up the railing and pulled herself onto the roof without any particular grace. Unlike her brother, she'd never been one to sneak out from the second-story bedrooms to run off with friends or lovers, so she lacked practice. She made it up, though, and joined Rias. From the elevated perch, the flaming words were easy to make out. Unfortunately.

Go home, joratt. Death awaits you here.

"I suppose you can read that," Tikaya said, groping for a way to make light of the situation, though worry weighed upon her heart. And anger as well. What bastard would have come onto her family's property to do such a thing? Though a hint of the mental sciences lingered in the air and was doubtlessly responsible for the perfect outlines of those letters in flames, any fire had the potential to get out of hand. What if sparks landed on the thatch roof of the house?

"My vocabulary has many holes in it, but those are words I knew long before I met you, yes."

"I'm sorry, Rias. I'm sure it's just one angry person who's misguided and not thinking. Or..." She stopped. She didn't want to justify the actions of whatever idiot had done this.

"As I was saying, it'll be best if I leave tonight." Rias touched her back gently and maneuvered past her to hop off the roof.

Feeling numb, Tikaya watched the flames until her father's bellow echoed up from the lanai below. "Everyone stop standing around. Get down here to put out this fire!"

By the time Tikaya climbed down, Rias and Yosis were gone.

CHAPTER 6

"IT'S FASCINATING," PROFESSOR LIUSUS SAID, her face so close to the black sphere, she kept bumping it with her nose. Her chin clunked the bamboo table on which the artifact sat more than once. She didn't notice. She held her spectacles in one hand and, with the other, kept shoving back gray strands of hair that fell into her eyes as she examined the artifact from every angle. It'd been at least ten minutes since she'd said anything to Tikaya or acknowledged her presence in the room.

Tikaya didn't mind. She knew Liusus had a passion as strong as her own, though her specialty was maritime archaeology rather than philology. They'd had occasion to work together often, and Tikaya considered Liusus a friend and mentor.

Tikaya leaned forward and touched a series of symbols on the outside of the object. A spherical projection formed in the air above the device, depicting one of the race's languages, the last thing she had been studying. Liusus stumbled back, hand to her chest, eyes wide. She bumped her chair, upturning it with a loud thunk that echoed through the library alcove, but she didn't seem to notice.

"That's not an artifact," she said, giving the word the special accent to refer to a practitioner-crafted device rather than an archeological find. "There's no sense of—"

"I know," Tikaya said. "It's all technology-based."

"Technology..." Liusus started to lean back over the table again, but her foot caught on the leg of the fallen chair. She stared at it for a moment, as if perplexed as to why a piece of furniture might be lying down there, then straightened it with an exasperated grunt. "Have you showed this to anyone else yet?"

Liusus eyed the surrounding shelves full of scrolls and textbooks, as if she feared some spy might be watching from behind the stacks.

"Yes, the police searched my bags when I returned, and the artifacts were flagged and sent over to Dean Teailat. He, his staff, and I had quite the discussion about them this morning." Tikaya had relayed the same story that she'd shared with her family, though there'd been far more questions related to the tunnels, language, artifacts, and ancient people. She'd given accurate accounts of everything. Someone had to know the truth about what the relic raiders and the Turgonians had been up to, and how dangerous the technology was, as she wasn't comfortable holding all that information to herself, though she did hope she could trust her colleagues to remain tight-lipped about everything.

"And they let you have them back?" Liusus asked.

"Sort of. I'm to keep them at the Polytechnic and only study them here until the department heads have met and discussed the situation. I'm still trying to arrange communication with the president. He definitely needs to know about all this, and I need his help with another matter as well."

"Yes." Liusus reclaimed her seat. "I understand your other matter is the talk of the island."

Tikaya grimaced. Her colleague had never married, nor, in the years Tikaya had known her, shown interest in physical relations; she'd hoped Liusus would be too fascinated with the artifacts to care about rumors concerning Rias. In the less than twenty-four hours that she'd been home, Tikaya had already received enough advice on that matter and had no wish to discuss it again.

"The fire in your yard must have been alarming," Liusus said, her tone sympathetic.

"Yes... Who have *you* been hearing all the details from?" Tikaya wondered which of her family members was blabbing to the world. Everyone might know about Rias, but what happened on their plantation ought not be fodder for the island gossip mills.

"It was in the morning newspaper."

"I didn't think you read the news. It's too recent, you've said on many occasions."

"That's correct," Liusus said, "but everyone was discussing it in the staff lounge this morning."

Tikaya sighed. "Wonderful."

"If it cheers you up, only one in three of your colleagues thinks the Turgonian has brainwashed you into bringing him here so he can spy while perpetrating the ruse of being your lover."

"Wonderful," Tikaya repeated. "What do the other two thirds think?" Why, she wondered, am I asking when the answer will only irritate me?

"Mixed reactions. A few outliers think you may be knowingly colluding with him, rather than being brainwashed—"

Tikaya rolled her eyes. Was that supposed to be an improvement?

"—but those were people who aren't aware of what your work in the war entailed. A couple of optimistic sorts who are aware of your cryptography contributions—and admire them very much—think you're working for the president and, under his orders, seduced the admiral in order to extract information for our people's benefit."

Tikaya snorted. That was new. And even more ridiculous than the rest. As if *she* could seduce someone. "Does anyone think we were thrust into an adventure together, against our wishes, and happened to fall in love along the way?"

Liusus scratched her jaw thoughtfully. "I don't recall that version. Not enough intrigue to capture people's fancies, I imagine."

No, of course not. "So, how are you doing? Is anything new happening in the world of marine archaeology? I haven't talked to you much this last year." Tikaya would have wanted to catch up with her colleague anyway, but she'd specifically sought Liusus out because of Rias's message.

"Yes, I've been busy looking over wreckage from a Danmesk Empire shipyard that was unearthed on the Bratar Coast, a good four hundred miles south of what was previously believed to be the southern most border of the empire. We believe volcanic activity buried a significant coastal colony there nearly two thousand years ago." Liusus took a breath, signifying that she was warming up to a lengthy lecture on the topic.

"Nothing closer to home?" Tikaya felt rude for cutting her friend off, and, in different circumstances, would have enjoyed hearing about the new dig, but she was quite certain that a civilization that had been dead for over fifteen hundred years wouldn't have a problem with Rias building a submarine.

"What do you mean?" Liusus asked.

"Around the islands. Our islands."

"Our history is well documented, given that our people were writing and keeping records when we first colonized the islands seven hundred years ago. The maritime museum even has one of the original settlers' ships on display, along with examples of dress, tools, and housing from the time period." Liusus tilted her head. "But you've been to the museum, surely, and know all of that."

"Yes, I was just wondering..." Tikaya removed her spectacles and took a moment to clean the lenses while considering if she should tell her colleague about Rias's suspicions. She believed she could trust Liusus, but she didn't even know what to ask. All she had to go on was Rias's hunch. "Rias sketched out plans for a submarine while we were on our way over here, and, out of all the items he had that might have given the authorities cause for alarm, it was those sketches that drew Jikaymar's attention."

"Jikaymar? The high minister in charge of foreign relations?"

"Yes."

Liusus spread her arms. "I imagine he sees a submarine as a craft that could be used to spy upon our people. You can't blame him for being alarmed. Was there anything unusual about the design?"

"Only that Rias believed he could make it work for long voyages. He said his people haven't been able to do more than putter around on the bottoms of ponds, because there's no way to create a viable underwater propulsion system with wood or coal as the fuel. He thought to acquire a Made power source from a local craftsman."

"Well, there you go. Can you imagine the potential power of a craft that married our Science with imperial metallurgy and engineering technology? The Turgonians may be warlike and brutal by our standards, but nobody would call them dumb. They have the best ships in the world. When it comes to the mental sciences, they're as superstitious as children in a graveyard on All Spirits Day, but that's a good thing as far as the rest of the world is concerned. I'm sure the high minister is horrified by the idea of Turgonian submarines that use Kyattese power sources. What if your admiral is designing a prototype, and he intends it to be the first of dozens or even hundreds that their military builds? Can you imagine what sort of advantage that would provide in naval warfare? They could be ready to take on the Nurians again by the end of the decade. And where would that leave our little islands? In the line of fire again."

Though Tikaya had been shaking her head all through the latter half of the speech, it took a lot to stop Liusus once her taro pot started bubbling over. "He's only interested in building it for us," Tikaya said. "Him and me. So we can work on intriguing puzzles and digs from the world of eld and then disappear beneath the sea if his past enemies catch up with us." As much as Tikaya had always considered herself a homebody, the idea of such explorations had grown on her, and she smiled as she explained it, not realizing until she finished that Liusus was watching her with a frank gaze.

"You were never this hopelessly quixotic when you were engaged to Parkonis."

At least she hadn't called Tikaya naive. Yet. "No, we were a very... practical couple. But Parkonis never gave me a reason to adore him... Rias is very..."

"Yes, I've seen the tintype."

Tikaya blushed. Was she the only one on the island who wouldn't have recognized him at first glance? "I was going to say supportive. He makes you feel bigger than you are instead of smaller."

"He's certainly bigger than average." Liusus's eyes glinted behind her spectacles. "I suppose all his body parts are proportional."

Tikaya's blush grew so fierce it threatened to singe her cheeks from the inside out. "I never knew you had such a wicked mind, Liusus." Figuring she'd best change the subject before she burst into flames, Tikaya switched back to the original topic. "If I wanted to research Kyattese maritime archaeology, where would be a good place to start? The Oceanography Wing of the library?"

Liusus studied Tikaya for a long moment before answering. "Yes."

"Thank you." Tikaya picked up the sphere and took a step toward the door, but Liusus's words halted her.

"There are detailed bathymetrical maps of the waters around the Kyatt Islands in there. I trust... they won't be used against our people."

Such as by a spy in a submarine? Tikaya sighed. "He's not working for the empire any more, Liusus. The emperor treated him like grimbal droppings, and he's no longer interested in obeying imperial orders.

And my kidnapping certainly didn't cause me to develop a fondness for Turgonians. Quite the opposite, I assure you. I have no interest in those maps."

"What *are* you looking for then?"

Good question. "I'm hoping I'll know it when I see it."

Liusus didn't look suspicious exactly, but she did appear concerned. Tikaya groped for a way to lessen that concern before leaving.

"Who was it that thought I could actually seduce a man?" she asked.

Liusus blinked a few times. "Professors Iolas and Koaneoa."

"Ah, one man blind and the other eighty years old. That explains much." Tikaya smiled and waved.

This time she made it to the doorway before Liusus's words made her pause.

"You're *not* homely, Tikaya. You're just tall."

"Yes, well, it's good that I found someone who's... proportional, eh?"

Tikaya left Liusus making choking noises that might have indicated surprise or laughter or both. She strode through the sprawling Polytechnic library, a three-story building of volcanic stone walls and banyan tree wood. Though the Kyattese generally preferred symmetry and logic when it came to construction, the library was one of the oldest structures on the island and had grown and evolved over the centuries, leaving it something of a maze to newcomers. Tikaya knew it well though and found her way to the northern wing on the second floor. A sign on the Oceanography room door made her pause.

Closed for repairs.

"Repairs?" Tikaya tried the door and found it locked. "What kind of repairs could a library possibly need?"

Nobody was around to answer her question.

As Tikaya strode up the cracked walkway of the Pernicious Miasma, lizards, rats, and other verminous creatures skittered in and out of the overgrown clumps of grass on either side. Stuck in the middle of a shallow basin, the inn was not the benefactor of any tropical breezes, so the smells of the nearby harbor—seaweed, fish, and the burning coal from someone's steamer—hung in the air. Warehouses arose on all sides, further hemming in the one-story building. A driftwood sign, half hidden by the tall grass, proclaimed it the Pragmatic Mate, but someone had painted Pernicious Miasma across the front in bold red letters. A piece of paper tacked to the side read, "Turgonians welcome" in the imperial tongue, though the nightly and weekly rates listed at the bottom were twice the normal prices.

When Tikaya grasped the doorknob, something sticky licked at her palm. She yanked her hand away with a grimace, wiping it on her dress. If the world were fair, the proprietor would be paying Rias to stay there.

A potted plant with more brown fronds than green nearly thwacked her in the face when she walked inside. Rusty iron bars covered a window to the left of the narrow hallway. Nobody sat at the desk inside the cubby, so she picked up a metal wand and rang a triangle dangling from one of the cross bars. Three lizards scurried across the floor and disappeared into cracks in the wall.

Several moments passed before a curly-haired blond man limped into the hallway, leaning on a staff as he walked. "Help you, ma'am?" he asked.

"Yes, did a Turgonian named Rias check in here last night?"

"Along with an older Kyattese practitioner? Yes. Most unlikely pair I've ever seen. We don't discriminate, but I didn't know whether to give them the local rate, the Turgonian rate, or the hourly rate."

It took Tikaya a moment to get past the image his words birthed, then come up with a response. "What rate do you charge the lizards?"

"They eat the flies and crickets, so they stay for free."

"I see. What room is Rias in?"

"Three, but I don't think they're in. They left early this morning. Surprising since they were out so late at the gambling hall."

"The gambling hall?" Tikaya hadn't known there were gambling halls on the island—the Book of Akahe frowned upon such vices—though she supposed the waterfront businesses thrived by catering to visiting foreigners.

"Yes, after the big man asked for directions, they were gone for hours last night."

"Any idea where they went this morning?" Tikaya asked.

"Nah, I don't pry into my guests' personal lives. Are you interested in a room?"

"No, thank you. Is there any chance you can let me in to see if he left a message?"

"Go ahead." The man unlocked the door to the tiny office and shuffled inside.

Tikaya waited to see if he would pull out a keychain and escort her to the room, but he sat down and pulled out a magazine full of pictures of nude women. Maybe Rias had left his door unlocked....

She turned into an even narrower hallway, this one bereft of attack shrubbery lining its walls, and searched for Room #3. None of the doors had locks. She supposed that explained why the proprietor hadn't felt compelled to show her to the room personally. The catch was broken on Room #3's door, leaving it ajar, and Tikaya pushed it open without needing to risk touching any sticky residue that might lurk on the knob.

The tiny windowless room—closet might have been a better word—claimed a dearth of furnishings. It didn't even have a bed. She was on the verge of cursing her cousin for recommending the place when she found the missing bed folded into the wall. A piece of wire stretching across one corner at the right height to garrote Tikaya held two hangers. Rias's trousers dangled from one. A crate in a second corner served as the only other piece of furniture. There was a pen on it, but no note to suggest where Rias might have gone. She checked the pockets of the hanging garment, even as she wondered what clothing he'd found to replace the military trousers, and smiled when she found a note folded in the pocket.

It held a pair of nonsense words. She tried the same key as he'd used with the previous note and decoded it: *Shipyard 4.*

Tikaya hadn't realized there were more than three shipyards in the harbor, and double-checked her decryption, but it appeared correct. Perhaps Shipyard 4 was near the privately owned docks at the far end of the quay.

She hustled out of the room, worried she'd miss Rias if he and Yosis had indeed left early that morning. The proprietor had pulled the curtains on his booth. She decided not to say anything in parting in case he was... busy.

Outside, Tikaya almost crashed into a big man heading up the walkway with canvas totes full of tools. A big *Turgonian* man, the bronze skin, muscled arms, and determined brown eyes suggested. Apparently in a hurry, he nearly strode right through her.

Tikaya gulped and skittered into the grass to let him pass. Though she doubted she was in further danger of being kidnapped, the role she'd played in thwarting the Turgonians' conquering aspirations meant she'd always be wary when one approached. This one had a grim, fierce aspect as well. Marine, she guessed, though perhaps a former one, since he wore loose cotton and hemp island garb.

"Oh, pardon, ma'am." He stopped to look her over. "Are you all right? Sorry, I was in a hurry to, uhm..." He eyed her more closely.

Uh oh. What if flyers were being passed around to Turgonians all over the world, displaying pictures of the "cryptomancer" with offers of reward? She glanced around. Nobody else was in sight.

"Pardon, ma'am," the Turgonian said again, "but are you the admiral's Kyattese woman? He said she was tall. And smart. And you look like both."

She looked smart? None of her family members or colleagues would say that, at least if recent events were anything to go by. Of course, spectacles seemed to be rare amongst Turgonians, so maybe that fit their definition of "smart." At least this fellow sounded more like an ally than an enemy.

"The admiral's Kyattese woman?" Tikaya asked. "I guess that's more or less accurate, though he's somewhat... retired now."

"I *know*," the man groaned. "He didn't explain it all, but I can't believe it. I thought, er, we *all* thought that he was dead. To know that he's here and alive, and—" the man's face, one she'd been thinking of as grim and fierce a moment before, split into a broad grin, "—he talked to me! He asked about what ship I'd served on in the war, and he knew *all* about the action we'd seen and even about the way Captain Levk used to sing when he was deep in his cups." The grin turned into a fond chuckle before the man seemed to remember Tikaya was standing there. "Oh, do you know where he went? These are for him." He hefted his totes, and equipment clanked, everything from saws and hammers to metalworking tools. "And don't tell that shifty bloke who's following him around, but my boss at the steelworks said he could come by anytime to use our Bragov Converter. My boss used to be a marine too, you know."

"I... am sure Rias will appreciate your support," Tikaya said, mildly stunned by the deluge of information. It didn't surprise her that Rias was already attempting to make allies and gather resources, but she hadn't realized it'd be feasible. It hadn't occurred to her that there might be Turgonian ex-patriots living on the island who held useful positions. "What was your name, sir?"

"Oh, Milvet." He thumped his fist to his chest and gave a bow that surprised her with its depth. She wasn't certain of the exact nuances but knew the degrees of torso inclination were adjusted based on the rank, military or warrior-caste, of the person receiving the bow. She had a feeling she'd been granted a lot of status on Rias's behalf. Didn't this Milvet care that Rias had disobeyed orders and was in exile? Or maybe he didn't know exactly. "Real good to meet you, ma'am. Do you know if I should leave this in his room or is he around?"

"I believe he's in one of the shipyards at the quay."

"Already setting to work, eh?" Milvet winked.

"Uhm, I suppose so."

Was Rias truly going to start building his submarine right under Yosis's nose? Surely not. That'd be asking for trouble, assuming the government even let him get started. Besides, he'd need a lot of good Turgonian steel to craft the hull, and that wouldn't be in large supply. This steelworks Milvet had mentioned was probably the only one in Kyatt and surely only worked with scrap metal rather than fresh ore. The volcanic islands didn't provide anything like that.

"I'm heading down there now," Tikaya said. "Do you want me to take those bags to him?"

"Oh, no, I couldn't ask a lady to carry my dirty tools. I'll go with you, ma'am."

Tikaya doubted it would be in her best interest to be seen wandering around with Turgonians, but she didn't see how she could turn down the earnest fellow. She certainly didn't want to dissuade anyone from becoming an ally to Rias; he'd have precious few of them here.

"Right," Tikaya said. "This way, then."

As they wound through the streets toward the waterfront, Milvet handled all of the talking, or perhaps one might call it burbling as he extolled Fleet Admiral Starcrest's virtues and spoke of all the times his own ship had been in the vicinity of the admiral's flagship. They'd reached the quay, and Tikaya was searching the signs for mention of a Shipyard 4, so she almost missed it when Milvet asked a question.

"Do you think he'll be coming back to Turgonia?"

"Huh?" Tikaya asked.

"Both of you, that is."

"Ah, I don't know what he told you," Tikaya said, not wanting to trample on whatever story Rias had given the young man, "but you do know that he's...?"

"In exile? Oh, sure, he told me that. And made me promise not to tell the world that he's alive if I travel back to the empire, but he's going to want to come home eventually, won't he? The emperor's powerful, sure, but if the admiral showed up in the capital, he'd have legions of people who would stand at his back and make it right clear that it'd be in the emperor's best interest to give him his lands and title back, if you see what I'm saying." Milvet offered a sly comradely smile, as if he were ready to sign up for one of those legions right then.

"We'll... have to wait and see what the future holds." Tikaya wondered if this young man was naive or if Rias truly could raise an army, one that could be used to coerce the emperor into rethinking the exile declaration. If it *were* a possibility... Well, it was sobering to think that Rias might be choosing Kyatt, where her people only wished to torment him, over returning home. "He said something about being more interested in helping the world than the empire the last we spoke of it," she said as they passed the last of the three shipyards she was familiar with and entered a tangled snarl of old wooden docks jutting out into the harbor. Where *was* Shipyard 4?

Milvet trekked happily along at her side, muscles bulging as he carried the gear. If the long walk with his arms weighed down tired him, he gave no indication of it. If anything, he looked tickled to have this opportunity to work for Rias.

"What's the dock number?" he asked.

"We're looking for Shipyard 4," Tikaya said.

"That's the little one down at the end." Milvet waved toward the end of the quay where a dilapidated block-and-tackle hoist system straddled an empty bay. "It's the original one for the island, isn't it?"

Tikaya squinted in the direction he was pointing. Compared to the private and public shipyards they'd passed, each capable of housing multiple vessels in various stages of completion, the spot ahead appeared to be little more than another dock. As they drew closer, she could see that the channel was enclosed with a gate at the end, but everything from the hoist system to the dock itself looked like something suitable for the maritime museum rather than actual use. It didn't even have a sign, just a crooked, sun-faded "4" carved into a weathered post at the head of the channel.

"Is this privately owned?" Tikaya asked. Strange perhaps to ask a foreigner, but Milvet seemed more familiar with the docks than she. Her own work hadn't brought her down here often.

"Think so," Milvet said. "I know the Dukovics control some of the old docks down here."

"That's a Turgonian name, isn't it?"

"Yes, ma'am. After the war, my people weren't real welcome here, even those who'd made homes here long before the fighting started, and suddenly they weren't allowed to dock their ships. Someone talked a native into buying a block on the quay and signing a contract to rent the berths out to Turgonians."

Tikaya hadn't realized there were that many Turgonians on the islands.

"I wonder if that's the ship the admiral mentioned." Milvet waved to the dock next to the tiny shipyard.

The only "ship" Tikaya saw was a giant pile of junk hunkering against the waves. Twisted metal arms and cranes rose from the deck of the old tug. At least it had been a tug once. Now, the entire deck was canted with water lapping over one end, and the vessel appeared about as seaworthy as a boulder. Rust coated the monstrosity like powdered sugar on a rum cake, except without any of the appeal.

"Are you sure that's... a ship?" Tikaya asked.

Milvet set his bag down, scratched his jaw, and said, "I might have been more flattering than I intended in using that word, ma'am."

Tikaya would have turned around, certain she'd decoded Rias's message incorrectly, but she spotted Yosis sitting in a deck chair next to a gangplank—a knotty old board—leading onto the dilapidated tug. Head back, eyes closed, mouth hanging open, he appeared to be sleeping. The hem of his white robes flapped in the breeze, revealing hairier legs than she cared to see. Yosis didn't stir to adjust his robes. Maybe Rias had worn him out with all his traipsing about the night before.

"After you, ma'am." Milvet nodded.

The man didn't look anything like Agarik, but his polite ma'ams were starting to remind Tikaya of him. For all that Turgonians might be warlike brutes, imperial mothers did seem to raise their boys to be polite, most of them anyway. She thought less fondly of Sergeant Ottotark and Captain Bocrest, though even Bocrest's crustiness had seemed less harsh in the end.

"Thank you," Tikaya said and walked up the dock.

She was close enough to shove Yosis's chair into the water—and she contemplated what punishment she might receive should she do just that—before he snapped his mouth shut and opened his eyes. The withering look he gave her made her wonder if he was a telepath.

"Good afternoon," Tikaya said, smiling to wipe any vestiges of a guilty expression from her face. "I've come to see Rias."

"You should not be allowed to collude with him. I've sent my first day's notes off and made my recommendations. I'll hear back shortly."

From whom, she wondered? The police? Or was he answering to another institution? "I can't wait to hear the results," Tikaya said, though his words roused concern. They couldn't truly keep her from seeing Rias, could they? She was a free citizen. And he was... They hadn't decided yet apparently.

"I doubt that," Yosis grumbled.

Clanks came from the bowels of the half-sunken vessel. A moment later, a hatch clanged open, and Rias's head poked out. All manner of rust flakes, dust, and cobwebs cloaked his hair, and a large smudge of grease adorned his cheek. Though Yosis had cast new worries into her mind, Tikaya couldn't help but smile at this sight.

He smiled, too, when he saw her, pulled himself onto the tilted deck, and crossed the gangplank in a single long stride. Elloil's handiwork was evident in his new attire, a sleeveless yellow shirt that wrapped across his torso, leaving a large open V below his throat, and vibrant green plaid clam diggers. She dearly hoped the garb represented an attempt to appear innocuous and didn't reflect his true color preferences. If it did, she might have to return him to the Turgonian marines, just to get him back into a uniform. Though, she had to admit that as vile as she found the colors, they didn't look *bad* on his olive skin, and the sleeveless shirt revealed a lot that was—she swallowed—worth revealing.

When he reached her, he swept her into a warm hug, though, after a quick glance at Yosis, gave her only a chaste kiss. The depth of Rias's smile and an eager I-have-news light in his eyes suggested she may not have gotten much more anyway.

"Milvet, thank you for bringing the tools. That's far more than I hoped for." Rias gripped the Turgonian's arm with one hand while keeping Tikaya close with the other.

"It was an honor and my duty, my lord," Milvet said.

"Rias, please."

"Yes, my lord. Er, sir. Uhm, Rias." Milvet shrugged sheepishly.

Yosis had not risen from his chair, but he observed the exchange with narrowed eyes.

"Look what I won," Rias said to Tikaya and stretched an arm toward the vessel.

"You won it?"

"In a game called Cockroach, a board game that pits two people against each other. You can choose to be either the plantation owner defending his crops or the insect army attempting to decimate the fields." He grinned again. "Who would have thought I'd find military strategy games on the Kyatt Islands?"

"Military strategy?" Tikaya asked, bemused. Cockroach was a game children played, and it surprised her to learn there was a gambling-hall version.

"Of course. As the plantation owner, I had to deploy my troops and use my resources to stave off the invading insect armies."

"Troops? Do you mean the... family members?" Tikaya asked, thinking of the freckled blond boy, girl, and spouse board pieces.

"Yes. Once I learned the rules—and that laying a trap in one's own silo to blow up the captured invaders isn't acceptable—winning was a simple matter."

"Did you say... blowing up the silo?"

"An undesirable tactic since preserving one's assets is preferable, but sometimes a small sacrifice is worth making if it facilitates the winning of the war."

"How do you blow up a silo, my lo—Rias?" Milvet asked.

Rias winked. "Spontaneous combustion. That's usually accidental, but one can certainly hasten it along by providing oxidation through moisture and air. Bacterial fermentation also works. The rules in Cockroach, however, do not appear to allow for such creativity."

"Yes," Tikaya said, "we don't like to encourage our children to go around blowing things up."

"A shame. Such skills can prove useful in life."

"Turgonian life," Yosis muttered. He produced his notepad and scribbled a few lines.

Rias only grinned, and Tikaya wondered if he might be deliberately provoking the professor.

"I better get ready for work," Milvet said. "Though there's not much going on there during the nightshift." He didn't say it to anyone in particular, though he widened his eyes slightly, and Tikaya assumed that was an invitation for Rias to come and do... whatever it was he intended to do.

Rias gave him a comradely wave, then offered his hand to Tikaya. Perhaps out of habit, Milvet saluted Rias before striding off. Yosis made a note.

"Do you truly think he'd be so obvious about all of this if he were planning something inimical?" Tikaya snapped at the professor.

"Perhaps," Yosis said, without bothering to look up from his notepad, "it is by being obvious that he seeks to lull us into a false sense of safety."

Tikaya opened her mouth, another retort on her lips, but Rias tugged her gently toward the gangplank. "Come see my prize."

She took a deep breath and followed him. If Yosis didn't bother Rias, she shouldn't let him bother her. Still, she couldn't help but grit her teeth when the professor followed them onto the old tug.

The rusty deck creaked ominously when they stepped onto it. Tikaya could scarcely identify the warped cranes and other lifting apparatuses. Aside from the rust bejeweling the hull, a slimy green coat covered much of the deck, and she had to walk carefully lest she slip more often than usual.

"Are you sure you *won* this?" Tikaya asked. "Maybe the other fellow pretended to lose so he'd no longer be responsible for the moorage fees."

Rias lifted his chin. "I'd know if someone sandbagged in a strategy game. The fellow had already lost his coin in previous rounds, and this was all he had left with which to gamble. Normally, I don't partake in such ventures, and I did feel underhanded in acquiring his belongings, but I have few resources myself these days and must think of our goals.

Given how expensive it is to purchase metal here on the islands, I estimate the scrap here to be worth nearly forty thousand ranmyas."

"And you think you can turn this scrap into your new... project?" Tikaya figured Yosis knew about the submarine, but was reluctant to mention it out loud regardless.

"I'll need to recruit helpers to provide the manpower, but with the use of a shipyard—" he waved at the slender channel next to his dock, "—I'm certain I can build... something. Whether it'll be quite as ideal as what I drew on paper, that remains to be seen."

"That's not much of a shipyard."

"It's more than I expected. Since your people aren't as advanced, er, since they don't build as many ships as my people, I feared the Kyattese version of a shipyard might be a beach with a nice slope." He mimicked shoving something big into the water.

"*He's* denigrating *us*?" Yosis asked.

"If I have the opportunity," Rias told Tikaya without acknowledging the professor's comment, "I can have a prototype done in a matter of weeks."

Tikaya imagined sitting beside him as he piloted a submarine made from a patchwork of tin cans, old copper pipes, and Mother's silverware. She tried to remain optimistic, since he was smiling at the idea of his project. "Well, you have one helper already, it seems."

"Two."

"Oh?"

"Milvet you met, and your cousin also promised to help." Rias stopped before the hatch. Water sloshed around below, and Tikaya hoped he wasn't going to invite her down.

"Elloil?" she asked. "He's promised to do manual labor for you?"

"In exchange for advice on his upcoming surfboard line. Apparently someone suggested my years of engineering, mathematics, and physics studies should be utilized in designing toys for children." Rias quirked an eyebrow.

"Actually, surfing is popular amongst all age groups here. There are even a few spry eighty-year-old grannies who take on the North Coast waves. If you designed a superior board, you might win the love of the Kyattese people, causing them to forget your previous misdeeds."

Yosis snorted. It was the closest to a human emotion he'd expressed thus far.

Rias considered Tikaya with a speculative gaze before sighing and saying, "Just to be clear, you *are* teasing me, right?"

Tikaya smirked, imagining him rearranging his mental to-do list to place surfboard design above the melting down of scrap for submarine materials. "About the likelihood of people forgetting your misdeeds, yes, but not about the popularity of the sport."

"I see." Rias extended a hand toward the open hatch. "Would you care for the full tour? Yosis has already received it, due to his unwillingness to let me go anywhere alone."

Tikaya leaned over to peer through the open hatch. Rusty holes in a bulkhead, some with warped bolts sticking out of them, were all that remained of what must have been a ladder; their tracks descended into murky water that might have been three inches deep—or three feet. She crinkled her nose at the fishy, mildewy scent wafting up from below. "Did he enjoy his tour?"

"Oh, yes. I believe he was immensely impressed with the craft."

Yosis's second snort contained even more emotion—and volume.

Tikaya had little interest in going down, but perhaps Rias wanted her to see something, or maybe he thought they could steal a private moment. She kicked off her sandals, hiked her dress up to her thighs, and tied it so it wouldn't get wet—so long as the water wasn't more than a foot or two deep. "After you."

Rias gave her bared legs an appreciative look and brushed his fingers down her calf as he lowered himself through the hatch. A delightful little shiver ran up her leg, and she thought again how unfortunate it was that he was staying in that lizard-infested closet instead of on her family's plantation. Maybe she could slip away one night to visit him.

With the ladder missing, Tikaya braced herself for a plunge into icy water. Rias caught her before her toes splashed down, however, cradling her against his chest. "This way, my lady."

Before she could decide whether she wanted to be independent and ask to be let down, he carried her out of the water. The cabin floor tilted as much as the deck above, and about half of the space remained dry, though that hadn't kept the barnacles, algae, and mildew from making themselves at home on the bulkheads.

Rias set her down. There weren't any lanterns, but sunlight seeped through holes that dotted the ceiling like stars on a clear night.

"If I'd known you intended to carry me to someplace dry," Tikaya said, "I wouldn't have taken off my sandals."

"Then I would have missed the leg display." Rias gave her a half smile, though it vanished quickly. He lowered his voice to a murmur and put his back toward the water and the hatch. "Did you get a chance to do any research?"

"I asked a few questions and tried to visit the Oceanography Wing in the Polytechnic library, but the door was locked with a 'closed for repairs' sign on it. I thought that quite unusual."

"Unusual as in worth breaking into on the sly because the information housed within might be relevant to one's current predicament?" Rias asked.

A soft splash behind them announced Yosis's presence. Not certain if he'd been there long enough to hear anything, Tikaya said, "Probably not. Besides it's not as if I'm the type of girl who partakes in midnight breakings-and-enterings. I have enough trouble to deal with right now."

"I understand." An apologetic grimace flattened Rias's lips.

Tikaya winced. She'd meant to hint that he could meet her at the library at midnight if he could sneak away, not to imply that he was the cause of her trouble. She'd talked him into coming to the islands, after all.

By that point, Yosis was staring at them, and she couldn't bring herself to clarify in front of an audience.

"The engine room is this way," Rias said, breaking the silence.

"Is there anything in there worth salvaging for the new engine?"

"No, I'll be designing that from scratch. It'll need to be extremely compact and efficient." Rias ducked a drooping ceiling beam and slipped into a cubby full of machinery that hadn't run in years. Maybe decades. "I will soon need to know specifications of, ah..." He glanced over Tikaya's shoulder, noted Yosis gamely tagging along, and shrugged and said. "Do you have any suggestions on who might be able to help me with a power source? I'll need the energy statistics soon."

"I can only think of two Makers who specialize in energy sources for powering engines."

"Does either of them owe you favors?"

"Not exactly." Tikaya grimaced. "One is Parkonis's mother. She's retired now and only teaches a few hours a week, but she used to be one of the best Makers on the island."

"Your ex-fiancé's mother? I can't imagine she'd care to do either of us a favor. Who's our other choice?"

Tikaya's grimace deepened. "My grandfather."

"Ah. So, if either of these options agreed to take on the task, I'd have to worry about them building something that would blow up at an inopportune moment, thus ensuring my death."

"If it helps, I think they'd both simply refuse to help. Neither has a long history of murdering foreigners."

Rias arched an eyebrow. Nobody was appreciating her attempts at humor that day.

"I'll ask around," Tikaya said. "Let me worry about that."

"This is ridiculous," Yosis said, shaking his hand. Apparently he'd been writing so quickly his fingers were cramping. "You don't seriously believe anyone is going to let you build a spy submarine from *within* our harbor, do you?"

"A spy submarine?" Rias asked. "No, but wouldn't your people appreciate one designed to aid in underwater exploration and salvage missions?"

"Not by you."

"Who better?" Tikaya asked. "Turgonian engineering is superior to ours, everyone admits that, and wouldn't you rather have him building a submarine for our use rather than for the empire's?"

Yosis responded with a glare.

"If it turns out well," Tikaya said, "he can make more and sell them here on the islands. I'm sure the maritime archaeology department would love one. Lots of people would. They might prove more popular than surfboards." She smiled, meaning the last part as a joke, and thinking it might draw an amused response from their stodgy watchdog.

"He won't be here long enough for that." Yosis stalked out of the room, banging his elbow on a warped flywheel on the way past. He cursed in several languages. Unfortunately his curses didn't fade in a way that would mean he'd left the area. No, he would continue to spy on them from the corridor.

"Help me out," Rias murmured. "Was that a death threat or a deportation threat?"

"Rias, nobody's going to try to kill you here."

"I'd rather face a duel, or even an assassin, than someone who makes threats from the shadows and lights a woman's lawn on fire."

Tikaya searched his face, trying to decide if his words implied he'd been threatened by more than words burned into the grass. Some anonymous enemy that he couldn't strike? Even if he could identify those lurking in the shadows, would he attack? He might fear the image he'd present to her people if he did so.

"Do you get to face assassins?" Tikaya asked, hoping he'd prefer levity to grimness. "I thought they plied their trade from behind."

"You just have to practice turning around very quickly." If he meant that as a joke, his face didn't lighten to show it.

Tikaya followed him out of the engine room, sad that her visit seemed to have stolen his good humor rather than improving it.

CHAPTER 7

TIKAYA'S STOMACH RUMBLED, EAGER FOR lunch, as she bicycled up to the front lanai. She eyed the blackened pieces of earth on the lawn—the fires had burned down in such a manner that the letters were still visible. She'd have to throw some compost out and smother the area with seeds. At least in their sunny climate, it wouldn't take long for something to grow out of the charred earth.

An unfamiliar bicycle leaned against the lanai railing. Tikaya hoped it was some innocent visitor, meeting with one of her family members, but an uneasy twinge poked her in the gut. She had a feeling it had to do with her.

She headed for the door, but a low, "Ho, Coz," made her pause on the threshold. Elloil sat in one of the chairs at the end of the lanai. "You missed lunch."

"I've had a busy morning." Tikaya reached for the knob.

"Parkonis didn't."

Her hand froze. "What?"

"He didn't miss lunch."

Tikaya glanced at the bicycle. Yes, it'd be a good match for someone of Parkonis's height. "Is he still in there?" It'd be cowardly to hide outside instead of going in to see him, but the temptation came to her nonetheless. "Did he seem... well?" The emperor's assassin might have kept his word to Rias and seen Parkonis returned to Kyatt, but there was no guarantee the time her ex-fiancé had spent with the Turgonians had been pleasant, especially considering he'd been working with those who'd launched an attack on the capital and had tried to thwart the marine sortie into the tunnels.

"He looked all right, though he had a fancy tale to share. It doesn't quite match up with the one you told."

"I'm not surprised. From what he admitted to me, and what I saw, the truth didn't flatter him."

"He was still spinning his truth when I came out for a smoke. There was a lot of I-knew-its and nodding from your brother, cousins, and father."

Tikaya groaned. Of course everyone would believe her lying ex-fiancé instead of her. Under normal circumstances, that might not have been the case, but they all *wanted* to believe Rias was the enemy. "Not you?" she asked.

"Nah, Parkonis called my surf shop a quaint hobby the first time he came to dinner. We're practically mortal enemies."

"Does *he* know that?"

"I don't think he even remembers my name." Ell stirred in the shadows. "He's talking to your mother one-on-one now. You might want to interrupt."

Tikaya must have been speaking in Turgonian too much of late, for a handful of curses involving Parkonis's dead ancestors and the smelters he could slag himself in tumbled from her lips before she could stop them. She was glad Yosis wasn't around with his notepad.

"Thanks for the warning," Tikaya said and turned the knob.

A few voices drifted in from an open door at the back of the great hall, but they sounded young. Guessing Mother would be spearheading kitchen cleanup, Tikaya headed in that direction. A familiar masculine voice drifted out through the swinging door. Her mother responded. Tikaya meant to walk directly in and confront Parkonis, but she caught herself stopping and pressing an ear to the door.

"Of course he's acting polite and pleasant," Parkonis said. "He wouldn't come in here being abrasive and self-absorbed. He's a genius."

"Most of the geniuses I've met are on the self-absorbed and abrasive side, dear."

Tikaya held back a snort. She wasn't sure if Mother was poking arrows at Parkonis specifically, or simply referring to the entire body of colleagues Tikaya had brought by the house over the years. Either way, she didn't sound ready to turn on Rias. Good.

"If that's true, then the fact that he's not should worry you," Parkonis said. "He's a mastermind and a manipulator of people—just look what he's done to Tikaya. He convinced her to turn her back on me and to bring him here, so he can do Akahe knows what. If the Turgonians get a toehold here today, it could mean the downfall of our people tomorrow. You have to talk to Tikaya. She's blinded by her infatuation and can't see that he's fooling her."

Even if Parkonis wasn't succeeding in winning over Mother, Tikaya figured it was time to enter and put an end to the conversation. When she pushed open the door, she imagined herself striding into the kitchen, thrusting a finger at Parkonis's nose, and telling him that his opinions weren't appreciated, but her hip caught on the corner of the counter on her way in, and she stumbled into his back.

"Ooph," Parkonis said, staggering forward and catching himself on the pastry table.

"Afternoon, dear," Mother said without commenting on the clumsy entrance. She stood over the sink, washing plates, but she turned off the water and wiped her hands on a rooster apron, complete with a fringe of feathers. One of Tikaya's nieces had decorated it, thus ensuring it would be in use for ages, however questionable the fashion statement. "Are you hungry?" Mother asked. "I've saved you a plate."

"Thank you," Tikaya murmured, though food was the last thing on her mind.

Parkonis had righted himself and turned to face her. He'd cut his unruly red-blond curls and shaved the beard since last she'd seen him. She didn't see any scars, bruises, or missing limbs that would suggest he'd been treated poorly of late. Her first instinct was to snap at him for coming here while she was gone—had he waited until she left that morning to approach the family?—and spreading lies, but she'd probably give him less ammunition if she acted like the bigger person. That should be doable. Even barefoot, she had three inches on him.

"Good afternoon, Parkonis." Tikaya clasped her hands behind her back. "I'm pleased to see you're well. I've been worried about you. After that chaos there at the end, I wasn't sure if... I was afraid that you wouldn't make it out." Her words were true, though she had to bite her tongue to keep from pointing out that he never would have been in danger if he hadn't gone off with relic raiders in the first place.

"I barely escaped," Parkonis said. "They dumped me, Gali, and the rest of the survivors in the brig of their warship, taking us south to the

Turgonian mainland, to be dealt with—that's what they called it—for our crimes against the empire. As if *they're* not the savages. Those bloodthirsty mongrels deserve to receive that which they've given over the years." He started to curl his lip, but seemed to remember something, for his eyes widened and he glanced behind Tikaya. "Is *he* here?"

She took that to mean he wouldn't call Rias a savage to his face. "No." She supposed she shouldn't be pleased that the story meant Gali wouldn't likely be by to pester her soon. For all she knew, the Turgonians would "deal with" their prisoner using a firing squad, and she couldn't wish that fate on anyone. "How did you escape?"

"That stone-faced teenaged assassin sailed down the coast with us and was in charge of prisoners. He was taking people off the ship, moving them to the train station for a ride to the capital for I shudder to think what punishment, but he got careless. He forgot he'd unlocked my cell, and when he herded off the others, I slipped out. It was night and most of the crew was off on shore leave by then, and I got away. I've been thanking Akahe every day for that bit of luck."

"You can thank Rias for that luck," Tikaya blurted before she could question the wisdom of it. Bringing up his name might be a mistake—defending him at every turn would only give credence to people's notions that he controlled her somehow, but she couldn't let Parkonis remain unaware of his assistance, not the way she feared her president was. Why should Rias be blamed for every death in the war and receive none of the credit for the lives he'd saved?

"Pardon?" Parkonis glanced at Mother, as if to catch her eye and give her a knowing nod, but she had her back to them. She'd been washing the same pot for five minutes, but she acted like she wasn't listening.

"At the end of the ruckus, Rias told the assassin to relay the message that if the emperor didn't leave me and my family alone, he'd make trouble. He also asked the boy to ensure you were able to make it home."

Parkonis opened his mouth as if he wanted to protest outright, but he glanced at Mother's back and seemed to decide on another tactic. "Well. If that's what you saw, that's what you saw, but is it possible that he made a point of having this conversation in front of you? Thus to win your favor?"

"He'd already won it by then. He didn't need to play tricks."

Parkonis winced, and she regretted her hasty rebuttal. He'd see it as an admission that she'd rejected him in favor of Rias, and that had to hurt.

She might wish that he'd disappear on another year-long field expedition, this time a legal one perhaps, but she didn't want to hurt him.

"Listen, Par." Tikaya stepped forward and hesitantly laid a hand on his arm; she feared he might jerk away, but he didn't. "I apologize if... It wasn't my intent then or now to hurt you. When I met Rias, I thought you were dead. As far as I knew, you'd been dead a year. And you let me believe that—let us *all* believe that." She didn't want to rub in his failings, but she didn't want him to believe he had a right to play the victim here either, not entirely anyway.

"Tikaya, it's not about that." Parkonis avoided her eyes as he said the words. "If you don't want me after the choices I've made, I understand, but to pick him as the alternative... I don't want to see you get hurt. I certainly don't want to see you bring shame to your family by being the one to... Could you live with yourself if a year from now, our islands have been conquered, our people enslaved, and Turgonians are building fortresses on our beaches?"

"That's not going to happen. Didn't you hear what I said? He specifically told the emperor that he'd make trouble if Turgonians harassed us." All right, Rias had told the emperor's seventeen-year-old henchman that, and he'd only tried to finagle protection for her family, not her entire island chain, but she truly believed Rias would stand up for her people if she asked it. And if they treated him as a valuable ally who'd defected from his people, not some spy.

Parkonis was shaking his head. The sadness—or maybe that was pity—in his blue eyes seemed genuine, but that only made Tikaya want to smack him. Why couldn't any of them trust her to judge a person correctly?

"Don't be blinded by your feelings, Tikaya," Parkonis whispered. "I believe this was set up from the beginning, and he saw your gulli–desire to find the good in the people and picked you as a likely target. Even if you're right and he *was* exiled, maybe he saw you—and our islands—as a way to earn back his emperor's favor."

Tikaya thought of Milvet, the earnest Turgonian she'd met that morning, and his words of how Rias could raise an army to march on the capital if he wished his lands back. "You're wrong, Parkonis. He wouldn't need to do that. He has resources. If he wanted to go back, he could." Tikaya didn't know how true that was, but it disturbed her nonetheless to know he might have options—that he could leave at any time if he decided she wasn't worth all the trouble.

"Tikaya..." Parkonis sighed and shook his head again, as if he were dealing with a particularly slow and stubborn child. "Just do me one favor, will you? Tell him, or, no, just ask him... What would he do if you decided to come back to me. See what his reaction is."

Tikaya remembered Rias's reaction when Parkonis had first shown up alive. He'd been disappointed—stung—until he'd decided he'd fight for her. She smiled at the memory of him arguing his virtues in an attempt to win her back when she'd never intended to leave him in the first place.

Parkonis frowned at her. "Just see what kind of pressure he puts on you to ensure you don't leave him. Even if you don't intend to—" the corners of his mouth twitched downward, "—it wouldn't hurt to test him, right?"

Except that it'd show Rias that she didn't trust him completely. He'd see Parkonis's test for what it was. Out loud, she said, "I'll think about it. But not right now. I have work to do." Like figuring out who she could find to Make Rias's power source. "May I see you to the door?"

Whether Parkonis found comfort in her promise or not, she couldn't tell. He sent one last long look at Mother before letting Tikaya guide him out of the house. Unlike the other glances, that one seemed to hold only sadness, as if he were regretting that she wouldn't be a part of his life any more. His fault, Tikaya told herself. He needn't have disappeared for a year without sending word to anyone. But what then? What if, when she'd been kidnapped, she'd known Parkonis was alive and waiting for her back home? She couldn't have considered Rias as anything more than an ally then, or if she had... she would have been the dishonorable one. Maybe she should thank Parkonis for his shortcomings, for giving her a way out.

After lunch, Tikaya bicycled north along the coast, heading for her grandfather's cabin and workshop on the far end of the plantation. She dreaded the idea of talking to him when he'd so vehemently displayed his displeasure over Rias's presence, but not quite as much as the idea of going to Iweue, Parkonis's mother.

The winding coastal road took Tikaya along a sandy shore, one that was popular amongst clammers. A low tide left much of the beach bare, and several people were busy with shovels and buckets. Most were relatives, but a bronze-skinned figure out amongst the freckled natives made Tikaya pause. The neighbor. Mee Nar. The man who'd taken his wife and left dinner a mere fifteen minutes before that fire was started on the front lawn. Her father had searched around the house after the flames had been extinguished, but hadn't found any evidence as to who might have started it.

Tikaya leaned the bicycle against a tree at the head of a path leading through tall grasses and out to the beach. Maybe it was time to ask the Nurian a few questions.

The ocean breeze tugged at the man's red and orange silks. Unlike Rias, Mee Nar apparently hadn't felt the need to clothe himself in native garb. Given that he'd attacked Rias, Tikaya felt uneasy approaching him. There were several other men, women, and children on the beach though. Surely he wouldn't do anything to her. Besides, with nothing more than a shovel for a weapon, he appeared innocuous enough. Damp sand clung to his bare calves and feet, and clumps flew as he thrust the blade into the wet earth. He dug a deep hole, then bent to pluck out two clams and drop them in his bucket.

The wind and the roar of the sea should have disguised Tikaya's approach, but when she was still twenty meters away, Mee Nar turned in her direction. Chance? Or was he a practitioner? One who could manipulate fire, perhaps?

Tikaya smiled and gave him a neighborly wave. He offered an open palm to the side, a Nurian civilian-to-civilian salute that was supposed to signify one bore no weapons nor was bringing the mental sciences to bear. In Kyatt, the Science was practiced for research and life enhancement. In Nuria, martial applications were common.

Tikaya picked her way around sandy pools and limp seaweed to stop a few feet away. "Hello, Mee Nar, wasn't it?" she asked in Nurian.

"Indeed, Ms. Komitopis." He responded in accented Kyattese, then dipped a knee and ducked his head in a bow. He kept his eyes upon her as he did so.

Tikaya knew that was how Nurians bowed—always maintaining eye contact—but she couldn't help but wonder if he wanted to watch her every move out of more than habit.

"How is the clamming going?" she asked. She *wanted* to ask, "Did you light my family's lawn on fire?" but thought that might be a tad forward.

"Quite well. Your islands are bountiful. My wife tells me it never snows, and I have seen how each season remains pleasantly warm, and the only change is that it sometimes rains more often. But even when it rains, it seems to finish by mid-morning, leaving the people to enjoy the sun in the afternoon."

"Yes." Tikaya had no interest in discussing the weather, but perhaps she could use it to lead into other topics. "I missed it very much when I was kidnapped and taken to the frozen wasteland that is the empire's Northern Frontier."

Mee Nar's face grew closed at the mention of the empire. "I imagine so. Many parts of Turgonia are as inhospitable as the people."

"You've been?"

"I was a prisoner of war interned in a camp outside of Port Malevek for six months."

"Ah, so you fought the Turgonians in the Western Sea Conflict." And had every reason to hate Rias...

"That is not what we called it, but yes. I served in the navy for twenty years." He scarcely looked older than she, but Nurians, Tikaya recalled, could enlist as young as fourteen. "I decided to retire after my time in the camp," he added.

"That bad, eh?"

"I was not important enough to be interrogated, but it was still... austere. The time made me think and realize I'd spent too much of my life at sea and too little time seeking love and a family. Back in '63, I was injured nearby and spent two months here recuperating. I found the women most accommodating." He smiled at some memory. "Beautiful, of course, but also not so obsessed with a man's status and place in society as my own people. Once my chief accepted my retirement, I came here and soon found my wife."

"What did you do in the navy?" Tikaya wanted to know if he'd studied the mental sciences.

"I was a simple sailor."

"Mundane work?" She'd heard the Nurians could use the Science to fill their sails with wind.

"I never studied the mental sciences if that's what you're asking."

"Ah, I was just curious."

"Of course you were." Mee Nar's expression remained bland, but something in his eyes made her believe he knew exactly what she was angling for, or at least that her questions masked more than casual curiosity.

"As a retired naval sailor," Tikaya asked, "will you feel obligated to report back to your people that one of their old enemies is living on the island?"

Mee Nar's eyebrows shot up. "*Living* on? I thought... ah, I was led to believe he was visiting temporarily."

Tikaya studied the sand rimming her sandals for a moment. The man's surprise seemed genuine. If he'd thought Rias was only going to be a short-term visitor, would he have thought there was a need to play tricks to scare him off?

"We are not... temporary," Tikaya said, so she could gauge Mee Nar's reaction.

"You will live here instead of in Turgonia?"

Tikaya wondered if he was merely curious as a neighbor, or if he was collecting information to send back to his government. You shouldn't have come down to talk to him if you were worried about that, she told herself. "You said it yourself. The climate isn't as desirable there."

"Yes, but you would have power and rank there, would you not? He's a hero to his people, I understand."

"His people think he's dead."

Mee Nar frowned. "Then his arrival on their shore will be a pleasant surprise, surely?"

Tikaya didn't want to explain the rift between Rias and his emperor. It wasn't her story to tell, and, in case Mee Nar *was* planning a letter back home, she shouldn't give him any extra fodder for it. After all, she'd come down here to learn about him.

"Either way, my work is here, and Rias is retired. I wanted to ask you if it'd be a problem if your children grew up with one of your people's most infamous enemies for a neighbor."

"It *would* be difficult to explain to my parents if they ever came to visit," Mee Nar said.

"Considering that you attacked him at dinner, you don't seem very concerned by the notion now."

"That was a reflex. You don't serve twenty years in the military without having a few reactions drilled into you, such as attack Turgonians on sight to protect those you care about." Mee Nar shrugged. "I didn't even recognize him at first. It was just... when he walked in wearing that uniform." Another shrug.

"If you *had* recognized him, would that have changed anything? Or would you have simply raised your bow more quickly?"

"It is true that dropping his head onto the Chief's throne room floor might earn me a title, or accolades and honors for my family at least, but... my life is here now, and I no longer crave such hollow things. Also, Starcrest is... *heesu ming*. You know the term?"

Tikaya knew it, but there wasn't a Kyattese equivalent. Her people had a lot fewer words for enemies than the Nurians and the Turgonians. "Honorable foe?" she suggested.

Mee Nar wiggled his fingers to imply that wasn't quite it, but might be as close as they'd get. "Every Nurian sailor hated to see his flagship on the horizon, because it almost assuredly meant defeat and capture. Even when the odds were against him, it never seemed to play out the way those odds suggested. He was more slippery than soap, and we called him King Fox for his cunning. He'd do whatever it took to make sure his ships came out ahead in a confrontation. Yet, we knew if we were captured, we'd be treated fairly until such time that our government bartered for our release. It was also known that if he gave his word, he'd keep it. I cannot speak from personal experience, but there are stories of times when he went against his emperor's wishes to keep his word to our officers."

If that were true, that might explain why the Turgonian emperor had been so quick to exile Rias for disobeying the order to facilitate the assassination of the Kyattese president. Maybe it had been the final blow that broke the sword.

"He was respected on both sides," Mee Nar finished. "To answer your earlier question, no, I wouldn't care to have my children growing up next door to Fleet Admiral Starcrest, retired or not, but I also wouldn't fear for their safety in his presence."

"That's a relief," Tikaya said, though she didn't know if she could trust Mee Nar's words. Was it possible he was only telling her this, so she wouldn't suspect him of the fire? He *seemed* sincere, but she wasn't the best judge of people, having always preferred books to social situations. It did strike her as sad that a foreigner might be more open to accepting Rias here than her own people. The Nurians had suffered just as much in the war as the Kyattese and had just as much reason to resent him. "Thank you for your time. Good luck with the clamming." She nodded toward his bucket.

Mee Nar bowed, eyes meeting hers again, and headed off with his shovel.

Tikaya returned to the bicycle and her journey. As she covered the last couple of miles to Grandpa's home, she mused upon the likelihood of more threats coming Rias's way. She doubted anyone would attack him, and that was almost a shame, because he'd prefer that. Instead, they'd pester him like a mosquito buzzing about, not drawing blood, but staying out of reach.

The sun was dipping behind the volcano when Tikaya turned off the main road and onto the dirt path heading up to a small bungalow nestled beneath coconut trees. A much larger rectangular building lay behind it, banging sounds and pulsing lights emanating from within.

Tikaya parked the bicycle and knocked on the workshop door. The bangs stopped, though the lights continued to escape through the windows, a mixture of blues and greens.

"What?" came Grandpa's crotchety voice.

Despite the uninviting opening, Tikaya turned the knob and poked her head inside. "Grandpa? It's Tikaya. Do you have a moment?"

A few seconds passed before Grandpa asked, "That joratt mongrel with you?"

She bristled at the slur, but knew it was pointless to correct him. Her mother had been trying for decades. "It's just me."

"Good. You throw him back in the ocean yet?"

"He's moved into a place of his own in town." Not exactly evading the question...

Grandpa grunted.

Tikaya let herself in. She had to weave past tables, cabinets, and waist-high toolboxes before finding him in a back corner, hunched over a workbench with a mallet and a chisel. Barefoot, with his shirt buttoned askew, he might, at first glance, appear senile, or at least forgetful, but Tikaya knew he was too caught up in his work to care about dressing. At least he was wearing pants today. With Grandma passed on, one never knew what state of civility—or lack thereof—one would find him in when visiting his home.

The tendons on the backs of his gnarled hands leapt as he carved an axe handle from a piece of driftwood. An obsidian blade lay next to it, the oily black stone imbued with a faint blue sheen. Though he could make energy sources such as Rias needed, Grandpa specialized in Making enhanced farm tools. Few finished pieces adorned the workshop; his implements were widely sought and tended to be purchased before he'd done more than sketched a design.

A communication orb sat on a pedestal by the end of the workbench. Usually dust or a cloth covered it, but not this time. Tikaya wondered who Grandpa had been talking to of late.

"You're too good for some Turg dog, girl." He leaned closer to his axe handle, squinting. He *had* spectacles somewhere, but he always refused to wear them.

"What are you working on?" Tikaya asked instead of responding to his suspicions. Grandma had been the only one to succeed in changing his mind about things, and even her victories had been rare.

"Axe for the Uluoe place."

"It's a handsome blade. You've imbued it with strength and sharpness?"

"That's right." When finished, Grandpa's stone implements were as strong as those made from Turgonian steel, and the blades never rusted or grew dull. "You need to chop anybody's sugar cane off, you come see me for the appropriate tool."

Tikaya knew he was referring to Rias, but she thought of that bastard, Sergeant Ottotark who'd harassed her all through the mission. "I wish I'd had one while I was being dragged around by those marines."

For the first time, Grandpa tore his gaze from his work. His blue eyes, still sharp despite his ninety years, bore into her as his hand clenched about the haft of the axe-in-progress. "Did those animals touch you?"

Though her first thought was of Captain Bocrest smashing her against the wall, she knew he meant more personal touching. "One tried, but I doused him in kerosene and threatened to light him on fire."

Grandpa's eyes grew round. For a moment, he only stared, but then he laughed. "Good, good, I wouldn't have guessed you had that sort of gumption in you, girl, but that's good."

Tikaya wondered if her mother would think so if she knew. Perhaps in Ottotark's case, she would approve, but what of the men she'd shot and killed during the escapade? What would Mee Nar think if he knew she'd killed Nurians? Granted, the assassins had been after her, to keep her from helping the Turgonians, but she'd killed people nonetheless.

"Grandpa, I'd rather not talk any more about what happened out there. I want to put my life back together and return to my research." And figure out a way to make Rias a part of that life and that research. She didn't mention that.

"That's good. Your mother was concerned when you were working our fields with the hands instead of at school, studying and teaching."

"I know. I'm ready to begin again. And, to help with my research, there's something I need." Tikaya took a deep breath, afraid he'd immediately guess her reason for the request. "Would you be willing to Make an energy source of sufficient means to power a... small ship?"

Grandpa propped a fist against his hip. "A ship? Don't you do your work at the Polytechnic?"

"Yes, but I told Ri—. Uhm, there are a lot of unsolved puzzles and mysteries out there in the field, old ruins and artifacts too large to bring back here to study. I wish to take Rias to them, to see if we can make headway where other teams have failed. He has unique skills that—"

"Take *Ri-as*," Grandpa snarled, saying the name the same way he spat out his racial slurs. "You came here to ask me to craft something to help that murderer? To complete his underwater spy boat?"

"Grandpa, he was a marine, not a murderer, and he's neither now. He's done with the empire. He wants to help me with my work." And who had told Grandpa about the submarine plans? Tikaya glanced at the communication orb.

"Why can't he build a normal ship then? Why does he want to snoop around underwater?"

"So we can evade the nations who'd shoot him simply because he was a Turgonian marine once."

"Not *a* marine," Grandpa said. "*The* marine who caused all our grief."

"If you asked him what really went on back at the beginning of the war, you might be surprised. Our president might not even be alive if not for him."

For a heartbeat, puzzlement drew Grandpa's thin, white brows together, but he shook his head again. "What he told you and what happened aren't likely the same things."

"Fine, we'll have to disagree on that." Tikaya glanced toward a window—daylight was dwindling, and she needed to bicycle to town for the midnight infiltration of the library she'd planned. She hoped Rias showed up to infiltrate with her. Not only did he seem the type to have more experience with such things, but she missed him. "Is there no chance you'll Make an energy source? For me?"

His only answer was to glower and fold his arms across his chest.

Tikaya sighed. This had been a waste of time. She'd have to ask the mother of the ex-fiancé she'd left back in the frozen north with a passel of vengeful Turgonian marines while she had returned home with her new lover. That would be a fun conversation, oh, yes.

She was relieved she could justify putting it off for another day. There was a library waiting for a midnight visitor.

CHAPTER 8

THE MIDNIGHT MOON AND STARS provided enough light to bicycle down the road toward town, but not enough to keep Tikaya from finding ruts and divots with her wheels. After falling into the grass twice, and dumping the lantern out of the knapsack she carried three times, she parked on the outskirts of the city and walked the last mile to the Polytechnic campus. A handful of whale oil lanterns burned along the street dividing it from the historic homes of the original colony, but shadows lay thick around the library, classrooms, and research buildings. Paths and roads wound through low vegetation, leading to doors and courtyards. The ground cover was kept clipped within a few inches, so wouldn't offer many hiding spots for someone sneaking toward the buildings.

Tikaya circled to the back half of the campus where she found a tree-dotted route. Using the palms and jackfruits to hide her, she veered toward the library. She didn't expect company out there, but one never knew. Besides, lamps burned behind a handful of windows in the research buildings, promising that a few souls remained there late. The library, fortunately, stood in darkness, including the second-story wing she wished to visit.

When she reached the last of the trees, Tikaya paused to check in all directions. A heartbeat before she stepped out onto the open path, a soft rustling reached her ears.

She froze. Rias?

She'd mentioned midnight infiltrations, on the chance he could escape, but she didn't think evading Yosis would be easy. Besides, she'd wager a Turgonian marine could sneak through the night without rustling. If someone was out here, it probably wasn't he.

Hugging the nearest tree, Tikaya peered in the direction from which she had come. High above, the palm fronds waved softly. Maybe she had simply heard fallen leaves being stirred by the breeze?

Another crunch sounded, as if someone had stepped on a leaf. Definitely not the wind. She eased around to the other side of the tree, thinking she might need to abort her breaking-and-entering attempt.

"Fruiting darkness," someone cursed. Someone familiar.

"Ell?" Tikaya whispered.

"'Kaya?"

"Over here." She shook her head as a dark shape eased into view. "What are you doing here?"

"Following you. What are *you* doing here?" The smoke smell clinging to Elloil's clothing identified him as much as his voice.

"Nothing you need to be concerned about," Tikaya said. "Why were you following me?"

"I was out on the lanai, enjoying a smoke, when I saw someone shimmy down the drainpipe from the rooftop above. I figured it was one of the boys sneaking out. Imagine my surprise when this glint of moonlight reflected off your spectacles."

"You didn't answer my question."

"Didn't I? Huh."

"Ell!" Tikaya's exasperated whisper came out louder than she intended. After glancing about to make sure they were still alone, she lowered her voice and asked again, "*Why* are you following me?"

"Your mother made me."

Tikaya leaned against a tree for support. She'd thought... Well, it had *seemed* that Mother was the closest thing she had to an ally in this. "Why?"

"She's worried about you. She doesn't want you going to the docks or the Pernicious Miasma at night where you'll—" Ell propped his fists on his hips and attempted a feminine pitch to his voice, "—get mauled by transients or stolen by another batch of villainous kidnappers. Those Turgonian brutes haven't got any reason to like her, you know." He dropped his arms and let his voice return to normal. "I didn't want to, but she made me promise to keep an eye on you. She said I wouldn't be invited to any more family dinners if I didn't. Oh, and I could forget about the money she'd promised to invest in my surfing business."

Tikaya rubbed her face. At least Mother's concerns seemed to revolve around her daughter traipsing through questionable neighborhoods, not visiting Rias. "Was it the food threat or the money threat that motivated you most?"

"She's a really good cook. And I'm still looking for a lady love who'll make victuals for me."

"You could learn to make them yourself."

"Were you not there when I almost lit the kitchen on fire with a pile of lemons?"

"Ah, yes, I'd forgotten about that. Though technically, weren't you trying to turn the lemons into a battery, not a food dish?"

"Yes, but I took the smoking dish towels as a sign that I wasn't meant to spend time in kitchens." Ell waved at the Polytechnic buildings. "If I'd known you were coming to work, I would have stayed on the lanai. I was enjoying a particularly fine smoke."

"As long as you're here," Tikaya said, "you can help."

"Doing what?"

"I'm going to sneak into a locked-off wing of the library. If you see anyone coming, I'd appreciate it if you'd warn me. Toss a pebble against the window or some such."

"*You're* going to sneak into a locked building?"

"Yes, why is that so shocking?"

"You've never done anything mildly illicit," Ell said. "Is Rias coming?"

"I'm not sure he'll be able to get away."

"Then how are you planning on getting in?"

Tikaya sniffed. "I've decrypted messages encoded by the brightest military minds in the world. I think I can thwart a simple door lock."

"You haven't a notion of how to bypass one, do you?"

"I brought a couple of hairpins. That's always enough in adventure stories."

"I'll just get comfortable then." Ell sat at the base of a tree, making a show of settling in. "Don't be afraid to give up. I want to hit the nine o'clock waves tomorrow."

"Oh, please. With your nocturnal inhaling and imbibing practices, you're never out there before noon anyway."

"True enough." Ell waved for her to continue about her business.

After giving the grounds another check for activity, Tikaya trotted to the back door of the library. As part of the faculty, she had a key for it, so she needn't worry about Ell witnessing her fumbling attempts at lock picking. Or so she thought. In the darkness, she dropped the key twice before finding the hole. She didn't hear Ell's snickers, but she had no trouble imagining them.

As Tikaya slipped inside the hallway, cool air caressed her cheeks. Without any light coming through the windows at the ends, the lava rock walls seemed pitch black. She paused to listen. Nothing stirred. Though she had a lantern, she felt her way along, not yet wanting to risk a light, not with other people up late, working on campus. After years spent at the Polytechnic, she could find her way in the dark anyway.

She crept past several doors, running her hands along the book-filled cases that lined the walls on one side. When the books ended, she knew she'd reached the stairs. She eased up them and passed through two archive rooms on her way to the Oceanography Wing. She padded around in the darkness until she found the doorknob. It was still locked with the sign hanging above it.

Tikaya slipped her knapsack off her shoulder and dug out the lantern. A few minutes later, she knelt before the door, a puddle of light illuminating the area as she poked and prodded in the lock with her hairpins. Reluctantly, she admitted that she didn't know what she was doing. Maybe she should have asked Ell to come up with her. He'd probably laid siege to a few secured doors as a youth. Or perhaps even more recently.

Tikaya knelt back, giving the door another once over. The hinges were on the outside. She hadn't thought to bring a chisel or screwdriver. "Ell's right, you're terribly inexperienced at this," she whispered. Maybe she could try Rias's tactic of using the lantern flame. Could she use the heat to loosen the hinges so they'd be easy to pop? There'd be no way to hide that someone had been there if she left the door leaning against the wall, but maybe she could put everything back together so the tampering wouldn't be too noticeable.

She stood, intending to give it a try, when a voice behind said, "It looks like a four-pin tumbler. Challenging for the tools you have, but not impossible."

After nearly kicking over her lantern in surprise, Tikaya spun and grinned. A few steps away, Rias leaned against the wall, as if he'd been watching for a while. He wore the same dubious clothing he'd had on that morning, though he'd added footwear: bamboo thongs with woven vine straps. Awful. But they only made her grin more widely, and she strode toward him, lifting her arms for an embrace. She did pause halfway through the motion to check behind him. The hallway was empty.

"I left him sleeping," Rias said and stepped toward her for a hug and a heated kiss that suggested he wasn't happy spending the nights apart either, especially with Yosis as his only alternative for companionship. When he drew back, Tikaya made a mew of protest, having forgotten where they were and what the priority was.

Rias tucked a stray lock of hair behind her ear. "I don't know how long my keeper will stay asleep, so we'd better hurry. I'm sure he can track me through this." He raised his wrist, displaying the glowing red stone set in the bracelet. "Unfortunately, it's proved more difficult to remove than Turgonian shackles."

Sighing, Tikaya drew back. "Yes, of course. Thank you for risking the trip."

"You're welcome." He tilted his head toward the door. "What's on the agenda for tonight?"

She thought of his kiss and what she'd *like* to put on the agenda, but said, "Research. It's good that you're here. This section of the library is huge, and I'm not sure what exactly we're looking for. Having a research assistant will be helpful."

"Research *assistant*?" Rias took the hairpins from her and bent them into new shapes. "I see my former career counts for little, and I'm going to have to start over at the bottom in this new field."

The gleam in his eyes suggested he was more amused than offended, so Tikaya teased him with, "If you do a good job making the morning coffee, I'll see if I can get you a promotion."

Rias held up the two hairpins, now contorted into unrecognizable shapes. "This is your torque wrench and your pick." He knelt before the door. "I'll handle this since we're pressed for time, but I'll explain what I'm doing in case you want to try picking a lock later. I've found it to be a useful life skill."

Tikaya recalled the numerous times on their journey that he'd escaped Captain Bocrest's prisons and shackles. "When," she asked, holding the lantern to shed light for him, "did a stalwart, law-abiding, military officer have occasion to learn to pick locks?"

"My familiarity with locking mechanisms began with one of my mother's favorite lectures, the one that always ended with, 'If you took it apart, you can blasted well put it back together again.' As to the picking, my older brothers found my youthful curiosity irritating at times and had a tendency to lock me in closets, cupboards, and storage chests. It vexed them terribly when I appeared at the supper table none the worse for the experience. The skill was thus worth mastering for that reason alone."

He talked her through the systematic picking process, and after a few minutes pushed the door open. Before he stood, Tikaya rested her hands on his shoulders and bent over to kiss him on the cheek. "I might just promote you before I've tasted your coffee."

"That's good because cider and tea are the primary drinks in the empire. I wouldn't know what to do with a coffee bean."

"Oh? Maybe Grandpa is right and Turgonians *are* barbarians." Tikaya stepped inside.

Rias snorted and followed her. Tikaya closed the shutters on the windows before lighting a few lamps and candles. Bookshelves lined the walls of the spacious chamber, with rolling ladders allowing access to tomes near the carved obsidian molding under the arched ceiling.

"This is *all* related to oceanography?" Rias eyed the towering stacks.

"Yes. Though I think we're going to be interested chiefly in the seas around the Kyatt Islands. That'll narrow things down."

"How much?"

Tikaya checked a directory. "Uh, that wall."

Rias considered the twenty-five-meter-long wall with its floor-to-ceiling shelves stuffed with books. "You may need more than one research assistant. Why didn't you invite your cousin to join you?"

"A lot of the historical tomes will be in Old Kyattese. Ell wouldn't be able to read that."

"Tikaya, I can't read it either. I can barely read *new* Kyattese."

"You've proven numerous times that you don't need to be able to understand a language to make useful insights." Tikaya swatted him on the backside as she headed for the shelves.

"Demanding woman," he murmured, but strode to the shelves as well. Instead of examining the book titles, he stopped before a tall case holding rolled scrolls. Maps most likely. That jangled a bell in Tikaya's memory.

"A colleague mentioned that all the topography and bathymetric maps for the islands and surrounding waters are in here. I think she was worried about them getting into Turgonian hands, especially since you're building a submarine and could find little nooks from which to spy, but maybe there's another reason she didn't want me handing them to you." Tikaya tried not to feel guilty about the fact that she was not only handing them to him but encouraging him to study them.

Rias slanted her a sidelong look. "Turgonia *has* your bathymetrical maps."

"It does?"

"There were old ones in the archives that I dug out, and then I sent a scout ship early on in the conflict to take depth readings at night and verify the accuracy. We had plans to occupy your island and knew there'd be less opposition if we didn't use the harbor. We were concerned with the underwater lava flows and how they may have changed the terrain, so my men were quite thorough."

"Oh." Tikaya shouldn't have been surprised, but she experienced a moment of numbness at the reminder that he, despite his cute stories of boyhood intellectual pursuits, was still the enemy admiral who'd caused her people so much pain during the war. Her exasperation at her family's unwillingness to welcome him was perhaps unfounded. "Well, take a look. I can't imagine yours are terribly accurate if your men were out there with knotted ropes. I'm sure our practitioners worked with the sailors making the recordings." After she spoke, she wondered if he'd find the comment... snotty. She'd implied, after all, that his people had primitive methods that weren't equal to the ones used by those who practiced the mental sciences. Offending one's only research assistant probably wasn't a good idea.

Rias nudged a few candles aside and spread the first of the maps out on the table. After a brief look, he said, "Actually, I think ours are more accurate." He scratched his jaw. "I don't suppose there's anyway I could get copies now."

"How can that be?" Tikaya had selected an armload of books and she brought them over, setting them down with a thump on the table. Dust flew up and tickled her nostrils as she peered over the map.

"About twenty years ago, a young captain was assigned the dangerous mission of creating an accurate bathymetric map of Nuria's east coast. Though dodging Nurian scout ships kept him busy, he found the rope method tediously slow and inaccurate and invented a primitive echo ranging device that used sound waves to determine the depth and shape of the undersea environment."

"And was this young captain someone with whom I'm familiar?"

"He was." Rias tapped the map. "A copy of this would be useful for navigating in and out of the harbor on our first voyage, especially if there's something out there—" he waved toward the ocean, "—we should investigate."

"I'm told there isn't, nothing of archaeological significance anyway. Our people have documented everything that's happened in the last seven hundred years, and before that the islands were uninhabited."

Rias lifted his gaze from the map. "Nobody had ever been here before?"

"According to the history texts, when my ancestors landed here, there wasn't any evidence that other humans had ever settled or even set foot upon these islands."

"After *my* ancestors chose to depart from the Nurian continent, they roamed the oceans and explored widely, looking for an uninhabited land before choosing what they eventually turned into Turgonia. I haven't studied that period of history extensively, but I'm surprised they didn't find your islands at any point in their travels."

"It's interesting that you said your people 'chose to depart' Nuria," Tikaya said, wondering if he'd be offended if she shared an alternate view of the history with which he'd been raised. "The Kyattese global chronicles tell us that the peoples who banded together to become the early Turgonians were those who were persecuted and shunned and even enslaved in Nuria because of their poor affinity for learning the then burgeoning mental sciences. They *fled* the continent in search of a land where they could live without worrying about Nurians."

Rias lifted a hand, palm up. "History has always been written to favor the viewpoints of those penning the texts. Were not your people also fleeing something when they left the Southern Hemisphere?"

"A plague, yes. It broke out after opposing factions started a war that decimated the continent. My ancestors were those who left after governments collapsed and chaos reigned. They vowed to find a new land where they could adopt a peaceful way of life and stay neutral in other nations' disputes. They found their way here seven hundred years ago, and we've always prided ourselves on starting over so successfully." Realizing she sounded a tad supercilious again, Tikaya mumbled, "Not that any of that matters now," and returned her attention the table. While comparing historical accounts was interesting, they had limited time in the library. She opened one of the books.

"What are your people hiding, I wonder?"

Perusing a map, Rias sounded like he was talking to himself, but Tikaya felt compelled to ask, "You just have a hunch, right? No proof of anything?"

"They're upset by my submarine construction plans."

"Because they fear you're still holding hands with the emperor and he'll want to use your submarine for purposes that'll be detrimental to our people."

"Yosis's comments aside, I don't believe for a moment that your high minister thinks I'd build my craft in front of them if that were my intent. I also suspect that the Kyattese diplomats stationed in Turgonia have ferreted out the truth about my alienation from the emperor—they *must* know I'm no longer his man. Your government is making up false concerns to camouflage something else. There's something down there that they don't want me to see."

"I'm not aware of any underwater secrets that my people are hiding from foreigners."

"Maybe they don't want *you* to know about it either."

Tikaya propped her fist on her hip in exasperation. So far, she had nothing more than his hunches to go on, and they seemed to be straying farther and farther from the likely. The only thing that supported the idea that something fishy was going on was the odd closing of the library wing. For all she knew, there was a burst pipe waiting to be fixed or some other innocent piece of maintenance requiring attention. "Maybe you're a paranoid Turgonian who's ascribing entirely too much intelligence to my government."

"I'll admit that there are a number of popular sage quotes involving paranoia and survival in my culture, but your government isn't full of fools. Regardless, if we do operate under the assumption that there's something down there, something that's not visible from the surface but would be visible with the help of an underwater craft, it'll narrow down our search a great deal." Rias tilted his head toward the overflowing shelves. "We'll only need to look up the history of water exploration around the islands."

"It's as good of a starting point as any, I suppose. Those books will be in Old Kyattese."

"I'll stick to the maps." Rias waved to the shelves, then paused and took a longer look. He rolled the ladder over and climbed up to a row of maps drawn on parchment, their edges yellowed and tattered with age.

"I'll grab some of the old chronicles from the other room," Tikaya said. "It's always possible the ones I grew up reading contain revisionist history."

Rias, perched on the ladder and already engrossed in a map he'd withdrawn, did not answer.

Tikaya yawned and glanced toward the shuttered windows. She didn't think dawn lurked on the horizon, but she and Rias had been buried in their research for at least two hours. Perhaps because she'd found so little of interest, she'd been spending a lot of the time worrying that Yosis would wake up, notice Rias gone, and hasten in this direction with some draconian punishment in mind.

"I may have something," Rias said. No fewer than twenty maps sprawled about him, some recent, some so old that the edges had crumbled when he opened them. "Your main island here has gained square footage over the decades, I assume due to the volcano's continuing leakage of lava onto the sea floor. Following these maps—there was a new one done about every hundred years or so—you can see the gradually increasing footprint on the east side."

"Yes, that's a fairly well-known fact here."

"What's interesting is that these first three maps all have a basin delineated just north of the underwater lava flows. Here, next to this inlet." Rias pointed to the same spot on different pages. "Then, four hundred years ago, the basin disappears from the maps. Not just one but all the subsequent ones."

Tikaya removed her spectacles, rubbed gunk out of her eyes, and leaned close to examine the tiny underwater terrain lines. "It's possible it was filled in. Every couple of generations the volcano gets frisky and spits out larger amounts of lava."

"Frisky? Is that the geological term?"

"I've never had occasion to learn the Turgonian words related to volcanology. If you'd like to switch to Kyattese, I can be more precise."

"Not necessary. It's just that the word frisky brought other thoughts to my mind." Rias wriggled his eyebrows.

Tikaya blushed, forgetting her weariness. "If we finish here, maybe there'll be time for exploring those thoughts more thoroughly before you have to get back."

"In that case, let us be most efficient in the study of these maps."

Tikaya traced the basin on one of the older versions and eyed the legend. "That would be a big area for lava to have filled in without a major seismic event."

"Deep too. Turgonian diving suits wouldn't allow one to descend even halfway down to the bottom, if the basin still exists, that is."

Tikaya scribbled the dates AC 374-469 on a scrap of paper, the years between the last map drawn with the basin and the first map drawn without it. "I'll dig out a geology text and see if anything significant happened during that gap. Are there any other discrepancies?"

"Not that I found."

"I don't suppose you memorized the bathymetric maps your people took and could verify or disprove the accuracy of this one?" Tikaya tapped the 469 version.

"Sorry, my ancestors gave me a reasonably good memory, but not an eidetic one."

"Ah, apologies. I sometimes expect too much of you." Had she the energy, Tikaya would have laughed at his chagrinned shoulder slump. He always seemed so disappointed when his education failed her in some way. She patted his arm to let him know she was teasing him. "We should leave before Yosis realizes you're gone. I'll head to the geology wing and grab a couple of books to take home. If that section isn't closed for repairs *too*, that is." In her wanderings around the Oceanography

Wing, she hadn't seen any problems that would have justified the locked door and sign. "Do you want to put those maps away and meet me at the door?"

"Cleaning up, is that one of the roles of assistants?"

"I don't care what Grandpa says; Turgonians *are* faster learners."

Rias snorted. "Take your time with the books. I want to copy this side of the island."

"Planning your first trip already?" Tikaya asked lightly, though her colleague's words came to mind. How many of her people would consider it treasonous of her to facilitate Rias's acquisition of the bathymetric maps? But, assuming his story was true, the Turgonians already had this information—*better* information—so it shouldn't matter.

"The craft will need a maiden voyage, and this isn't that far from your harbor."

Maiden voyage, sure. He wanted to know what was down there.

Tikaya had to admit that the strings of her curiosity were being plucked as well. Though they'd found nothing major, the small discrepancies were making her believe there *was* something to Rias's hunches. She put away the books she'd looked at, and headed for the geology department, hoping to find a historical accounting of seismic activity on and near the Kyattese Islands. On a whim, she veered into the civil history room first. There hadn't been newspapers back then, but the government had maintained annual journals, recording significant events. They were more political than geological, she was sure, but an earthquake or volcanic anomaly would have affected the populace and therefore been mentioned. When she located the appropriate date range on the shelves, she found herself staring at a gap in the middle. It was only a one-book gap, and she might have missed it if she hadn't been perusing the years with intent, but 397 was gone. As a historical reference book, it shouldn't have been checked out.

Tikaya lifted her lantern and gazed at nearby tables, thinking someone might have left it out, but they were all empty.

"All right, 397," she murmured, "what happened to you?" Or, more specifically, what happened in that year that someone wanted forgotten?

Her mind filled with research ideas, histories of other fields that she could cross-check, but she'd been in the library too long already. Rias needed to get back, and he was probably waiting for her to finish before leaving. Besides, none of the other rooms was locked, so she could come back and investigate during the day.

Nodding to herself, Tikaya strode back to the bottom-floor door through which she'd entered. Rias wasn't there.

"Still tracing?" She thought she'd been gone long enough for him to finish, and then some.

She returned to the stairs. A thump came from somewhere on the second floor. Worry knotted Tikaya's gut and she broke into a run. Taking the stairs three at a time, she sprinted toward the Oceanography Wing. Rias had closed the door on his way out but not made it farther than that. He was curled on the floor, clenching his temples.

"Akahe curse that man," Tikaya growled, knowing Yosis had to be responsible. She dropped her knapsack and raced to Rias's side. "Rias?" she whispered. "Are you...?"

He gasped and shook his head so hard he almost clunked it on the floor. "Heard... cousin's warning... too late. I can't... block... it." He clawed at his wrist.

Though her first instinct was to stay and help him somehow, the only way to stop his pain was to stop Yosis.

"Stay here," she barked, though it was unnecessary. He wasn't going anywhere.

Tikaya lunged to her feet and sprinted down the stairs. Rage fueled her, and she flew out the library door like a champion sprinter. Right away, she spotted the white-robed figure on the dark path nearby. Her vision narrowed to a black tunnel until she saw nothing but Yosis. His gaze was toward the second-story windows of the Oceanography Wing, and he didn't see her coming. *Good*, Tikaya thought, the word a snarl in her mind, and she ran at him like an arrow loosed from a bow.

She smashed into him so hard, they both hit the ground and rolled several meters. Her battles at Rias's side must have taught her something, for she came out on top, straddling Yosis. She smashed the heel of her palm into his face before he got his arms up in a semblance of a block. With anger and frustration still coursing through her veins, she simply aimed for a different target. She punched him in the gut numerous times before an indignant yell of, "Ms. Komitopis!" pierced her fury-clouded mind.

A moment later, someone grabbed her shoulders and hauled her off Yosis. Blood charged through her body, and she almost took a swing at this newcomer as well, but cold awareness cut through her rage. Striking one's fellow citizens was illegal on the islands, and she had witnesses who had seen her beating up on Yosis. Lots of witnesses, she realized, as she peered about at policemen carrying lanterns along with a couple of government officials that she recognized from the war room. Their hair was tousled and clothes rumpled. One woman wore a bathrobe. Yosis must have sent out some sort of alarm when he woke to find Rias missing.

Several sets of eyes stared at Tikaya, some stern, some shocked, some outraged. Yosis staggered to his feet, one hand pressed against his abdomen, the other clutching his nose. Blood ran from one nostril and dripped down his arm. The lantern light shown brightly enough to reveal several droplets spattered on his white robes. Tikaya couldn't bring herself to apologize.

"Ma'am?" the ranking policeman asked one of the officials. "Do we take her to—"

He broke off and cast an uneasy glance over Tikaya's shoulder. Rias had come up behind her without a word or a sound. Blood trickled from the side of his eye and his ear, and Tikaya ground her teeth, not regretting her attack on Yosis for a second. If there weren't policemen edging closer, she'd be tempted to punch him again.

Rias eyed the professor, but Tikaya couldn't guess what was going through his mind. None of the rage she felt seemed to burn in his eyes. How could he be so calm?

"Take them both to jail." Yosis had moved away from Tikaya and Rias and was standing—*hiding*—behind one of the patrollers. "You see what kind of animal she's become under his influence?"

"*His* influence?" Rias asked mildly. "*I* haven't pummeled anyone." He rested his hand on Tikaya's back and gave her a half smile. She blushed, though she had the impression he was pleased that she'd beaten up some fellow on his behalf.

"What were you doing in the library at night?" the ranking policeman asked.

Tikaya opened her mouth to proclaim that she was on the faculty and could visit the library any time she wished—no need to mention the second-floor lock picking, but Rias answered first. "Searching for a private spot. Between her family-filled home and the thin walls of the Pragmatic Mate, we've found it difficult to... visit with each other."

Tikaya blushed harder. She could understand making up a story to cover their true interest, but she didn't want all of these strangers imagining her... *visiting*.

"Are you telling me that you were using the *library* for some sort of... tryst?" the policeman demanded.

"We are both academically inclined," Rias said. "And those posh reading chairs on the first floor are quite comfortable."

That earned a round of glowers, and a lip curl from the official who was probably even then vowing to never read in those chairs again.

Tikaya nudged Rias with her elbow. "Stop helping," she whispered. As it was, this news would likely spread all over town. If she was going to go visit Parkonis's mother, she didn't want the woman thinking she'd become the sort who... violated library reading chairs with men.

"Ma'am?" the policeman asked again.

"Though I'm inclined to have Ms. Komitopis put in jail," the female official said, "her father would create a fuss over that. Take her home and leave someone to ensure she *stays* there. If Professor Yosis wishes to file a complaint of assault, we'll have a judge attend to it."

Stay at home? How was she supposed to find a power source for Rias if she had to stay at home?

"I want a full psychiatric evaluation done on her," Yosis said.

Tikaya slumped. As satisfying as beating him into the ground had been, the repercussions were going to be unpleasant. She imagined a flock of telepaths descending on her home to "evaluate" her.

"And him?" the policeman asked.

"Yosis's summons was heard," the official said.

"What does that mean?" Rias murmured.

"I'm not sure," Tikaya said.

"My colleagues are coming?" Yosis asked. "Excellent."

"Reinforcements?" Rias guessed.

Something about the smug expression on Yosis's battered face made her think it might be worse. A moment later, Yosis turned his head toward the street. A cluster of men and women in the white robes of the Practitioner School strode onto the Polytechnic campus. A pair of gold braids were sewn into the sleeves of each person, a couple of inches above the hem. Tikaya's stomach sank. These were faculty members from the College of Telepaths.

The policemen stepped back, perhaps happy to hand the Rias problem off to someone else. The practitioners joined Yosis, bent their heads, and conferred for a moment before forming a line facing Tikaya and Rias.

"It is time to see why this enemy of our people is *really* here," a white-haired telepath said.

Though Tikaya already stood in front of Rias, she eased over so she more fully blocked him from them. "What are you planning to do? He's my guest here, and even if he weren't, there are laws about using invasive mental techniques on people."

"On Kyattese citizens, yes, but he is not a citizen."

"There are treaties about employing those techniques on Nurians and Turgonians as well," Tikaya said.

"Ah," the white-haired man said, "but I've been informed that he's no longer a Turgonian citizen. The police said you made a statement to that effect during your questioning, is that not true?"

Tikaya stared at him. Dear Akahe, what did they plan to do to Rias that they needed to go fishing for loopholes in the law?

"He has also told me that he's in exile," Yosis said. "As odd as it seems, he'd have more protection here if he were still a Turgonian citizen." The professor smiled sweetly at Rias around his split lip. "You wouldn't care to change your stance would you? Admit that you're still the emperor's man?"

"I am not," Rias said without hesitation.

Emotion welled in Tikaya's throat. Rias might tell a story about a lovers' tryst to protect what he doubtlessly thought was some greater good, but he wouldn't lie to save himself.

"He's my *guest*," Tikaya said. "I invited him here to meet my family. Taking him off for... whatever inimical mind probes you have in mind is unacceptable."

Rias stirred at the mention of "mind probes." Maybe she shouldn't have been so blunt. Whatever mental intrusions he suffered in the past couldn't have been a pleasant experience. Mind rape. She didn't think her people would be cruel, but the very act of drilling into someone's thoughts... It couldn't be anything other than painfully invasive.

"Inimical?" said the white-haired man. "Really, Ms. Komitopis, there's no need for histrionics. I assure you, we are professionals. We merely seek the truth."

The truth. Gali had also sought the truth when she probed Tikaya's mind.

Tikaya looked at Rias over her shoulder, tempted to tell him to sprint into the darkness and find passage off the island before they could find him. He could send a note, let her know where he landed, and she would go to him. Even if it meant leaving her family and her career for the foreseeable future. She opened her mouth to say as much, but Rias winced.

"Come," Yosis said. "Now."

"He's not a hound," Tikaya snapped at him, fingers curling into a fist again. She wondered how long his range was. When had he first attacked Rias? Within a hundred meters of the library? Two hundred? A mile? She didn't know how long Rias had been hunched on the carpet, in pain. She shouldn't have left him alone up there.

"Perhaps not," Yosis said, "but, like a hound, he'll learn that pain comes with aberrant behavior. Appropriate behavior offers the cessation of pain."

Yosis either thought Rias couldn't understand him or that he was an idiot. Or maybe he knew that Rias understood him and was arrogant enough to think he could break him even with that awareness.

"We'd best call it an evening, Tikaya," Rias murmured and walked toward the practitioners, his hands clasped behind his back. He gazed over his shoulder at her. "Perhaps we'll have a chance to revisit the chairs another time."

Two policemen stopped him and patted his waist and pockets before allowing the practitioners to take him. Nothing came of the search. Had he not had time to finish tracing the map? Or maybe he'd hidden his work on his way out. He'd mentioned the chairs twice.

A policewoman headed in Tikaya's direction. Searching for that map would have to wait.

The officials turned away, apparently feeling their work was done. Tikaya jogged over and planted herself in front of the female who'd been giving orders. "Ma'am, I request that you assign someone different to follow Rias around. Professor Yosis seems to have some sort of vendetta. Either that or he's just a small man who's relishing this chance at power far too much."

"Ms. Komitopis, I suggest you go with the police and stay home and out of trouble. Your time spent with the Turgonians and your actions of late have many people questioning your loyalties and what you seek to accomplish in bringing a hated enemy here."

Tikaya, beginning to question what she sought to accomplish as well, didn't have an answer. Perhaps it was time to give up. She and Rias could return again in a few years, when time had softened the pain of the war—and people's hatred of Turgonians. She watched the practitioners stalking away, Rias hemmed in between them, his head and shoulders above the tallest of them. His size mattered little. They had him. If she chose to leave, how would she get him away from them?

When Tikaya didn't respond, the official stepped past, heading for the street.

"Can you at least tell me when the president is due back?" Tikaya asked. He was the one person who could wave his hand and see to it Rias was treated well, and he was the one person who owed Rias a favor. If he knew about it.

"That is unknown. Goodnight, Ms. Komitopis."

The policewoman who remained cleared her throat and pointed Tikaya toward a different road, the one leading to her family's plantation. A short, sturdy lady with pale brown hair, the woman didn't appear as threatening as the practitioners, but her presence could certainly keep Tikaya from continuing the research she and Rias had started that night. An agate rank button pinned on her uniform shirt glowed faintly, reminiscent of moonlight, and Tikaya recalled that the police could communicate with each other from different parts of the city. Yes, her every movement would likely be reported.

Tikaya sighed and headed toward the tree where she'd left her bicycle. After the practitioners and officials disappeared into the city, Elloil ambled out of the bushes, pushing his own bicycle.

"Ho, there, Tikaya," he said. "Where have you been? Mother sent me to look for you." He turned his shoulder toward the policewoman and mouthed something that might have been, "I tried. Didn't you hear my warning?"

Tikaya only shrugged. Maybe Rias had heard it, but it hadn't come soon enough to help.

"Are you all right?" Ell asked after she'd collected her bicycle.

"Of course not." Tikaya gazed toward the dark, empty street that had swallowed Rias and his pack of watchdogs. "I'm waiting for him to wake up, decide I'm not worth all this pain, and disappear. I don't think there's a prison that could hold him, if he were determined to escape."

"Yes, you are."

"Are what?"

"Worth it." Ell smiled.

Tikaya tried to feel better at his assertion, but couldn't manage it.

CHAPTER 9

TIKAYA SAT ON THE STEPS of the lanai, gazing out at the sea and ignoring the stack of books at her side. Her colleague Liusus had brought a pile of work over that morning, certain she'd find her confinement restless. Given that Liusus had not approved of Tikaya's interest in "maritime archaeology," she had expected frowns of disapproval, but apparently nobody knew that she and Rias had been in the Oceanography Wing. He must have put everything away and locked the door before Yosis's attack. Tikaya had been too embarrassed to ask if the entire island thought she'd been polishing Admiral Starcrest's sword in the Polytechnic library.

"Nobody's been able to figure out what to do with that sphere," was what Liusus had said when Mother dragged the two of them inside, insisting Liusus have lunch before returning to work. "When I told them that it lights up and shows pictures, it was amusing to see so many stuffy old archaeologists and philologists completely agog. Once the smoke around your Turgonian blows away from the island, the dean will be leaning on the government, begging, imploring, and otherwise bribing them for permission for you to come back to work."

Tikaya had mulled over whether she could use that somehow to escape house confinement. Under normal circumstances, she'd love to return to work to study alongside her colleagues, but she was too worried about Rias to think about the ancient technology. Once Liusus left, Tikaya ignored the stack of books and let the mystery of his disappearing basin fill all the space in her head. She itched to get back to the Polytechnic and find everything she could on that missing year.

The policewoman, however, sat on the end of the lanai, munching on taro chips and lemonade. Tikaya tried not to find it a betrayal that

Mother was feeding her keeper. Mother fed everyone. If the Turgonian emperor showed up at their door, he'd likely have a platter of roasted pork and grilled pineapple in his hands before he could sit down.

As if the thoughts had produced her, Mother pushed open the sliding screen door and came out with a pitcher. "More lemonade, dear?" Without waiting for a response, she filled Tikaya's glass and the policewoman's as well.

"Thank you, ma'am," the woman said, though she cast a furtive glance toward the road, as if she were worried some superior would chance upon her enjoying refreshments while on duty.

"Tikaya, dear," Mother said, "you haven't eaten." She tilted her chin toward a plate sitting on the railing. "How are you going to gain your health back when you don't eat?"

"My health is fine, Mother. I'm just busy thinking."

"You spend too much time thinking. You always have." Mother set the pitcher down and settled on the steps next to Tikaya. "What is it today? Your young man or the trouble you've stirred up?" She glanced toward the policewoman.

Despite herself, Tikaya smiled at hearing Rias called her "young man." "They're inextricably intertwined right now, but I'm most worried about him. The College of Telepaths has him. They could be forcing their way into his head right now."

"I'm sure that won't happen, dear. That's not ethical, and the treaty—"

"They're ignoring the treaty. Because he's no longer a Turgonian citizen, they think they can."

Mother frowned. "That's abhorrent. I'll talk to your father. As a Komitopis guest, your fellow should be afforded some protection."

"*If* Father would be willing to claim him. That seems... unlikely."

"I'll talk to him when he comes in from the fields tonight."

"Rias has been a prisoner before," Tikaya said. "Tortured and mind-assaulted by the Nurians. I didn't think... I wouldn't have brought him here if—"

"I'll talk to your father, dear. I promise. If he wants to continue enjoying my cooking and good favor, he'll listen."

"Thank you, Mother." Tikaya doubted her gratitude sounded sincere. She didn't want to underestimate her mother's ability to influence people, especially those who lived within her domain, but she doubted

Father would prove malleable on this topic. Besides, tonight might be too late. The telepaths may have already done their work on Rias.

"It'll turn out," Mother said. "We may not have an aristocracy, the way the Turgonians and Nurians do, but our family has played a significant role in Kyattese history since the beginning. The government won't ignore us."

Tikaya gazed past her mother and at the door carving highlighting the first landing. "Yes, that's true, isn't it? A Komitopis captained one of the colony ships, and many of our ancestors have served in office over the years."

Mother nodded. "As president several times, among other positions."

And what, Tikaya wondered, had her ancestors been up to in the 390s? In 397, specifically. "You keep a journal, don't you?"

Mother cocked her head at this change of topic. "Yes, I write it in almost every day."

"Do you know if other people in the family have? Throughout history?"

"Yes, of course, it's commonly done. Unlike some of the first colonists that let their ancestors go rural, the Komitopises have always prided themselves on literacy and education."

Tikaya lowered her voice. She doubted the policewoman had any knowledge of government intrigues, but who knew what she would report back? "Do we have an archive of family history or anything like that?"

"An archive? That's an optimistic word for it, but there are crates full of books and family relics in the attic." Mother offered a crooked smile. "Crates full of utter junk too. Organizing it all would be a project for..." She lifted her eyebrows. "Perhaps for someone confined to the house and seeking to distract one's mind from grim thoughts."

"Mother, are you trying to trick me into cleaning the attic?" In truth, Tikaya was delighted to have an excuse to run up there and hunt around. She wondered if her mother knew that and had made the suggestion for the benefit of the policewoman.

"Of course not, dear." Mother's eyes grew wide and her smile innocent. "More lemonade?"

"Maybe later." Tikaya helped her mother up. "This is the original house our family built, isn't it? So there might be items dating all the way back to the original colony up there?"

"The original house, yes, though it's grown and expanded quite a bit over the years. I honestly have no idea what's up there, though the older stuff would be in the west wing. That was the original bungalow."

"Thank you."

Tikaya nearly ran into the house and up to the second floor where a creaking pull-down ladder led to the attic. Faint light seeped in through vents at one end. Dusty crates filled the dark space, and she tripped before she'd taken a step. She recovered, clunking her head on the low gabled roof, and thought about retreating for food and water and other spelunking supplies after taking in the sheer bulk of furnishings, crates, trunks, and various—as Mother had called it—junk that stuffed the space. There weren't any aisles. There were simply areas that would be easier to climb over than others.

Once Tikaya lit a few lamps, she began the hunt for bookcases and other book depositories—such as the ash can she upended, dumping out magazines filled with hand-drawn nude women.

"Lovely. My family members thought it important to collect the earliest forms of Kyattese pornography." Regardless, she eyed them long enough to date them. Less than seventy years old. "Ugh," she muttered at the thought that they might have belonged to Grandpa or one of his brothers.

The find meant that section of the attic contained relatively recent memorabilia. She crawled deeper, passing everything from exotic art brought in from far off ports, to trunks containing wedding dresses, to a taxidermy octopus that fell off a wardrobe and onto her head, eliciting a startled squeal. Her outburst roused some bats, and they flapped past in a flurry, wings brushing her head, before disappearing through the vents.

"Not a mission for the squeamish." Tikaya checked a disassembled bed frame for the craftsman's name and date. "547. Making progress."

When she reached a painting from a popular artist from the late 300s, she stopped. With the cessation of movement, the quietness of the attic grew noticeable. Tikaya wiped slick palms on her dress. It might have been the exertion causing her to sweat, the fact that there was little airflow in the warm attic, or the notion that she just might find a clue to her mystery up there. Surely, no government busybody with something to hide had thought to check in her family's attic for books that needed to be removed.

The corner of a cobweb-choked bookcase against the wall came into view. Hidden behind wooden pumping equipment from some long-retired well, it would have been easy to miss. Tikaya crawled over trunks and boxes—and clunked her head on the descending ceiling several more times—for a closer look. The books she pulled out were from the right era, with leather straps around the bindings to keep the parchment pages from warping and buckling from changes in humidity, but they were all by well-known authors. They were titles on religion and mythology for the most part, nothing that would shed light on conspiracies from 397. She needed the hand-written journal of some ancestor.

"Ms. Komitopis?" came a muffled voice from the attic entrance. The policewoman.

"Yes, I'm here."

"Ah, good. I feared you might be attempting to escape through some secret exit."

Tikaya glanced toward the nearest roof vent. "Unless I grow wings and shrink, I don't think that'd be possible."

"An unlikely occurrence given how fond your mother is of proffering food."

"Quite." Tikaya sought something to say that would convince the woman to leave her alone. Or maybe she ought to try to coerce her into helping search. A tempting thought, but the last thing she wanted was to make discoveries that someone might report back to the police headquarters. "I've been tasked with a time-consuming job."

"Can you take a break?" her mother asked, voice muffled by distance. She must be in the hallway underneath the trapdoor. "Your cousin wants to see you."

"Ell?" Tikaya guessed. "Can you have him come up here?" She didn't know if that was wise, but she didn't want to leave the attic now.

"No, one of those sprites-cursed concoctions is dangling from his lips. I won't have that smoke in my house."

Tikaya sighed. "Be down in a minute."

She looked around, making note of nearby objects, so she could come back to the same spot, and crawled away from the bookshelf. The hem of her dress snagged on something. She tried to twist her leg and pull it free, but the object held her fast. She reached down between trunks and found a pile of old whaling gear. She grabbed the hilt of the tool entrapping her hem and pulled it out, intending to toss it aside. But she froze and gaped at her find instead. It wasn't a tool; it was a sword in a worn leather scabbard that had been nibbled by rats.

Due to Kyatt's relatively peaceful history, she hadn't chanced across any weapons. This had to be a gift someone had received in trade or...

Tikaya pulled the blade free, and her breath caught. Though dulled by time, the fine steel was unmistakably Turgonian. Other nations had been dabbling with steel during that time period, but the empire had mastered efficient production methods early on. Their old swords illustrated the fact, when one was lucky enough to find one. The Turgonians had always been secretive with their metallurgy technology, with laws forbidding the selling of weapons and tools across the borders. Something like this had probably come off a soldier who had fallen in an overseas skirmish. But there hadn't been any battles on the Kyatt Islands back then. How had this weapon found its way into her family's attic?

Maybe some Nurian war hero had acquired it, then bartered it away, or given it as a gift. But her ancestors had largely been farmers, not traders or world explorers. She stuck her head down between a sofa and a wardrobe to dig deeper into the pile of fishing gear. Beneath the harpoons and hooks, she unearthed a leather messenger bag. Her heart sped up again. Though the history of clothing wasn't her specialty, she had a colleague who studied military archaeology and maintained a small museum in his office. Tikaya had seen this very bag and knew it was Turgonian marine issue from the late 300s.

She eased it out and unbuckled the straps. Mindful of the piece's age, she tried to take care, but her fingers were shaking with the excitement of the find. It might be nothing, she told herself. But it could have to do with everything.

"Tikaya?" Mother called.

She twitched in surprise, and the flap came open, spilling its contents.

"Elloil says it's important and that he can't stay long."

"Just a minute," Tikaya called. "I... caught my dress. It's more treacherous than a dig at an ancient Nurian battlefield back here."

An old cap had tumbled out of the bag as well as a leather journal and letters threatening to disintegrate with age. Horrified that she'd dumped them so carelessly, Tikaya feared that touching them would make matters worse. She picked up the cap. It didn't look like part of a military uniform, but a bill designed to keep sun out of one's eyes might make it a sailor's garment. The straps on the leather journal were secured with a small lock. Someone's private diary? She rifled through the bag, looking for a key, but nothing else remained inside.

"Maybe I'll get to put Rias's lock-picking instructions to use, after all," she said.

"Ms. Komitopis?" That was the policewoman, a note of suspicion in her voice.

"Yes, yes, coming." Tikaya put the journal, cap, and letters back in the bag and carried it most of the way to the trapdoor. Before reaching the exit, she tucked the gear behind a painting where she could find it again later. She started toward the door, but changed her mind, went back, and pulled out the journal. She untied the sash belt of her dress, slipped the book into her undergarments, and arranged the material and belt so that others shouldn't notice the bulge. It'd probably be fine if she left it, but who knew if that policewoman might come up and snoop around?

"You're becoming as paranoid as Rias," she muttered, picking her way toward the trapdoor.

When Tikaya climbed down, her mother was waiting, the policewoman not two feet away—and eyeing the attic opening suspiciously.

"Ell's on the back lanai," Mother said.

"What does he want?"

Mother spread her arms. "He doesn't talk to me, possibly because I so often let him know how disappointed his mother is in his career choice."

"I thought you two were sharing confidences now."

Mother blinked. "What do you mean?"

Tikaya glanced at the policewoman, wishing she'd disappear. "He said you sent him off to keep an eye on me last night. Or maybe just in general," she added when no hint of understanding entered her mother's eyes. "To keep me out of trouble."

"No..." Mother sniffed. "As if I'd send *that* perennial teenager to keep someone out of trouble." She strode down the hall, muttering about sloth and family underachievers.

A bang sounded from downstairs—a door hitting the wall. "Tikaya, what're you doing in there? I've got to get to the beach—giving some visiting foreigners some lessons."

Tikaya hustled through the house, though Mother's words had roused new suspicions in her mind. If *Mother* hadn't sent Ell to follow her, who had?

Ell was pacing on the back lanai, bluish smoke wafting from a cigarette. "Tikaya," he blurted when she stepped outside. "I've got news for you. Rias is..." He trailed off when the policewoman stepped outside. "Oh, right. Forgot about that."

Forgetting her suspicions for a moment, Tikaya grabbed his arm. "What about Rias?"

"He's, uh..." Still eyeing the policewoman, Ell took out his tobacco tin. "Well, they let him go."

"They *did*? Did they... the telepaths, what did they do to him? Is he all right?"

"I don't know exactly, but he seemed the same as usual when I saw him."

"You saw him?" Tikaya barely resisted the urge to grab Ell by the collar of his oversized hibiscus-dyed shirt to shake more details from him.

"Indeed so." Ell must have sensed her urgency—her fingernails were digging into his arm after all—but he took his time rooting around in his tin, pulling out two already rolled cigarettes. "Smoke?"

"You know I don't..." She stopped, catching the slight widening of his eyes. "Fine, I'll take one if it'll get you to spill the news."

"Good, you know I hate to smoke alone."

Ell pressed two cigarettes into her hand. Tikaya recognized one as a fake, a tightly rolled paper with nothing in it. Keeping her back to the policewoman to hide the motion, she slipped the extra into her pocket. She held the real one up, so Ell could light it for her, then held the noxious thing to her lips, pretending to inhale.

"Where'd you see him?" Tikaya asked.

"He's back at the shipyard."

"They're going to let him return to work on his submarine?" Tikaya couldn't believe it.

"Not exactly. He didn't say much about the telepaths, but I guess he's been giving permission to finish building a *ship*, not a submarine, and to hurry up about it. Once it's seaworthy, he's to sail away from Kyatt and never return."

Tikaya rocked back on her heels. "He said that? It was his choice or...?"

"Some high minister's order, I gathered."

"And he agreed to it?" she whispered, gripping the railing.

"I don't figure he had a choice." Ell put a hand on her shoulder. "Sorry, Coz. I know you were hoping for... I don't know, marriage or something, I guess. I liked him a lot too. He treated me better than—" he glanced toward the house, "—lots." He lowered his hand. "I need to grab some food to take with me. Don't tell your mother, all right?"

Ell hustled into the house. Tikaya, imagining Rias leaving forever, barely noticed him go. Would Rias ask her to leave with him? Was she ready to go if it meant forever? Or... what if he *wasn't* planning to ask her? What if whatever he'd suffered at the telepaths' hands had convinced him that she wasn't worth it, that it was time to go home?

The fake cigarette—before she formed premature conclusions, she needed to see if that was a note from Rias. She turned and headed for the house. The policewoman, who'd stood beside the door during the conversation with Ell, followed her inside. Tikaya thought about going back to the attic, but the lighting was poor, and her escort might decide to follow her up the ladder this time. She veered into the water closet, opened the window for light, and yanked out the rolled paper. She released a relieved breath when she recognized Rias's handwriting. By now, she could decrypt the code quickly and read the words straight through.

Tikaya–

I know you are concerned, but I am well. The telepaths were debating over what to do with me (at the same time, I was debating whether to simply consent to their intrusions of my free will) when High Minister Jikaymar strode in, said nobody would be touching my head, and dragged me off to the side. He told me I could go where I wished, but that it'd better be to the docks. He wants me off Kyatt as quickly as possible, and he's allowing me to build a ship, but bluntly stated that I'd be stopped, one way or another, if I attempted to create a submarine.

I don't have to tell you that these allowances are surprising, if not ideal. The paranoid, as you would call it, side of me wonders if it's all part of some trap they hope to spring. If not, I must assume someone spoke to Jikaymar on my behalf. Is it possible your president has returned?

*With love,
Rias*

Tikaya stuffed the note into her pocket and strode out of the water closet. She had to go see Rias, but she wanted to retrieve the rest of the items in the attic so they could examine everything together. As she turned into the hallway, she almost crashed into the policewoman. Oh, right. Tikaya *couldn't* leave the house. How ironic that Rias was now free to walk about, and *she* was confined. She couldn't count on him coming to visit her right away either, not when her family had made it clear that he wasn't welcome. Did he even know she was confined to the house? He'd been pulled away before her sentence had been given, hadn't he?

"Is everything all right, dear?" Mother asked from the doorway to the kitchen, the kitchen that overlooked the back lanai. She held a spoon dripping batter in her hand, so she'd been working in there. Tikaya wondered how much of the conversation her mother had overheard.

"I need to get a message to Rias," Tikaya said. "Do you know if anyone is about who isn't busy?" She didn't know who that might be, as she hadn't seen many people that day. The house was quiet due to planting time.

"Where is he?" Mother asked.

"He might be back at the Pernici—, er, Pragmatic Mate, but he'd more likely be eating, sleeping, and working at Shipyard 4." Sleeping being questionable, Tikaya thought.

Mother's gray eyebrows twitched at the slip-up. She was well aware of the name of the hostel—and the dubious neighborhood it occupied. "That's hardly a fit place for an upright young man."

"The hostel or the shipyard?" Tikaya asked with a smile. "If you'd seen the not-entirely-floating shipwreck he acquired, you might find the Mate a superior abode."

The pursed lips turned into a disapproving pucker. "I need to go to the market. I can relay your message."

Tikaya hadn't meant to send her mother off on errands for her, but as long as she was offering... "I don't suppose you could give a message to Parkonis's mother, as well? As soon as it's permitted—" she glanced at the policewoman, "—I need to go over and see her, but I'd hate to stop by unannounced." Actually, it was more that she'd hate to find that Parkonis was living with his mother until he settled in somewhere again. Tikaya couldn't stomach the thought of knocking on the door and coming face-to-face with two sets of disappointed stares.

"Iweue?" Mother's spoon drooped. "Are you sure she'll want to see you right now? Or me?"

"No, but Grandpa wouldn't help, and she's the only other person I know who could Make an energy source to power a big engine. And Rias needs one." Tikaya realized that might not be true if he no longer intended to build a submarine. Perhaps a standard Turgonian boiler and furnace system would suffice. She needed to talk to him before making further plans.

"I suppose it couldn't last," Mother said.

"What's that?"

"You being the least needy and demanding of my children. Your brothers always craved attention, whereas you simply wanted to be left alone with your books and puzzles. Father and I worried now and then, you know."

"Oh." Awareness of the policewoman standing by caused warmth to creep into Tikaya's cheeks. She didn't want to have her failings deconstructed in front of strangers. "There's no need to worry about me. I'll just wait here while you go talk to Rias. I appreciate it. Thank you."

"Parents *always* worry. We were relieved, though, when you started seeing Parkonis. I thought I'd finally get those grandchildren I'd pictured for so long. I used to tell your father that I feared you didn't know one must plant a seed to grow a tree, and that suitably virile pips are scarce in the dusty archives of the Polytechnic."

Tikaya winced. How had her mother drifted onto this topic again? And was that a smirk on the policewoman's face?

"Yes, Mother. Would you like me to start the runabout for you? Bring it around front?"

"Though you and Parkonis *did* always seem more like friends," Mother went on, caught up in some memory as she gazed out the window. "You didn't stare at him across the dinner table, as if you wished the family would disappear, so you could tear off his clothes and assume a horizontal plane."

"*Mother*!" Tikaya whispered. By now the policewoman's smirk had turned into a hand-covering-her-mouth attempt to hold back laughter. Tikaya's cheeks were no longer simply warm; they were being seared by a surge of molten lava. "I did *not* look at Rias like that. I was too busy being uncomfortable relaying our adventure to twenty pairs of judging eyes."

"Dear, if that's true, I can't *imagine* how you look at him when you're alone and... comfortable."

Escape, Tikaya thought. She had to escape. "I'll go get the runabout for you. The afternoon's already growing long. You don't want to delay. What if the market closes?" She headed for the front door, but her mother continued to muse.

"Though, I *can* understand the feeling. Parkonis was—*is*—a nice lad, but a touch scrawny and scattered, don't you think? Your new fellow is quite handsome, especially when he's roaming about shirtless. Intriguing stories behind those scars, I imagine. That one on his eyebrow, it looks like someone must have been trying to kill him."

"I'm fairly certain someone was trying to kill him on *all* of the instances he received scars, Mother. And, shouldn't you *not* be speculating on shirtless men when you're married to Father?" Shouldn't you not? Tikaya groaned to herself. How sad that a linguistics specialist could fumble her own language so.

"Don't be naive, dear. Of *course* a woman's allowed to speculate. I'm certain that Akahe doesn't judge us for what's in our minds, and being married doesn't mean we must suppress our fantasies. Why a good fantasy can enhance one's intimate relations with one's spouse. It's all perfectly acceptable."

Tikaya had no response for that. She hustled out the front door, nearly slamming it in her haste to escape. As much as she'd wanted an advocate for Rias, having her sixty-year-old mother displaying salacious interest in him wasn't *quite* what she'd had in mind.

CHAPTER 10

TIKAYA HAD WANTED TO DELVE into her attic finds as soon as possible, but Mother left her with a number of cooking tasks to perform in her absence. She could hardly object when Mother was out running errands for her. If the policewoman hadn't been lingering, Tikaya would have tugged out the journal, cut open the lock, and devoured the contents while stirring soup on the cooktop. It wouldn't be the first time she'd read while attending to household chores, though all the scalds, cuts, and spilled pots had resulted in numerous parental warnings on the folly of such practices. As it was, a couple of hours passed, and numerous kin came and went before she could escape the kitchen.

Hoping she could leave her watchdog below, Tikaya left the soup to simmer and headed for the trapdoor. When she reached up to push it open, she met resistance. A shiny new padlock dangled from the latching mechanism.

She stared at it, dumbfounded.

The attic hadn't been locked two hours earlier. At least, she didn't think so. Was it possible her mother had come ahead and unclasped a lock before asking Tikaya to "organize"? But, no, she'd lived in the house most of her life. There'd never been a lock on the attic. Her brothers and cousins had gone up there to smoke during their rebellious teenage stages, which Ell had yet to grow out of. No, somebody had locked the trapdoor within the last two hours.

The hallway floor creaked as the policewoman stopped a few steps away.

"You don't know anything about this, do you?" Tikaya doubted the woman carried padlocks in her pockets or would presume to secure a room in someone's house, but she didn't know who else to suspect.

"No, ma'am."

"Did you by chance see anyone head this way while I was cooking?"

"At least a dozen people were in and out of the house this afternoon."

For a long moment, Tikaya stared at the lock. Unbelievable. She'd ask at dinner, though she couldn't believe this was a coincidence. Someone in the family must have heard she was up there. Someone who knew about the Turgonian artifacts? Or was there something else up there that she had yet to discover, something important? She thought of Ell—he'd gone into the house, supposedly for food, hadn't he? Had Mother let him know she'd been up in the attic when he came? He couldn't possibly be in on some familial conspiracy, could he?

Growling, Tikaya stalked down the hallway, brushing past the policewoman and heading for the other wing of the house. At least she still had the journal. Maybe it would hold the answers she sought.

When she reached her bedroom, she paused with her hand on the knob. "Mind if I have some privacy?" she asked the woman tagging along after her.

"So long as you don't decide to escape out the window." The policewoman smiled, but there was a speculation in her gaze, as if she thought Tikaya might do just that.

"I promise to stay inside."

"Very well."

Tikaya shut and locked the door. Before she took the three steps to her desk, she'd practically torn her undergarments off in her haste to pull out the journal. It wouldn't be long until dinner, and whoever had locked the attic might confront her then or forbid her to research the family history further. She didn't *think* anyone would search her room, but one never knew...

Intending to force open the lock, Tikaya pulled a letter opener out of the drawer, but she paused. The three-hundred-year-old journal wasn't as ancient as many of the artifacts she'd studied, but it *was* a piece of history. Tamping down her growing sense of urgency, she fished a couple of hairpins out and applied Rias's picking techniques.

Despite its age, the diary lock was in good condition and proved far simpler than the one at the library. It released with a soft click.

"Hah," Tikaya said. "So, at the age of thirty, you deviate from pure academics to embark on a life that involves beating up professors and prying into people's diaries." For a moment, she wondered if she should blame Rias's warmongering Turgonian influence, but she was too busy unfastening the leather straps and easing open the book to wonder for long.

With the first page, she knew it was indeed a personal journal, one written in Middle Turgonian, the letters large and wobbly, as one might expect from an accounting written at sea. When she spotted the date at the top of the first entry, a flutter danced through her stomach. 17 Frost Moon, 342. The Turgonians had started their calendar after their first major acquisition on their new continent, fifty-five years after the Kyattese "After Colonizing" dates had begun. That meant her new find was from 397, the year of the missing book in the library.

Tikaya settled onto her bed to read. It'd been more than ten years since she'd studied Old and Middle Turgonian, so it took a few moments to get into the rhythm, but she was soon skimming through the opening pages. Darkness descended outside her window, but she barely noticed.

When a knock sounded at her door, it jarred her out of the world she'd delved into, and she almost dropped the book. Clanks and voices came from the yard out front. Tikaya leaped from her bed and checked the window.

The family's runabout had returned, its engine glowing a soft blue with the energy source that powered it. Her mother had opened the rear and was piling groceries into—Tikaya's heart gave a relieved flip—Rias's arms. The lizard-tracking device no longer adorned his wrist, and there was no sign of Yosis.

She clenched a fist. "*Good.*"

Mother said something, and Rias, arms laden with a crate and an impressive number of sacks, walked around the runabout. He gave it a long thoughtful look on his way to the front lanai. Tikaya wondered if he was dreaming up ways to improve upon the design or simply hoping he never had to ride in the thing again. With its wooden wheels, bamboo frame, and engine parts carved from—if memory served—whale bone, the vehicle must lack the finesse—and smoothness—to which he was accustomed.

In the hallway, someone knocked again, this time with a swift sternness that suggested a reply should be prompt. Tikaya had hoped Rias might glance up at her window, but he didn't see her, so she hustled toward the door. She almost opened it before realizing she still held the journal.

"Just a moment," Tikaya called. Her delays would seem suspicious, but she didn't see a way around them. She searched for a safe place to stash the book. Given that someone was wandering about, locking doors, she didn't want to leave it out. Unfortunately, unlike her brothers, she'd never hidden dirty posters, tobacco, or other parentally forbidden items in her room, so she'd never created a secret niche. When the knock came again, she resorted to stuffing the journal into her undergarments again. She grabbed a decorative sash for her waist, and then, to draw the eye from the area, a flamboyant flower brooch that she'd adored when she was eleven or twelve. It was garish but suitably distracting. "A girl needs to dress up when her beau comes to dinner after all."

Tikaya unlocked the door and strode into the hallway, an apology for the policewoman on her lips. But her father was the one standing there, scowling.

"Do you know what the soup is doing?" he demanded.

"Er." She'd forgotten she left that pot on the cooktop. "Simmering?" she asked hopefully.

"Boiling all over the place and making a mess in the kitchen."

"Sorry, Father. I'll clean it up." She wanted to add, "Right after I see Rias," but the depth of that scowl suggested the addendum would be unwise.

"You'll sleep in your room tonight as well," he growled and stomped toward the stairway. "*Alone*," he added as he descended.

Sighing, Tikaya hustled toward the stairs. It seemed she was catching up on the youthful indiscretions she'd forgotten to pursue as a teenager, including sneaking out and irritating one's parents. The policewoman stood in the hall, her hands clasped behind her back as she imitated a potted plant. So lovely to have a witness for one's life.

By the time Tikaya cleaned up, the family had gathered around the table. With so many watching, she didn't hug Rias, instead only gave him an awkward hand pat on her way past. She ate swiftly, hoping everyone would finish soon so she could excuse herself for a more private conversation with him, though she didn't know how much she dared discuss with the policewoman still around.

Ell didn't show up for dinner, and she wondered where he was. As much as she hated to think suspicious thoughts about family members, the shiny new lock on the attic had her hackles up.

Rias asked a few polite questions at dinner, and responded with a thankful smile whenever Mother included him in the conversation, but mostly he remained quiet. Given how often Father's glower shifted in his direction, that wasn't surprising.

At one point, Rias asked his across-the-table seat mate Ky, "How long have your people had vehicles?"

Tikaya's brother shrugged. "Two or three centuries at least. They're rare because it's a lot of effort for a practitioner to Make a power supply. Most people ride bicycles or pull wagons with donkeys."

"That rickety vehicle is actually a sign of our family's prosperity," Tikaya said dryly.

"Nothing wrong with our runabout," Father said, sparing a new scowl for her.

"No, sir," Rias said. "If you were of a mind, you could make the ride smoother by installing..." He glanced at Tikaya and asked, "Shock absorbers?" in Turgonian.

She offered an unwieldy translation. Her people didn't have an equivalent, as far as she knew.

"I could take a look at it and see if I can come up with something," Rias offered.

"That sounds lovely." Mother's voice held true pleasure, and she beamed a smile at him.

For a few heartbeats, Father's expression seemed to soften and turn speculative as well, but he shook his head, and the scowl climbed back onto his lips. "We don't need any Turg improvements."

After that, the dinner conversation limped along. Tikaya was relieved when Mother dismissed the children and put an end to the moribund event. She couldn't grab Rias's arm and lead him to the back lanai fast enough. The policewoman trooped after, though Mother stopped her with a raised hand.

"Dear, you look tired. Why don't you sit down, and I'll bring you a spot of rum cake?"

The policewoman pointed at Tikaya. "I need to—"

"Here now, you can see through the window from this chair. Won't that do? It's only polite to offer privacy to young couples."

Father appeared at Mother's shoulder. "What are you doing? Devil's spit, don't *help* them."

"Come, Loilon," Mother responded, "we've raised three children. Surely, you've learned that they'll do what they wish, and it's better to let them do it under a watchful eye than to force them to slink off into the night where they'll get in trouble."

Tikaya thought Mother would give her a disapproving frown when she finished speaking, but she leaned around Father to eyeball Ky and Tikaya's other brother, Kolio, instead.

"What?" Ky asked innocently from the dining room.

"We'll discuss this further." Father guided Mother away with a hand on her back.

"Of course," Mother said, something in her voice suggesting she wasn't worried about coming out on top in the brewing argument.

Grateful for her mother's interference, Tikaya joined Rias in the courtyard. The fountain burbled, a half moon cast beams upon the water, and a soft breeze stirred the fronds of the plants and trees. A perfect evening for a little romance, but the questions that had been threatening to bubble over in Tikaya's mind—similarly to the soup in the pot—spilled out as soon as they were alone.

"Did the telepaths truly leave you alone? What'd the high minister say to you? Did he threaten you or did you reach an agreement? Where's the tracking device? And Yosis? Is he done following you? Are you free to go wherever you wish? Are you truly giving up your dream of building a submarine?"

"Hm." Rias took Tikaya's hand and led her to a stone bench. "This is our first private moment..." He glanced at the windows overlooking the courtyard, through which the policewoman and several of Tikaya's teenaged cousins observed. "Rather, this our first *semi*-private moment, and you wish to interrogate me?"

"*Rias.*" She gripped his forearm with both hands. "We can practice lip osculating later. If you tell me what happened with all those telepaths, I'll show you what's under my dress. As a Turgonian, I'm sure you'll find it fascinating."

"Er, yes, as a man, I'm sure I will, but..."

Tikaya rolled her eyes, shifted so her back faced the windows, and tugged his hand over so he could feel the outline of the book beneath her sash.

"More intrigues? Very well, I shall endeavor to respond to your inquiries in an adequate manner." Rias tilted his face toward the moon for a moment. "Yes, the telepaths left me alone, though I sensed a number of cursory probes as a few tried to gauge my top-level feelings. I don't believe they learned much. There's an advanced class at the academy for high-ranking officers as well as those who work in beyond-borders intelligence operations. It's taught by an ex-Nurian wizard hunter. You learn a few rudimentary techniques for resisting mental interrogations."

"At a *Turgonian* academy? I didn't think your people acknowledged that the mental sciences existed, much less that there's a need to defend against them."

"They don't openly, no. It's a top-secret class. As to the rest of your questions, I do not know who the high minister was in contact with, but I must surmise that it was someone of influence. He didn't look happy about it, but he removed the tracker and said I could walk around without an escort. The stipulation for my freedom was that I agreed not to build a submarine and that I promised to leave by the end of the month unless they recanted and invited me to stay."

"The... month?" Tikaya sagged against his side. "And they want you gone for*ever*? I knew that'd be a possibility, but I'd thought—*hoped*—that... with time, my people would get used to having you around, and you'd at least be able to come back for frequent visits and..."

"I did too. I didn't want you to have to choose between me and the home you love, but I suspected this would be the case. That's why..." Rias reached out and touched one of the fronds draping over the bench, brushing it gently—sadly?—with his thumb.

"What?"

"Why I haven't asked you to marry me," he said.

"Oh." Tikaya remembered him bringing up the subject once in a room full of bodies when she'd asked him to distract her from the grisly surroundings and some particularly taxing mental work. He'd been joking then, sort of, but she hadn't forgotten that he'd mentioned it. But she was still trying to get used to the idea of sailing off and having adventures with him; she'd always wanted to raise a family here.

Rias cleared his throat. "Given the lack of encouragement in that monosyllabic response, perhaps it's just as well that I haven't asked."

"No, no." Tikaya leaned closer and kissed him. "I was thinking, sorry."

"I suppose I've learned by now that I'm not quite as intriguing as what goes on inside your head."

"That's not true. All right, that's not *always* true. These are just intriguing times. Let's talk about our future together later, shall we? I *do* want to spend it with you. And I want to see what kind of potato-gun-making, lock-pick-wielding, bathtub-armada-creating children I might have with you. I'm just not certain I can see raising them on a submarine. Or without the support of my family. You sound like you might have been... *trying* to your mother."

"*Me?*" The shadows didn't quite hide the magnitude to which Rias's eyebrows climbed. "I wholeheartedly deny the likelihood of such an accusation. Of course... my denial might be less wholehearted were my mother not thousands of miles away and unlikely to chat with you any time soon."

"I'm actually composing a letter to her." Tikaya was only teasing him, but perhaps it wasn't such a bad idea. One ought to introduce oneself to one's potential mother-in-law, shouldn't one?

"You are? Then... why don't I get back to answering your initial questions? Yes, let's do that. I haven't seen Yosis since this morning. He stalked off when he heard the high minister's mandates. I did have the impression he wasn't done with me. Jikaymar suggested I finish my ship swiftly, leaving unspoken the implication that unsavory things might happen to an ex-Turgonian commander who stayed around."

"So you're building a ship now? Wouldn't it be faster to simply spend a few more nights in the gambling hall and win enough to purchase one? You can't possibly finish one from scratch by the deadline you've been given."

"I doubt it would be that easy—you can usually only win everyone's money once before word gets around and people start avoiding you. Besides..." Rias glanced at the windows again and lowered his voice. "I haven't given up on my submarine. I'm simply altering the design, so it'll appear to be a surface-based craft."

"Ah ha, I knew you wouldn't abandon that idea so easily."

"As to the build time, it'll be tight, but I've recruited a crew of sorts to help. There are more ex-Turgonians living in the city than I would have guessed, many of them former marines who chose to marry a native and settle here, much like your Nurian neighbor. They've all proven willing to assist me so far."

"Not surprising. What about my cousin, Ell?" Tikaya asked, remembering the locked attic. "Has he been helping you?"

"He has, yes."

"Keep an eye on him," Tikaya said.

"Oh?"

"Just in case he's someone's eyes."

"I don't get that sense from him, but I'll be careful and compartmentalize my team." Rias shifted his weight on the bench. "My new design is compact, so it won't take as long to build as a warship or something of that size."

"Your... new design? You have one already? Didn't you just learn that you had to change it this morning?"

"Yes, I had time to revamp it on the ride out here. So long as the bumps I received to my head while sitting in your family's conveyance didn't cause damage that will render my calculating skills untrustworthy."

Tikaya snorted. "I knew you thought the runabout was awful."

"Just... incomplete." Rias touched her sash. "Have I answered your questions adequately? Are you going to slap my hand if I slip it under your dress to see what you're hiding?"

"Have I ever?" Tikaya checked the window. The youngsters, perhaps bored by the dearth of physical activity, had disappeared, and only the policewoman remained. Unfortunately, she seemed to take her job seriously, and she watched them like dedicated surfers surveying the ocean for a promising wave. "We better put on a show for her," Tikaya whispered. "Can you slip it out and take it to your hostel room?"

Rias eyeballed his sleeveless shirt and clam diggers. "I suppose I can employ a similar method to yours, so long as nobody's looking too closely at my groin area."

"Don't walk past my mother on the way out."

"What?"

"Never mind. It's a journal that was written over three hundred years ago by one of your countrymen. He'd retired from the military and was sailing on an exploration vessel. They were seeking gold, ancient treasures, and signs of some sort of lost colony. The latter intrigued me, because, for all that I've studied history, I hadn't heard of any such thing. Do you know of it?"

"It's a fable," Rias said, "one of many my mother read to me as a child. According to our history, there were eight waves of ships that left Nuria, all intending to colonize different parts of what's now the Turgonian West Coast. After a generation or two of conquering, assimilating, and carving out places for themselves, they eventually found each other again and formed a central government. The history books claim that all of the original colony waves were accounted for, but the fable says that there were actually nine waves and that one never made it. The story tells of a great storm that forced the small fleet off course and eventually sank the ships. Every now and then, someone goes looking for evidence of the lost colonists, because the fable also tells of priceless antiques that had been taken from the old world." Rias shrugged. "I suspect it's simply a tale kept alive by wistful treasure hunters."

"Many cultures have such stories," Tikaya said, "some based on a grain of truth but some totally fantastical. I don't know about a lost colony, but according to this journal, this exploration vessel was here in 397—that's 342 by your calendar. It'd be an impressive coincidence if their quest didn't have anything to do with the altered map and the missing government journal from that year."

"Did this countryman of mine find anything?" Rias asked. "How did the journal end up in... Where did you say you found it?"

"Our attic. I'm—"

A door banged, and Tikaya flinched.

"It's getting late," Father said. "Finish up, send your... suitor home, and come to bed."

Suitor. That was an improvement. Maybe Mother had won the argument. The door thudded shut again. At least he was giving her a couple more minutes. "Ever notice how you're *always* a child in the eyes of your parents? So long as you're staying under their roof...."

"I have experienced similar scenarios during my homecomings, yes." Rias turned his shoulder and leaned in to stroke her face with one hand while resting the other on her thigh near the book. "It doesn't matter how many military medals and accolades you receive; your mother still expects you to clear the table and take out the trash."

Tikaya might have chuckled, but her body had instantly grown aware of the warmth of his hand through her dress. "Er, yes, as I was saying, I didn't get to read all of it before dinner, but the book will be safer with you."

"Safer?" Rias's roaming fingers paused. "What do you mean?"

Tikaya, aware that Father might be back out at any moment, gave him a quick synopsis of the afternoon's events.

"You suspect your cousin?"

"He's been around—and around *me*—far more than usual."

"And here I thought he simply found *me* intriguing."

"I'm sure that's true too." Tikaya tapped the back of Rias's hand, reminding him that his fingers were supposed to be delving under her dress. She supposed she could get the book out herself without her observer noticing, but thought Rias might perform the move more adroitly. Akahe knew it was within her range of talents to fall off the bench while trying to extricate the tome.

Fortunately Rias obliged, his warm fingers slipping beneath the hem to find bare skin. He lowered his lips to hers for a kiss as well, perhaps figuring the policewoman would be more likely to watch that than his hand. Tikaya certainly didn't mind. Too soon, he pulled back.

"Wait, did you say this journal was written in three-forty-two?" Rias whispered. "It'll be in Middle Turgonian then."

"Is that a problem?"

"Only if you want me to be able to read it."

"It's not that different from the modern tongue. I'm sure you'll be able to work it out. If you're as smart as I believe you are." Tikaya took his face in both hands, smiled, and leaned into him to resume the kiss.

"There better be maps and pictures," he muttered around her ardor.

Before she could decide whether she wanted to respond, his roaming fingers inched higher, finding the book, but also delivering a few teasing strokes that made her breath hitch and her body flush. "*Rias,*" she whispered against his mouth. "You can't do such things if you're leaving."

The door slammed open again, and Tikaya jerked away from Rias like a guilty teenager.

"Enough, Tikaya," came her father's voice.

She wanted to tell him to go away, that, by all the blighted banyan sprits in the forest, she was thirty years old. Besides, he'd never objected to her spending late evenings in the courtyard with *Parkonis*. Of course, she'd had her own room in the city then, and necking sessions at the homestead had been rare. It didn't matter anyway. The book was gone. When she glanced at Rias's lap, he gave her a nod. Mission accomplished.

"Coming, Father." Tikaya stood and smoothed her dress.

Her father had gone back inside, but the policewoman stood on the lanai. A second woman in uniform had joined her. The night shift?

Rias stood up and captured her hand. "Ms. Komitopis, would you be available for a date in three days hence?"

"A date? I'm confined to the house and under watch."

Sure, *he* might be free now, but Tikaya had still assaulted a professor.

"Perhaps you can figure out a way to sneak away," Rias said softly.

"I'll... see what I can think of." Tikaya remembered that Liusus had said her colleagues were missing her, or rather missing her expertise when it came to the alien artifacts. She could try sending Dean Teailat a note. He had some sway in the city; maybe he could speed the judicial process along. "What did you have in mind for this date?"

"I thought we might take a stroll up the coast, and you could show me the sights. I've heard you can stand on the rocks and watch live lava plop out of tubes, then sizzle as it falls into sea."

Ah, he wanted to explore the shoreline near the basin that had disappeared from the maps. "It's not as exciting as you'd think," Tikaya said, hoping he understood that to mean that she'd been to the area and seen nothing suspicious or intriguing. Surfers hit the breaks up there every day and kids tramped all over the caves in the nearby cliffs. After more than three hundred years, any evidence of historically significant happenings would be long gone.

"You only say that because you grew up here. I'm sure I'll find it fascinating." Rias smiled, kissed her in parting, and strolled out of the courtyard, choosing, with his book burden, to walk around the house rather than through it.

"Fascinating?" Tikaya murmured. Dear Akahe, what did he have in mind?

CHAPTER 11

TIKAYA TOOK A DEEP BREATH and climbed the steps to Iweue's lanai. It'd been two days since Rias's evening visit. That morning, a new policewoman had come by, relieving the old one of duty, and handed Tikaya a message. Apparently, her plea to Dean Teailat had worked. She had a month of community work to look forward to, along with eight weeks of counseling sessions in which she'd learn to control her "inappropriate rage," but at least she could walk around without an escort. Of course, she was *supposed* to be back working at the Polytechnic, not visiting Parkonis's mother.

Tikaya pulled the doorbell ringer, a braided seashell chain with a pewter book dangling on the end. She'd loved that ringer once—as it showed how much Iweue adored reading—but now it reminded her how much she'd *liked* having Iweue for a future mother-in-law, and she'd seemed to like Tikaya too. If the woman had been a condescending nag, it would have been much easier to walk away from the family. Showing up today and asking for something on Rias's behalf would likely wound Iweue. Tikaya could only hope she'd be in a cheery mood thanks to Parkonis's recent return from the dead.

A thump sounded within the thatch-roof bungalow, followed by a call of, "Coming."

Tikaya reminded herself that she was on a necessary errand and that it wouldn't do to feel chagrin at the fact that Iweue was home. When the door opened, she forced a bright smile, though she doubted it disguised the wariness that hunched her shoulders.

"Good afternoon," she said.

Iweue, a graying woman with her hair swept into a bun, leaned forward to squint through the screen door, almost dropping the book clutched to her chest. She patted about, checking the pockets of a loose blouse and an apron before finding her spectacles in their usual perch above her brow. "Tikaya?"

"Yes, ma'am." The formal title slipped out before she caught herself. Parkonis's mother had always insisted on being called by her first name, even by her students at the College, preferring that to ma'am, and certainly not Mrs. Osu, thank you very much, for that surname had come by way of a deadbeat husband who'd wandered off to one of the small islands to lounge about the beaches and avoid work and responsibility, a story Iweue had explained often. Even so, Tikaya wasn't certain the woman would appreciate first name usage from her any more.

"Iweue, please." With her spectacles now affixed, she looked Tikaya up and down. "It's wonderful to see that you've returned home safely. And that you're well. There are rumors all over the island, and I've heard... so many things, really, from Parkonis. I'm not certain what to believe about, er, is there no hope for you two, Tikaya? Underneath it all, I think he misses you and would come back if... your new... relationship doesn't end up lasting."

Tikaya didn't know what to say. She had expected disappointment and maybe condemnation from Parkonis's mother, not for her to ask if she'd take her son back. The mature thing to do would have been to discuss the situation; instead Tikaya avoided it completely by asking, "Rumors?"

Iweue pursed her lips thoughtfully—probably seeing through Tikaya's reluctance to discuss the matter—and said, "Yes, rumors. Here, sit down." She waved to a pair of rattan chairs and a small table at the corner of the lanai.

Before their rumps had more than touched down, Iweue launched into details. "Parkonis says that his team was there on a sanctioned—" her eyebrow twitched at the word, "—relic hunt with several others from the archaeological community when Admiral Starcrest showed up with a company of marines and started slaying people left and right. This being the group who had kidnapped you from your parents' plantation, Parkonis felt quite justified and heroic in kidnapping you back from their vile midst. But you were uncooperative in helping our own people thwart the Turgonians. For the safety of all of her allies, his colleague Gali was forced to use her telepathy training to enter your mind—"

Iweue's eyebrow twitched again, this time at the word forced, "—and found out Starcrest had duped you into working for him. Parkonis claims that Starcrest is here now, under the guise of courting you, to delve into Kyattese secrets and seek a weakness that imperial forces, led by himself, can swoop in and exploit."

"That's... similar to the version of events I keep hearing," Tikaya said. "I suppose I should have guessed that the government didn't make up such an elaborate tale of its own accord. Bureaucrats aren't known for their creativity."

"Yes, Parkonis reported to them immediately upon his return." Iweue folded her hands in her lap and waited. For Tikaya to offer her own version of events? It *was* promising that Iweue didn't seem to have formed an opinion yet.

Though Tikaya was starting to grow weary of telling the story—maybe she could put together a pamphlet to hand out to folks—she launched into it again, adding in a few more details of the ancient civilization and puzzle-solving because Iweue had often shown interest in her work when she and Parkonis had come for dinner.

"Hm," Iweue said after the story's conclusion.

Tikaya wondered if that meant she'd lost belief in the tale somewhere along the way and had continued listening only out of politeness.

After a moment, Iweue asked, "Did he mention his wife to you?"

"Huh?" Tikaya blurted. Of course Rias *had* mentioned his former wife, but nobody had asked about the woman yet—how did Iweue even know?—so the topic surprised her. "I mean, he did, yes. Early on. He said the marriage had been dissolved as a result of him losing his name, warrior-caste status, and ancestral lands." Realizing that implied he hadn't necessarily wanted the marriage to end, Tikaya rushed to add, "He said he didn't regret that. I gather it was something of a relief because she wasn't faithful. It'd been a relationship arranged in his youth, and they'd turned out not to have anything in common."

"She wasn't *faithful*?" Iweue leaned forward so quickly, her spectacles slipped down her nose. She stared at Tikaya over the rims.

Not certain what response Iweue wanted or expected, Tikaya only said, "Yes..."

Iweue sank back in the chair and adjusted her spectacles. "That's hard to imagine. He's a great hero over there. I'd think being his wife would have been very prestigious, second only to wedding the emperor himself."

"Uhm." The last thing Tikaya wanted was some scenario in which Rias's wife regretted her past indiscretions and showed up on the docks to ask for him to return. How had they ended up on the subject? She'd come to discuss components for powering engines, not Rias's past loves. "I suppose some warrior-caste women, being born into a privileged aristocracy, may not appreciate the gifts Akahe—er, their ancestors—bestow on them." Tikaya tilted her head. "I didn't know you were an expert on Turgonian marriage practices."

"Not an expert, no, but I've read..." Iweue flipped a hand, as if to dismiss the notion, but a thoughtful expression drifted onto her face. "Actually, why don't I show you?"

Before Tikaya could agree or disagree, Iweue slipped out of her chair and into the house, leaving the screen door banging in the breeze in her haste to reach... what? Curiosity propelled Tikaya after her host.

Little had changed in the small home, though Tikaya barely had time to notice the woven grass rugs, the beach-themed wall decor, or the bamboo and rattan furniture—all littered with books—before Iweue zipped through the living area and up a ladder to the loft. Bookcases, their shelves bent under the weight of so many tomes, filled the low walls and formed aisles through the space. In some spots, lesser encyclopedias and compendiums were simply stacked on the floor. Tikaya followed her guide through the maze to the back of the loft where a lamp and a plush chair waited. Iweue put her hand on a case built into the back wall. Numerous history and Science tomes with bland black and brown leather bindings filled it.

"As you may have noticed," Iweue said, "I've been collecting over the decades. I keep saying I'll donate some of my books to the library, but it's difficult to part with one's treasures."

"I've always found that to be true," Tikaya said politely, not sure what else to say. Though she had a fondness for all sorts of books herself, she wondered at the point of this diversion.

"I so crave good adventure yarns that I read novels from a number of different cultures. I must admit, I find our own authors tend toward the academic; some are very imaginative, but you wonder if they've ever actually had any adventures themselves. And they can be quite verbose.

I don't care how much symbolism one can find in a dead fish washed up on the beach—there's just no reason to spend paragraphs describing it."

By this point, Tikaya had no idea where Iweue was going with the conversation, so she merely nodded.

"I've found that Turgonian novelists, though terse and not known to pen books of great literary merit, at least when judged by other nations, have a knack for telling stories in a succinct way that moves the story along and makes you want to turn the page."

Tikaya gave another encouraging nod. Iweue's rambling seemed to be coming to a head.

"Of course, it grew terribly hard to acquire such novels during and after the war—and it's considered quite unseemly to own them today. I was encouraged by colleagues to burn my copies, if you can imagine. Ghastly notion, that. I did make their placement in my library more... discreet."

With that, Iweue pulled out a particularly drab looking tome entitled *On Manipulating Alchemical States*. A soft click sounded, and the bookcase swung outward. Surprised, Tikaya stepped back to evade its bulk. Iweue pushed it all the way around, revealing a second case full of books on the backside. These were more slender texts, some with quite vivid colors. Tikaya didn't think she'd ever seen a book with such a luscious pink binding.

"*The Rapier and the Rose*, by Lady Dourcrest?" she read.

Iweue cleared her throat. "Pay no attention to those books. They're terribly salacious. Not at all worth your time to read, but the merchant captain who smuggles, er, brings the latest Turgonian publications to me when he passes through always includes that author's latest titles. The way he smirks and admires my physique when he hands them over... I dare say he's trying to put suggestions into my head." Iweue sniffed.

Tikaya tamped down a smile. "And do you read them?"

"Of *course* not."

"That one has a bookmark in it."

"What? Oh, it must have come already inserted. No doubt some lewd passage to which the captain wished to draw my attention." Iweue pointed to the top shelf. "*These* are the titles I thought might interest you."

As Tikaya read the first one, her mouth dropped open. "*Captain Starcrest in the West Markiis?*" She skimmed the shelf, and her jaw sank lower and lower. There had to be more than thirty titles. "*Fleet Admiral Starcrest and the Nurian Armada?*"

"That's from later in his career. I'd start at the beginning. The ones by Lord Bearcrest are best." Iweue plucked a book from the shelf. "Here. *Lieutenant Starcrest and the Savage Saboteur.*"

Tikaya stared at the row of books. She'd known Rias was considered a hero amongst the Turgonian marines, but these stories... They implied he was a household name in the empire. There were probably children who were, at that very moment, reenacting his exploits in backyard adventures. That Turgonian metalworker's words came to mind, the suggestion that Rias could take back what was rightfully his if he chose to stir up trouble. It might be a difficult road, but when had he ever shied away from a battle where the odds were against him? What if... What if the only reason he'd chosen not to return home was her? What if they'd never met? Would he have gone straight to marching on the capital to demand his title and rights back? Was she costing him a chance at regaining his old life?

"What was that?" Iweue asked.

Tikaya realized she must have muttered some of her questions aloud. "I was... wondering about the books. Are they biographical?"

"Oh, I don't think so. Just stories loosely based on actual events in the admiral's career. The author admits he didn't have any interaction with Starcrest—who, it sounds like, spent most of the twenty-odd years of his career at sea, making him rather unreachable—but he did do research to ensure the battles and historical events were as accurate as possible. That seems to be quite important to Turgonian readers." Iweue selected two more novels. "Here. This is another one from when he was a lieutenant, and then the story of how he obtained his captaincy, largely by being one of the few survivors of the battle of—oh, I don't want to spoil it for you. Why don't you read them? How novel to think that you could actually ask him how true the adventures are, hm!"

Tikaya stared at the books. It was bizarre to think that she knew someone—was *loved* by someone—who had popular novels written about his exploits. Further, he had been someone so important that an author, even a Lord something-or-other-crest, wouldn't think to pester him for an interview to get the facts. "Have you read them all?"

"Oh, yes. As I said, they're romping tales. I read several books a week, you know. Especially now that I've retired from teaching and that the children are grown up. It can be a touch lonely in the evenings."

"Perhaps you should invite that Turgonian merchant captain up for tea once in a while."

Iweue sniffed. "Really!"

"Forgive the insinuation." Tikaya waved her hand. "Thank you for lending these to me. I'm certain they will be interesting to read." Whenever she found time to break away from the rest of her research. That thought reminded her of the reason for her visit. She was about to ask after a power supply when a new thought pranced into her mind. "They didn't... ah, do any of the adventures mention... the wife?"

"Briefly. Mostly to describe her beauty and mention how Starcrest was pining after her during his long months at sea."

"Oh, please." Tikaya doubted Rias would pine after anyone if there was even the faintest problem around to keep his mind busy.

"Also, the authors all decided he was quite faithful to her."

Tikaya made a face at the books in her hands. Maybe she didn't want to read them after all, not if they included passages of Rias waxing nostalgic on his distant wife. Well, she *had* asked.

"They're just stories, of course," Iweue said. "They show him as a noble and honorable man, but a tricky one as well. The tactics he pursued to keep his men safe and outthink—and sometimes utterly destroy—the enemy were often cunning, sometimes unorthodox and... Let's just say it's clear he would be perfectly capable of fooling someone, even an intelligent someone, and it wouldn't be any fault of hers if she fell for his tricks."

Just when Tikaya had thought Iweue might prove a supporter of Rias. She did not lift her gaze from the books when she asked, "Are you saying you believe Parkonis's interpretation of events, after all?"

"No, Tikaya, just that you should proceed with wariness. If the man still feels loyal to his emperor..."

"He doesn't. The reason he's *here*, that he was ever in trouble to start with, was because he refused to cross certain lines for that beast. Emperor Raumesys's mistakes are the rest of the world's gains. Rias won't return to him—he was offered that opportunity already and refused it. *We* could have him if the president would get back here, call off the College and ministers, and talk to him."

"*Have* him? Are you suggesting we start a permanent naval force?"

"He can do more than order boats around," Tikaya said dryly. "I'm actually here to speak to you about something he's building and to ask... are you still Making?" Tikaya hadn't noticed any tools littering the house the way they did her grandfather's workshop. What if this trip had been for naught?

"Now and then. It takes a lot out of me, and there are younger folks with as much knowledge, and they have new ideas."

But none of them had a reason to help Rias. "Rias needs something more compact than a boiler and furnace to power the ship he's building."

"Does he now?" Iweue stroked her chin and glanced at the shelf—perhaps imagining some ship she'd had a role in building being mentioned in a future novel. "That would be... a great deal of work, but interesting work. It's been some time since I Made an energy source for powering more than well pumps and irrigation systems. I believe I could do it, but I'll need at least a week of uninterrupted work time."

"Are you willing to undertake the task?"

"I might be, in exchange for something of value."

Tikaya had little money and hated the idea of asking her family for coin, especially given that nobody seemed to want her and Rias to end up together, but she'd figure out a way. She owed him... more than she could ever repay. "Such as?" Tikaya prompted.

"I want a ride."

Tikaya almost dropped the stack of books. "A what?"

"I want a ride on the ship when it's done."

The submarine, Tikaya thought, but she wasn't about to admit to that. By the time they were ready to take on passengers that secret would be out regardless.

"I'm sure I can arrange that." She smiled and added, "I know the captain, after all."

CHAPTER 12

WOODEN SURFBOARDS RATTLED IN A long, bamboo carrying cart attached to the back of Ell's bicycle. He rode ahead of Rias and Tikaya, leading the way to "entirely excellent waves." He'd invited himself along on the lava-sight-seeing trip, and Tikaya wasn't pleased about it, not when she still wondered if someone had hired or otherwise coerced Ell into spying on them. After inquiring amongst numerous family members who lived in the house, Tikaya had learned nothing about who placed the padlock on the attic trapdoor, only that nobody knew anything about it. Mother had seemed bewildered and suggested that perhaps Grandpa had done it to keep the grandchildren from climbing up and hurting themselves on the old fishing gear. Unlikely timing, that.

"You're going to adore surfing, Rias," Ell called over his shoulder.

Rias's only response was to exchange glances with Tikaya. When he'd shown up at her door at dawn for their "date," he'd been wearing a hollow bamboo tube on his back, one typically used for carrying artwork or maps. Whatever he had planned for the day, it had little to do with water sports.

"You have to learn anyway, if you're going to design boards," Ell added.

As if that were his top priority. Tikaya shook her head at her cousin's back. She and Rias had been strolling to the bicycle shed when Ell had come racing down the path toward them, having apparently spent the night at the house. He'd asked where they were going, because he'd been planning to talk Rias into a surfing lesson that afternoon. When Tikaya had attempted to quell him with a succinct, "We're going on a date," he'd failed to be quelled and simply asked where. When Rias had mentioned the lava cliffs, Ell had clapped, proclaiming the waves there perfect, so he could come along and give Rias a lesson that very day.

"The East Coast isn't a beginner area," Tikaya said. She didn't want to see Rias smashed against the rocks for his trouble.

"I know safe spots. I'll take care of Rias. Besides, he looks like a born athlete. I'm sure he'll be fine."

"He hasn't seen me swim," Rias told Tikaya.

"I've seen you swim. Amidst burning shards of wood from ships you've recently crashed."

"I can wave my arms in the correct motions, but I'm not a natural. My tendency is toward sinking."

"If you humor him for an hour, maybe he'll leave us alone." And if he didn't... that would suggest Tikaya was right in suspecting Ell, and that she'd have to figure out a way to question him. The idea of interrogating a relative didn't appeal, so she pushed the thought aside for later contemplation. She nodded toward the basket on the back of Rias's bicycle—it held a picnic hamper and the bamboo case. "Is the map you copied in there?"

"Yes, and some modern ones from your physical oceanography department. I pored over them last night and have some ideas on—"

"We're here," Ell announced, dropping his feet to the ground.

Only the fact that they'd been pedaling uphill kept Tikaya from crashing into the surfboard cart. She cast another exasperated look at her cousin's back and looked for something to lean her bicycle against. There wasn't much. The ground was nothing but black lava rock, and only a few scrubby clumps of grass grew from pockets of dirt in the crevices. Below the road, waves broke against the fifty-foot-high cliffs. They curved inward, forming an inlet, but most of the action was out in the open sea. Despite the early hour, dozens of surfers straddled their boards, waiting for waves beyond Obsidian Hollow, the name for a stretch of black sand beach at the beginning of the cliffs. A steep path wound down to it in switchbacks. Other bicycles and two runabouts were parked near the trail sign.

"Excellent." Rias hopped off his bicycle and took a few steps toward a point overlooking the inlet.

"The trail down is over there." Ell pointed at the sign.

Rias paused. "I wish to see the sights first. Is this where the live lava spills into the sea?"

"Yes." Tikaya doubted he had any interest in the lava, but went along so they could fool Ell. "There are numerous spots along the cliffs. All sorts of caves dot the walls too," she added. "There are outfits that lead tours out here for visitors. They usually end up at Squall Lodge on the other end of the cliffs. There are hot springs with mineral baths that supposedly have restorative properties."

Now Ell sported the exasperated expression. "Really, 'Kaya? *Mineral* baths? That's where old people go. I know he's got a few years on you, but I don't see a cane."

"I do have a few old war wounds that act up from time to time." Rias smiled. "Are these mixed-sex, clothing-optional baths?"

"Actually they're clothing-prohibited baths," Tikaya said. "It's quite the romantic spot. I went out there once with—ah, I visited once briefly."

Rias's eyebrow twitched.

"They're romantic if you're *old*." Ell gave Tikaya a was-your-brain-damaged-during-your-kidnapping look. "And don't mind seeing the wrinkly old bodies of the patrons. Let's go surf." Ell waved to the sea.

"I will shortly," Rias said. "I simply wish to see the lava."

"It's boring," Ell said. "Drip, smoke, drip, smoke."

"Yes, but I'm fascinated by volcanology, specifically the ways in which one might tap geothermal reservoirs as a source of energy. My people have drilled around the Kraftar Geysers on our mainland, finding liquid magma a hundred meters deep, and scientists posit that natural heat could be employed similarly to that which we gain from burning coal. We could power our steam machinery and warm homes in the winter without having to mine for fuel. Given our current reliance on coal stoves and hypocaust systems, such an efficient energy source would prove a great boon."

Ell stared as Rias spoke. At the end, he shrugged his shoulders helplessly at Tikaya. "What are you supposed to do when he goes on like that? Nod? Grunt?"

"I've found that he appreciates it when you listen in enraptured appreciation and ask questions at the end."

"Enraptured what?" Ell blinked a few times, then shrugged again. "I'll be in the water. Give me a wave when you're done sightseeing and you're ready to have some *fun*."

"Hm," Tikaya said when Ell had pedaled out of hearing. "I didn't know you could sound so passionate about something in which you have no interest."

"Not *no* interest," Rias said, resuming his walk toward the point. "Just little interest right now."

Tikaya caught up with him, wishing she'd worn something sturdier than sandals as she picked her way over the uneven black rock. The former lava fields were mostly level, but they were littered with hardened ripples, buckles, and fissures. "I was moderately certain you hadn't brought me up here to watch plops of lava fall out of a tube."

"No." Rias extended a hand to help her across a wide crack. "Though I appreciate your willingness to listen in enraptured appreciation no matter what the subject."

"That's what lovers do."

"That... hasn't been my experience."

"That must be why you came looking for me." Tikaya stopped a few feet from the edge of the cliff. Warm wind, misty with sea spray, gusted down the coast, tugging at her long braid and ruffling the hem of her dress.

Rias strode up to the precipice and peered over the edge. "I wasn't looking exactly; you were just conveniently placed in an adjoining cell."

"But you *would* have looked for me if you'd known I existed, right?"

"Oh, yes." Rias removed the stopper from the hollow bamboo case and pulled out a rolled map. "Had I known the Kyattese cryptanalyst decoding our secret messages was a beautiful woman, I would have started sending encrypted letters of adoration along with our secret missives."

Tikaya choked on the idea, imagining how bewildered she would have felt deciphering something like that. "That wouldn't have gone over well in the war room."

Rias grew silent after that, head bent as he studied his map. The wind whipped at the corners, trying to tear it from his hands, but he didn't seem to notice. Tikaya knelt at the edge of the precipice, eyeing the cliffs as well as the dark blue waters beyond. Of course, nothing of the missing basin was visible from the surface. The old bathymetric maps had shown it nearly a mile off the coast and hundreds of feet deep. What Rias hoped to find in these cliffs she didn't know.

Tikaya returned to his side and considered the flapping parchment in his hands. The map displayed ocean currents around the main island.

"I'm prepared to listen in enraptured appreciation any time you're ready to share," Tikaya said.

Rias smiled though he continued studying the map. "Am I correct in assuming all of those caves down there have been thoroughly explored? And that archaeologists would have long since removed any significant findings?"

"That's likely, yes."

Rias returned the map to the tube. A few other papers were rolled up inside. "I want to look anyway."

"Look at what?"

"A hunch."

"About what? And based on what?" Tikaya asked.

"About... things." He must have seen her prop her hands on her hips in exasperation, for he added, "Do you remember me mentioning a search algorithm I worked out based on tides, currents, prevailing winds, and the like?"

Mostly she remembered Yosis zapping him with the bracelet when he started talking about it. "Something for finding wrecks, wasn't it?"

"Wrecks, yes, and perhaps significant amounts of flotsam and jetsam."

"Like you said, anything in those caves would have been discovered long ago."

But Rias was already returning to the bicycle. He opened the picnic hamper and pulled out climbing gear. Two lanterns and an oilskin pouch followed. What'd he have in the pouch? Matches?

"I thought you had a romantic picnic lunch for us in there," Tikaya said.

"Not this time. This way," Rias said cheerfully as he passed her, a coil of rope slung over his shoulder and a bag of jangling metal appurtenances in one hand.

"You're going down to the caves?" Tikaya jogged after him.

"I thought *we* might go down. There are only a couple I want to check out."

Tikaya couldn't bring herself to tell him that her last climbing experience—the one that had seen her poisoned by a giant practitioner-controlled bird-of-prey—hadn't left her enamored of the sport. Not when the adventurous wink he threw over his shoulder told her how much the prospect excited him. She wouldn't dampen his spirits.

Rias walked nearly a half mile along the cliff tops before dropping to his belly and peering over the side. Tikaya checked to see if they'd be in view from the surfing area, should they drop a rope and descend. They didn't need to give Ell any fodder, in case he was indeed reporting back to someone, perhaps the same someone who had been removing clues all week, someone who might find it suspicious that Rias had chosen this particular spot for his sight-seeing picnic. Tikaya couldn't see most of the surfers and hoped most of them couldn't see her.

"Let's check this one first." Rias opened the bag and dumped rope and hooks for creating rappelling harnesses, as well as a number of bolts and a drill.

"Who outfitted you with climbing gear?" Tikaya asked, amused by how easily he seemed to be navigating these foreign waters and acquiring what he needed.

"Someone in town who takes visiting botanists into the rainforest on the west side of the island."

"Turgonian?"

"A native but a mongrel half-breed, according to him." Rias finished drilling bolts, attached the rope to them, and tossed the end over the edge. He'd created seats for himself and Tikaya. He helped fasten hers around her waist and between her legs, an awkward proposition given that she wore a dress, then hooked her to the rope. "Use that hand to brake. The other's your guide."

"Got it. How many people are working on your ship today while you're off sight-seeing?"

"Eight. But we're not constructing anything yet, simply forming the pieces that will become the hull and bulkheads in the steel mill. Ready?"

"After you."

In a few bounds, Rias found his way down the cliff to a ledge. It protruded from one side of a cave opening a couple of feet above the water. He must have timed this exploration to match up with a low tide.

Tikaya removed her sandals and eased over the edge. With her hands gripping the ropes like vises, she inched down the cliff.

"Loosen your braking hand if you want to go faster," Rias called up.

"No, no, it's fine. I like this pace."

Several seagulls glided past, one squawking at her. Yes, she wagered she put on quite a show as she inched her way down the cliff. Several minutes later, she reached the ledge.

"Sorry," Tikaya said, because Rias was waiting outside the cave, no doubt watching to see if he needed to assist her. "Given my propensity for tripping on land, I view scaling and descending cliffs as something that should be done slowly and carefully."

"There's no hurry." Rias unfastened her from the rope. "We're on a leisurely date, remember?"

"Ah, yes." Tikaya crinkled her nose as the scent of sea lion droppings drifted out of the cave before them. "For some reason, I'd forgotten."

Daylight slanted into the cave, gleaming against damp black walls. Inside, the crinkles and buckles exhibited in the field above had largely been eroded by the ocean's constant influence. A channel of seawater flowed in and out with the tides, filling a large pool. No wider than three feet, the ledge they stood upon followed the waterway on one side, eventually disappearing into the shadows. The black walls made even the lighted area near the cave mouth feel dark and ominous. Nonsense, Tikaya told herself. Ten-year-old children played in these caves, especially the ones close to Obsidian Beach. She had nothing to fear beyond stubbing a toe on a rock and falling into the water.

"What are we looking for?" she asked.

"It's unlikely that we'll find anything, but I estimate that these three caves—" he waved to include theirs as well as others to the north, "—would be depositories of any flotsam that might have come ashore from the southern end of that basin."

"You think there's a shipwreck out there? One those Turgonian explorers came looking for three hundred years ago?" Tikaya thought of Rias's story of lost colonizing ships.

"Something happened out there. Something that's kept generations of mapmakers from being allowed to accurately report their depth findings."

"Maybe the basin was filled in somehow. Why are you assuming there's a wreck? Did you find something in that journal?" Tikaya had wanted to ask earlier, but had dared not with Ell riding nearby. "Some clue about all this?" She recalled that Rias had suggested their "date" before he'd had a chance to see the book. What did he think would lie in the depths of these caves? And how far back did this one go? A long ways, she supposed, since it had originally carried lava flows. In theory, it could extend miles, all the way to the volcano itself. These particular caves were tens of thousands of years old, though, and time had likely brought down ceilings and blocked passages.

"From what I understood of the journal," Rias said, "it was the story of an affair between one of your married ancestors and a Turgonian sailor on a treasure-hunting expedition."

"An affair?" Tikaya tripped over a rocky protrusion and caught herself on the wall. "I didn't get that far. The author was describing his voyage and arrival here in the first few pages."

"The journal gets rather torrid once he meets Uouri." Rias took a couple of tries at pronouncing the name, then gave up and stopped to light the lanterns. They'd gone around a bend, and the entrance was no longer in view. "The young woman apparently found him dashing and handsome in comparison to her stodgy farmer husband. Also, according to the author's lurid descriptions, she was unexpectedly skilled at copulation methods."

"Must have been one of my cousin Aeli's forebears." Tikaya's mind wandered into curious musings at what Rias, an ecumenical man in his own right, considered lurid and torrid. "I'll need to get the journal back from you then. For further research."

"Research, eh?"

"Er, yes. About my ancestor. It sounds like she may have been historically significant by family reckoning."

"Well, then, the *research* section starts about halfway through. It's quite descriptive. I hadn't realized how flowery Middle Turgonian could be."

Glad the shadows hid her blush, Tikaya asked, "What happened to them in the end? And does any of it tie in with our missing year?"

"The last entry describes the pair's plans to escape the island together. His treasure-hunting ship had finished searching for signs of the lost colony and was ready to depart for its next port. She was going to meet him at the docks where they planned to sail away together on his vessel."

"That's it?" The ledge on their side of the channel dipped away, and Tikaya hiked up her dress to follow Rias into thigh-deep water. Currents tugged at her legs as the tides fluctuated. Barnacles scraped at the bottoms of her feet—maybe she shouldn't have left her sandals up above. "If the journal and the man's sword ended up in my attic, that doesn't bode well for the relationship. Perhaps her husband grew wise to the affair and decided to stop it."

"Murder?" Rias asked.

"Violence isn't my people's hallmark, but I imagine a man who'd learned his wife was sleeping with some foreign sailor could be moved to extreme acts." Despite her words, Tikaya had a hard time believing any of her ancestors would have shot a man full of arrows, then snatched his belongings like trophies for the attic. Perhaps the bereft Uouri had taken the letters, sword, and journal herself and hidden them away as keepsakes. "Even if there had been a murder, why would any of that matter now? Why hide the record of the entire year? I can see where my family might be embarrassed if news of the affair leaked out, but in a minor manner, I should think. How upset can you be over something that happened ten generations ago?"

Rias didn't answer right away. He had to duck his head and maneuver around bumps in the ever-lowering ceiling. Their tunnel was angling slightly downward. That was surprising—Tikaya had assumed that, if anything, it would slant upward. She eyed the walls, wondering how much deeper they'd be able to go. So far, Rias's lantern hadn't illuminated anything more intriguing than graffiti that hadn't yet been washed away by the tides. She caught a mention of a professor at the Polytechnic and what embarrassing things someone hoped would befall him. Tikaya had taken classes from the man years ago and found herself nodding in agreement at some of the suggestions.

The water kept rising as they descended, and it lapped at her thighs now. The barnacles had been replaced by algae that squished beneath her bare feet. Rias took her to such lovely places.

"From what I could tell," Rias said, finally answering her questions, "our lovelorn sailor was so focused on his affair that he wasn't documenting the ship's expedition thoroughly, but perhaps you can find something when you read through. I struggled to read the language."

"I *did* notice," Tikaya said, "from my original flip-through of the entire journal, that there were more than three months' worth of entries from the time he reached the island until he stopped writing. Why would your people have been here so long? In two weeks, you could sail around all the islands in our chain and have time left for hunting, fishing, and lounging on the beach."

"That suggests they either found something to cause them to spend more time here, or they believed they'd find something and didn't want to stop looking too soon."

"Yes. Uhm, Rias?" The ceiling had continued to drop while the water level rose, and the current tugged at Tikaya's waist. They'd entered a wider area, the channel turning into a pool. "How far back are you planning to go? Though I'm certain you're aware of this, I feel compelled to point out that this cave will be underwater when the tide comes in. I shouldn't like to hold my breath to swim all the way back to the entrance." In water that would be inky black. The thought stirred uneasiness, and she had to remind herself that tides didn't come in that swiftly.

Rias lifted the lantern and pointed toward a wide ledge on one side of the pool. "Let's climb out there for a moment."

By the time they reached the spot, the end of the passage showed up in the lantern light. Though she knew Rias wanted to find something interesting, Tikaya was glad they wouldn't have reason to linger.

They crawled out of the water and sat on the ledge—the low ceiling didn't offer room for standing. Seaweed, dead crabs, and broken sand dollars littered the rocks. Rias considered the back wall and watched the pool with intensity. Tikaya was almost to the point of asking if he'd seen something moving around in there when he slipped off his shirt.

"We're disrobing?" Tikaya asked. "If you're thinking we should practice the torrid, three-hundred-year-old copulation techniques described in that journal, this wouldn't be my first choice of locations."

Distracted, Rias only said, "I'm going to check something. Back in a moment." He removed a couple of matches from his oilskin pouch, laid them on the lanterns, then tightly tied the knots closed on the pouch and tucked the remaining matches into a pocket in his clam diggers.

Before Tikaya could ask what he expected to find, he slipped into the water, head disappearing beneath the surface.

She eyed the dark walls around her ledge. The idea of making some discovery down there intrigued her, but she doubted it would happen. The tides scoured the caves clean every day, and they must have been explored countless times over the years.

Long seconds meandered past—minutes?—and Rias did not resurface. Tikaya crept to the edge and peered into the pool. The lantern light did nothing to illuminate the dark water, but surely she'd see ripples from his movement if he were down there. Where had he gone? Further into the lava tube via an underwater entrance? If he didn't find some pocket of air inside, he'd be in trouble. As heroic a constitution as he had, even he couldn't hold his breath for more than a minute or two.

"*Rias.*" Tikaya gripped the lip of the ledge. "Drowning on a date would be a *stupid* way to die."

Leaving the lanterns, she slipped her legs into the water, intending to submerge and see if she could see where he'd gone. Before she'd gone more than a step, Rias popped up in front of her, short hair matted to his head. He wiped water out of his eyes but didn't draw in a huge gasp of air. He must have found some pocket of air nearby.

"Going somewhere?" he asked.

"To look for you of course. I thought a giant squid might have eaten you."

"The waters are a touch shallow here for them." The soft light from the lanterns failed to show any humor on his face. He considered her for a moment, his face grave. "I have a couple more matches. I think you'll want to see this."

"You think?"

"It's not a sure bet. Not like romping puppies or wrestling kittens."

"Is it worse than that room in Wolfhump?" Tikaya asked, referring to the bodies she and Agarik had found, the frozen corpses mutilated from garish combat with crazed human beings.

Rias brightened. "No. Not now, anyway."

"Not *now*?" Tikaya mouthed.

Rias pointed toward the water under the back wall. "It's about a twenty-second swim. There's nowhere to get lost, as it continues on as a lava tube, but it curves downward and then back up, so it's easy to scrape your hands. You can hold onto my leg if you want."

"I'll be fine." If it was as straightforward as he said, she could make it without a guide. Besides, she ought to save her wimp moments for truly frightening scenarios. Like climbing back up that cliff later.

"Can you swim with your spectacles on? You'll want them when we come up on the other side."

Tikaya wasn't as certain about that, but she took them off and clenched the wire frame between her teeth. She'd hadn't thought to bring another pair along and would hate to lose them down here.

Rias took a deep breath, then dropped below the surface again. Despite her assurance, she didn't want him to swim out of reach, so she followed after promptly.

They'd left the lanterns on the ledge, and the light didn't extend far. Tikaya had to grope her way through the darkness. With one hand running along the bottom and the other stretched ahead, she found the opening Rias had mentioned and kicked her way into it. In the cold blackness she kept her fingers outstretched and fluttered her feet for forward momentum. The tide surged about her, one moment helping her progress and the next hindering it, but her fingers soon bumped into bare skin instead of rock. She identified Rias's leg and pulled herself upright beside him, her feet finding the bottom.

He hadn't yet lit a match, so utter darkness greeted Tikaya. The air was cooler than outside and musty as well. Old. It smelled old. She thought of poisonous gases that could accumulate in sealed tunnels and hoped Rias didn't plan on staying long. A shiver ran through her. It was from the coldness of the water and the air, she told herself, though perhaps her senses were warning her that she wouldn't like what she was about to see.

Rias hugged her with one arm, then moved away. "I'm going to strike a match."

Tikaya wiped water out of her eyes and hooked her spectacles over her ears. "Ready."

A couple of soft scrapes sounded, the noise oddly loud. Little of the roar of the sea penetrated the walls around them.

"Too wet," Rias muttered. "Let me see if—"

Light flared. At first Tikaya noticed the flame and the match held between Rias's fingers. Then her eyes focused on what lay behind them. Bones. Skulls. Partial and complete skeletons. She swallowed. *Human* skeletons covered with the dust of the ages. So many bones were wedged in crevasses or laid on ledges that she would have believed someone had brought them in bags and dumped them. Could so many have come in on the tide? How would they have—

Rias grunted and dropped the match. Blackness engulfed them again.

Tikaya took a deep breath, not certain whether she preferred the view now or before. Either way, the image would be imprinted on her mind. Suddenly her cousin's proffered surfing lesson was sounding like a pleasant way to spend the day.

"Kittens *are* less disturbing," Tikaya said, trying to sound nonchalant, "but you've certainly lit my curiosity here."

Rias wrapped an arm around her. "This would have made my former wife scream."

"A not inappropriate response to a cave full of bones." One Tikaya might have made if he hadn't prepared her for the notion of something bad. "I was busy debating whether they'd been placed here or if the tide—some storm perhaps?—could have brought them in."

"The sea, I believe, though there must have been a lot of corpses if so many found their way into this cave."

"That's why you were thinking shipwreck," Tikaya said. "Your colony ships? Did some storm get them before they could reach land?" And did the incident pre- or post-date the arrival of her own people?

Rias shifted away from her. Soft clunks sounded. Was he... sifting through the bones? Why?

"Last match," Rias said and struck it. In his free hand, he held a skull with a hole in the side. He shook it, and something rattled inside. "Arrowhead. A stone one."

Tikaya skimmed the scene again, looking for any other clues she could take out with her, but the light winked out before she could do more than gawk at all the bones. "I can't believe nobody has ever found this."

"Perhaps people haven't been encouraged to look."

With more and more evidence stacking up to support Rias's hunch that all wasn't as it seemed on the Kyatt Islands, Tikaya couldn't bring herself to disagree. Someone knew what had happened out there all those years ago, and was going to great lengths to make sure she and Rias didn't find out what it was.

PART II

CHAPTER 13

IT HAD BEEN A LONG time since so much work filled Tikaya's desk, and it doubtlessly accounted for the fact that she couldn't find a pen. Any of them. Pages of notes battled for space with the old Turgonian journal, family lineage trees, and teetering stacks of Kyattese archaeology and history books. After more than two weeks of reading and note-taking, Tikaya was finally compiling a summary of her findings. The damaged skull Rias had pulled out of that cave presided over it all, empty eye sockets staring at her as she worked.

The obsidian arrowhead sat on a shelf above it. Based on the style, she'd placed it as Kyattese and estimated it at seven hundred years in age, but it differed from sketches of other arrowheads from the time period. It was sharper, finer, and smaller than the giant lizard- and boar-hunting projectiles of the era.

"It looks like it was made for hunting people," Rias had said in a note. He hadn't been by for a while, but he'd sent encrypted messages almost every day. She'd come to look forward to receiving them, like one might anticipate love letters, albeit these "love letters" focused on ancient mysteries, modern bureaucrats, and pesky telepaths showing up at his shipyard.

"My people have never hunted human beings," Tikaya had written back, though not with the same certainty she would have felt a few weeks earlier.

Rias hadn't brought it up again. Subsequent notes had detailed the progress he was making with the submarine-that-looks-like-a-surface-ship. He'd mentioned little of troubles, but Tikaya sensed he was leaving things out. One day, he'd informed her that he'd switched to living aboard the ship. That same day, a colleague at the Polytechnic had shown her a newspaper that mentioned a fire at the Pragmatic Mate.

More than once Tikaya had thought of bringing the arrowhead to the Polytechnic or the archaeology museum to seek out physical specimens to compare it to, but she'd had little time for extracurricular activities. After leaning on the police to get her back at work, Dean Teailat had been keeping her busy from dawn to dusk—often later—every day. Her colleagues were not only studying the sphere and the ancient language held within but deciding what to do with the information. Should it be locked away or shared openly in hopes of furthering man's understanding of nature and the world? As much as Tikaya wanted to be out helping Rias, and delving deeper into their subaquatic mystery, she couldn't walk away from the decision-making process when it came to that alien technology. Her colleagues hadn't seen the horrible things it could do, and too many of them were leaning toward publicizing their notes and inviting experts from around the world to study them.

Tikaya pushed away the thoughts; she'd been worrying about the technology at work all day. This was the time she'd set aside to study her and Rias's mystery. She'd best make use of it. Iweue had sent the energy source to the shipyard a couple of days earlier and, in his last note, Rias had alluded to a maiden voyage. Tikaya wanted to have as much information as possible for him when the submarine was ready, even though she worried about what they might find out there, or more precisely that they might dig up something that would mean she was no longer welcome in Kyatt. She bent back over her work, refusing to grow weepy-eyed thinking about being exiled and never seeing her family again.

Just as Tikaya finally found a pen, a knock sounded at the door.

Tikaya pushed a few papers over the Turgonian journal and propped a history book in front of the skull. "Come in."

Her cousin Aeli sauntered into the room, a letter clasped her in hand. She wore a flowing ankle-length skirt—one might have called it modest—with a sleeveless top that left everything except her breasts bare—definitely *not* modest. Tikaya had confirmed that the adulterous Komitopis who'd been the love interest in the Turgonian's journal was indeed Aeli's ancestor. Who knew such tendencies would breed true through the centuries?

"Thank you for coming, Aeli," Tikaya said after her cousin flopped down on the bed.

"But of course. You don't often ask for *my* help. In fact, you never have. I can only assume you're seeking advice in regard to your relationship with your strapping Turgonian."

Tikaya had been on her way over to shut the door, and she almost tripped and used her face to do the task. "My what?"

"Your relationship. You know what an expert I am on matters such as pleasing a man in the bedroom. Or on the beach. Or in the waves. Wherever you choose, though knowing what a prude you are, I imagine a bed is involved. Likely with little ruffling of the sheets."

"*Aeli*!" Tikaya shut the door with a bang. She'd intended to close it to keep the discussion quiet anyway, but this was a topic she was even more certain she didn't want escaping into the hall.

"You've found yourself a handsome stud, one most certainly accustomed to less... cerebral mates, and you're worried that he'll grow bored with you. Or perhaps he already is." Aeli patted the bed. "Come, I have all sorts of suggestions that you can try."

Cheeks flaming, Tikaya stalked over to the desk and pushed aside the book hiding the skull. "I asked you here about *this*."

Aeli's lips moved a few times before she managed to say, "*That*?"

"And *this*." Tikaya held the arrowhead up to the window—the sun was dipping toward the horizon, but enough light remained to highlight the obsidian. "Despite your unambitious secretarial status of late, you *did* study anthropology at the Polytechnic, and, as I recall, your thesis was on mental science dating methods for fossils, artifacts, and rocks to determine the time periods of past geological events."

Aeli's eyelashes fluttered a few times. "That was the exact name of my paper. You read it?"

"You're my cousin, and it's in my field. Of course I read it. I thought you'd go on to study with—" Tikaya shrugged. "It doesn't matter. I'm not comfortable going to my usual sources at the Polytechnic right now, so I'd appreciate it if you could date these items for me. I believe they're from the earliest years of our colonization, but the popularity of historical artifacts amongst collectors of late has caused some unscrupulous sorts to learn how to create—and sell—plausible fakes." Not to mention the dubious career of for-profit relic raiding that had grown up in the last generation.

"All right." Aeli held out her hand. "Let me see the arrowhead first. That—" she tilted her chin at the skull, the hole in the cranium clearly visible, "—is ghastly."

"Then I'll wait until after you've finished to mention where we found the arrowhead."

Aeli's lip curled, but she wrapped her fingers around the artifact and closed her eyes. Tikaya caught herself bouncing from foot-to-foot and forced herself to sit down at the desk. She'd seen other practitioners date items and knew it would take time. Also, Aeli had trained predominantly in telekinesis, not Seeing, so it'd take her even longer. At least she seemed to remember how to apply the Science. The last Tikaya had heard of Aeli using her skills, it had been to cause the seams and belts of handsome young Polytechnic students to fail at inopportune times. That had been two years earlier and had resulted in Aeli losing her job and being encouraged to enroll in counseling for her addiction to "wanton living," as the student newspaper had called it.

A while later, Aeli said, "Your estimate is correct."

Tikaya had resumed compiling her notes, but she dropped her pen and spun around in her chair. Beads of sweat moistened her cousin's brow, and her freckled face had grown pale. Tikaya handed her a glass of tea Mother had brought by earlier. Aeli guzzled it.

"I'd say this was made within months of the original landing," she said. "I can't tell if it was before or after, but obsidian implies island origins."

"Thank you. Did you get... anything else from it?" Some seers could sense how an object had been crafted and used, though Tikaya didn't know if her cousin's skills were that well developed.

"I saw *that*." Aeli scowled at the hole in the skull. "The moment of impact. Then darkness. Ages of darkness."

Tikaya leaned forward. "You saw the arrow kill that man?"

"It wasn't a man. It was a woman. And Tikaya?" Aeli collapsed fully onto the bed.

"Yes?"

"I hope you like mysteries, because it looked like a Nurian."

Tikaya leaned back in her chair. "Turgonian, I'm guessing."

"No, she was darker skinned and shorter and—"

"Thirty-odd generations ago, which is where we're placing that arrowhead, the Turgonians basically *were* Nurians. They spent the next seven-hundred years interbreeding with the taller pale-skinned natives of their current continent."

"Oh. Huh." Aeli sat up. "I guess that's right."

"Could you tell..." Tikaya wasn't sure she wanted to know the answer to the next question, but pushed on anyway. "Could you tell who shot the arrow?"

"No. The only aura around it that I sensed was the impact point. That was vivid. I could almost feel the crunch of stone piercing flesh and bone." Aeli shuddered and set the arrowhead on the desk. "Really, Tikaya, I would have much preferred it if you'd wanted advice on creative ways to please a man."

"Maybe next time." Tikaya tapped a fingernail on the arrowhead. "So, the Turgonians *were* here seven hundred years ago."

"And we were shooting them. How odd. I wonder what it was all about."

"We don't know for certain that one of our Kyattese ancestors fired the arrow," Tikaya said.

"Who else would have been around and knapping obsidian arrowheads back then? The Turgonians were using copper or iron for weapons, weren't they?"

"Yes, but it's possible they ran low on supplies and had to make do with what was here. Maybe this was some squabble between crews on their own ships and had nothing to do with our people."

"It seems more likely that the Turgonians tried to start their conquering and invading earlier than the history books say, and that our people drove them off to defend their new home."

"If that's so, why isn't it mentioned in *our* history books?" Tikaya asked. "And why were our ancestors shooting women?"

"The Nurians have female warriors. Maybe the Turgonians did too back then."

Tikaya decided not to argue further. She didn't yet have enough evidence to posit a different hypothesis. Besides, the hypothesis creeping into her mind wouldn't be a popular one if it proved true.

Paper crinkled. "I almost forgot," Aeli said. "This letter's for you. Aunt Mela told me to bring it up."

Tikaya recognized Rias's writing on the address. "It's been opened," she said when she accepted it.

"Has it? Huh." Some of Aeli's paleness had faded, and she winked.

"Did you find it entertaining reading?" Before looking, Tikaya knew it was encrypted, as all of Rias's messages had been thus far.

"I found it a bunch of gobbledegook. When I first saw the man, I couldn't believe he'd be interested in you..."

"Thanks."

"...but if he encrypts his love letters, perhaps you're made for each other."

"Someone finally noticed. Could you tell Father and Grandpa?"

"I will if you read it to me." Aeli wriggled her eyebrows.

"You'd be bored. They're not about ruffling sheets." Tikaya unfolded the page and started replacing the substitution letters in her head. "He's just checking on me and asking about the family."

"I don't believe you. That sounds far too boring to bother encrypting."

There were a few inquiries about their mystery too, but Tikaya didn't mention that. "Oh, here's some fodder for your lusty imagination." Tikaya grinned as she summarized. "He says he's looking forward to once again calculating the coefficient of friction with me once all this is resolved."

"Calculating the what of the what?"

"The coefficient of friction. You know, in math. It describes the ratio of force of friction between two bodies and the force pressing them to..." Tikaya sighed at her cousin's blank expression. Of all the people who shouldn't miss an innuendo. "Never mind."

Aeli flopped back onto the bed again, her skirt flapping. "You *are* made for each other. Unbelievable."

Tikaya decoded the rest of the note. "Oh. He wants me to come to the docks at sunset. His ship is ready to sail. Already? I can't believe it. I've barely seen any of—" Tikaya ran to the window. The sun was already setting. "Why didn't you give me this earlier?"

"No need to thank me for examining your arrowhead. I'll just leave you to dress in something appropriate for an evening out. Hint: *that*—" Aeli pointed at Tikaya's ankle-length skirt, "—is *not* it." She ducked through the doorway, perhaps anticipating a pillow being hurled after her.

As if Tikaya were that juvenile. She threw her pen.

"Thank you," she called out the window as Aeli bicycled away.

Then she hustled to gather a few notes and hide what work she intended to leave behind. If Rias was ready to sail, and had indeed crafted a vessel that could investigate the ocean's secrets, maybe Tikaya would finally have a chance to stop guessing at this mystery and to find some answers.

By the time Tikaya reached the quay, the sun had fully melted into the ocean, emblazoning the western sky with reds and oranges. A woman in a city worker's short-sleeve blouse and skirt moved from lamppost to lamppost, filling reservoirs with fresh whale oil and tapers, then setting them to light.

Tikaya's bicycle tires bumped along the wooden boardwalk as she pedaled toward Shipyard 4. She had to weave past groups of students and numerous couples strolling hand-in-hand. At first, she thought everyone was simply out enjoying the sunset, but there were a lot of people for that. Drum and conch-shell tunes drifted from somewhere ahead.

Trying to recall if she'd forgotten some festival, Tikaya slowed as she approached the shipyard. Dozens of lamps and torches had been lit around it and the adjacent dock, pushing back the approaching evening. Numerous people milled in the area, forcing her to leave the bicycle parked several docks away. Tikaya didn't see many Kyattese in the crowd. The multicultural group included more than a few Turgonians, though, not only ex-soldiers but women and children as well. A Turgonian carrying a bulging toolbox and wearing a bristling tool belt ambled past, flashing a gap-toothed smile at Tikaya. Another helper Rias had recruited?

As she walked closer, she realized the music was coming from the dock beside the shipyard. The scent of grilling seafood and pork wafted to her nose as well.

Rias had planned a party? A launch party? That wasn't exactly the way to keep away people who might notice his steamer had the ability to turn into a submarine...

"Pardon me," Tikaya said as she slipped around and between groups of people, suffering more than one clunk in the ribs from elbows involved in excited gestures. The smell of spiced rum reached her nose—more than one person carried kitschy coconut mugs as well as skewers of shrimp and pork. "May I pass, please?" Tikaya asked when she reached a thick knot of people. The docks left little room for slipping past congregating crowds. "I have a... I know the..." What would Rias call himself? "I have an appointment with the captain."

Between the music and dozens of conversations, nobody heard or noticed her. She cleared her throat to try again, but a familiar head appeared above the crowd. People stepped aside, making room for Rias. Naturally. Unlike her, he had all that formidable Turgonian brawn along with his height. Though the clothing he wore made him appear less formidable than usual... Dear Akahe, she hoped that Ell had picked out that hibiscus-dyed shirt and that he hadn't chosen it for himself. She intended to look into his eyes and ask if this outfit was part of a master plan or simply an unpleasant accident, but her gaze snagged at his chin. In the days since she'd last seen him, Rias had started growing a beard. More of a goatee, she decided. It was in the incipient stage, but his black hair made it stand out.

"What do you think?" Rias stopped in front of her and took her hand.

His presence created an insulating bubble, and people eased away from Tikaya. "I don't know," she said. "I have to get used to it. It's, uhm..." She lifted her fingers and stroked his chin. "Kind of bristly."

The corner of Rias's mouth lifted in a wry half smile. "I meant the *Freedom*. Our ship." He lifted an arm toward the berth at the end of the dock.

"Oh." Tikaya dropped her hand, aware of chuckles and shared nods on either side of her. Who *were* these people? "I haven't had a look yet. There's a crowd all the way back to Dock 58."

Rias chuckled, though the mirth didn't reach his eyes. There was a tightness about their corners and a tension in his posture. Because of the party? All of the people swarming about? "When Milvet asked if he could invite the families of the workers for a celebration, I was imagining a small gathering. Certainly not anything that included a music troupe." Rias shrugged and led her the rest of the way down the dock.

When they reached the end, the *Freedom* came into view, and Tikaya halted to gawk. There was no sign of the rusted wreck from three weeks earlier. The dark gray ship that floated in the berth was...

Sleek. That was the word that popped into her mind. Like a dart. No, a javelin. An arrow-shaped deck comprised the back half, while ladders in the middle led up to a wheelhouse and down to a cabin. A man wielding a spatula worked a portable grill set up on deck next to the music troupe. The entertainers left little room for much else. Tikaya guessed the entire vessel was only meant to carry four people. Her gaze roved fore and aft as she tried to figure out how it might become a submarine. For that matter, how would it sail? She'd assumed he'd build a steamer, even if it was a fake steamer, but the sleek craft lacked a smokestack. Maybe that hadn't been necessary with the energy supply.

"What do you think?" Rias bit his lip.

"It's fantastic," Tikaya said, realizing he was watching her, holding his breath it seemed as he awaited her response. "I never thought I'd say this about a mode of transportation, but it's quite handsome."

She'd never seen Rias smile so widely. The warmth in his eyes stole the strength from her knees, and she swallowed, more than a little effected by the fact that her praise meant so much to him.

Tikaya leaned over the edge of the deck, trying to peer through the water toward the craft's aft end. "What sort of propulsion does it have?"

Rias's smile beamed even brighter at this display of interest. "A screw propeller system much like we—the empire—uses on ice breaking ships. Compact and powerful, capable of..."

When he stopped speaking, Tikaya followed his gaze to the companionway leading to the sunken cabin. A string of blond-haired men and women strode onto the deck, speaking rapidly and gesticulating to each other as they maneuvered past the entertainers and toward the gangplank. Tikaya recognized most of the faces. Five were on the faculty at the Polytechnic, mathematics and engineering professors, and from the toolkit the last man carried, she guessed him a shipwright or some sort of naval expert. If anyone could suss out the fact that this was a submarine in disguise, that group could.

"Inspection?" Tikaya guessed.

Rias's eyes had grown tighter. Someone who didn't know him probably wouldn't have noticed the change, but he was worried. "Sent by your government, yes."

"You must have anticipated that they'd check up on you."

"I was hoping they'd send someone like Yosis, not experts in the field."

"But you were prepared in the event that they didn't, right?" Tikaya asked as the men stepped off the gangplank and made their way through the crowd toward Rias. They were gesticulating and chattering to each other—definitely excited about something.

"We'll see," Rias said.

Tikaya chewed on her lip as the men and women approached. What would happen if the high minister learned Rias had never planned to build a ship?

The shipwright and an engineer named Professor Yaro jostled for the position directly in front of Rias. In an impressive bit of elbow jabbing, the professor captured the spot.

"It's not a steamer," he blurted.

Tikaya winced.

Rias glanced at her out of the corners of his eyes, then focused on the professor. "No, it's not."

"I've never seen anything like it," Yaro said. "None of us have. There's no boiler at all. The machine for powering the engine, what do you call it?"

Rias glanced at Tikaya again, this time with one of his am-I-understanding-the-language-correctly looks. She shrugged back at him.

"Are you referring to the generator?" Rias's tone made it sound like he thought this a trick question.

"The generator?" Yaro asked.

"Yes... It would have been inefficient to build a boiler when that orb's energy can be converted into electricity."

"Into what?" Yaro looked to Tikaya for a translation.

Except that she didn't have one. She'd heard the term, but couldn't think of an equivalent in her tongue. "Like what the shock eels produce? Or more like a static charge?" She shuffled her feet and poked his arm to demonstrate.

Rias blinked slowly a few times. "The Drokovic Jar hasn't made it to the islands yet?"

"The what?" Yaro asked.

"It's a device for storing static electricity between electrodes on the inside and the outside of the jar." Rias pantomimed with his hands as he explained. "We used it for many early experiments on electricity. Generators—" he pointed to his ship, "—are relatively experimental themselves in the empire, but they convert mechanical energy, such as might come from a steam engine or in this case a battery into electrical energy that can power the motor that runs the propeller as well as other ship's systems."

His explanation went on for a few more minutes, and Tikaya was hoping nobody asked for a translation, because she'd have to think a while to make up compound nouns that might work. But it seemed Yaro and the others were too busy devouring the concept to care that they didn't know all the words.

"You must share the schematics," Yaro blurted at the end.

His colleagues nodded vigorously. Tikaya wondered if any of them remembered why they'd been assigned to investigate Rias. The high minister would probably receive enthusiastic reports on the wonders of electricity when he asked for details on the craft Rias had made—and blank looks in regard to questions about submersible abilities.

"Well," Rias said, eyes narrowing, "that's something we could talk about."

Tikaya might have struggled with the earlier terms, but she had no trouble translating "talk about" into "negotiate over" in her mind.

"Ho, there, cousin," came a familiar voice from Tikaya's side. Elloil ambled into the middle of the conversation without worrying about whether he was interrupting anything important. He thrust a rum-filled coconut into Yaro's hand. "What's everyone being so serious about over here? This is a party." He plucked more beverages from a tray a woman held and armed the rest of the professors.

Yaro and the others frowned down at their drinks. "But we were talking about the—"

"A subject for later discussion, gentleman," Rias said, "and ladies." He gave the two women a nod. "I must give Tikaya a tour and tend to my guests."

Tikaya doubted Rias planned to have anything to do with the guests, but the professors seemed to accept this excuse, and they trundled off up the dock, heads bowed again as they conversed with each other.

"Maybe it's fortunate you didn't get Yosis after all," Tikaya said. "He might not have been so easily distracted by a shiny new engine."

"True," Rias said.

"Now, now, enough of this boring people with engineering minutia." Ell had produced two more coconut mugs and extended one toward Tikaya. "Have some rum!"

"Tikaya does not find my minutia *boring*," Rias said a touch stiffly, though Ell only smiled and waved the cup toward them again. The drummer's beats had grown louder, and Ell probably hadn't heard the protest anyway.

Tikaya slipped her arm around Rias's waist. "You can tell me *all* of the details later. Are we going to be able to try out the—what did you call it? The *Freedom*?—tonight?" She hoped he had more than floating around the harbor in mind, though she didn't know how they'd be able to test the submersible feature with so many people around. "Once the crowd grows bored and wanders away?" Unfortunately, given the lively conversations and the amount of rum flowing, that might not happen any time soon.

"That's the plan, yes. How does one end a party on your islands?"

"Wait for everyone to pass out?" Tikaya guessed. She hadn't hosted many parties in her life.

"That sounds time-consuming," Rias said.

"How does one end parties in the empire?"

"Eventually a duel or a brawl breaks out, blood flows, and the sawbones is called. If enough people are injured, that dampens the festive mood and people wander home." Rias extended his hand. "Ready for the tour?"

Tikaya accepted his hand. "You Turgonians are a strange folk."

"Yes." Rias smiled and led her to the gangplank, a drawbridge-type structure that looked like it could be folded back into the deck of the ship when not in use.

"That's clever." Tikaya gave it an admiring nod as she stepped off. "A vast improvement over the rotting board."

"I hope you'll find the rest of the ship equally clever. The enforced revisions gave me pause for a day, but I've been dreaming up parts of this since I was—"

"Pork skewer?" Ell and a buxom raven-haired woman sauntered up with trays laden with food. "They're fabulous." He stuck one into Tikaya's grip.

"Uhm, thank you." Tikaya tried to think of a polite way to shoo them away. Perhaps Turgonian fisticuffs wasn't such a bad idea after all.

"Not me," Rias said with a wave when Ell tried to foist rum on him. "I'll be piloting the ship out of dock soon. Why don't you have the troupe pack up?"

"What? It's not even fully dark yet. This launch party could last until midnight. Or dawn."

"Move them to the dock," Rias said, letting some of his old commander tone creep into his voice.

"All right, all right. But at least give Tikaya the tour first. She hasn't been out here yet has she?"

Rias acknowledged this with a wriggle of his fingers and nodded for Tikaya to head for the wheelhouse.

"And don't bore her with engineering stuff," Ell advised. "Show her the fun things. Like where the Science will be performed." He grinned and turned back to his helper—or perhaps she was his date.

Wanting to see how the craft could turn into a submarine, Tikaya chose down instead of up for their first stop.

"Was that a euphemism for sex?" Rias held her refreshments while she descended the ladder into the cabin.

"Yes."

"Oh, because I did include a study nook where one can read texts or decipher ancient mysteries and such," Rias said. "You can even extend tools to take samples from the ocean. I was thinking of calling the spot the science station, but... perhaps not now."

"Don't alter your names because of one lewd surfer." Tikaya found herself in a narrow low-ceilinged corridor brightened by soft, steady illumination. She touched one of the small jar-shaped lamps mounted to the wall. "Are these practitioner-made?" Few houses on the islands had such lamps because of the effort—and therefore expense—that went into crafting light sources. She'd assumed Rias would have been too Turgonian to add anything Kyattese besides the energy source.

"Sort of." Rias had dropped into the corridor behind her. "I noticed Iweue's energy source was a touch bright."

"Like a small sun?" Kyattese practitioners all seemed to think brighter was better, perhaps so nobody could miss noticing the culmination of their efforts.

Rias tapped the bulkhead. "There are mirrors back there that reflect the light into lamp receptacles."

"Good idea."

Rias dipped his head to acknowledge the compliment. "They can burn oil in a pinch, but I was pleased to come up with a way that—

" he glanced at the companionway and lowered his voice, "—avoids consuming oxygen."

Tikaya hadn't spent much time contemplating the problems that might come with traveling beneath the surface, but she was glad Rias had. "What about the oxygen *we'll* consume?"

"I have plans, but for now we just won't be making any extended voyages beneath the surface."

Tikaya was sure her face didn't portray any sort of disapproval—after all, it was amazing that he'd already accomplished so much in such a short period of time—but Rias rushed to add, "I'm working on a device that can eliminate carbon dioxide and moisture from the air, but I'm inventing it from scratch, so it'll take a little time and experimentation. My people haven't yet had a need for such things. And your people... well, the raw materials are scarce here. Do you have any idea how difficult it is to make a container for pressurized oxygen out of coconuts and bamboo?"

"I, er, did you actually do that?"

"Let's just say I found an alternative for the primitive, er, limited engineering supplies on the island."

Tikaya quirked an eyebrow at the word fumble. With her people so quick to dismiss the Turgonians as savages, and pride themselves on science and Science research and discoveries, it was strange to think that he might find the islands... provincial. Of course, had Kyatt been blessed with ore or other copious natural resources, history might have evolved differently.

"We'll be fine for short excursions," Rias said. "Just, ah..." He scrubbed a hand through his hair. "Should you ever be interviewed about this, my maiden shipbuilding project, don't mention the plants in the engine room, please."

"The... plants?"

"As I said, the carbon dioxide eliminator is still incipient, but there's all that light from the energy source, so I thought some greenery might thrive. I didn't expect Virka—that's Milvet's wife—to bring quite so many specimens. She's a horticulturist here, I'm told. And, well, just don't tell any other engineers about my kludgy solutions, please."

"I'd never betray you so," Tikaya said. But, kludgy? Please. He'd even impressed *her* people with his craft. Generations of would-be acolytes would be copying his ideas. "Now, I'm eager for the rest of the tour."

Rias guided her through the compact but plant-filled engine room, showing off his generator, motor, and other machinery. He explained everything, though he didn't mention the one thing Tikaya was most curious about.

"How does it dive?" she finally asked.

"You can't see it from the outside, but there are four sets of docking clamps. We seal everything, and the lower half of the ship simply detaches." Rias waved his hands, as if to demonstrate on some smaller version of the craft that floated in the air before him. "I doubt the combined vessel would stand up to the rigors of the sea indefinitely, but we only need it to fool your people for a while."

"Are you saying the entertaining deck isn't a permanent construct? That'll fluster my cousin in his future party-planning ventures."

After leaving the engine room, Rias walked to an empty bulkhead in the bow. "The underwater navigation controls are behind here. I'll show you when we're alone."

"Is the wheel up top capable of steering the ship then?"

"Yes, until the transition lever is thrown."

Tikaya had never fancied herself a naval enthusiast, but she found herself eager to see the craft in action. "This sounds amazing, Rias. I can't believe you did all this in a couple of weeks. Have you slept any?"

"Rarely. It's hard to sleep when your brain is overflowing with ideas. As for the rest, you might want to wait to see if we successfully pull out of the harbor before you praise me."

"Speaking of that, how are we going to—"

"How's the tour going?" Ell called from the companionway.

"We're fine," Tikaya called back, then finished asking Rias, "—escape all of these people?"

"Once we make ready to pull away, I'm hoping the musicians and the barbecue chef will decamp."

"About my cousin." She eyed the companionway, wondering if Ell was lurking just out of sight. She'd been careful to keep her voice low when asking about the submersible aspect, but had it been low enough? "How much has he been around?"

"He's come by most days."

"And been helpful?"

"He's been eager to please."

Tikaya couldn't remember any teacher, mentor, or employer ever saying that about Ell. "Does he know...?" She waved at the walls.

"Nobody except you knows."

"How is that possible? Weren't some of them here every day, helping construct it?"

"In the Turgonian factory, every laborer has a particular gear or cog that he's an expert at making. He spends his days churning out his assigned pieces without ever having to know how it'll fit with the other pieces or what the final product will look like."

"This ship isn't nearly as big as a factory; I can't imagine how you kept everyone from noticing what you were doing down here."

"Not easily. And there have been..." His gaze flicked toward the companionway. "Spies."

"Ell?"

"I don't know if he is or not. I don't sense deception or subterfuge from him, but there *have* been nocturnal visitors to the site."

"How do you know?"

"I left harmless booby traps that would be triggered if intruders came through. One morning they'd been tripped. After that, I built locking mechanisms for the wheelhouse and cabin. Also, there was the incident at the Pernicious Miasma."

"I've been wondering about that," Tikaya said. "The newspapers mentioned a fire."

"In my room, yes. Someone was in there, searching for my schematics I'm guessing. One of the Turgonians staying there saw the door open and peeked inside. He spotted someone rummaging through my clothing. Being a Turgonian through and through, he attacked the intruder instead of questioning. They fought, and my man says he would have won but a second fellow came in and clubbed him in the back of the head. The intruders escaped, but, in the process of the fight, knocked lamps on the floor. Given all the rum vapors dousing the floors and furniture of that hostel, I'm surprised the whole place didn't burn to ashes."

Tikaya listened to the tale grimly. She wished Rias were staying at the plantation. Though there seemed to be a spy within her own family, she'd worry about him less if they were sharing a roof—or a bed, as would be preferable. What if the activities of these spies escalated? If they figured out Rias had disobeyed the minister's wishes and built a submarine, might he himself become a target?

"Were these intruders Kyattese?" Tikaya asked, imagining minions sent by High Minister Jikaymar.

"Nurian."

"Nurian?" Tikaya blurted. How many nationalities were a part of all this intrigue?

"Yes, my witness was certain, though they did wear island garb, a more sedate style than I've adopted, I'm told."

Tikaya snorted. "Everyone wears a more sedate style than you. I didn't even know you could buy lime-green clam diggers."

"Yes, just so you know, I'm not intentionally choosing such garish colors. My funds are limited and clothing options available in my size are even more limited. Also... I believe Ms. Eleke at Brazen Beach Attire is having some fun with me."

"That's..." Tikaya plucked at one of the bone buttons on his shirt—each one featured a palm tree carving. "Very likely. Did the intruders find anything when they were there? Or did the fire make it impossible to tell?"

"There's nothing to find. The schematics are in my head." Rias led her to a pair of hatches on either side of the steps leading up to the deck. "Last stop."

He twisted an inset handle and pushed a hatch open.

A muffled cry of surprise came from within. A man and woman were sitting on a bunk, arms and legs entwined like the aerial roots of a banyan tree. The man tried to lurch to his feet, but with the woman's legs over his, he ended up tumbling to the floor instead. He popped up so quickly he clanged his head on the low ceiling.

"Sir!" It was Milvet, his hair mussed, his face flushed. "I thought you were, uhm, that you'd be... Uh." He flung a hand toward the woman, a dark-haired beauty with the handsome broad, bronze features of people from the southern island chains. "You remember, Virka. I was just showing her around. She'd been wondering what you did with the plants. And why I've been working so much extra and didn't have time for, uh, home life."

Rias considered the pair, the discarded coconut cups on the floor, and arched a bland eyebrow. "I see."

"We were just looking for a quiet—"

"Hush, dear." The woman rose from the bed with more aplomb than her husband, pinched him on the rump, and told Rias, "It's a fine ship. Thank you for the lovely party. We'll be leaving now."

Rias and Tikaya stepped aside as she sashayed out. Milvet tumbled after her, clanking his head, and a few other body parts, in his haste to hurry after her.

"What *is* it about this place?" Rias asked when he and Tikaya were alone. "The people are randier than sailors pulling into port after six months at sea."

Amused by the entire exchange, Tikaya said, "Pleasant climate, beautiful scenery, and we eat a lot of oysters. They're a known aphrodisiac."

Rias straightened the bed and picked up the coconut cups. "Perhaps allowing the gathering was inadvisable. I thought, though, that letting so many people onto the *Freedom* would convince observers that I have nothing to hide."

Tikaya's amusement evaporated at this reminder of lurking spies. "Do you think it's possible Milvet and his lady were only pretending to be amorously engaged and were, before we entered, in here with their ears pressed to the hatch?"

"I don't know. I made the hatches thick and watertight, in case there's a need to seal off compartments. Come, let's invite the revelers to move to the dock."

The music troupe had already decamped, and it didn't take Rias long to usher the rest of the people off his ship. That didn't begin to end the party, though. If anything the crowd had grown larger. Someone had rolled a rum barrel down the docks and was filling cups as quickly as the amber liquid flowed out of the bunghole.

"Have a seat, my lady." Rias gestured her to a bench on the deck.

Tikaya imagined that once they were out on voyages together, she'd have to learn how to share all the duties, but Rias seemed content to have her seated while he hopped about like a cricket, handling all the departure preparations on his own. He smiled every time he passed her, reminding her of a youth getting ready to show off some prized project to his parents. A soft hum vibrated through the craft as the engine started up, much quieter than the rumbles of the ironclad warship on which Tikaya had been a prisoner.

Rias appeared on deck again, untied the lines securing them to the dock, and hopped into the wheelhouse. Tikaya climbed up beside him. As the *Freedom* inched away from the dock, a cheer went up among the onlookers. Tikaya leaned into the shadows so she could watch those onlookers without being observed herself. While many people were clearly having fun, a few faces held more serious miens. Kyattese faces, she noted, not surprised but a little sad. One or two might be spies, but some were probably folks who simply loathed Turgonians and hoped Rias's ship exploded on its maiden voyage.

The thought sent an alarmed start through her. What if someone had booby-trapped the engine or energy supply? "Rias? Did you ever figure out what those nocturnal visitors did when they came aboard?"

The grim look he gave her said he'd long since considered the question. "I *hope* they were just looking around. I hadn't installed the energy supply at that point, but most of the engine was finished. I went over every inch of it and the rest of the ship, looking for signs of sabotage." Rias lifted a polished bone swimming mask. "I even pretended to spear-fish in the harbor this morning, so I'd have an excuse to check the hull."

Tikaya relaxed an iota, but felt compelled to add, "There are ways one could sabotage a vessel using the mental sciences, possibly ways that wouldn't be detectable to touch or the human eye."

"I feared as much and started the engine this afternoon, before people showed up, to make sure nothing untoward occurred. I wouldn't want to endanger you if it could be helped. I almost didn't invite you out for this." He waved toward the mouth of the harbor.

"I would have felt slighted if you'd invited my cousin to your party and not me."

"I thought as much. In regard to otherworldly sabotage, would *you* be able to detect it?"

"I'm... not sure. I didn't sense anything other than the energy supply during your tour, but it's such a significant source of power that its field could overshadow lesser devices in the vicinity."

Rias turned the wheel to guide the craft around the last of the docks and angle it toward the sea beyond the harbor. "Could *that* be sabotaged?

I have wondered at the wisdom of accepting such a significant piece of equipment from your ex-fiancé's *mother*."

"Parkonis's mom wouldn't blow you up. She's read your books."

"My what?"

"*Lieutenant Starcrest and the Savage Saboteur*, among other titles. She seemed to have the whole collection."

"Those are *here*?"

"Specially ordered. It seems Iweue is a fan."

"That's.... unanticipated," Rias said. "I did wonder how you convinced her to craft me such a powerful artifact."

"She expects a ride later. It definitely didn't sound like she wanted to blow you up." Tikaya scratched her chin. "She might blow *me* up if Parkonis moves back in with her, but that's a concern for later."

"Hm."

Tikaya could no longer make out individual faces amidst the crowd on the dock, but the torches burning in the area pushed back the darkness, so she *could* see bodies turned in their direction, watching intently. Rias slipped something into her hand. A spyglass. For all his excitement over sharing this moment with her, his mind seemed to be running down the same railway track as hers.

Tikaya leaned farther into the shadows and arranged the spyglass so she could skim over the revelers. She lingered on anyone watching the ship, especially those who seemed to be alone and who weren't enthusiastically enjoying their rum. Near the back of the crowd, she spotted a familiar face.

"I don't suppose you invited High Minister Jikaymar?" Tikaya asked.

"No."

"It seems he invited himself then." Tikaya returned the spyglass. "Why don't I take another tour of the vessel and see if I can sense anything?"

"Good idea."

Tikaya hesitated, feeling she should remind him that, as someone who'd never trained in the Science, her senses were of limited use, but decided to wait and see if she discovered anything first. She climbed down to the cabin and started at the front, touching the bulkhead Rias had said hid the submarine navigation controls. From there, she worked her way back, trying to open her mind and stretch out her senses, the way she'd heard practitioners describe the act. All the while, she wished she'd thought to invite one of her more skilled family members, though, with locks mysteriously being fastened to attic doors behind her back, she didn't know who to trust.

A half hour passed while Tikaya checked every bulkhead, then moved into the engineering area and poked around the copious numbers of securely fastened potted plants. The energy source emitted light and power like a small sun. Reluctantly she admitted that if someone had tinkered with it, she'd never know. Lastly, she came up to the deck and leaned over the railing, getting as close to the propeller as she could without jumping into the water. She closed her eyes, trying to sense anything suspicious, but felt nothing more than the spray of the sea splashing her cheeks. They'd pulled out of the harbor and moved into more vigorous waters.

"Anything?" Rias asked when she rejoined him in the wheelhouse.

"Not that I could tell."

"At this point, we can disengage from the top and descend. Do you want to continue or wait for another night?"

Tikaya eyed their surroundings. They'd headed east from the harbor mouth. Rocky hills hid the docks and the city from view, and the moonless night cast the *Freedom* in shadow. Thinking of the dark gray paint Rias had chosen, she decided they'd be nearly impossible to see out there, especially given the vessel's low profile. Without masts or sails to be visible against a starry horizon, observers would have trouble distinguishing them from the waves.

Tikaya picked up the spyglass again. This time, she searched the dark hills. Here and there, a torch burned. People watching their craft? Or simply folks heading home after a day spent in town? Lush vegetation grew along the hilltops, and even with the spyglass, Tikaya couldn't make out the details of the torch bearers.

"I doubt they can see us," Rias said, "but either way, they'll continue to see the top of the vessel. I'll drop its anchor before we detach. People should just think we're out here canoodling."

"If the submarine doesn't work, we can give that a try."

"Doesn't *work*?"

He sounded so affronted at the possibility that Tikaya had to laugh. A mechanical error would probably leave him far too consumed with troubleshooting to consider canoodling. "I mean due to sabotage, not because of any failing on your part."

Rias's *hmmph* sounded vaguely mollified. He checked a couple of gauges on the console. "Are you ready? We'll only go down a few meters and for a short time on this first run."

Tikaya lowered the spyglass and noticed a tremor in her hands. Nerves at the idea of diving into the ocean depths? Or from knowing she hadn't been able to perform as thorough a check for booby traps as this deserved? "Ready," she said, despite those nerves.

Rias slipped a hand under a console, and something clacked. "Time to go below."

CHAPTER 14

TIKAYA AND RIAS ENTERED THE main cabin, and he shut the hatch behind them, spinning a wheel several rotations, his arm muscles flexing as he tightened it. In addition, he threw two heavy latches. A twinge of claustrophobic unease ran through Tikaya. Without access to the deck, the cabin suddenly felt tighter, the lights dimmer. Several clinks emanated from within the bulkheads, followed by a soft tremor and a last resounding *thunk-clang*.

"Those noises are normal, right?" The hatch lacked a porthole, or Tikaya would have had her nose pressed to it to check the results.

"Yes."

She touched the hatch. "Is this the only way out?" Given how much muscle he had thrown into tightening the wheel, she wondered how hard she'd find it to open on her own, should some emergency require her to do so. "What if there's a leak and we have to escape quickly? A leak due to sabotage, that is."

Rias took a couple of steps, reached above his head, flipped a hidden switch, and slid aside a panel between two beams. An escape hatch, the other side of which must have been buried beneath the wheelhouse, was set into the hull. "If we're at the surface, this won't be underwater. We'll enter and exit this way."

"And if we're not at the surface?"

"You'd flood the submarine if you tried to get out. Also water pressure is problematic to the human body below certain depths."

Problematic. As in instantly deadly. "Let's hope for no leaks then."

Rias regarded her gravely. "Do you still want to go forward with this?"

"Oh, yes. I just wanted to be aware of the options." Or lack of options, Tikaya added to herself. Then, deciding she wasn't showing enough enthusiasm for the adventure—and his new craft, smiled and said, "If we get bored in the confined space, there's always that canoodling."

Rias returned the smile. "I doubt you'll be bored. There's a porthole in the science station as well as the navigation chamber, and lighting outside to illuminate our surroundings. You're about to see the ocean in a way very few have. Perhaps no one in the world."

"Can glass withstand the pressures of water down... however deep we're going." She pointed in the direction of the ocean floor.

"I wasn't planning on skimming the bottoms of deep sea trenches in the *Freedom*—it'd take some of that black alien metal to withstand that kind of pressure—but there may be times when we want to drop a couple hundred meters to reach a wreck, and the hull should be able to handle that. As for the windows... Milvet arranged for the glass, and he claims a Maker enhanced it, but he couldn't give me specifics as to how many PSI it could withhold. I would have preferred real glass, as formulas tell me what to expect. As is... I've made my best guess and factored in as much redundancy as possible."

Rias thumbed a hidden switch, and the forward bulkhead split vertically down the middle, each piece sliding away on a concave track. He fastened a couple of latches, securing them to the hull. In the bow, controls and instrument panels had come into view, along with two chairs mounted to the deck. One of the portholes he'd mentioned allowed a view of the black waters outside.

"It's going to be dark down there," Tikaya said, then realized she was stating the obvious.

"Yes." Rias sat in the seat with the majority of the gauges and controls in front of it and flicked a few switches. "I want to wait until we're beneath the surface before turning the lamps on. We don't want to be visible to onlookers. We're close enough to the top that you could use the periscope I installed if you want to check on the upper shell of our ship. We should have cleared it by now."

"It looks like you've planned for every contingency."

Rias paused and tilted his head thoughtfully. "There's at least one thing I just realized I forgot. Allow me to apologize for that in advance. You didn't drink much of that rum, did you?"

"No... You didn't forget to build a head, did you?"

"It's there. It folds out of the wall next to our cabin. But I might have forgotten to... stock it."

Tikaya smirked. "Well, it can't be much worse than trying to find leaves on a frozen tundra in the Turgonian Northern Frontier."

"I was hoping I'd improve your life, not force you to reminisce about hard times. We won't stay down long. I just want to see..." Rias flicked another switch, and a faint sound reached Tikaya's ears—water gurgling? "Have a seat." He gestured toward the other chair. "Water is filling the ballast tanks. We'll start descending shortly."

Tikaya sat on the hard metal chair and promptly decided to suggest cushions as a later upgrade. She interlaced her fingers in her lap, crossed her legs, and tried to appear calm as she gazed through the viewport, waiting for the promised descent. The tightness of those interlaced fingers might have betrayed her nerves.

"Five feet," Rias said. "Ten."

At first, Tikaya didn't notice a change. The floor didn't tilt, nor was there any increased thrumming of the engines. The view of black water outside of the porthole remained the same as well—she imagined it'd be a much more intriguing view by day. Rias was watching a gauge—something like an altimeter? Except for depth? Tikaya leaned closer for a better look at the instrument panel.

Rias flicked a switch and a soft bong echoed from somewhere. He tapped a nearby display. "This is a version of that echo ranging device I mentioned."

"That the young captain invented?"

"Indeed so."

"For taking bathymetry readings of the ocean terrain?" Map-making practice shouldn't prove necessary, as the waters in front of the harbor were well-documented—and traversed often enough that Tikaya doubted any legerdemain-practicing cartographers could have fudged the maps.

"We could do that," Rias said, "but I'm more concerned about not crashing into said terrain."

"Ah." Good plan. That sole porthole didn't offer much of a view. There was a reef that circled a good part of the island and who knew what else out there? Numerous ships had been wrecked during the war, and while some had been salvaged many of the deeper ones had been left to gather barnacles on the sea floor.

"We've reached a depth of twenty meters." Rias checked all of his gauges again and seemed satisfied by what they told him. The soft bongs continued. "The floor isn't much farther down. I'm going to keep us at this depth. We'll turn on the lamps, I'll show you the science station, and we'll—"

A shudder ran through the craft.

Tikaya gripped the edges of her seat. "Double check the readings to make sure we're *not* running into things?" Her gaze latched onto the viewport, but darkness still reigned outside of it.

"Hm." Rias checked the gauges again. "We shouldn't be."

Another shudder coursed through the *Freedom*.

"Could there be a hiccup with the engines?" Tikaya asked.

It was amazing how much indignation a former Turgonian marine could infuse into one quick glance. "I think something's bumping us."

"We'd hear scraping sounds if it were a rock or a part of a wreck, wouldn't we?" Tikaya asked.

"I'd imagine so." Right, it was his first submarine ride too.

"Then what—wait, did you say something is bumping *us*? Not that *we're* bumping something?"

Rias lifted his hands from the controls. "I've stopped all forward and downward propulsion."

"The currents would move us some though, wouldn't they? Maybe we're snagged in seaweed."

"No. Something bumped us." Rias flicked a new switch, one labeled *lamp*.

For the first time, the darkness outside lessened. Tikaya left her chair and leaned her hands on either side of the viewport. From somewhere beneath the glass came a beam of yellowish light the same hue as Iweue's energy source. It illuminated less of the water around them than she would have wished. They weren't deep enough for her to see the sea floor, though a large coral nodule covered in colorful polyps rose at the edge of the light. She was surprised they'd traveled out far enough to reach the reef. Were they close enough that they might have hit a stray coral colony? That might account for the shudders.

"See anything?" Rias asked.

Tikaya pressed her face as close to the glass as her spectacles would allow.

A snake-like appendage slapped the viewport.

She shrieked and leaped away. Her leg caught on her chair and she fell backward, tumbling to the deck.

"I'll assume that means yes," Rias said.

From her back, propped on her elbows, one leg hung over the chair, Tikaya managed an inarticulate grunt and pointed at the viewpoint. Nothing was there.

"I saw something," she insisted.

"Yes, I gathered that from the shriek." This time Rias leaned in for a closer look.

"It wasn't a shriek." Tikaya scowled at his back. "It was... a high-pitched exclamation of surprise."

"You'll have to explain the difference to me sometime."

"It's a Kyattese distinction." Tikaya climbed to her feet. "Do you see it? It looked like a snake. No," she said, changing her mind as she remembered where they were, "a tentacle. One belonging to an octopus or a squid, though, if it's the former, that would technically make it an arm." Lovely time for vocabulary distinctions to pop into her mind. "That doesn't matter. What's odd is how *big* it was."

Rias looked at her.

"Giant squid and octopuses are more common in deep, temperate waters, aren't they? I've never heard of anything more than a foot or two long making an appearance here."

"Perhaps, due to being startled, you overestimated its size."

Another shudder pulsed through the submarine. The craft lurched to the side.

Tikaya stumbled again, this time catching herself against the hull. "And perhaps I *didn't*."

The view of the coral outside had shifted several feet to the side. Rias leaned close to the viewport again. This time the vista did not remain empty. The tentacle, a slimy grayish-green appendage, slapped the glass and stuck to it. Tikaya wouldn't have minded if Rias shrieked a little, or at least grunted in surprise, but he merely issued a thoughtful, "Hm."

"That's definitely from a creature more than a foot or two long," Tikaya said. "Do you think it's wrapped around us?"

"It seems so."

Rias clasped his hands behind his back, his legs spread so the intermittent vibrations—was that creature trying to drag them off somewhere?—didn't upset his balance. Tikaya chose to keep a white-knuckled grip on the edge of the console.

"You're correct," Rias said. "Giant squid and octopuses have occasionally harassed imperial ships, but always in northern latitudes. And usually, according to hesitant suggestions in reports from captains who've survived the encounters, under the influence of otherworldly persuasion, or so they believed."

Tikaya didn't like the implication that some of the captains who encountered the creatures *didn't* survive. "Do you mean to imply that some practitioner convinced this critter to visit?" She thought of the ice condor that had poisoned her in those desolate Turgonian mountains. It had been controlled by Nurian assassins practiced in the mental sciences.

The tentacle disappeared from the porthole, and the *Freedom* jerked again. This time the movement took the submarine closer to the coral.

"Would you be able to tell?" Rias sat back down at the controls and pushed a lever. "If a practitioner was controlling it?"

"Another animal telepath might be able to, but if someone is controlling it, he or she is far out of the range of my senses." Tikaya thought of all those people gathered on the docks. It could be any one of them. The high minister—was he a practitioner? She couldn't remember. "But if it smashes us against that big hunk of coral, I think we'll have an answer."

"I understand octopuses are quite intelligent. Perhaps it's mistaken us for the shelled prey it favors, and it simply plans to hurl us against the coral to break the submarine open and extract the innards for a meal."

"That's not any more reassuring than the practitioner hypothesis," Tikaya said. "Here's an idea: why don't we try to escape its clutches."

"I have been trying." Rias tapped a lever that he'd pushed to its maximum position.

"Oh. It's... holding us?"

"So it seems." Rias eyed a panel near the hull to his right.

Tikaya squinted to read the label. "Weapons?" What kind of weapons had he managed to lug down the docks in front of everyone and load onto the boat?

"Torpedoes," Rias said.

"Tor-what?" Tikaya had never heard the Turgonian word.

"They're self-propelled weapons driven by compressed air that can travel at speeds between fifteen and twenty knots. There's a charge in the head that explodes upon impact. It was named after the torpedo fish."

"By whom?" Tikaya asked, suspicious that he knew the origins of the name. Though she'd reconciled herself to Rias's martial past—mostly—it chilled her to imagine him sitting at a desk, designing weapons. "The same captain who invented that echo ranging contraption?"

Rias cleared his throat. "Actually, he was a lieutenant at the time, and the project was foisted on him by a particularly bloodthirsty superior officer." He seemed to be studying his controls and avoiding her eyes—maybe he could guess that it discomfited her to think of him inventing new ways to kill people. "I built these on board when nobody was around, and I have some stationary mines that I can deploy too, but neither will do any good against something wrapped around our hull. We'd just blow ourselves up with it."

"Let's save that for a last resort."

"Unfortunately, I was thinking of the possible need to defend ourselves against Nurian warships, not hungry sea life." Rias sounded annoyed with himself.

Tikaya gripped his shoulder. "As evinced by the empty tissue holder in the head, one man can't think of everything."

Rias snorted.

"Maybe it'll get tired of toying with us and swim away." Unless it truly was being controlled by a practitioner, Tikaya thought grimly.

Without warning, the *Freedom* was thrust forward in the water. Rias lunged for the control panel and yanked the wheel that controlled lateral movement. He spun it all the way to the right, but the coral outcropping came up too quickly. They glanced off it with a bang and a screech. The deck lurched, and if Tikaya hadn't still been gripping a beam she would have flown to the other side. An image of the hull bursting open and water flooding inside flashed into her mind.

Rias calmly maneuvered the controls to right the craft. He pushed another lever. "I think it let go to hurl us. I'm attempting to move away and rise before it catches us. It'll take time for the air to push out the water in the ballast tanks, but we can travel forward at—"

A warning bleat came from the echo ranger.

Rias spun the wheel hard. As the submarine turned, a myriad of colorful coral skimmed past.

"Sorry," he said, "I had a map of the reef in my head, but the octopus must have moved us more than I—"

A shudder raced through the craft again. Rias sighed.

"At least it doesn't seem to be strong enough to crush us," Tikaya said. "Or maybe it hasn't thought to try."

Rias spared her a glance, and she wondered if it meant her random thoughts weren't helpful.

"Why don't I check out that science station you mentioned and see if there's something that might be useful in prying stowaways off the hull?" Tikaya suggested. "You mentioned tools for collecting samples, didn't you?"

"Yes, one of my helpers just finished installing extendable arms with gripping hooks and shovels. But they're designed to pick up small samples, not pluck off gigantic octopuses." Intent on piloting the vessel, or perhaps keeping the creature from hurling them against the coral again, Rias didn't look at her as he spoke.

"I'll see if I can come up with something. Holler if you need me. Or if it succeeds in opening the sub like a tin of sardines."

"That will *not* happen."

Tikaya hoped he was speaking to the craft's superior engineering and not simply choosing to remain optimistic.

"Some maiden voyage," he added under his breath. The words didn't reassure Tikaya.

She hustled to the rear of the craft, to a hatch on the opposite side from their cabin. She flung it open and found herself in a cubby half the size of the sleeping area. Metal cupboards filled the walls, their doors all secured with clasps. She picked up an upended stool and set it before a desk secured to the deck in front of a porthole. The desk had a few control levers along the sides, presumably for manipulating those extendable tools.

Tikaya spun a wheel to unlock a porthole cover and found herself staring at the gray-green body of the octopus. "Lovely."

The hum of the engines increased, and a soft tremor ran through the craft, one that had nothing to do with the creature's attack.

"I'm pushing the engine," Rias called, "to wrest back some control. I'm going to steer close to the coral and try to scrape the octopus off."

Now why did that sound as dangerous for them as for their attacker?

"I understand," Tikaya called back, already opening cabinet doors, seeking inspiration in case Rias's plan didn't work.

A surprisingly thorough collection of specimen jars, digging tools, maps, and mapping equipment waited within, as well as alchemy substances useful for dating archaeological finds. Rias must have talked to a field researcher, or maybe he'd found someone to put the collection together for him. The man certainly knew how to recruit useful people.

The *Freedom* turned hard enough to send Tikaya stumbling into a wall. A bump and a scrape followed, and a ripple went through the gray flesh flattened against the porthole. The octopus was only adjusting itself, not releasing them. More hard turns and bumps followed. At least Rias had regained some control, though the deck vibrated hard enough to rattle Tikaya's teeth, and she wondered how long the engine could maintain the output required to fight the octopus. Maybe the creature would tire and give up first.

"There's a wishful thought," Tikaya muttered, then raised her voice so Rias would hear. "Do you have enough control to take us to the surface?"

"Possibly, but it's pressing down on us with a lot of weight. We've hit the ocean floor twice now. It's as if, when it's not hurling us against the coral, it's trying to smother us."

"If we could make it to the top..." What, Tikaya? How would the situation be improved up there? Unless they could drive the submarine up a beach like a runabout, the octopus wouldn't likely let go.

"Do you know someone waiting up there with a harpoon launcher?" Rias asked, his tone dry, even as he navigated them close to something that elicited another shuddering bump. Again the octopus shifted its grip, but did not let go.

"No," she responded. If anything, someone waiting up there might want to help the creature finish them off.

Tikaya opened a long, tall cabinet and found shelves filled with books, tightly packed so they wouldn't fall out. After a quick perusal of the titles, she plucked out an encyclopedia on sea life and flipped to the octopus section. Maybe they had predators she and Rias could mimic or fears they could exploit.

"I'm getting some different readings from ahead," Rias called. "You said there are wrecks down here?"

"By the harbor mouth, yes. There was fighting near the island at the end of the war, and the president sacrificed a few ships to fire to blockade the harbor at one point." Her first thought was that Rias should know all about those events, but then she remembered that he'd been on Krychek Island during the last year of the war. After he'd disappeared from the theater, the Turgonians had been at their worst, ignoring treaties and using more direct and desperate tactics in an attempt to subdue her people. That was a lot of what the Kyattese remembered and why people might never welcome Rias. Thoughts for another time, she reminded herself when another shudder coursed through the craft. She sat down to read.

"I'm going to head in that direction, then," Rias said. "There'll be more chances to scrape this fellow off, and maybe he'll have a claustrophobic streak."

Doubtful, Tikaya thought as she skimmed through a paragraph on ways octopuses defended themselves, which included hiding in holes. They also expelled ink, camouflaged themselves by changing color, and poisoned creatures with venom. "They have all sorts of defenses," Tikaya muttered, "but how do you *kill* one?"

The next bump was so hard that it hurled her from her stool. "Did we hit the ground?" she called.

"Yes," Rias said. "The structural integrity should remain intact through quite a bit of abuse, but this is a more taxing maiden voyage than I had in mind."

"I guess that means canoodling is out."

"Unless you think that would be useful against the octopus."

"The book doesn't mention it." Tikaya located her page again. This time, she stayed on the deck to read.

"Finding anything useful back there?" Rias asked after a few moments. "It's taking all my concentration—" a squeal of metal rang through the hull as they bashed against something, "—to keep this thing from preparing us for a suitable meal."

He sounded so equable. Tikaya struggled to keep her own thoughts calm. If he could joke, surely the situation wasn't too dire. She snorted, remembering that he'd made jokes when they'd been outnumbered, outgunned, and trapped on an enemy vessel before.

"Still looking," she responded as she continued to skim the octopus entry. In an attempt to show him that she could also stay calm and make jokes when their lives were in danger, she tapped a paragraph and added, "Apparently, octopus wrestling is a Turgonian sport increasing in popularity on your west coast. There's even an annual competition in Tangukmoo. Too bad we missed that when we passed through."

When Rias didn't respond, she assumed he thought the factoid too silly to comment upon. A moment passed, and she'd moved further down the page when he spoke again. "Would a dagger in the eye kill one?"

Tikaya almost dropped the book. He wasn't thinking of going *out* there, was he? "Rias, that was a joke, not a request for you to wrestle with this one. The octopuses in that area are a maximum of eighty, ninety pounds and aren't poisonous to humans. Whatever's out there must be five times that size if it's giving us such trouble."

"Given the force it's able to apply, I estimate closer to fifteen times that size."

"Either way, you're *not* going out there. Besides, I don't know how to steer your boat."

"Yes, shortsighted of me not to give you a lesson during the tour. I'm—" A loud crunch sounded, drowning out his words. Outside the porthole, the octopus shifted so that it only partially covered the opening. Tikaya glimpsed little more than dark water, though she thought she caught sight of something jagged before they moved past it.

"What was that?" Tikaya asked.

"We've gone through a hole in the hull of a wreck."

"Was the hole there *before* we went through?" Tikaya asked.

"Yes, though our stowaway broadened it."

"Be careful. Some of the wrecks out here are your people's, and they'll be made of metal, not wood."

"Noted," Rias said.

Another crunch sounded. Tikaya returned to reading. "Octopus predators include sharks, eels, some whales, and large fish," she muttered to herself, then snorted, trying to imagine the fish that could eat this creature. "Eels," she said again, tapping the page.

Wait, she'd been thinking of shock eels earlier. They could zap their prey with electricity, right?

With the inkling of an idea forming, Tikaya flipped to the eel entry. "There. Shock Eel. ...more closely related to catfish than true eel...

organs able to produce electricity... positively charged sodium... ion channels." She stopped after a few more sentences. She didn't need to know *how* the creature made electricity, as Rias's generator was already supplying it. If they could use it to...

"Rias," Tikaya called, "can you electrify the hull?"

A quiet moment passed, and she stepped out of her cubby.

"Rias?"

"Yes, sorry, I'm thinking. Absolutely, it can be done, but it should have been done in the shipyard. From down here, I'm not sure... Well, maybe. Here. Come pilot."

Tikaya groaned. "I should have known that would be required at some point." She jogged into the navigation area.

Rias stood and was pointing out controls before she even sat in the seat. "Rudder for left and right, diving planes for up and down, engine thrust, and—" Rias lunged and made a quick adjustment, steering them toward a hole so they didn't crash through the barnacle-covered wooden hull of a wreck. "You'll figure the rest out. The wrecks are giving the octopus something to think about, so you might want to keep weaving through them."

"Oh, good, an obstacle course. The ideal training environment for an inexperienced navigator."

Rias patted her on the shoulder. "You can handle it."

He disappeared into the back before she could grumble a response. Just as well. Tikaya needed her concentration. It didn't take more than three seconds for her to decide she didn't have time to figure out what the needles on the display for his echo ranging system meant. Instead, she rose from the seat and peered out the viewport. For the moment, nothing blocked the opening. She made small experimental adjustments to the control levers and prayed to Akahe that the octopus wouldn't smother the window with an arm.

The vessel jerked abruptly, and Tikaya felt the resistance in the control wheel. She wrestled with it to keep the craft in position. Another jerk came, the octopus trying to pull them toward the reef again.

"Oh, and stay away from Turgonian wrecks," Rias called, his voice muffled. "There may be mines and other unexploded ordnance in and around them."

Mines? A bead of sweat slithered down her spine. "You know, there are times when I really hate your people."

"Sorry."

Tikaya's adjustments to the wheel had little effect. The extra weight—and any force the octopus was applying—must affect the sensitivity. Out of the corner of her eye, she spotted a gauge with a needle pressed into a red area. She took a deep breath and fought for calm. And focus.

Despite their smothering tag-along, the outside lamps continued to work, illuminating the ocean floor for several meters ahead. Another wooden wreck came into view, and Tikaya nudged the rudder control, thinking to skim alongside it. Warier than Rias—especially in lieu of his last warning—she couldn't bring herself to search for an entry spot. The last thing she needed was to get them stuck. Maybe she'd try veering close enough to force the octopus to scrape against the barnacled hull. Rias had been doing that, and it hadn't had much effect, but she only needed to keep the creature busy for a while, not defeat it.

When the *Freedom* drew close, however, the octopus enacted a plan of its own. With an abrupt heave, it shoved the submarine, driving it into the hull. The *Freedom* crashed through with a great snapping of wood, and the force hurled Tikaya sideways. Her fingers flew from the controls, and she barely kept from landing on the deck again.

Cursing, she lunged back to the viewport, glancing out as she wrapped a hand firmly around the rudder lever. They'd smashed all the way through the side of the wreck. The light played over algae- and barnacle-smothered wood—lots and lots of wood. It snapped and jabbed at the *Freedom* with every foot they covered.

"How's it going up there?" Rias called, his voice even more muffled than before.

Tikaya imagined him crawling behind access panels, running or rewiring cables. "I'm, uhm, experimenting with different strategies."

She fought with the wheel, trying to find the hole they'd just made, so they could escape the clutches of the wreck. But the octopus or currents or a combination of both were determined to push the submarine deeper. Seaweed grew up everywhere, blotting out the already limited view and dimming the exterior lamps' influence. A school of startled fish burst out of the shadows and fled. More wood crunched, and Tikaya winced at each impact. No matter how sturdy Rias had made the submarine, surely it couldn't hold up to this abuse forever.

A solid wooden post loomed out of the darkness. Cursing, Tikaya spun the wheel to the maximum point. This time, the octopus must have been distracted, for she was able to turn the submarine. The nose of the craft still glanced off the beam, but didn't strike it head on.

Ahead, fish swam out through a hole. Hoping it represented the opposite side of the wreck, Tikaya angled toward it. It was too small, she realized too late, and they crunched through, enlarging the opening as they went. She groaned. They weren't outside yet, but in another portion of the ship. That had been a bulkhead, not the hull. She glimpsed fish again in her light, and followed them, hoping they'd lead her out.

By now sweat bathed her face and burned as it dripped into her eyes, but she dared not lift her hands from the controls to wipe it away. "Any progress back there?" Tikaya called.

If Rias responded, she didn't hear it.

Finally, she found another hole, one large enough to steer the craft through without destroying anything else. She eased out of it, with only a small bump—the octopus brushing the wood rather than the hull of the submarine striking it, and blew out a relieved breath when open water appeared around them.

Her relief was short-lived. Something huge and black appeared in the lamplight. The side of a Turgonian warship.

Rias's warning of explosives flooded into her mind. Tikaya yanked at the rudder control so hard she feared she'd tear it from the console. Though the octopus didn't seem to be fighting her, the extra weight still made the response slow. She grimaced as they floated closer. Engine, which lever had he said controlled engine thrust? That one. Yes. Hoping to slow them, Tikaya pulled it all the way back. They accelerated. She cursed again and thrust it in the opposite direction.

"Lessons, I definitely want *lessons* next time before being left alone up here!"

Again, Rias didn't respond. Tikaya growled and checked the viewport. The Turgonian ship was too long, their momentum too great. They'd end up glancing off its side. The hull wouldn't have explosives on it, would it?

"Up," Tikaya whispered, realizing she had another option.

She grabbed the lever that controlled the dive planes. This time she tested it slowly, not wanting to bury their nose in the sand. Slowly, the view through the glass inched up the black side of the ship. Too slowly. Tikaya could see every barnacle and the corrugations of rust pockmarking the hull. She pressed her face to the viewport, hoping to spot the railing, hoping they'd clear it. A huge gun came into view instead. Tikaya gulped. The hull might not have explosives embedded into it, but there might be shells loaded in that gun. If one of those exploded... Even Rias's sturdy engineering couldn't hold up against that kind of power.

"Ready?" came a call from the rear.

"Blessed Akahe, yes!"

Maybe if they lost the octopus, the *Freedom* would rise more rapidly. Tikaya tried to turn the rudder so they'd veer away from the gun, but with the engine thrust halted, nothing responded quickly. A whole bank of the weapons came into view, lining the hull, less friendly than bristles on a porcupine. The submarine drifted toward those guns, their course inevitable. She couldn't tear her gaze from the viewport.

Between one blink and the next, blackness blotted out the view. Her first thought was that the lamp had been extinguished, but a faint tremor ran through the submarine. Ink, Tikaya realized. The octopus had released the ink in its sac. Had it fled as well? She couldn't see anything through the blackened viewport.

Footsteps pounded on the metal deck. "Did it work?" Rias burst into the navigation room. "It felt like it let go."

"I think so, but we have another problem." Tikaya pointed at the viewport, but the black ink hadn't fully dissipated. "We're on course to run into—"

Rias leaped to a control panel on the wall next to her seat and threw four switches.

"—the side of a Turgonian warship," Tikaya finished. "What's that do?"

"Fill the ballast tanks with air so we'll rise, but it might not be fast enough." Rias squinted through the porthole.

Beyond the fading ink, the rusted railing of the warship came into view. Tikaya stood, fingers pressed against the console. They'd risen past the guns. Maybe they'd clear the entire ship. A smokestack loomed, though, canted toward them on the wreck's tilted deck.

Rias slid into the navigation seat, and Tikaya was more than happy to let him take the job back. He fired up the engines again and steered them toward the gap between the smokestack and a second one with its side torn open. They bumped against the first stack, but Rias didn't flinch. Tikaya heaved a sigh and sagged against the wall.

"I was afraid to touch anything on that ship," she admitted when he glanced at her, "after your mention of unexploded munitions."

"Ah. They shouldn't be dangling from the smokestacks."

"You wouldn't think so, but with Turgonians, one never knows." Tikaya bent down and wrapped a hug around Rias from behind, pressing her cheek to his. She decided not to admit that she'd nearly scared herself to death a couple of times when piloting his creation—he always seemed to think her above that sort of thing—but she let her relief show in the tight embrace.

Rias was adjusting the controls to take them to the surface, but he paused to grip her arm and lean his temple against hers. "It's true that there *have* been instances of defeated Turgonian captains booby-trapping their ships to ensure enemy parties would, ah, blow up, as it were, when attempting to board."

"Blow *up*? Wouldn't that have caused some of the crew to blow up as well?"

"All of them, yes. And usually the ship as well, but that kept the enemy from acquiring secret orders or taking the vessel as a war prize."

Though Tikaya didn't break the hug, she did pull her head back, watching Rias out of the corners of her eyes. "They didn't do such things under orders from their admirals, did they?"

"There was no need to give such orders, the idea having long since been instilled in them during their academy days." Rias pointed at the viewport. Rivulets of water ran down the outside. Now on the surface, the submarine bobbed and swayed with the waves.

After that crazy adventure, Tikaya almost expected it to be dawn, but darkness still hugged the sea. A chronometer on the wall behind Rias's chair informed her that it'd only been an hour since they'd left the dock. The rum was probably still flowing. Odd to think that all that chaos had gone on beneath the surface and the people above probably had no idea about it. Most of the people anyway. Someone had been controlling that octopus.

Brought back to the reality that they'd only survived one attack and that the war might just be beginning, Tikaya released Rias from her hug and stood up, though she left her hands on his shoulders. "Did *you* ever booby trap one of your ships?" she asked. After all, he'd gone to that academy as well, and at a younger—and perhaps more impressionable age—than normal. "Or were you too gifted to ever find yourself in that predicament?"

"Oh, I found myself in that predicament more often than you'd think, since I had a stubborn determination not to simply equal but to exceed the expectations set forth in my orders. I tended to poke my nose into a lot of burning buildings. But I was always convinced that I could trick or scheme my way out of the situation without blowing up my ship or surrendering my crew."

"Since you're here with me, nearly being eaten by an octopus, it must have worked most of the time."

"Yes. My amazing knack for getting myself into trouble was surpassed only by my supreme luck when it came to getting out again, often with results that impressed my superiors. Fortunately, I've grown more sedate of late." Rias leaned his head back and smiled at Tikaya.

"Are you truly telling me that the Rias I know today is a *sedate* version of the old one?" Tikaya remembered the way he'd led her through a Nurian warship, determined not simply to escape it but to destroy it in the process and, oh, the one sailing alongside as well. "Are you sure you didn't simply drive your superiors crazy? Maybe they promoted you through the ranks so quickly so they wouldn't have to deal with you as a subordinate any longer."

Rias blinked a few times, then let out a round of laughter that rang from the metal walls. Tikaya thought it might be his way of expressing his relief that they'd survived the octopus—sturdy submarine or not, he *had* to have been worried too—but she hadn't heard such amusement from him since they'd arrived in Kyatt, so she savored it. He even wiped tears from his eyes.

"I haven't had anyone suggest that notion to me," he said when the laughs stilled, "but if I get an opportunity to return to the empire someday, I'll be certain to run the idea past a few of my former superiors."

His expression grew wistful, and Tikaya's pleasure faded. He must be thinking about how much he missed his home and his old colleagues. Her recent thoughts—that she was asking too much to keep him here—returned and filled her with sadness. She cleared her throat and attempted to tamp down the melancholy feelings. "We'd best get back to the party before all the rum is gone."

Rias chuckled. "Indeed. I was abstaining before, but I could use a swig now."

"Me too," Tikaya murmured.

CHAPTER 15

B Y THE TIME THE *FREEDOM* floated into its berth, most of the revelers had drifted away. Or, Tikaya thought as she glimpsed a familiar scowling figure, maybe they'd been *driven* away. She'd thought High Minister Jikaymar might be waiting, but it was someone worse. Her father.

He stood, fists against his hips, wearing what had become a permanent sneer of late. He turned his scowl on Rias, as if he were some juvenile delinquent who'd taken Tikaya out to roam the countryside until all hours, alternating between necking and bashing in old ladies' mailboxes.

"Good evening, sir," Rias said before hopping onto the dock to secure his craft.

Though they'd reattached to the upper portion of the ship, Tikaya gave the *Freedom* an uneasy look fore and aft, almost expecting to find an octopus arm dangling from a corner or some other sign that would prove they'd been beneath the water's surface. Not that it mattered. Despite Rias's camouflage, someone had known the craft had the ability to submerge—and had been ready for it to do so. If, on their next run, they tried to explore the inaccurately mapped waters near the cliffs, what further troubles would they find?

"It's late and you didn't tell your mother where you were going." Father's scowl wasn't much softer when it landed on Tikaya.

She wished she could think of something to say to lighten his mood, to bring back the father she remembered. He'd always been a quiet man, one to spend long days out in the fields or in the distillery, always preferring work to the emotional chaos of being in the house with so many family members, but he'd always been fair as well as stern. He'd usually had a smile for his only daughter. Since she'd returned with Rias, Tikaya hadn't once seen him without his shoulders hunched to his ears and his eyebrows drawn down in a V.

"I know, Father." She joined him on the dock. "You didn't need to come all the way down here. I would have returned."

Squeaks sounded as the men who had been manning the portable grill wheeled it toward the boardwalk. "To the peace after the war," one called to Rias in Turgonian. It was a common before-drinks salutation in the empire, and Tikaya didn't miss the significance of it being used in this context. Rias lifted a hand and offered only a wry, "Indeed" in response.

"It's late. Finish up quickly and go back to your hotel," Father told Rias, apparently not finding anything odd about ordering around someone who'd once held the rank of fleet admiral. You—" he stabbed a finger at Tikaya, "—come." He stalked toward the boardwalk.

Tikaya knew her father wouldn't approve, but she gave Rias a goodnight hug, lingering long enough to say, "Be careful."

"Indeed," Rias murmured again, returning the hug with one arm since he was holding a mooring line in the other. "I'll send word when I've finished repairs and... additions."

Tikaya imagined him adding all manner of weapons to deal with wayward sea creatures that might attack them. She hoped the government would let him. Now that someone *knew* that he'd gone against their agreement, Rias might find the roadblocks in his path had turned into flaming tar and caltrops. She snorted to herself. She was thinking in terms of Turgonian metaphors now. She hoped no telepaths were about, sniffing at her thoughts.

"Love you," she whispered and kissed him—because her father was scowling from the head of the dock—on the cheek.

She refused to hurry to catch up. She didn't want to anger Father, but she wanted him to have time to think of how unreasonable he was being. Couldn't he see that? Couldn't any of them?

"Night, Ms. Komitopis," one of the Turgonians said with a wave for her as she passed.

She lifted a hand to acknowledge him, but would have preferred people let her pass in silence. Especially Turgonian people. Her father continued on without further glares or comments.

"Where's Ell?" she wondered when she caught up with him. She would have thought he'd be one of the last to leave. Maybe his lady had dragged him away. Or maybe he'd had something to do with the incident. He certainly came and went at inopportune times.

Actually... when Tikaya took another look at the last of those gathered, she realized that *only* Turgonians remained. They were cleaning up discarded cups and tossing garbage into bins. During the event, there'd been a mix of people. Not many Kyattese natives, true, but lots of other foreigners. She wondered what had happened to dampen the party and cause it to end early. Wrathful octopuses or not, she and Rias hadn't been gone *that* long.

"Sent him home," Father said, drawing her eye from the docks.

"And he listened?" Tikaya asked. Even when Ell had been a boy, he hadn't been very good at listening to her parents or his own.

Father didn't answer. He picked up his pace. Tikaya wondered if Mother had promised him she'd clear the house of youngsters for the evening if he hurried home quickly.

As they left the boardwalk and headed toward a beachfront street with runabouts parked on the sides, Tikaya resolved to come back down and help Rias in the morning. Dean Teailat could let her have a day off.

"Get in." Father was holding open the passenger door to the runabout, and he jerked his chin for her to hurry.

"I—"

A boom sounded behind them, louder than a cannon being fired.

Tikaya spun back toward the quay, her jaw plummeting. Orange flames roared into the night, leaping as high as the hilltops behind them, the brilliant intensity brightening the harbor for hundreds of meters in every direction. Shouts of surprise and cries of pain rose over the rumble of the ocean.

From the hill overlooking the waterfront, Tikaya was too far away to read the dock numbers, but she *knew* where the explosion had originated. Nobody else would have been a target.

Her legs seemed to have rooted to the earth, but she forced them to move. He could be injured. He could be—

No, no thinking like that, she told herself.

Tikaya started to run toward the quay, but an iron grip caught her by the elbow. Father.

"You're *not* going down there," he said. "It's too dangerous."

There was no surprise in his voice. No horror. He'd known, she realized numbly. He'd known it was coming. That was why he'd been hurrying her away. That was why he'd sent Ell home. Had he warned all the other Kyattese to leave as well? Was he the one who'd been keeping an eye on her at home too? The one who'd locked away the secrets in the attic?

Later. It was something to worry about later.

Tikaya yanked on her arm, but his fingers, strong and calloused from years in the fields, had the tenacity of iron.

"It's gone, girl," Father said. "It's for the best. One day, you'll understand."

"Under*stand*?" Tikaya cried. "If I *ever* understand why someone would blow up a good, honorable man whose only crime was being born on the other side of an ocean, I'll shoot myself."

She stomped her foot onto her father's instep. Her sandal lacked the bone-crunching heft of Turgonian combat boots, but her anger lent it power. Her father gasped and his fingers loosened. This time, Tikaya succeeded in yanking free of his grip. She sprinted down the street, pausing only long enough to tear off her sandals so they wouldn't slow her down.

"Tikaya!" came her father's cry from behind.

She didn't glance back. With her bare feet pounding on pavement, then grass, then finally the wood planks at the beginning of the boardwalk, she sprinted toward those flames. She dodged people who were fleeing in the other direction, bumping elbows and shoulders, but barely noticing. Someone tried to grab her arm.

"Woman, you're going the wrong way," a man yelled. "Get out. The whole harbor's going to burn."

Not likely, Tikaya thought without slowing. The cold, calculating minds who had planted the explosion wouldn't have wanted to harm the Kyattese people or destroy any more of their own property than necessary.

Ahead, the height and breadth of the fire had lessened as whatever ultra-incendiary fuel it had initially been burning dwindled, but flames continued to roar and wood snapped, flinging burning shards in all directions. The breeze sent smoke inland, stinging Tikaya's eyes. Her vision blurred, but she kept going as far as she could. Shipyard 4 and Rias's dock were gone. Utterly and irrevocably. The docks on either side were burning, their pilings and boards charred like skeletons in a funeral pyre. A portion of the boardwalk had collapsed, and water blocked Tikaya's route. She kept running, of a mind to jump off and swim to the remains of Rias's dock, despite the flames licking every broken board and piling, despite the heat searing her cheeks with the power of molten lava.

Before she reached the jumping point, a board broke beneath her foot, and her leg plunged downward. Jagged wood gouged her flesh. Pain flashed up her leg, but she scrambled back, tearing the limb free without worrying about injuring herself. She had to—

Someone grabbed her from behind.

Her breath snagging in her throat, Tikaya whirled. She hoped it was Rias and was ready to fling herself into his arms. But it was her father, sweat streaming down his face.

"*Tikaya*, there's nothing you can do out here except get hurt. That freak of a ship is gone."

"I don't care about the slagging ship," Tikaya growled, hardly noticing the Turgonian curse on her lips. "I have to find Rias."

"If he listened to me, he went back to his room before any of this happened."

"His room was burned down! He's been sleeping out here." Tikaya thrust her arm toward the flames gnawing at the scorched pilings, all that remained of Rias's dock.

Surprise flicked across Father's face before he clenched his jaw in grim acceptance. "That's unfortunate then, but he knew he wasn't welcome. You never should have brought him here."

"*I?*" Tikaya dragged her sleeve across her eyes and nose, knowing the smoke wasn't entirely to blame for their running. Father was putting this on *her* shoulders? "I shouldn't have brought the man I love and that I plan to marry home to meet my family? I'm sorry, but I thought that was the expected thing and that it'd be appreciated more than me disappearing to Turgonia or some other Akahe-forsaken country for the rest of my life. I thought you and Mother would like to see grandchildren if we had them. I thought—" Her voice broke with a choking hiccup. She was shrieking and she knew it, but she couldn't find control.

"Sir, ma'am, please return to shore," called a voice from out on the water. A fireboat had drawn near, the first of several angling toward the flames.

Footsteps sounded on the boardwalk. Policemen were jogging toward Tikaya and Father.

"There's nothing we can do here," Father said, giving her arm a tug. "Let these people handle it."

Tikaya curled her toes around the edge of the boardwalk, as if she could grow roots and become as immovable as a giant palm. Wood floated in the water all around them. More than wood. A body drifted out from beneath the boardwalk, face-up, sightless eyes staring at the sky, flesh burned away like wax on a candle.

Tikaya clenched her teeth and squinted her eyes shut. It wasn't Rias, but it was one of the Turgonians who had been helping clean up. If those men hadn't escaped the flames, how could he have?

Soft curses reached her ears. She caught her father saying, "...made a mess of it," under his breath.

Tikaya pried her eyes open. She scanned the water, not just searching for bodies but for the *Freedom* as well. With a wooden ship, there would have been floating boards. But the submarine was made of metal, even the detachable deck and wheelhouse. If its hull had been damaged, it would have sunk like a rock. She lifted her head. What if the body of the craft had survived the explosion? What if it was down on the bottom of the harbor, still intact but filling with water? With Rias in it.

"Can you help me get her home?" her father asked someone.

With her back to him, Tikaya barely heard it. She couldn't go home. She had to organize a search, a dredging of the harbor. And if nobody would help her, she'd dive down herself. How deep was the water there? Twenty feet? If the submarine had sunk straight down, she could—

A hand gripped hers, and something cool came to rest on her arm. "Ma'am? There's nothing you can do here. My men are here, and this is our job. Let us help."

"No, you don't understand." Tikaya turned and found herself staring into a policewoman's eyes. They were sympathetic, but Tikaya didn't want sympathy; she wanted a search team at her disposal. "It's possible he's still alive. We need divers to search the bottom of—" A yawn halted the rest of her sentence. How could she be tired *now*? She frowned down at the hand resting on her arm. The hint of something blue peaked out from beneath the policewoman's palm. It took Tikaya a moment recognize it as one of the patches they used to subdue agitated criminals. In her own agitated state, she hadn't noticed the telltale tingle of a Made item.

Tikaya cursed and tried to pull her arm away, but the leaden limb barely responded. When she stepped back, she couldn't feel her foot and she stumbled. Someone caught her from behind. Her father? No, a policeman. He gripped her armpits while the woman took her ankles. Tikaya tried to fight, but the weariness weighing down her limbs wouldn't be bucked. They carried her down the boardwalk, away from the fire and away from Rias. Frustration charged her soul, but her body wouldn't respond. Before they reached the end of the quay, unconsciousness robbed her of thoughts as well.

Tikaya woke in her room with her head throbbing and her tongue dryer than lava rock baking in the sun. Afternoon light slanted through her window. *Late* afternoon light. She jolted upright in bed, instantly aware of how much time had passed. Curse those policemen and curse her father for playing a role in all of this. From the very beginning, he'd been on their side. Their? She didn't even know who they were. She had a vague notion of High Minister Jikaymar and others in the College of Telepaths, but that was it. And she still didn't know how much of this had to do with whatever ugly portion of history they were covering up and how much had to do with Rias being Rias.

Rias!

Tikaya lunged from her bed and grabbed clothes from a dresser. She had to—

"What, 'Kaya?" She paused, underwear dangling from her fingers, to consider the grim realities.

By now, he'd either found a way to survive on his own, or...

She didn't want to think about *or*. After all that he'd lived through, all the attacks he'd endured, she refused to believe he'd succumbed to explosives planted on the dock. Unfortunately, if he was alive and well, she had no idea where to find him. She glanced at the sun outside her window. She'd been out at least twelve hours, probably more like sixteen. Too much time had passed. He could be anywhere.

She'd have to do what she could here and wait for him to contact her. Her thoughts went to the lock on the attic. If the answers she'd sought hadn't been in the journal, maybe they were in those letters. She used a trip to the washout to check the house and see who was home. Mother's humming came from the kitchen downstairs, and children's voices drifted in through open windows, but nobody was about on the second floor.

Tikaya fetched a few hairpins and crafted them into the tools Rias had shown her. Picking a lock that dangled over one's head wasn't the easiest thing, especially given that her sole expertise in the area lay in thwarting the security system on a three-hundred-year-old diary. Her arms soon burned from holding them overhead. She stuck with it, though, and a satisfying *click* reached her ears. She unclasped the padlock, pushed the door open, and pulled herself up. In the darkness, she had to grope her way to the spot where she thought she'd left the rapier and satchel. When she patted around and didn't find anything, she grew concerned that Father had removed the items—curse her, why hadn't she done this days ago? She clenched her jaw, determined that she'd search her parents' bedroom if she had to, but she remembered that she'd tucked the rapier and satchel down out of sight. She dipped her hand between two pieces of furniture and found the items. As soon as she had them, she scurried out of the attic. She dropped as softly as she could into the hallway below, then winced when the door fell shut above her with a thunk. Afraid the noise would draw someone, she stuck the sword scabbard and satchel between her legs and reached up to slip the lock back into place. It snapped shut, and she turned to head to her room, only to halt in her tracks.

Her mother stood in the hallway, not three feet away.

"Uhm," Tikaya said. "Good afternoon?"

"After the night you had, I doubt it." Mother regarded the scabbard and satchel. "Let's talk, dear."

Trying not to feel like a child caught stealing cookies from the jar, Tikaya rearranged her purloined gear and trailed Mother down the hallway. She eyed the stairs, thinking of bypassing the lecture and heading out to look for Rias, but Mother might have information that could prove useful in finding him.

They entered Tikaya's room. Mother sat on the side of the bed and patted the quilt next to her. Tikaya shook her head. She couldn't sit. She set the sword down and paced.

"I'm sorry for your loss, Tikaya."

"Oh." Mother didn't realize that Rias wasn't dead. Or at least that Tikaya refused to accept that Rias was dead, not until she saw the smashed remains of his submarine and his body washed up on the beach. The image pumped a fresh feeling of dread into her. What if those things had happened while she'd been unconscious? What if Mother knew for certain of which she spoke?

"He seemed... Well, he's not what I'd envisioned when I told you to bring me home a son-in-law and a father to my grandchildren, but I saw that he made you happy."

"Yes," Tikaya murmured, even as she sought a way to end this conversation. If Mother wasn't going to object to her pilfering artifacts from the attic, she wanted to get on with examining them. She fiddled with the strap on the dusty satchel.

"Now that he's gone, it'd be wise if you stopped investigating whatever it is you're investigating." Mother eyed the desk. "I didn't say anything about the skull, but—"

Tikaya lifted her head. "You saw that?" She'd been careful to hide it every time she left her room.

"I dust in here, dear. I'm fairly certain I came in to collect dishes several times last week without you noticing. You're not the tidiest of people when you're wrapped up in a mystery." She held up a hand before Tikaya could voice an objection. "As I was saying, whatever history you're trying to dig up, I get the feeling everyone would prefer it didn't surface."

"I've gotten that feeling too."

"And?"

"And that makes me all the more curious to know what everyone's hiding."

Mother shook her head slowly. "That curiosity is what got your young man killed."

He's not dead, Tikaya almost said, but she didn't know that. Not truly. She closed her eyes. What if...?

A touch on her arm brought her mind back to the room.

"Let this one go, Tikaya," Mother said. "It's not worth dying over. And your father's worried that'll happen to you."

"Father *knew.* He knew about the explosion at the dock. Ahead of time."

"And he tried to save you, to pull you away from there, didn't he?"

"Mother, do *you* know what it is they're trying to hide? And who exactly is involved? Is Father...?" Tikaya closed her eyes. She didn't want to believe her own father could be responsible for an attempt to murder Rias, but...

"I don't know, and he won't tell me." The bed frame creaked as Mother shifted her weight. "You know I married into the family, so I'm not an original Komitopis. Even after all these years, it's possible there are family secrets I haven't been privy to." She glanced at the sword on the bed. "Your father's not sharing anything with me about this, but since you returned with Rias, he's been tenser than a boar cornered by hunters. He did tell me that everything he's done has been to protect the family. And you. He specifically said that you're in danger and need to go back to researching ancient and *distant* cultures."

Tikaya sighed. "I understand, Mother. I'll think it over."

She glanced out the window again. She couldn't see the setting sun from the room, but lengthening shadows promised night would be upon them soon. Time to shoo Mother away so she could take a look at those letters. No matter what she said, Tikaya *was* going to get to the bottom of this. If Rias really was gone, she'd make sure she found out why he'd been murdered.

Mother patted her leg and stood. "I trust you'll do the right thing, dear. Just... stay safe."

As soon as the door shut behind her, Tikaya dug into the satchel and pulled out the letters.

CHAPTER 16

NIGHT HAD FALLEN AND THE family had gone to sleep when a soft clack drew Tikaya from her reading. She stood up, picking her way past the two dozen letters scattered about on the floor, and checked the hallway. Darkness lay thick in the passage, and she heard nothing beyond the snores coming from her parents' bedroom.

"Your imagination," she muttered, though she couldn't help but hope Rias would stroll through the door.

Tikaya returned to her cross-legged position on the floor amongst the letters, all recently opened. She'd felt like a deviant prying into someone's personal wax-sealed envelopes, but none of them had ever been posted. Before she'd opened the satchel, she'd assumed they would be letters from the Turgonian soldier who had written the journal, but only one held his signature at the bottom. The rest were from other crew members, including two from the ship's captain. The letters from the crew were addressed to wives, parents, or siblings back in the empire—the collection led Tikaya to assume that her lovelorn soldier had been chosen to take the missives ashore and post them. While a few of those letters had held clues as to the crew's mission in Kyatt—find the ships from the long-lost colony and bring home any treasures within the holds—it was the two messages from the captain that had occupied her attention for several hours. They were addressed to a Fleet Admiral Dovecrest, and they were encrypted.

At first Tikaya had assumed the old code would prove easy to crack—how sophisticated of cryptographers could treasure-hunting civilians from three centuries prior have been?—but the deciphering was going slowly. The admiral to whom the letters were addressed must have provided a key for the captain to use if he found anything worth sharing with the military. Naturally, that made Tikaya want to know what they contained more than ever.

The clack sounded again.

Tikaya lifted her head. "That's *not* my imagination."

The noise hadn't come from the hallway but from outside. From the window.

Hope poured into her limbs, and she sprang to her feet. Rias? Who else would be tossing pebbles at her window?

She scurried around the bed, unlatched the pane, and shoved it open. A strong wind blew in from the sea, and clouds scudded across the sky, blotting out any moon that might have shed light over the yard or the cane fields beyond. With the family in bed, there weren't any lanterns burning along the walkways, and Tikaya squinted, trying to see if someone stood below her window. She didn't see anything, though she could make out the dark smudges that remained on the front lawn, evidence of the fire a couple of weeks earlier.

"Over here," came a low whisper, so soft she almost didn't hear it over the wind, but she recognized that voice, and she almost scrambled out the window in her haste to greet its owner.

Rias stopped her with a touch and slipped inside to join her. "It's been raining and the roof is slippery," he explained.

Only the knowledge that sleeping kin occupied the adjacent bedrooms kept Tikaya from bursting into laughter—for all she knew, he'd been *dead*, and he thought she cared about the treacherousness of the *roof*? She slung her arms around him in a hold that a Turgonian wrestler couldn't have bested and buried her face in his shoulder.

Rias returned the embrace, though he didn't seem as overcome with emotion—of course, he'd known all along he hadn't been dead—for he lightly observed, "It's good to know that news of my death wasn't enough to force you to retreat to your bed and weep inconsolably into your pillows. I think."

"I knew you weren't dead," Tikaya said, voice muffled by his shoulder. It took another deep breath before she could loosen her grip enough to lean back and gaze into his eyes.

"Truly? Because *I* wasn't certain I was going to survive at first."

Indeed, a new scab ran from his forehead into his hairline, and a bruise blackened one eye. He'd changed back into the somber black Turgonian military uniform, a pistol, dagger, and ammo pouches hanging from his belt. He looked like a man ready to go to war.

"What happened?" Tikaya asked.

"It seems your guess that there might be a trap waiting to be triggered was correct, only it was on the underside of the dock instead of on the *Freedom*. I was fortunate to be down below when the explosion went off. If I'd been on the dock or even on the deck..."

Tikaya nodded. "I saw the bodies of... I saw bodies."

"You were there?"

"I ran back down to the harbor when I heard the explosion. My father tried to stop me—I realized later that... that he knew it was coming." Tikaya licked her lips. Maybe she shouldn't have admitted that, especially given that Rias looked to be in the mood to stop his attempts at diplomacy and start filling people full of pistol balls. "I pulled away from him and sprinted down there. I didn't see the *Freedom*. At all. I was ready to dive in and search for it—for you—by myself, but the police showed up and someone used a calming patch on me. It knocked me out, and they brought me back here. How did you—your boat wasn't anywhere to be seen when I got there."

"No. The explosion caused the dock to lurch sideways and it collapsed onto the *Freedom*, tilting it onto its side. Me too." Rias touched the fresh scar. *Tilting* wasn't likely a violent enough word to describe the event. "Water flooded into the cabin. My first instinct was to throw the switch and put the *Freedom* into submarine mode. I didn't know if it'd work from there. It did, but tons of water was trapped inside, and it sank straight down. I had to revamp the system for pumping water out of the ballast tanks and use it on the interior. The oxygen tanks were damaged. I wasn't sure if they'd blow up on me or if I'd have enough air to breathe, but I had a feeling it'd be better to remain at the bottom of the harbor instead of coming up. For all I knew, someone was waiting up there to finish the job if the explosions didn't kill me."

"From what my father said—and Rias, I'm *so* sorry I didn't realize he was part of this and that—" Her voice cracked and she wiped at her eyes. Curse the volcano, all she'd done was apologize to him since he stepped foot on her island. Why had she ever thought bringing him here would work out?

"Sssh," Rias murmured, his gaze flicking toward the door. "It's all right." He lifted a warm hand to her face and brushed a tear away with his thumb. "It's not your fault. I'm the one who defied them and continued to build what seems to be the main source of their agitation. I'm having problems with following orders and minding authority in my old age."

Tikaya snorted and made a note to lower her voice. "You're *not* old."

"I feel it after the last twenty-four hours. I spent most of the night at the bottom of the harbor, wondering if I'd run out of air and worried someone would send divers down to make sure the *Freedom* was destroyed. There were fireboats, and there was a private yacht sailing around on the outskirts of the activity too. Someone keeping an eye on things. Finally at dawn, I was able to get the submarine to limp out of the harbor, bumping and scraping along the bottom of the ocean. I stayed shallow and followed the coast up to those cliffs—"

"You didn't go down into that basin, did you?" Alarm flashed through Tikaya, partially at the idea of swarms of octopuses assaulting the *Freedom* and partially at the thought that he'd leave her behind and try to solve the mystery on his own.

"Not when I was standing in a foot of water and wondering if I'd even be able to surface again, no. I slipped into one of those caves and climbed out. The *Freedom* requires repairs, and I need more tools than I had on board. I need to add a few modifications too. I also need my—" he glanced at the mess of papers on the floor, "—letter-purloining co-navigator."

Good. She wasn't going to miss this expedition. "They're from that soldier's satchel. Two were written by his captain. In code. I'm working on the decryption and hoping there'll be some useful clues within."

One side of Rias's mouth quirked upward. "Are those the letters you mentioned being locked in the attic?"

"Yes. Someone's lock-picking lesson came in handy. I—"

A floorboard creaked in the hallway. Tikaya froze. She hadn't locked her door. Anyone could walk right in.

The knob rattled and turned. Rias released her. Tikaya lunged around the bed, hoping to block the view into her room before her visitor came in. She was two steps away when the door opened.

Mother stood there in her nightgown, eyes bleary as she held hands with one of Tikaya's little nieces. "Tikaya, what are you still doing up?" Mother frowned at the lit candles all over the room and the letters littering the floor.

"I couldn't sleep." Tikaya didn't look over her shoulder, not wanting to bring attention to Rias, though he must have hidden somehow. Even sleepy, Mother couldn't miss seeing a six-and-a-half-foot Turgonian standing at the foot of the bed.

"Grammy, I'm *thirsty*," the little girl complained.

Mother allowed the child to tug her away from Tikaya's doorway, but not before frowning and saying, "Blow out those candles and go to bed. And remember what I said. It's best to let it go. For your sake... and all of ours."

"I understand, Mother. Thank you." Tikaya closed the door and locked it this time.

The window opened, and Rias slipped back inside. Raindrops glistened in his black hair. "Ready to sneak out?" he whispered.

"Sounds fun," Tikaya whispered back. Oddly, it was the truth. To think, she'd missed out on such adventures by staying home, being good, and obeying her parents during her teenaged years.

"Are our actions putting your family in danger?" Rias nodded toward the hallway.

Tikaya's sense of having fun evaporated as she considered her mother's parting words. "She said she doesn't know what's going on exactly, just that Father has been tense. And, as I said, he knew about..."

"Perhaps someone is blackmailing him, forcing him to work against us."

Tikaya paused. She hadn't considered that. Maybe her father was acting to protect the family and had little choice but to cooperate. If so, that made his actions at least somewhat less reprehensible in her eyes.

"I'm not sure, but they're not giving me any answers. The answers are out there." She waved toward the ocean.

"Agreed. Do you need help packing anything?"

"No, just give me a moment." While she put the letters and journal in the satchel, Rias added the sword scabbard to the weapons on his belt.

"Do you still have your bow?" he asked.

In the act of blowing out a candle, Tikaya hesitated and rotated her face toward him. "Do you think I'll need... Are we planning to shoot people?" It had been one thing when, in their previous adventure, they'd been fighting for their lives against Nurians who wanted to assassinate her; killing her own people was a different matter.

"People? No. Unless I miss my guess, we'll never see any of your *people*. They don't seem to care to confront a man face-to-face."

A hint of condemnation twisted his lips. A warrior through-and-through, he must find such tactics distasteful. She remembered how much he'd detested the idea of his emperor employing a back-stabbing assassin.

"If they can send a giant octopus against us, a creature far from its native clime," Rias said, "there's no telling what else we might face."

Good point. "My bow's in a shed out back. I can get it on the way out. We'll visit the smokehouse too. It sounds like we'll need a couple of days' worth of supplies." Tikaya grabbed matches and candles and added them to the satchel.

"If we're *given* a couple of days," Rias said.

"You think they may already know you and the submarine survived?"

"You know the capabilities of your practitioners better than I do. I've dealt with shamans and wizards in battle on the seas before, but..." Rias spread his arms, palms up. "It's different when some of the enemy are related to your lady and challenging them outright isn't a possibility."

The floor in the hallway creaked again. Tikaya blew out the last candle, and the room succumbed to darkness. She felt her way to the window and Rias, patting him on the chest. She hoped he knew it was meant to be reassuring and also to thank him for putting up with all of this.

They waited a few moments, until whoever had been in the hallway had gone back to bed, then slipped outside and into the darkness.

Tikaya balanced the bow across the handlebars as she bicycled side-by-side up the coastal road with Rias. Wind gusting in from the sea threatened to hurl them off the gravel and into the weeds. Rain came and went in fits, leaving them drenched and shivering. The cold couldn't compete with the frigid temperatures of the imperial Northern Frontier, but wind and wet clothes certainly didn't make for an enjoyable nighttime ride. She was tempted to suggest staying in one of the plantation's outbuildings until the storm blew past, but knew Rias wouldn't entertain the idea. Pedaling hard, he was forcing a grueling pace. He was certain they didn't have any time to spare. After gathering their initial supplies, they'd stopped only once, to risk sneaking into her grandfather's workshop to retrieve the fine tools Rias needed for repairs.

A hint of predawn light had come to the sky by the time they reached the northern edge of her family's property. Instead of continuing along the road that would take them to the cliffs, Rias veered up a bumpy, dirt drive.

"Wait," Tikaya blurted, dropping her feet to the ground. "Where are you going? That's where the Nurian neighbor lives."

Rias stopped but didn't return to the main road. "I know."

"He's *not* going to want to see you."

"Few people here do." Rias gazed up the dark hillside. It was a small lot, more rocks than vegetation, so it was easy to see the cottage even in the gloom. "I'll feel better going into this if we have the assistance of someone who can sense magic and perhaps use some if we're in a pinch."

"Mee Nar said he was a sailor, didn't he? Not a practitioner. Besides, didn't you say Nurians were the ones responsible for burning down the Pragmatic Mate? Because they were trying to find the *Freedom's* schematics?"

"Yes," Rias said, "I believe Mee Nar knows about that infiltration as well. Perhaps he directed it."

Tikaya almost pitched sideways in surprise. "Then why would you go to him now?"

"Because, if he's a spy, I have information he wants."

"You think he's a *spy*? He's married and expecting a child."

"Spies rarely announce their intent to spy," Rias said dryly. "He probably met the girl and volunteered for the mission, hoping for a long-term placement."

"To watch *my* people? Why?"

"The Nurians, like the Turgonians, have spies around the world to make sure they're not surprised by other nations."

"What can he learn out here?" She waved to the rural home.

"He works in the city, does he not?"

Tikaya didn't know. How did Rias know more about her neighbor than she did?

"Choosing a home out here may have been part of his ruse to appear semi-retired and harmless," he said. "But this location overlooks the shipping lanes and offers proximity to an old, prominent family."

"On what are you basing your suppositions?"

"That he told us he's a warrior, when he's actually a practitioner." Rias tilted his head toward the hill. "If he says no, we'll continue on, but it's worth asking."

Tikaya pedaled after him, but added, "Why do you think he's a practitioner?"

"He probed my mind after we squabbled in your house."

"Like a telepath?"

"Exactly like a telepath. Not a strong one, I suspect, or he could have been in and out without me sensing him, but I think he sought information or, at the least, wanted to read my intent in being there."

Tikaya hadn't sensed that, but then the room had been full of people and she'd been a tad distracted. If Rias was right and *could* somehow convince Mee Nar to help, it might keep them from triggering traps. She was chagrinned that she'd missed whatever had been planted under the dock. A real practitioner would be far more helpful than she in that capacity.

"But if he *is* a spy, shouldn't he be the last person you ask for help? How can you trust him?"

"Because I know what he wants."

They parked their bicycles and climbed the single step to the covered lanai. If nothing else, it was good to get out of the rain for a few minutes. Rias lifted his hand to knock.

Before his knuckles touched wood, Tikaya whispered, "Do you have any parting instructions for me in case he kills you with his mind?"

"If he were that strong a wizard, he wouldn't have attacked me with his bow in your house. But in the event of my death, now or later in the day, I request that you defeat these meddling bureaucrats, uncover the secret they're hiding, stop them from threatening your family, and... send that letter to my parents."

"Is that all?"

"Also—" Rias nudged her shoulder with his, "—I'd like to think that you'd pine eternally, refusing to accept the embrace of another, knowing that he could never measure up to me."

"Well, that's a given." Tikaya squeezed his hand.

Rias knocked on the door.

The small cottage could only have one or two rooms, so it didn't take long for footsteps to sound on the other side. A curtain moved in a window near the door. Tikaya tensed. If Mee Nar saw who was on his stoop, he might greet them with a weapon. Maybe she shouldn't have left the bow on the bicycle. Rias had the sword and pistol on his belt, she reminded herself.

When the door opened, she tensed, but Mee Nar stood there, empty-handed, his black hair down about his shoulders instead of up in a topknot. Though he bore no weapons, tension tightened his face, and his fingers were curled, almost into fists. His wife was nowhere in sight.

"Enemy Chief Fox," he said in Nurian, using his people's name for Rias, though the rest of his words were in Kyattese. "What brings you to my home?" He didn't add, "at this hour," but his gaze did flick toward the dark sky.

"I'm in need of assistance," Rias said. "I thought of you as someone who might be trusted to help."

Mee Nar's jaw sagged. Several seconds passed, and his mouth opened and closed several times before he decided on, "*Why?*"

"You're not Kyattese," Rias said.

Tikaya watched him, wondering if he'd thought through this conversation before knocking on the door. This didn't seem like a particularly compelling argument.

Mee Nar snorted though. "No, no I'm not."

Tikaya had some sense of an understanding passing between them, and, for the first time that she recalled, she wondered what exactly the rest of the world thought of her people. Did the Nurians and Turgonians have some common beliefs?

"What do you want?" Mee Nar asked.

"Someone to come with us for a couple of days and keep an eye out for practitioner attacks while I repair my watercraft and we prepare for a short journey."

Mee Nar twitched in surprise at the mention of practitioners. He opened his mouth, perhaps to deny any personal experience with the

Science, but simply shrugged and let it go. "You are perceptive for a *nik-nik-too*," he said, using the Nurian term for someone who either had never studied the Science or lacked aptitude for it.

"Not perceptive enough to handle Kyattese who wish me and my craft ill."

"Yes... I heard of the explosion. I'd hoped you'd died."

Tikaya almost choked on his bluntness.

Oddly, Rias smiled. "Not enthused at the prospect of having me for a neighbor?"

"No."

"Even if it would give you all sorts of information to send home to your chiefs?"

Mee Nar's eyes narrowed, but he didn't answer the insinuation that he was a spy. Instead, he said, "To assist you, I would have to miss work. I have a wife here with a child on the way. What would you offer in exchange for my help?"

"What would you want?"

Mee Nar considered Rias thoughtfully. "Tell me about this watercraft that is worrying the Kyattese so. It goes underwater, yes?"

Rias nodded, clasped his hands behind his back, and proceeded to describe the *Freedom*. The amount of detail he offered surprised Tikaya, both because she hadn't realized his Kyattese had come along so well in the last few weeks and also because she couldn't believe he was volunteering so much information to a man he'd said was probably an intelligencer.

Mee Nar rubbed his jaw as he listened. "I see why the Kyattese are concerned. Boats like this could be used for spying and sneak attacks. You built weapons into it, yes?"

Interesting—he *did* seem to be fishing for as much information as possible. Unless the man had a secret passion for engineering, maybe Rias was right. A Nurian spy for a neighbor. Tikaya's home certainly had changed a lot in the last few years. Or maybe she just hadn't been paying attention to the world around her.

"Some weapons, yes," Rias said. "For defense. I designed it for science and exploration purposes."

Mee Nar's response was somewhere between a snort and a laugh. "Exploration, yes. No doubt."

"Perhaps informing your chiefs of its existence would cause them to look upon you favorably."

"Perhaps. But if I am to help you, I want more."

"Such as?" Rias asked.

"I want the schematics."

Tikaya snorted. Sure, he did. She didn't know how Rias had known, but he seemed to have guessed correctly.

Hands still clasped behind his back, Rias dropped his chin and studied the threshold. "I must have a moment to consider this."

"Understandable," Mee Nar said.

Surprised he hadn't outright denied the request, Tikaya trailed Rias off the lanai and back to the path where they'd parked the bicycles. He put his back to the house and gazed out at the sea.

"What are you going to do?" Tikaya asked.

"Stand here thoughtfully for a few moments in discussion with you, then agree to give him the schematics."

"Er. Really?"

"It was to be my bargaining tile from the beginning."

Tikaya studied his face. Just when she thought she had him all figured out... "Won't that be seen as a betrayal by your emperor? Aren't you worried the Nurians will use the technology to build submarines of their own and spy upon, or attack, your military? Your former military," she amended and a new thought came to mind. "Or are you doing this to snub the emperor? As revenge for the wrongs he's bestowed upon you?" Even as she spoke the words, she shook her head. That didn't seem like him. Oh, maybe he'd snub the emperor if he got a chance, but to do something that would put soldiers and marines at risk, men who had once served under him...

Rias gazed into the face of her scrutiny. "I intend to send copies of the schematics to the empire as well."

"Oh," Tikaya said, not quite certain she understood. "But they won't be willing to use a Made power source, will they?"

"Perhaps not, but they'll be inspired to work out something else. Just as the Nurians will not have easy access to the Turgonian steel used in the construction. They'll be inspired to work out something else. In the end, decades hence, they'll both have submarines of a sort, and they'll develop methods of detecting each others' submarines and nullifying each others' advantages. Little will change in the end, but perhaps by making the basic schematics freely available, I can avoid seeing more of my hostel rooms burned down."

"Hm, I guess it sounds better than selling the information to the highest bidder."

"Glad I have your heartfelt approval." Rias offered a faint smile.

"Do my people get a copy of the schematics too?"

"It depends on how much they annoy me over the next couple of days. And whether we live long enough for me to write them down."

"They're still in your head only?"

"The final ones, yes." Rias returned to the lanai where Mee Nar leaned against the doorjamb. "I agree to your terms."

"You *do*?" Mee Nar asked. "You must be desperate for my help."

"I trust you would not be in this position if your chiefs did not deem you capable."

Mee Nar's lips flattened at this further insinuation that he was a spy. "I'll need to see the schematics."

"I haven't had a chance to write them down. I will do so when we've completed this mission."

Mee Nar frowned. "This mission where you believe your life is in jeopardy?"

"Yes. I propose you do your best to keep us alive, so that I'm able to write everything down for you."

The frown deepened. "I should demand you do it now."

"We don't have time." Rias eyed the sky, which, though still cloud-filled, had grown lighter since they'd arrived. "The Kyattese will soon know that the *Freedom* and I aren't wrecked on the bottom of their harbor. They may *already* know. Please gather supplies for a couple of days and join us." Rias nodded and headed toward the bicycles without waiting for agreement.

Mee Nar grumbled under his breath, but he went inside, and drawers and cupboard doors banged and thumped as he complied.

CHAPTER 17

TIKAYA SAT ON A MOSTLY dry rock ledge near the mouth of the cave where Rias had docked the submarine. She had the captain's letters and a notepad in her lap, protecting them from intermittent spurts of rain as she worked on the decryption. The worst of the weather had passed, though clouds still hugged the island, gathering around the top of the volcano. Behind her, thuds and bangs drifted out of the cave, evidence of Rias's work. Mee Nar was in there, too, going over every inch of the submarine. He'd already searched the interior and, when last Tikaya had checked, was swimming around on the outside. She tried to ignore the noise and concentrate on her work, though her gaze kept lifting to the sea and the cliffs rising around them. They were north of the mystery basin and the cave they'd visited before, but close enough to make her nervous. If those plotting against Rias knew he was alive, they'd guess to check here. Apparently, Rias hadn't had many choices in how far he could go, though, not with the damage done to his craft, and the cliffs had been a logical place to hide, due to the sheer number of caves. They'd left their bicycles in bushes miles back, specifically so no one heading up the road would guess someone had descended the cliffs nearby.

Tikaya grew entrenched in the decryption work and was startled when someone touched her shoulder.

"How's it going?" Rias asked. Something about his tone, or maybe it was the amused twinkle in his eyes, told her he'd asked more than once.

"Slower than I'd hoped." Tikaya rattled the pages. "If anybody's done a chart on the frequency of vowels and consonants in Middle

Turgonian, I've never seen it, so I'm having to compile that first. It's not the same as in the modern language; the alphabet isn't even entirely the same. It further complicates matters that the ink has faded over time, and it's hard to pick out some of the letters."

"Can I help?" Rias rearranged the sword on his belt, so he could sit beside her. He was barefoot and had removed his shirt, providing an arresting sight that distracted her for a moment. "Is that a no?" Rias handed her a piece of the ham they'd taken from her family's smokehouse.

"Er, no." Tikaya blushed and accepted the offering. It was time for a lunch break apparently, for he had a couple of slices of his own. "Thank you. As for help, I don't know. Unless you want to read some of this aloud to me?" She lifted the journal. "I'm using our randy sailor's diary to create an alphabetic frequency chart, but maybe hearing the language spoken will give me something that I'm not seeing."

Rias took the book, but didn't open it right away. He was peering around the ledge. "Where's your bow?"

"I left it by my pack in the cave. Why?"

"I'll get it for you when I head back in. You should keep it close."

"Are we being prudent or has trouble already found us?"

"It might be nothing, but a shark swam past Mee Nar when he was in the water."

"Oh?" Tikaya asked. "It's true there's no reef around this part of the island, but they don't usually come this close. The surfers hardly ever see them, and that cave is fairly shallow."

Rias nodded. "I wondered if your animal-loving practitioner—or *practitioners*—might be using sea creatures to scout the area."

"If so, they might have our cave pinpointed already."

"Perhaps not. We killed it swiftly." Rias touched the sword.

Tikaya stared at the cave mouth and imagined him leaping from the hatch of the submarine to wrestle with a shark. Distracted by his shirtless state, she hadn't noticed that his trousers and hair were damp. "How did I miss hearing that?"

"You have a knack for channeling intense focus when it's required to solve a problem."

"That's a nice way of saying I was oblivious to my surroundings." As usual.

Rias only smiled and lifted the book. "Do you want to hear any particular passage?"

His eyes crinkled, and Tikaya blushed, remembering the penned details of the physical relationship the sailor had shared with her ancestor. *Aeli's* ancestor, she reminded herself. Having Rias read one of those passages—and there had been a number of them—might be... intriguing under other circumstances, but this wasn't the time.

Tikaya cleared her throat. "No. Actually, I can do it myself. Read the book aloud, that is. It's more important that you finish your work."

"I don't know about that. I want to know what's in those letters. That basin out there, if it is indeed there, is large. It'd be nice to have a clue as to where to look to find... whatever it is we're searching for. I have a vague notion that there's a seven-hundred-year-old wreck down there and that those three-hundred-year-old treasure hunters managed to pull some secret off of it, something important enough that your government has been leaning on mapmakers ever since, so that there's no evidence that the basin even exists."

"I know." After finding all those bones in that cave, Tikaya had the same notions. "I'll finish with these." She waved the letters. "If the information is there, I'll find it. Before you're ready to sail out."

"I know you will." He gave her an appreciative smile, one that promised he had faith in her skills and that also warmed her heart—and a little more. She caught herself holding his gaze, admiring the gold flecks in his brown eyes, growing aware of his half-clothed state, and thinking about how long it had been since—

This time Rias cleared his throat. Instead of giving her back the journal, he flipped it open to read. "A boring passage. Perhaps that would be wise, don't you think?"

"At least until we've finished here," Tikaya whispered, a touch breathless.

"Oh, yes, I remember this one. His attempt at a poem describing the clouds as seen during his watch in the crow's nest. This fellow didn't have the Turgonian warrior's heart, which is I suppose why he let some irate husband kill him. Oh, wait, the poem is in Old Turgonian, isn't it?" Rias tapped the page. "I better read a sample of the then-modern tongue, eh?"

"Wait." Tikaya placed a hand on the journal to keep him from turning the page. "I'd forgotten about that poem. Was he just trying to capture some nostalgic feeling of the olden days, or was there a reason why he switched to that tongue? The history books say your language changed fairly rapidly, linguistically speaking, from Old to Middle over about a hundred and fifty years, as your people spread out, adopting new words and even switching the verb-subject orderings to that of one of the civilizations they encountered. By the time these letters were written, Middle Turgonian was well-established. But maybe..."

Rias seemed to track her musings, for he said, "I don't know about the transition from Old to Middle, but Middle was maintained for academic and formal military writings long after modern-day Turgonian had been adopted by the common man. As a boy at the university, I had to fumble through a couple of mathematics treatises written in Middle Turgonian by a stodgy old professor who refused to update his work, claiming the ideas were clearer when explained in their... I'm boring you, I can see."

Tikaya had turned her eyes toward the letters, but she jerked them back in his direction. "No, not at all. I'm just wondering if it's as simple as that. If it is..." She flipped to a page in her notes. "I need to rework my frequency analysis data, this time for *Old* Turgonian."

Rias chuckled. "I'll leave you to work then."

Before the new ideas could swallow her attention completely, she kissed him and said, "Thank you."

"Starcrest," Mee Nar called from below the ledge. "You have a problem."

"I guess that means the lunch break is over." Rias stood up. "What is it?"

Mee Nar held up a tiny dark nodule. "A tracking device. It was disguised as a rivet."

Rias digested the news without a word, his face a mask.

"I'm sorry," Tikaya told him. "I didn't sense anything like that when I checked. If it'd been on the inside, maybe..."

"I missed it, too, and I actually swam around out there. It's not your fault." Rias touched the back of her head before hopping down from the ledge.

"It's good work." Mee Nar dropped the tiny device into his hand. "Very subtle."

"How do I disable it?" Rias asked.

"I can show you the sophisticated way we do it in Nuria."

Rias handed the device back to him. "Go ahead."

Though Tikaya was eager to get back to the letters, she watched the exchange, her curiosity piqued. Mee Nar dropped to one knee, placed the fake rivet on the rock, pulled a sturdy knife from a belt sheath, and smashed the device with the hilt. A tiny spark flew out, but nothing more serious happened. He held up the flattened device for inspection.

"Interesting," Rias said. "That's how we do it in Turgonia too."

"Perhaps your two nations have more in common than you thought," Tikaya said.

The two men shared edged smiles.

"Let's get back to work," Rias said. "We may have less time than ever."

He and Mee Nar disappeared into the cave, and Tikaya hunched over the letters, determined to do her part.

Tikaya smiled as she worked on the last paragraph of the second letter, though she caught herself squinting and leaning closer to the page. The light was fading anyway, thanks to the sun dropping behind the volcano. She'd have to find a candle soon, but maybe she could finish in time... She was almost done. Old Turgonian, who would have thought? Once she'd figured that out, she'd made quick work of the basic route cipher. The letters confirmed that there were wrecked Turgonian ships in a basin a half a mile away from the cliffs, the same area now missing on the maps, and the last paragraph looked like it might hold more detailed instructions for finding the spot.

With her new key balanced on one leg, the letter on the other, and her journal in her lap, Tikaya almost failed to notice the warning tingle that flicked at the back of her neck. She jerked her head up and lunged for the bow Rias had set beside her.

Expecting an attack to come from the water, she stood up and checked in that direction first. The waves lapped at her ledge, and it alarmed her to see how high the tide had come in while she hadn't been paying attention. Another half an hour, and a wave might have swooped over her ledge and stolen all her work.

Tikaya shook her head. Not important now. What had twanged her senses? She didn't see anything in the water. She froze. Rias. What if something was about to attack them?

Bow in hand, she whirled, intending to leap into the cave to warn him, but an ear-splitting screech sounded behind her. She fumbled and almost dropped her weapon. She spun around, anticipating an attack at the back of her head—that cry had been *right* behind her. A huge white-chested hawk leaped from the ledge, stirring Tikaya's hair with its great wing flaps. At first, she thought it meant to attack her, but it flew away from her. With something clenched in its talons.

The letters. Ugh.

"Rias!" Tikaya shouted, but what could he do?

She snatched an arrow from the quiver, nocked it, and lined up the shot. Steady, she told herself. The hawk was heading for the cliff tops. She'd only get one shot...

Tikaya adjusted her aim for the wind and its movement, then released the arrow. It spun away, and she held her breath.

The arrow caught the hawk in the chest, halting its wing flapping. Tikaya's feeling of triumph only lasted a moment, for the bird plummeted, falling into the water a hundred meters away.

"Blighted banyan trees," she snarled. For lack of any better options, she took note of the cliff features near the hawk, dropped her bow, kicked off her sandals, held her spectacles to her face, and dove into the water. She wasn't going to lose those letters before she finished decoding them.

Tikaya plowed through the waves, her head up as she paddled, trying to keep the dead hawk in sight—and her spectacles on her face. Water ran down the lenses, adding to the difficulty of seeing anything. She didn't think the body would sink, but the current might carry it out into the sea. Or, if it'd released the letters as it fell... Wet paper *would* sink.

Tikaya swam faster. A wave washed into her face, almost knocking off her spectacles. Cursing again, she readjusted them. If she lost them, she might not find her way back to the cave and Rias. Or if there were other creatures out there, ready to thwart her efforts, they might attack before she reached land again. Had Rias heard her shout? She'd hate to need rescuing, but sure hoped he was available for the job if required.

When she thought she'd reached the right spot, she treaded water, trying to kick up high enough to see over the waves all about her. A quick flash of green caught her eye. The fletching on her arrow. Tikaya paddled in that direction and was relieved to see the bird still attached to that arrow. She grabbed the end of it and lifted the dead creature, surprised by how lightweight the huge hawk proved. She almost sobbed in relief when she spotted the letters still clenched in its talons. Prying them out proved challenging, especially since they were soggy and she didn't want to tear them, and she tried not to feel uncomfortable over the fact that she was mauling some dead bird in the process. Finally, she pulled the pages free. She released the hawk and searched the cliffs, alarmingly distant now, trying to pick out their cave in the deepening shadows.

Through the water droplets spattering her spectacles, she spotted a dark figure waving. Tikaya waved back and paddled toward Rias, the soggy letters clutched in one hand. She was going to feel like a fool if they were too damaged to read by the time she returned.

She had to fight the current on the way back, and her arms and legs burned from the effort, but she reached the ledge. Mee Nar had joined Rias, and they helped her out of the water. Candlelight came from inside the cave. Time to move inside to finish her decryption efforts.

"What were you..." Mee Nar started, then spotted the limp letters.

"Did it attack you?" Rias asked.

"No, it just wanted my work. Completely unacceptable." Tikaya snatched up the key and her notes—at least *they* were still there—and stalked past the men. "Watch my back while I finish, please."

"Yes, ma'am."

Rias picked up her bow and quiver and trotted inside after her. Tikaya went straight to one of three lanterns on the ledge beside the *Freedom*, dropped to her knees, and spread out the letters. Fortunately, the old ink was indelible at this point and hadn't faded after the immersion, but she struggled to lay out the pages without ripping them. Too bad the Turgonians hadn't been using vellum any more by then.

The men stopped behind her and spoke in soft tones. She barely heard them. She was even less aware of her own shivering as water dripped from her chin and onto the stone ledge. Only when she sat up did she realized Rias had draped a blanket around her shoulders. She clutched it about her wet dress with one hand and lifted her paper with the translation in the other.

Mee Nar was standing guard by the cave mouth, crouching on a boulder that remained out of the water. With the tide in, the ledges on either side of the pool where the *Freedom* floated were scant. She noticed that Rias hadn't bothered to bring along the top portion that had allowed it to look like a ship. Perhaps it lay at the bottom of the harbor. The long, sleek cylinder that remained resembled no craft Tikaya had ever seen.

"I don't know if you heard Mee Nar," Rias said, "but he apologized for not sensing the bird's approach until too late. He said he was focused on the water and the cliffs above us, and the hawk barely registered."

"I understand. It's fine."

"He's also been trying to find where the practitioners are hiding to launch these attacks. If he locates them..." Rias set his jaw. "I'll visit them personally."

Tikaya pulled the blanket tighter. "Better to find what they're hiding rather than risk a confrontation where people could be injured."

"After all this, *injuries* aren't what I had in mind."

Tikaya couldn't blame him. Still, she'd prefer to avoid bloodshed. If there was any chance that, after this was all over, she'd be allowed to step foot on the island again, killing people would crush it. "If we dig out their secret, it might take the fight out of them."

"Or it might convince them to increase their efforts to kill us to permanently silence us," Rias said.

"Turgonians are a pessimistic sort, aren't they?"

"I believe paranoid is the word you've used previously." Rias nodded to the paper clenched in her hand. "Was there anything useful?"

Tikaya brightened. "Oh, yes. Nothing explains exactly *what* led our three-hundred-year-old treasure hunters to the Kyatt Islands, but they were convinced they'd find signs of their lost colony here. I got the impression that they'd gone back to study the logbooks that remained from the other colony ships, found dates for the storm that took them off course, and compared them to the departure dates and prevailing winds and currents to figure out..." She caught Rias eyeing the hatch of the submarine, and blushed. "Sorry, you're probably not interested in that part."

"Oh, no, I like it when you include all the details," Rias said. "It makes me feel less bad about babbling about my own interests. I was listening and being impressed that these treasure-hunters went to such lengths. They must have had..."

"Someone like you on board?" Tikaya smiled.

"Sounds more like a research specialist." He nodded at her.

"Regardless of the how, they found evidence of a single wrecked ship that they believed had been attempting to sail away from the island."

"Away? That suggests some likely routes." Rias gazed toward the cave mouth. Darkness had fallen outside, but he was probably picturing the topographical and bathymetric layouts in his head. "No longitude or latitude recordings, I suppose?"

"I don't think they were that precise back then. I know my people were navigating by the stars. Wayfinding, they called it. But..." Tikaya tapped the last paragraph of her notes. "The captain wanted others to find the wreck, so he left very precise descriptions of the landmarks in sight and the sunken ship's distance from the cliffs. It's supposedly a half a league due east of a butte with a fissure splitting it in the middle."

"He *wanted* others to find it?" Rias asked. "Why would a treasure hunter share the location of his find?"

"The short answer is that his crew couldn't reach it. With utter luck—ropes and hooks—they pulled up a few pieces of the old ship, but they estimated it to be two hundred meters down. They didn't have diving suits back then—and I don't think there are even any diving suits today that allow people to go that deep, are there?"

"Not even close," Rias said. "My people have suits that require a sea-to-surface connection, a tube through which air is pumped down. I've heard the Nurians have used magic to create self-contained suits, but nothing that can withstand the pressures at that depth."

"Can the *Freedom* go that deep?"

Rias blew out a slow breath. "If it's two hundred meters, yes. If it's much more than that..." He lifted a shoulder. "When I started all this, I was simply thinking of a vessel that could sail a couple of dozen meters below the surface and avoid the prying eyes of Nurians in their crow's nests. I figured most wrecks we'd want to investigate would be in coastal waters and not too deep." Rias stuck his hands in his pockets and eyed the submarine glumly.

Tikaya gripped his forearm. "It's a wonderful craft, Rias. I'd certainly prefer to spend more time on the surface than below it. Sunsets and starlit skies are far more romantic than the dark depths of the ocean."

He smiled faintly, though still seemed disappointed in himself. "We may be able to reach it. We'll see how exact those old measurements were. So the captain sent word to Turgonia to ask for help in recovering the wreck?" His eyes shifted upward thoughtfully. "I'm not sure we had salvage ships capable of pulling craft up from such depths back then—even today, they usually use divers to set the hooks—but the captain might simply have been hoping."

"The treasure hunters were also pressed for time. They were having trouble with my government, due to the months they spent sailing around our waters. It was done in secret in the beginning, though my people eventually figured out they were out there and objected to their presence. According to the letter, the captain made up a story about how they were pursuing pirates that had sailed into Kyattese waters and disappeared, but he feared the Kyattese had stopped believing the ruse and that he had limited time. He specifically states that they seemed agitated about the explorations."

"And these letters were never mailed," Rias said, "suggesting the entire crew might have disappeared shortly after. Our lovelorn sailor may have fallen to one of your irate ancestors, but what of the rest? Attacked by a giant octopus? Or, I suppose for a ship their size, a kraken might have been more likely."

Tikaya had a hard time believing her people had simply made an entire ship of treasure hunters disappear, but admitted, "Animal mastery has long been a skill my people have had." She thought about the fact that the hawk's attack meant someone knew exactly where she and Rias—and the *Freedom*—were now. "There's one more thing. The last lines of the last letter read, 'The Kyattese are hiding more than a wrecked ship. I suggest you bring the fleet for a full investigation.'"

Rias gazed into her eyes. "Are you sure you should be sharing your findings so openly with me?"

The question surprised Tikaya. At this point, they were surely in this together. "Why do you ask? Are *you* planning to send an encrypted letter to someone back in Turgonia?"

"I don't know. It depends on what we find and how it affects the empire."

"I can't imagine it'd be anything that would endanger anyone, not after all this time."

"Hm," Rias said neutrally.

Tikaya chewed on her lip, wishing he hadn't raised the issue. Now she wouldn't be able to put it out of her mind. He might not have any loyalty to his emperor any more, but he'd admitted more than once that he still cared for Turgonia—his family and countless old friends lived there. What if whatever they found forced them to choose sides? And her side ended up being different from Rias's?

"I'm going down there," he said. "Are you certain you still wish to accompany me? Even if it means... we may have a tough decision to make?" He must have been thinking thoughts similar to hers. "You may be seen as someone who's betraying your people if you reveal these long-held secrets."

"I've been made aware of that repeatedly, yes," Tikaya said, "but whatever group is protecting these secrets has come close to killing me right along with you, so I don't think they deserve my loyalty. I wouldn't do anything to harm my people, but... after all this, I *have* to know what's down there. I don't know that backing away at this point would protect me or make me any less of a traitor in these people's eyes. And if they *are* blackmailing my father or threatening my family..."

Rias pulled her into a hug. "Let's see what's down there before we worry about this further. A few more hours, and I'll be finished with—"

"Something approaches," Mee Nar called from the cave entrance.

"Or maybe I'm finished now," Rias said.

A high-pitched animal squeal raised the hairs on Tikaya's arms. She'd gone with her brothers on hunts often enough to recognize it, and, by the time Mee Nar jumped into the air, leaping over something, she'd grabbed her bow.

Rias had his weapons out too, the sword in one hand, the pistol in the other. He fired before she caught sight of the javelina. The *first* javelina. Others stampeded into the cave, racing through the shadows, straight toward Rias and Tikaya.

The darkness made it hard to pick out more than blurry bodies with glimpses of dark, bristly fur, beady eyes, and sharp yellow tusks. Tikaya nocked an arrow with hands steadier than she expected. She'd faced wild pigs before, at least. Albeit not in such tight quarters.

A gunshot rang out, the noise deafening as it echoed from the cave walls. One animal flopped over, but the rest of the herd continued toward them, eight, no ten powerful javelinas.

"Get on the boat," Rias said.

Tikaya loosed an arrow, then leaped onto the *Freedom*. The top of the submarine wasn't meant for walking on, not like the deck had been, and she almost slipped into the water on the far side. Being up there might not protect them anyway. A three-foot gap stretched between the craft and the ledge, but, as far as she knew, javelinas had no trouble swimming.

As if to reinforce her thoughts, a squeal rent the air right behind her. Tikaya spun back toward the ledge. She hadn't had time to nock another arrow yet. Rias leaped the gap, stabbing down into a swimming pig's back while he was midair. The creature squealed and disappeared beneath the surface as Rias landed beside her. Other javelinas surged toward them. Tikaya shot another arrow, taking a swimming pig between the eyes.

She glanced about, trying to find Mee Nar, but full night had fallen, leaving more shadows than light. One of the creatures kicked over one of the lanterns as it raced off the ledge and into the water, further dimming the cave. Tikaya hoped the rest of them weren't smart enough to figure that out. Fighting them in the dark would be impossible.

Beside her, Rias's sword sliced down, hacking into a brawny javelina's neck as it tried to climb the slick side of the submarine to reach the top. The sword stuck, and he had to kick the creature free with his boot. Two more animals climbed over the sinking pig, eager to take its place.

"How many *are* there?" Tikaya yelled, struggling to pick out another target in the poor illumination.

Light flared, almost blinding in its intensity. A gout of flame burst across the ledge, angling into the water at Tikaya's feet. A bevy of squeals assailed her ears, even as the smell of singed flesh invaded her nostrils. Not stopping to question the help, she used the light of the conflagration to pick out new targets, firing three arrows in rapid succession. Rias put his sword to quick work, ending the lives of the creatures writhing in pain from the fire.

The flames died out, leaving dead javelinas on the ledge and more blackened bodies floating in the water. None of the creatures moved.

Tikaya checked her quiver to avoid looking at the carnage. She was beginning to share Rias's desire to find the practitioner, or practitioners, responsible for this and end the battle in a more direct manner.

"Just a retired sailor, eh?" Rias asked Mee Nar who was picking his way around bodies toward the *Freedom*.

"One acquires a few skills when one isn't busy swabbing the deck and trimming the sails." Mee Nar pointed toward the sea beyond the cave mouth. "There are lights out there. A ship I'm assuming."

Tikaya lowered her bow. "Were the javelinas just a distraction? To give the ship time to find us?"

"They're not approaching the cave," Mee Nar said. "They're waiting out there."

"North of here? About a half a league offshore, straight out from the butte with the split in the middle?" Rias asked, giving Tikaya a significant look.

"It's hard to tell at night, but that sounds about right," Mee Nar said.

Rias fished a spyglass out of his pocket. "Wait here." He hopped onto the ledge and trotted out of the cave.

"Will he use his underwater boat to attack them?" Mee Nar asked.

Tikaya had been about to jump back to the ledge herself, but she froze, alarmed at the thought of Rias's torpedoes slamming into the side of a Kyattese ship. "I don't think so. I..."

"I saw he has a lot of ordnance in there," Mee Nar said.

Thus far, Rias had been acting defensively, but what if they'd pushed him too far? Could she blame him if he chose to attack the people who had tried to blow his craft—and *him*—into countless pieces?

"We've had to fight some underwater creatures," Tikaya said. "It might simply be for them." Though... if Rias had added a switch to more easily run an electrical charge through the hull, that ought to be all the submarine needed to defend against enthusiastic aquatic huggers.

Mee Nar waved at the cave entrance. "I'll have to leave if he chooses to attack. As much as I'd like to deliver those schematics to my superiors, I wouldn't be able to continue to operate here if I openly sided with Starcrest." He grimaced. "I'm not even sure my people would let me come home if they learned I'd openly sided with Starcrest."

"He's not going to attack anyone," Tikaya said. She hoped the statement was true.

Rias ran back inside, bounding over javelina bodies so quickly that Tikaya slid out an arrow, her gaze darting toward the entrance. She expected some rabid animal to race in on his heels, but nothing came.

"If you're coming with me, get in," Rias barked. "We're going down." He untied the *Freedom*, leaped onto its hull, and spun the wheel to open the hatch.

"What's happening?" Tikaya scrambled toward him.

"Do you intend to attack that ship?" Mee Nar asked.

"I haven't decided yet. They're dropping glowing orbs over the side. Explosives is my guess."

"To destroy the evidence?" Tikaya asked. "Or do they think we're already down there and want to hit us?"

"Both goals are likely." Rias hopped through the hatchway.

"Why do I have a feeling this isn't going to go well?" Tikaya muttered.

CHAPTER 18

TIKAYA DROPPED HER BOW AND quiver into the submarine, though she couldn't imagine having a use for them inside, then climbed down herself. A dozen questions threatened to spill from her lips. Like Mee Nar, she couldn't see being a part of this if Rias meant to take actions that could result in deaths. But she couldn't pass up the chance to see what was down there either, not after weeks of digging into this mystery. For the moment, she kept her mouth shut. She'd stop Rias if he intended to do more than scare the people out there with warning shots.

She lifted a hand, intending to pull the hatch shut, but Mee Nar dropped in beside her.

"I'm sure I'll regret this," he said. "No, I'm *already* regretting this."

Tikaya wouldn't have minded if he'd stayed behind—her people might be even more distressed to find out that Nurians as well as Turgonians were snooping into their past—but she and Rias might need Mee Nar's help. She doubted mundane Kyattese technology could produce an explosive device that would drop hundreds of meters into the water and detonate. No, they'd be facing some practitioner's deadly work down there.

"Close the hatch," Rias ordered from navigation. He'd already started the engine.

Tikaya secured the hatch, then perched on the seat next to his. Mee Nar, wandering through the craft and muttering to himself in Nurian, was slower to join them. By the time he reached navigation, Rias had already steered them out of the cave. He flipped the switches to fill the ballast tanks with water.

"We're going under?" Mee Nar squeaked. He cleared his throat and said, in a more normal register, "I mean, don't you want to get a close up look at that ship first?"

"We'll get a look soon enough," Rias said.

Outside the front porthole, dark water replaced the view of the waves.

"Oh." Mee Nar clenched an overhead beam with a firmer grip than the ride required.

Tikaya admitted a bit of pleasure, or at least mollification, that a Nurian warrior and practitioner who had spent countless years at sea was more nervous than she had been when it came to diving beneath the surface in a submarine. Of course, he might simply know more about what they were about to face. That thought was sobering.

"What are you planning?" Tikaya asked, concerned about the grim expression on Rias's face.

"To get close enough to determine if they *are* dropping explosives."

"And if they are?" she asked.

"Disable their ship to encourage them to stop."

Already on the edge of her chair, Tikaya shifted uneasily. "By shooting at them? Is there a way to disable them without causing casualties?"

"It's a wooden sailing ship, so not likely. There's no engine I can target, so I may have to inflict substantial damage to incapacitate them."

"Rias... we can't do this. We don't even know for sure what's down there and if it's worth this."

"One torpedo may be enough to make them hesitate, giving us a chance to go down. They won't have a target if they're of a mind to shoot back, and they won't know if we're near or far with more weapons."

"Rias," Tikaya repeated. "We need to know what we're protecting before we take action that could kill people."

He turned in his seat, seeming calm and reasonable, but determined as well. "I don't want to attack your people any more than you do, but we're *not* going down there to investigate if someone's dropping charges all around us. Octopuses and water pressure, we can withstand, but not explosives dropped on our heads."

Mee Nar cleared his throat. "If they are Made devices, I should be able to sense them as they approach. I can give you directions so you can avoid them."

"And if they hit the wreck and destroy it before we get a chance to investigate?" Rias asked.

"We have to risk it," Tikaya said.

He'd already turned back to the controls, and he flicked on the underwater lamp. The submarine surged forward, toward the Kyattese ship, Tikaya feared.

"All right," Rias said, "but let's give them something to think about before we go down."

"Something to think about?" Tikaya asked. "Like a cannonball down the gullet?"

"Technically, we have torpedoes, not cannonballs," Rias said.

Mee Nar frowned.

"Neither is acceptable, Rias," Tikaya whispered harshly.

A few long seconds passed, and she couldn't tell if he was mulling over alternatives or simply refusing to reply because he knew she wouldn't like his answer. Finally, he tilted his head thoughtfully and met her eyes.

"Did you have a chance to familiarize yourself with the tools in the science station?"

"I looked at them when I was seeking octopus-fighting inspiration," Tikaya said, "but I didn't try any of them."

"There's a cutting tool. Why don't you go make friends with it?"

Tikaya's first thought was that he wanted her out of navigation so he wouldn't have to explain his actions to her, but a hint of a smile had found its way onto his lips. A mischievous smile.

"What do you want me to cut?" she asked.

"I designed it for boring into the hulls of wrecks, figuring that we might encounter old vessels with archaeologically significant items inside. Of course, I was imagining us traveling to remote and exotic parts of the world to find these items, not into the water a few miles down the beach from your parents' house, but regardless, that tool may prove useful now." Rias's smile widened. "I imagine your people will have a hard time focusing on hurling charges over the railing when their ship is in danger of sinking."

"You want to drill a hole in their hull?" Tikaya asked.

"Actually, I thought you might handle that. It'll take some tricky maneuvering to slip in close enough for the tool to reach the hull without bumping into the ship and alerting the Kyattese to our presence. You seemed uncomfortable the last time you were in charge of navigation."

Mee Nar gave her a startled look, as if surprised she'd been allowed to touch the submarine's controls.

"It's not my fault you still haven't given me proper instruction in that regard," Tikaya said.

"Soon." Rias pointed behind her, toward the science station. "You'll do it?"

She supposed it was a better option than watching a torpedo burst through the hull of her people's ship. "How *big* of a hole?"

Rias paused, and she imagined him running an equation in his head, then held up his hands to form a circle in the air. "One they'll notice, but that they should be able to patch before they get into too much trouble. And while they're making repairs, we'll go exploring."

As Tikaya headed back to her new station, she caught a comment from Mee Nar. "Depending on the skills of the practitioners aboard and what they're focusing on, they may notice our presence no matter how careful you are not to bump the ship."

"Perhaps you can give those practitioners something else to think about?" Rias suggested.

"You want me to get into their heads? I had some rudimentary instruction in that area, but telepathy isn't my strength. I'm sure they'd sense me meddling. I'm best at offensive attacks, flamboyant ones in particular. It's what impresses my people."

"Yes, my ships were on the receiving end of some of those fireballs," Rias said dryly. "We're almost there. If there's something you can think of to help—even if it's only to give me a warning that they know we're here—I'd appreciate it."

Here? Already? Tikaya opened the hatch and slipped into the tiny science station. A lamp outside the porthole was already on, and she peered into the water, wondering if they were close enough yet to see the Kyattese ship.

A distant boom reached her ears. Though she didn't see a flash of light or feel the effects of a shock wave, Tikaya assumed the sound meant Rias was right; her people were dropping explosives. That boom must have come from deep down, too. What if she and Rias were already too late?

A shark swam into view, one beady eye visible above a partially open mouth that revealed rows of sharp teeth. Coincidence, Tikaya told herself when it disappeared from sight. Something bumped against the submarine, and she gripped the desk with both hands. Maybe she'd been wrong.

"Company?" she called.

Another shark drifted past.

"Yes," Rias responded. "The water around their ship is teaming with sharks."

"I noticed. Do my people know we're here?"

Rias and Mee Nar conferred in a low tone.

Tikaya leaned close to the porthole, this time peering above them, figuring Rias would come in from below, but she didn't see anything. He would probably cut out the lamps when they drew near. That would make sawing holes difficult. She sat down. Yes, familiarizing herself with the tools ahead of time would be a good idea.

"It may not be a practitioner, but simply the carnage that's attracting the sharks," Rias called. "We've seen dead fish and other creatures floating up. I'm sure those explosives are doing damage to the sea life down there. A brutal tactic, given your people's peaceful reputation."

Tikaya grimaced. She knew he wasn't judging *her*, but she couldn't help but identify with those making these choices. How not? As far as she knew, they weren't rogues or foreigners; they were operating with the full knowledge of key members of her government. They represented her people, her country, and... her. "Yes, it is," she said. Then, compelled to make an excuse for them, she added, "They must be desperate."

"We're going in," Rias said. "We're about thirty feet down right now, and I don't want our light to be visible to someone looking overboard, so I'm turning off the lamps. When we're under them, I'll risk turning yours back on so you can see."

"Understood."

Hardly feeling ready for the task, Tikaya found levers that controlled the pair of articulating arms she'd briefly explored during their last trip. A soft click sounded as something on the outside opened, and the "arms" unfolded to stick out into the water. One of the sturdy, black-painted implements held a claw with pincers that could open, close, and rotate to grip things. The other held the cutting tool Rias had mentioned. Tiny serrated teeth circled a long, cylindrical blade with an oval tip.

The outside lamp winked out, and darkness interrupted her assessment of the implements. Even the interior lighting seemed to dim. Tikaya could do little but wait. The *Freedom's* engine was quiet, even at full speed, but she sensed the craft slowing down.

"We're under them," Rias said, his voice lower than before, as if he feared those on the ship might hear him.

Tikaya doubted that could happen, but she found herself answering in kind anyway. "I need a little light to see what I'm doing."

Before she'd finished speaking, a faint illumination grew outside. Rows of dark green boards came into view, not a foot from Tikaya's porthole. Knowing they might not have much time, she extended the saw. The tip touched the wood but didn't do anything. She eyed the controls, trying to figure out how to move it back and forth or up and down, something that would cause the teeth to bite into the wood.

"Rias?" she asked.

"Under the desk." Soft footfalls approached her station, and Rias appeared at her shoulder. He pointed at a switch with three different positions. "Those move the teeth at different speeds. The energy orb powers it. You just direct the blade."

"Thank you. Is it—"

"Starcrest," came a strained whisper from the front.

"Never mind, I'll figure it out," Tikaya said.

Rias squeezed her shoulder and jogged back to the front.

Tikaya fiddled with the switch. Outside, the serrated teeth started spinning around the blade. The submarine had drifted a foot away from the ship, and she had to extend the arm farther before the tool touched the hull. It bit in with impressive speed and power, and almost immediately she felt the give as it pierced through the board to the other side. Moving the blade to cut out a circle was harder than piercing the original hole had been, especially given the length of the arm and the fact that the ship kept floating in and out of reach. She could feel Rias trying to keep close without bumping the wooden hull, and knew he was doing the best job that he could.

Gradually her crooked line took on the dimensions of a half circle. A little longer, and she ought to be able to—

Something slammed into the submarine. The force threw Tikaya backward in her chair, and the cutting blade was torn from the hole.

"Company," Rias called.

"They know we're down here," Mee Nar added.

"I guessed that." Trusting they'd handle the "company," Tikaya leaned back toward the porthole, her hands gripping the tool controls.

Just as the blade found the hull again, a shark rammed into the articulating arm. Startled, Tikaya almost fell out of her chair. She pressed her face to the porthole, afraid the strike might have broken the arm. It remained in tact, but, that close to the glass, she spotted dozens—hundreds?—of sharks milling around out there.

"Is the hull electrified?" she asked.

"No, not with you at the tools," Rias said.

Right, the current could probably travel up the metal and into her body. Ouch.

"The sharks shouldn't be able to damage us though," Rias called, then lowered his voice to talk to Mee Nar. "Any idea what they're going to try? Besides sharks?"

Tikaya didn't hear the answer. She directed the tool toward the hole again, hissing when more sharks came in, bumping the arm with their bodies. She took an irritated swipe at one, drawing blood, and it swished its tail and shot away in a streak. Rias's words about the carnage her people were causing came to mind, and she promptly felt guilty.

A couple of clunks sounded. The submarine had eased closer, scraping against the ship's hull. Rias must no longer care if they bumped it. Taking advantage of the nearer target, Tikaya angled the tool in again.

"You're getting it," came Rias's voice, this time from the hatchway. He stepped into the science station. "Good."

"I can handle it," Tikaya said, focusing on the porthole. "You should stay up front."

"I'm experimenting with my extendable clamps. We're attached to them now. Mee Nar's trying to distract their practitioners. He says there are at least four." Rias set a metal object on the desk with a clunk. He unlatched a cabinet door and plucked out something else.

"What are you doing?" Tikaya asked, eyes riveted to her work outside.

"Giving them something to think about."

"More than the leak?" Tongue between her teeth, she guided the saw closer to the start of the circle. Almost there. Another inch and—

A shark's blue wedge face pressed against the porthole. Tikaya gasped. Knowing it couldn't do anything didn't keep that leering face full of teeth from alarming her.

"*Rias*," she said in exasperation. Of course, he couldn't do anything about it either, but he was in the cabin, so he received her complaint. "It's blocking my view."

Rias laughed. "So it is."

Tikaya was about to give him a how-can-you-find-this-amusing glare when her gaze fell upon the cannonball-shaped object on the desk. Welded seams ran around it and a tiny flap stood open while Rias poked around inside with pliers and a screwdriver.

Tikaya stared. She had seen pictures of enemy ordinance during the war, and some of them looked a lot like that. "Is that... a mine?"

"Yes. I've removed the powder charge. I thought I'd see if I could insert it into the hole as a warning. Maybe put a little note in the middle."

"A *note*? Like what? We didn't blow you up this time but we could have?"

"Something of that sort. Just to give them plenty of time to think over their situation."

Something else thumped against the hull.

"Right now, I'm more concerned about *our* situation." Tikaya pointed at the porthole—the shark was still floating right outside.

She angled the cutting tool up to poke the finned intruder. At the first touch, it burst away from the window, but, unlike the first shark, it returned. That huge maw opened and snapped down on the articulating arm.

"Demon-spawned sprites," Tikaya blurted and tried to pull the tool back into its cubby in the hull. The shark refused to let go. It shook its body from side to side, like a dog trying to rip a rope from its master's grip.

Though she feared it was already too late, she grabbed the controls for the second tool. She could barely see with the shark thrashing about in front of the porthole, but she tried to bring the gripping claw in to... She didn't know what she hoped to do. Distract it. More by accident than skill, she jabbed it in the lower belly hard enough to surprise it. The shark's mouth opened long enough for Tikaya to yank the cutting tool back into the hull. She couldn't tell if it'd been mangled beyond use yet, but the blade was still rotating, and it grazed the shark's nose. This time the creature disappeared, leaving only bubbles behind.

"Good work," Rias said, "you got him in the balls. That tool will need repairs, but see if you can slice out that last couple of inches there. That's all we need for now."

"Already on it," Tikaya said, pushing the saw toward the wood again.

Awkward vibrations shook the arm, and the saw lacked the smooth cutting efficiency of before. She struggled, but made progress while Rias finished his modifications to the mine.

"Do sharks actually *have* balls?" Tikaya asked.

"Of course they do, as evinced by its alarm at your precise placement of that grasper."

"I'm sure it was just startled by having something poke its underbelly." Tikaya finished carving the circle—if one could call the lopsided, crooked outline a legitimate geometric shape.

"That wasn't its underbelly." Rias smirked.

"Do you actually *know* how sharks reproduce, or are you simply teasing me?" If Tikaya hadn't been busy with more pressing matters, she would have grabbed that encyclopedia on sea life. Instead, she maneuvered the claw toward the damaged hull, hoping she could pull out the wood, rather than punching it in; the sailors would have a harder time making repairs if they had to fashion a plug.

"Sharks reproduce via internal fertilization." Rias knelt and unlocked a tiny hatch underneath the desk. He placed the mine inside a cubby, closed the hatch again, and hit a switch beside it. Several clunks sounded, as if the metal ball were being cycled past a number of safety hatches. "The back of a male shark's pelvic fins has a pair of intromittent organs called claspers, which are essentially the same as a mammalian penis." Rias stood back up and made the mistake of meeting Tikaya's eyes—she imagined her brows had climbed into her hairline—and he seemed to remember he was talking to a woman. He blushed and his academic lecture turned a tad shy. "The sharks swim side by side, with the male, uhm, well, it bites the female to get a good grip, and one of the claspers goes in and delivers sperm to the female's, uhm, woman area."

Woman area? Tikaya held back a smirk of her own. "I see. I didn't realize you were so well versed in the reproductive natures of sea creatures."

His blush deepened. "Twenty years at sea, and you learn a few auxiliary tidbits of information. Do you need a hand with that?"

"No, I have it." Tikaya had wedged the tips of the claw around the sides of her circle, and she pulled out the "cork." She glimpsed a dark hold before water flooded in, obscuring the view. Dark was good. It should mean nobody was in there, watching her handiwork. The crew might know a submarine was under them, but they apparently didn't know what it was *doing* yet.

"May I?" Rias waved to the controls.

Tikaya slipped out of the seat. He nudged another switch under the desk, then guided the grasping tool out of view. Soft scrapes and clunks came from the hull. That she heard them made Tikaya aware of the utter quietness around them. Chaos had to have erupted on the Kyattese ship at the first sign of the submarine's approach, but she couldn't hear a thing.

Water started streaming past the porthole. The submarine bumped and drifted, drawing alternately closer and farther from the ship's hull. At first Tikaya thought some vigorous waves had come their way, but then she realized the other ship was moving. Because they were attached, they were going with it.

"They're trying to escape us," Rias said. "We'll let go as soon as..." He leaned closer to the porthole. "Should have included some mirrors so I could see—there."

The claw came back into view, now holding the mine. Rias thrust it through the ragged gap and released it. Tikaya thought she could detect light in the hold now, but the waterline was above the hole, so she couldn't make anything out for certain.

"That ought to keep them busy." Rias pulled the tools back into their compartments in the hull. "Mee Nar, want to release those hooks we put out?" He faced Tikaya. "Ready to go down?"

"Yes, though there's one other thing I'm wondering about."

"I'm absolutely certain the mine is diffused and won't cause harm, yes."

"That's not it." Tikaya propped her fists on her hips.

Concern wrinkled Rias's brow. "What?"

"The male shark *bites* the female? And she *allows* that?"

"Oh," Rias said, though he didn't look like he knew if he was completely off the hook. "Well, it's in the water, you see, and they don't have hands or legs or any other way to, uhm, hold on. Not like we do. Er, we could. If you wanted to... get creative underwater."

"Underwater? Completely? Even that diary doesn't mention that."

"Yes, I suppose one would have to either be quite, ah, swift or have some sort of device for breathing underwater. One could take tanks of compressed air down. There are prototypes in the empire for diving suits like that, though they're terribly awkward and heavy." Rias dropped his chin into his hand and tapped his jaw with one finger. "As I said earlier, they're meant for salvaging wrecks, but I imagine one could come up with a much lighter suit and system for recreational diving."

Tikaya tapped him on the shoulder.

Rias blinked and looked up. "Yes?"

"Did you truly just go from a discussion of sexual positions to designing some new diving prototype in your mind?"

"Er, maybe?"

"You must have mystified your wife," Tikaya said before she thought better of it. He never seemed that distressed when he mentioned how incompatible they'd been, but she would never wish to remind him of painful moments.

"Yes," was all he said. "I've mystified a lot of people with my interests. Fortunately, you seem unfazed." Rias offered his arm and nodded toward the navigation cabin.

"Fortunately," she agreed amiably, taking his arm. The Nurians had even less mundane technology than the Kyattese, so poor Mee Nar was probably being mystified up there himself.

"Just so we're clear," Rias murmured as they headed back up front. "No biting?"

"We'll see."

"We have a problem," Mee Nar called before Rias could respond to her comment.

Mee Nar was pointing at the front porthole when they came in. Sweat gleamed on his brow and his loose shirt stuck to his back. A red sphere floated in the water inches above the *Freedom's* nose.

"Is that one of the explosives?" Tikaya asked.

Rias had already lunged into the primary navigation seat.

"Yes," Mee Nar whispered, his voice strained. "They threw a bunch out as soon as we detached. Most of them didn't come close, but..." He licked his lips.

"I guess they didn't like your mine gift." Tikaya gave Rias a grimace that she hoped portrayed an apology for distracting him with that silly conversation. He gave her a quick headshake, as if to say he was to blame.

"I'm keeping it from dropping farther," Mee Nar continued, "but I can't disarm it, not when it's this close. I don't know if it explodes on impact or on a timer."

"Does this thing go in reverse?" Tikaya asked, trying to remember if Rias had mentioned a control for that. She was fairly certain he'd just driven it forward and used the rudder to turn in a circle when they needed to change directions. With that sphere hovering so close to their nose, there was no way they could go forward. It'd smack right into the porthole and blow up.

Rias flipped the switches that controlled the water-to-air ratio in the ballast tanks. "This *thing* goes down."

"Sorry," Tikaya murmured. Apparently calling an engineer's latest invention a thing wasn't the way to his heart.

The sphere rose out of sight as the submarine descended. Rias nudged the propeller lever, and the vessel glided forward.

"You can release it now," Rias told Mee Nar. "We're not—emperor's balls!" He turned hard to avoid a second sphere, this one dropping into view ahead of them rapidly.

The submarine changed headings faster than a sailing ship, but not nearly as fast as Tikaya would have liked at that moment. Standing behind Rias, she caught herself sinking her fingernails into the back of his chair. Slowly the sphere drifted off to the left of the viewing area, or, rather, they drifted away from it. Only when it dropped out of sight did Tikaya let out a relieved breath.

"That was—"

A boom thundered below them and to the port side. The craft lurched, the deck tilting so hard it almost threw Tikaya off her feet, even with her grip on the chair. Mee Nar tumbled into the bulkhead. Rias's hands never faltered—he rode out the bucking wave and brought the craft back to a horizontal position. His gaze skimmed over the gauges and displays.

"Did that do any damage?" Tikaya asked.

"Nothing that's showing up."

"That wasn't really a no was it?"

"No," Rias said. "Any deficiencies will become clear when we descend to lower depths."

"Because the hull will implode and we'll die?" Tikaya asked.

Mee Nar threw her a wild-eyed look.

"Something like that," Rias said. "Mee Nar, are there any more of those out there? I can't pick up objects that small with my echo ranging device."

"You should come up with a catchier name for it," Tikaya said. It was a stupid thing to say, but somehow it was better than standing there imagining more of those mines dropping onto their heads. Wasn't that the whole reason they'd sneaked in to disable the ship? To avoid this situation?

"Mee Nar," Rias repeated, turning in his chair.

The Nurian was still staring at them, his face pale, his breathing rapid. Maybe the morbid exchange hadn't been wise.

Rias was tall enough to grip the other man's shoulder without standing up. "Mee Nar, you said you could detect the charges around us." His voice was penetrating, and he stared straight into the Nurian's eyes. "We're depending on you here. All of us. And your wife and child will be waiting for you to come home safely."

Mee Nar's stare shifted to Rias's grip. For a moment, he looked like he might pull away and dart off into some hole to hide, but he held out his hands and drew in a big gulp of air. "Yes. Yes, I know. I understand."

"Guide me." There was definitely a tone of command in Rias's voice. He gave Mee Nar a nod and turned back to the controls.

Mee Nar took a few more deep breaths. Tikaya was tempted to offer him a shoulder to lean on, but after Rias's words, he seemed to regain some of his composure. She remembered her own moment, trapped on a Nurian warship, and how she'd almost fallen apart after shooting—*killing*—people and how he'd calmed her down. Strange to think that a veteran warrior would need similar treatment, but she supposed the submarine—and the tons and tons of water above them—presented a unique experience.

"There are none above us dropping." Mee Nar's eyes were closed, and his hands gripped the console as he concentrated. "One is approximately fifteen meters to the starboard."

"Understood." Rias guided them toward the port. "Are there any below us? I want to descend now."

"Not close enough for me to detect. There don't seem to be many left. I think they threw a bunch over the side, hoping to hit us before sailing off to make repairs."

"I'm taking us down then. It won't take them long to recuperate up there."

Mee Nar's gulp was audible, but he nodded. "I'll keep my senses open."

"Thank you," Rias said.

Since Mee Nar seemed content to stand, with a death grip on the console, Tikaya slipped into the seat beside Rias. "How far down are we now?"

Rias glanced at a gauge. "Only thirty meters."

"And we're going down to two hundred?" Tikaya might be sharing some of Mee Nar's claustrophobia in a moment. "It occurs to me that the landmarks in the letter won't be very helpful down here. Are you going to be able to find the wreck?"

"We'll see. I'd say something cocky like I have the map in my head, but I ran into the coral reef on our last excursion, so I better not talk too soon."

"Well, you were distracted by a giant octopus hurling us about."

"My commanding officers never would have accepted such an excuse," Rias said.

"Over the eons, women have learned to be accepting of men's flaws."

Rias gave her a sidelong look. "That must be a Kyattese-only philosophy. I never noticed it amongst imperial women."

Tikaya alternately watched a depth meter and the viewport as they descended. Thanks to nightfall, the water outside had been dark all along, but there was an oppressive, absoluteness to it now. And a stillness. The only sounds came from the soft hum of the engines and from creaks and groans that Tikaya tried not to find alarming. Rias's face gave away nothing.

"How much pressure are we under?" Tikaya asked softly, not wanting to disturb Mee Nar.

Eyes still closed, the Nurian seemed to be taking his task seriously. Maybe he needed the work for a distraction.

"Atmospheric pressure is approximately fourteen point seven pounds per square inch at sea level," Rias said, "and it increases by fourteen point seven psi every thirty-three feet." Rias glanced at the depth meter. "We're nearing two hundred meters, so approximately 291.994 psi."

"Approximately," Tikaya said and smiled.

Rias didn't return the gesture. Maybe he was thinking about all those pounds of pressure on the hull of his craft. Tikaya studied his profile. He wasn't paying attention to the viewport at all; his gaze swung back and forth from the depth meter to the readings on the echo ranging device. Hoping to see a promise of the ocean bottom before they reached the submarine's maximum operating depth? What *was* their maximum operating depth? Rias hadn't told her.

"The last two spheres have blown up," Mee Nar said. "I was tracking their descent."

"It's random then?" Tikaya asked. "When they blow up? Or were they adjusted to a shallower depth to target us?"

"I don't know," Mee Nar said.

Rias didn't acknowledge the Nurian's announcement. As Tikaya watched him, a question floated into her mind. Maybe distracting him wasn't a good idea.

"Have we reached two hundred?" Tikaya asked.

"Yes."

"And no sign of the wreck?"

"No sign of the bottom."

"Oh. I checked the letter twice to make sure of my translation. I'm sure it said two hundred meters."

"I believe you. Their measurements weren't likely accurate." Rias glanced at his gauges. "Two hundred twenty meters."

Tikaya swallowed. She wanted to let him know that it was all right to give up. As much as she desired to know what was down here, she desired to live more. Quiet filled the cabin, creating an eerie sense of solitude, or maybe isolation. If they disappeared down there, never to return to the surface, nobody would ever know what had happened to them. She wished she'd left a note for Mother, instead of simply disappearing into the night.

She could hear Rias's breathing. It remained steady and regular; he'd appear calm to someone who didn't know him well, but she could read the tension in his rigid posture. It warned her of danger in a way his words did not.

"What are you thinking?" Tikaya murmured.

"Among other things? That I regret bringing you down here."

"I would have been annoyed if you'd gone without me."

"There are worse things to be," Rias said.

Like dead. Tikaya didn't say it out loud. Another groan emanated from the hull. The ominous noise was louder than before, she was sure of it. "We can turn back," she said. "Curiosity is only an admirable trait until it gets you killed."

"We can go deeper," Rias said.

Tikaya stood for a better look outside the porthole. The life in the waters outside had dwindled. The sharks had disappeared along with the schools of fish that had flitted through their light earlier. What did swim through the beam of illumination were strange creatures with rows of uneven, bristly teeth and misshapen bodies, nothing she'd seen fishermen selling in the market. In their own ways, the fish were as strange and alien as anything they'd seen in those ancient tunnels in the empire. Like something from another world, a bizarre world that had few commonalities with the one she knew. A bioluminescent squid—at least Tikaya *thought* it was a squid—jetted away at their approach.

She pressed a hand against the hull to lean in for a better look. The icy temperature of the metal numbed her fingers and she pulled them back. It was only then that she noticed the puffs of air in front of her face with each exhalation. She wrapped her arms around her body. Who would have thought she'd need a jacket and mittens off the coast of the Kyatt Islands? She almost made the joke to Rias, but his face was grimmer than ever.

"Mee Nar," Tikaya said, "do you want to watch the porthole in the science station and see if there's anything coming up—or down, as it'd be—in that direction? We must be getting close to the bottom."

"All right," Mee Nar whispered.

Tikaya never would have guessed a Nurian warrior and practitioner could sound so meek. And afraid.

Rias's gaze shifted away from the instruments just long enough to regard Tikaya with knowing eyes. Yes, she wanted to ask her question and she didn't want Mee Nar to know the answer, not when he'd grown so alarmed at the mention of the submarine failing.

"What's the maximum depth the *Freedom* is designed to handle?" Tikaya whispered when they were alone. "I *know* you have an exact number in mind." According to the depth gauge, they'd just dipped below two hundred and fifty meters.

Rias blew out a long breath. "I rate it at a maximum operating depth of two hundred and eighty meters."

A surge of alarm charged through Tikaya's limbs. Dear Akahe, they were almost there already. She struggled to keep her breaths slow and calm, not wanting to fall apart the way Mee Nar had—or worse. "And there's still no sign of the bottom? We have to go back. This isn't worth dying over."

"If the captain's letter said they pulled up something, it couldn't have been much deeper. Their estimates couldn't have been *that* far off."

"How sure are you that we're in the right spot?" Tikaya asked.

"We're in that basin; we would have hit the ocean floor by now if we weren't."

"How deep is the basin?"

Rias didn't answer.

"I know you know. You studied the old maps closely enough to know when the basin turned up missing. You must know its depth."

"Four hundred meters at its deepest, but there's a ridge coming up."

Tikaya glanced at the depth meter and a fresh wave of alarm washed over her. "We're almost to two-seventy-five."

"The ridge is—"

"You said two-eighty was the maximum, right?" Tikaya interrupted, her heart in her throat. "This is insane. Take us back up."

"The maximum operating depth is the depth at which I deem it's safe to operate. The crush depth should be closer to three-twenty-five to three-fifty."

"*Should* be?"

"It *won't* be before three-twenty-five," Rias said. "We crafted the strongest Turgonian steel alloy that's ever been invented for the hull."

How he could have melted that wreck into any semblance of a strong alloy, she couldn't guess, but she wouldn't doubt him when it came to metallurgy.

"So... we should be fine as long as we stay above that point?" Tikaya asked.

He was speaking calmly, but that tension was still in his shoulders. He wasn't telling her something. "On paper, yes, but I haven't tested it anywhere near this deep. If one of the tanks ruptures or there's a mechanical failure or... Emperor's teeth, a thousand different things could go wrong, and if one of them does, and I can't fix it quickly, we can easily drop below crush depth, and the *Freedom* ends up as another wreck on the bottom of the ocean."

Tikaya wished she hadn't goaded the reason for his concern from him. It was obvious as soon as he said it, but she hadn't been thinking of the possibility that they might not be able to return to the surface. She'd imagined them as a balloon being held underwater, just waiting to be released to shoot back up. But they weren't a balloon; they were a couple of frail human beings encased in a steel cylinder. And steel sank. Tikaya found herself imagining what it'd be like to die down here. Would it be like drowning? With water rupturing the hull and rushing in to smother them? Or would their bodies, without the protection of the vessel, implode under such pressure?

She shook her head and banished the unhelpful thoughts. She slid out of her chair, stood behind Rias, and put her hands on his shoulders. "We'll be fine. None of those things will happen."

Rias snorted. "What makes you so sure?"

"You built it."

"Tikaya... I'm not infallible. Trust me."

"Would you be this worried if I weren't here?" she asked, thinking of his comment about regretting bringing her down.

Rias hesitated before admitting, "No."

"And if I were safe on the beach, would you be excited and thrilled to be down here testing it and searching for the wreck and probably going deeper than any human being has ever gone before? Even if it meant risking your life?"

"Maybe."

"I'd be devastated if you died down here while I was sitting up there, braiding my hair, so let's pretend I'm one of your marines right now and nothing else."

"Hm." Rias checked a different gauge—had his range finder finally found the bottom? "I never discussed *biting* with my marines."

"Yes, I understand some of them found that regrettable." Tikaya thought of the letter she'd written to Corporal Agarik's family; she wished she'd posted it and Rias's letter already, in case... Well, the letters were in her room. If she proved incorrect about Rias's infallibility, her mother would find them and take care of the task.

"Tikaya?" Rias asked softly.

"Yes?"

He tugged his gaze away from the instruments and met her eyes. "If we make it out of this, will you marry me?"

"Erp?" It wasn't the most eloquent thing she could have said, but he'd startled her.

"I was going to wait until... to see if there was any chance we could make things work with your family and your people, and to wait until I had established some sort of stability, financially and otherwise, in my life, but plummeting into the ocean depths to unknown dangers makes a man rethink his priorities, and I... I'm talking rather rapidly, aren't I?"

"Yes," Tikaya whispered. "And you should probably be monitoring our descent." What a stupid thing to say. But her heart was thundering against her ribs, and she needed a moment.

"Yes, of course," he murmured, facing the console again.

Tikaya had been imagining—*hoping*—Rias would propose to her one day, but at the same time, she kept thinking that he'd have such a better life if he returned to the empire where he'd have the support of his family and friends, and where he'd be a hero instead of a target for angry Kyattese citizens. How was it anything but selfish of her to ask him to give up all that and stay with her?

"You're not saying anything," Rias observed. "In the world of asking for dates and proposing marriages, that's generally a bad sign."

"I'm wondering if it's fair of me to ask you to choose between Turgonia and me."

Rias glanced at her. "What do you mean?"

"Well, I've talked to Milvet, and I see how you are around the Turgonian expats, or rather how they are around *you*. I believe it'd be feasible for you to return to Turgonia and recruit the men you'd need to take back your lands and force the emperor to return your warrior-caste status to you. You could have everything from your old life again. I feel like it's not fair to ask you to give that up and to force you to try and find a place in a world where everyone wants you dead."

As she spoke, Rias made adjustments at the controls and faced his console, but he kept his ear toward her. "You never asked me to choose between the worlds," he said. "I chose of my own accord. I want to be with you, Tikaya. As for going back to the empire, I suppose if you had some notion of being the wife of a well-to-do warrior-caste gent, I could try to get my lands and title back, but... blood and battlefields, Tikaya, it's *cold* there six months out of the year. Like touch-your-tongue-to-a-lamp-post-and-it'll-be-stuck-there-until-spring cold. Then in the summer, it's so hot, you might as well be working in a smelter. Sure spring and autumn are decent, but they're *short*. I'd much rather stay here and figure out a way to make things work with your people."

Tikaya's jaw drooped open as he spoke. "I—it never occurred to me that you wouldn't want to go back if you could."

"Well, now you know. Think on it, will you, and maybe give me an answer to the other thing, too, eh?"

Tikaya recovered some of her equanimity and leaned against his chair. "I seem to remember you promising that there'd be music, a nice dinner, and candlelight if you ever proposed to me."

"I have some dried fish in the back. As to the rest, it seems I must add to the list of items I forgot to pack. I—" Rias leaned forward and tapped a gauge. "I think we've reached—"

"There's something out there," came Mee Nar's cry from the back.

The hull creaked and groaned again.

"Let's level out while we check it out, shall we?" Tikaya asked. "No need to keep descending, right?"

"Already done." Rias turned toward the starboard.

Their light played over a ridge smeared with brownish plant matter or maybe that was mud. Branches of strange seaweed and mushroom-type growths ran along the sides with wild spicules thrusting from the top. A foot-long piggish creature with numerous short stubby fins, or maybe they were legs, shuffled along the ridge, probing the mud with tentacles. Further along, something that looked like a cross between a crab and a spider hunkered in a dark nook.

"Bizarre," Tikaya whispered, awed by the utter strangeness of the life. "How can anything live down here? I mean, if the pressure is so great that it could crush a steel hull..." She glanced at Rias, feeling a little ashamed by her lack of knowledge. She should have read that marine encyclopedia front to back before this trip.

But Rias didn't seem any more knowledgeable than she. "They must have the same pressure within their bodies as is exerted on them from their environment, though it's admittedly hard to fathom. With their molecules squeezed together so, they'd have reduced fluidity in their—" He shrugged. "I don't know. They've adapted somehow."

"No light makes it this far down either, does it?" Tikaya asked. "We're below the euphotic zone. This is amazing, Rias. As far as I know, nobody has ever been able to study these creatures. The aquatic biology students and professors at the Polytechnic should be lining up to ask you for rides down here, not letting government dullards try to blow up your submarine."

"You're welcome to suggest that to them when we return."

Footsteps clanged on the deck behind them.

"Find the wreck yet?" Mee Nar asked.

"Looking now," Rias said.

"You see those fish out there? Those are the ugliest, strangest I don't even know whats."

"Any sign of explosives from our friends above?" Rias asked.

"I haven't sensed any, or seen any signs that they've exploded down here."

"Maybe the pressure crushed them before they could reach the ocean floor?" Tikaya suggested.

"It seems as if your people would be smart enough to compensate for that," Rias said. "We—wait, got something. There's a big change in the ridge topography ahead." He checked his gauges, then peered through the viewport.

Tikaya pressed her shoulder against his, eager for a glimpse of the wreck. After all these weeks of sneaking about, searching through elusive—and missing—archives, and fighting against invisible foes, she couldn't wait to see the source of all their troubles.

What glided into view, however, was not a ship. It was a crater. Almost hidden by a cloud of silty dirt, a huge concave gap marred the ridge. All the plant life was obliterated, and countless dead fish, squid, and other creatures Tikaya couldn't identify floated about the area. Rocks and pebbles trickled down the sides, leaving little doubt that the crater had just been created.

"I was wondering how powerful those spheres were," Rias muttered.

Tikaya pulled back, sickened by the view. How could her people, people who prided themselves on pursuing peaceful methods, both with other nations *and* with nature, make this choice? She could imagine Turgonians blowing up swaths of the countryside to test new weapons, but not the Kyattese. Her people didn't do such things. They just... didn't. She sat down hard.

Rias had paused the submarine long enough to pull out a scrap of paper. He scribbled an equation on it, then plugged in a few numbers.

"Are you calculating whether one of those spheres would blow us down to the South Pole if it hit?" Tikaya asked.

"Given the dampening effect the water's pressure would have, the explosive potential is... Impressive. I didn't think your people had any weapons like that. They didn't hurl anything with that power at us during the war, unless you made advances during the last year when I was in exile."

Tikaya was sure he didn't mean to condemn her with that "you," but it made her wince anyway. As if she'd been a part of this... "Apparently, my people are making progress."

"Or are only willing to kill sea life and nosy intruders, not attack enemy warships with everything they've got." Rias set aside his paper and took the controls in hand again. "Mee Nar, you're still keeping a magic-seeing eye out for those spheres, right?"

"Yes," Mee Nar said from behind Tikaya. "Your leak must be keeping them busy. I haven't sensed anything new being dropped."

"Good, though we can't count on that lasting long." Rias had nudged the submarine into motion again and was watching the echo ranging display. "Something else is coming up."

This time, Tikaya didn't lean in for a better look. She was afraid they'd find crater upon crater down there.

"I sense something," Mee Nar said.

Rias's hand froze on the control lever. "Dropping from above?"

"It's... No." Mee Nar stood with his eyes closed, chin drooped to his chest. "It's already at our level, and I think... Yes, I'm positive. It's not moving."

"A dud?" Tikaya wondered. "That dropped down but didn't explode?"

"Are we in danger of running into it?" Rias asked.

"I don't think so," Mee Nar said. "It's on the ridge. Or on something on the ridge. Oh, that actually might be what you're looking for."

Tikaya frowned. What did that mean? She poked Rias. "Get closer."

"Weren't you the one telling me to go back up a moment ago?" Rias asked as he guided the submarine farther along the ridge.

"That was at least five moments ago, and you didn't take the opportunity when you had the chance. It's been rescinded."

A deep moan emanated from the hull, and Tikaya's humor disappeared. Mee Nar shifted uneasily too.

"We've reached the end of the ridge," Rias said. "But there's something... Yes, there it is."

Outside of the porthole, a lumpy shape had come into view, its form so covered in centuries of mud and silt that Tikaya wouldn't have identified it, if not for the masts. Even they were obscured by seaweed growing up around them. The ancient ship lay on its side, no holes obvious in its hull, at least not on the half she could see. Unlike modern Turgonian ships, it lacked portholes and spaces through which cannons could fire as well. If there were oar holes—and there should be on a vessel that age—grime had long since covered them up.

Shedding light upon the ship was a six-inch-wide glowing red sphere. It perched on one of the few sections of railing that weren't broken, waiting to explode.

CHAPTER 19

TIKAYA STARED AT THE ORB. She couldn't believe it had landed so precariously without falling off the railing. Or exploding. Yet.

"I hope it *is* a dud," Rias said. "Or it's going to be inconvenient."

Inconvenient? Tikaya thought of the crater they'd passed, and shuddered.

"I wouldn't touch it," Mee Nar said. "It's emitting a lot of power."

"It couldn't have been made to explode on impact." Rias guided the submarine along the wreck, showing them more of the ancient structure, the wood impressively preserved despite all the grime and growth on and around it. "Or it would have done so when it touched down. And then there are the ones above that exploded early in their descent."

"Maybe it's random," Mee Nar said.

Rias took them up and over the ridge so they could see the back side of the wreck. "Is it possible someone is up there controlling when they explode?"

Mee Nar shook his head. "That would take a great deal of concentration, concentration that would have been difficult to maintain given the leak and other excitement that must be going on up above."

"We'll just do our best to avoid it then."

While the men spoke, Tikaya was scouring the wreck with her eyes, searching for the clues that had prompted the treasure hunters to pen letters to the Turgonian military. "There aren't any holes in the hull or on what we can see of the deck. The masts aren't even broken. What caused it to sink?"

"A good question," Rias said. "It shows little damage from the landing too. No debris field around it. That would have been different if it'd landed on top of the ridge, but it looks like it sank into plenty of mud on the side instead." He pointed to the bottom of the hull. "It's about ten feet deep."

"I assume there's no way for us to step outside of this vessel without being crushed," Mee Nar said. "How are we going to get in to look around?"

Rias waved to the back. "The cutting tool wasn't completely destroyed by the shark attack. We should be able to bore a hole in the hull."

"One wide enough for us to pass through?" Tikaya asked. "Would that even be possible? This ship looks to be in better shape than the two-year-old ones in the harbor."

"Yes, from what we've seen so far, it's in pristine condition." Rias slowed the submarine to a stop—they'd circled the wreck and come back to the sphere, which glowed ominously at them, like a guard dog growling at the gate of a junkyard.

Tikaya gave a short laugh. "Are we sure it's the right ship?"

"Oh, yes," Rias said. "That's a colonial era penteconter. I had a model of one as a boy. The oars must be around somewhere, buried under the silt perhaps."

"Time," Mee Nar said.

"You sense something?" Tikaya asked.

"The Kyattese ship is heading back to its position above the wreck."

And above us, Tikaya thought.

"Let's cut into the hull." Rias closed his eyes for a moment. "If my model was historically accurate, the captain's cabin would be forward, on the port side."

"Who's going to do the cutting?" Tikaya feared she already knew the answer to her question, and she eyed the sphere warily.

"You have as much experience as I do at this point," Rias said.

"And rather less experience navigating." Tikaya sighed and headed for the science station again. "Mee Nar, let me know... Give me a warning if you can." She feared that if the sphere fell off the railing, or randomly decided it'd found the right moment to explode, there wouldn't be *time* for a warning.

"I'll try." Mee Nar sounded even less optimistic than she felt.

Tikaya hesitated before maneuvering the claw and cutter out of whatever storage slots Rias had built into the hull. She remembered that he'd been able to get the mine from inside to outside but doubted that would be safe at these depths. "Are you sure these cutters will work down here? Can I grab something with the claw?" Would there even be anything in there to grab? What if the pressure had destroyed whatever evidence existed inside that hull?

"The tools should work—I had my helper make them sturdy, and we didn't use anything that'll contract or expand," Rias called back. "But don't open that hatch to bring anything inside. There's an airlock, and it should technically work, but if you find something just hold onto it with the pincer, and we'll go back to the surface to—"

Mee Nar interrupted him. Tikaya couldn't hear what he said, but she could guess. The Kyattese ship was up to something.

She slid the cutting tool out of its cubbyhole. It took more effort to move it through the sluggish water down there, and the shark's attack had left it with a wobble, but she managed to get the saw to the ancient hull. She held her breath when she started it up, but the sharp blade bored into the wood. Wood and centuries' worth of ocean gunk. The saw's bites stirred up a grayish-brown cloud, and soon Tikaya couldn't see a thing outside the porthole.

"Great," she said. "I couldn't cut a decent circle even when I *could* see what I was doing."

"Easy," Rias warned. "The sphere is wobbling."

Tikaya gulped and slowed down. They'd attributed randomness to the timing of those explosives, but maybe they weren't granting those practitioners up there enough skill. What if that one had been sent down and placed precisely there to act as a booby trap? Disturb it and...

She shook her head and focused on her work. It was slow going. There was no way she could cut a hole large enough for the submarine to float through, especially not with that sphere poised to fall. She could only hope that they'd be able to find something helpful when they opened up the hull. If nothing else, she could cut a few smaller holes, and they could check various spots.

The hull of the *Freedom* moaned again. Tikaya eyed the walls warily. She told herself they were level, not going any deeper, so nothing should snap now. Despite the chilly air, she caught herself wiping sweat off her brow.

"Your progress?" Mee Nar asked from the hatchway.

"Hard to say. I can't see much. Tell Rias to make a saw that can suck up the dust it makes next time."

Mee Nar grunted and withdrew.

Abruptly, the resistance vanished, and she was cutting through air. Had she succeeded in slicing out a circle?

Tikaya pulled the tool out and squinted, trying to see through the haze. Guessing as to the outline of her cutaway, she gave the hull a poke with the saw. A ragged oval fell inward. A cloud of sediment and debris shot up, and Tikaya winced. She should have grabbed the cutout with the claw, not pushed it in.

Something dark shot out, bumping into her porthole. She stumbled back, fearing some new attack, but it was only one of those misshapen fish. It righted itself and flitted away.

Tikaya found the directional controls for the lamp, and angled the light into the hole. Rias had guessed right; it was a cabin, though she had no way to tell if it had belonged to the captain. It did seem to be on the larger side, though she couldn't see from wall to wall. She wished they could get closer, but with that booby trap waiting to fall, they dared not bump the craft.

A few dark humps were all that remained of the cabin's furnishings. Mollusks or other creatures that ate wood must have devoured them over time. Her hopes of finding anything useful faded.

"What's the hull made from?" Tikaya called. Now that she'd seen the lack of furnishings, she was surprised the outer shell of the ship remained intact. Perhaps the paint or whatever varnish they'd used back then had protected it.

"Teak was abundant in Nuria," Rias responded. "That'd be my guess. Is there anything left in the cabin?"

Tikaya extended the claw tool to its maximum reach and probed around at deck level on either side of the hole. Since she couldn't change her position to see more of the interior, blind groping was the best she could manage. The claw *did* bump against things on either side. She fumbled about, trying to find a grip so she could drag one of the items into view. Though Rias had failed to adorn the science station with a clock, Tikaya was aware of the seconds ticking past.

When she succeeded in hooking something, she pulled it out carefully. And warily. She thought of the bones in the cave and had visions of dragging out a seven-hundred-year-old skeleton. But, no, there was too much life about down here for that. Something would have eaten the human remains long ago. Not exactly a comforting thought.

Tikaya eased her find into the light and discovered it was... a ceramic wine amphora.

"Wonderful," she muttered.

She couldn't work up any archaeological interest in the artifact; she'd seen dozens, if not hundreds, of similar amphoras, so unless ancient secrets were etched on the sides, somewhere beneath the centuries of gathered grime, she doubted they'd found anything useful. She set it down and probed for something else.

Three amphoras later, her groans were loud enough to reach the navigation cabin.

"Problem?" Rias called.

"Unless this colonial captain was an utter lush, I think we've opened the wrong cabin."

"It might be a steward's cabin. I'll move us forward."

As Tikaya retracted the claw, she heard Mee Nar's snort and utterance of, "If this ship is full of wine, then I'm *sure* it's Turgonian."

"Ceramic just happens to withstand the centuries well," Tikaya said. "I'm sure there were other things in the room as well."

"Like kegs of mead?" Mee Nar asked.

"Tikaya," Rias said, "you were right. I believe my side trip to fetch this Nurian was in error."

"At least I'm not the one foolish enough to contemplate firing a torpedo at some Maker's exploding artifact."

Tikaya sat up straighter. "What?"

"I wasn't *seriously* contemplating it," Rias said.

"I should hope not," Tikaya said.

"Unless I could modify the torpedoes to shoot at a much greater speed, thus to carry the sphere out of range of the wreck before exploding."

"Rias?"

"A joke," he said. "I wouldn't fire them at this depth anyway."

Tikaya shook her head. "I'm ready for you to move the submarine forward."

"Understood," Rias said, soberness returning to his tone.

The hole she'd opened up slipped from view, and the *Freedom* stopped ten feet farther along the hull.

"Just so you know," Rias said, "you're directly under the sphere now."

"How lovely." Tikaya started sawing again. At least if the sphere dropped and exploded, she wouldn't have time to know what was happening before it was over. "So comforting."

"They're *right* over us," Mee Nar said. "They must be tracking us. Or the wreck. Or their orb."

"It doesn't really matter which," Rias said. "Let me know if they start dropping more explosives."

"If the creator is up there and figures out this one is sitting down here, waiting to be detonated," Mee Nar said, "then they won't *need* to drop more."

Tikaya pulled out a hole in the hull, this one even more ragged than the first. She slipped the claw inside and fished about, hoping for something more useful than wine. A chest full of journals perhaps, though she admitted a book wouldn't have likely survived the water, unless it had been sealed in something air- and watertight. She groaned when she pulled out another ceramic container.

"More wine?" Rias asked.

"This might be your mead. Or food. I don't know." Whatever it was, she didn't think it'd be worth grabbing as their *one* item that they could haul to the surface.

"They've dropped a round of spheres," Mee Nar said.

Tikaya thumped her fist on the console. "Cursed banyan sprites, I don't have anything."

"Go in again," Rias said. "It'll take a moment for them to fall down here."

"Not that long of a moment," Mee Nar said.

"Just let me know when I have thirty seconds."

"They're falling fast."

Tikaya jammed the claw back into the hole, barely remembering not to knock hard against anything—not with one sphere already down there with them. She patted about on the slanted deck, wishing she could *feel* what the pincers touched, not simply sense that they were bumping against things.

"Now," Mee Nar said.

"Tikaya?" Rias asked.

She grabbed the closest thing. It scraped and bumped along the deck slowly. Either the claw tool wasn't working as well, or this was something heavy. Hope arose within her. Then it caught against something. She cursed.

"Tikaya, we need to go," Rias said, his voice steady but underlain with contained urgency. "Is it safe to pull out?"

"One second..."

Tikaya yanked again, but her find wouldn't budge. Remembering the second tool, she swung the saw in, hacking into the hull, creating a wider hole.

A thump and a grunt came from navigation. "Starcrest, get us out of here!"

"Calm down, Nar."

Tikaya finished cutting and thumped on the new cutout with the saw. There was no time to worry about whether bumps would rattle the sphere on the railing free, not when dozens more were plummeting down. Cutting the wider hole let her find a better angle, and she was able to pull her prize free. Though gray with grime, it looked like a chest. Praying that she'd found something worth risking themselves for, she worked the claw through a thick metal—or was that stone?—ring on one end. She closed the pinchers, hoping they could pull it up with them without the contents being dumped on the—

"Starcrest, it's falling!"

Before the words were out, the submarine was moving. It lurched forward so fast, Tikaya fell into her seat. She almost lost her grip on the controls, but, not knowing if she'd entirely secured the ring, she refused to let go.

"Look out," Mee Nar called. "It's—"

Tikaya held her breath. They must have knocked the sphere on the railing free. Had it struck the ocean floor? It couldn't have exploded or she would have felt it.

The submarine pulled away from the wreck, turning as it went, and she caught a glimpse of it. The glowing orb had dropped into the mud beneath the ship. And it hadn't exploded. Tikaya released the breath she'd been holding. More might be coming, but at least they'd evaded—

A flash of crimson light assailed her eyes. Tikaya stumbled backward, tripping on the chair, and going down. Before she hit the deck, a wave of force slammed into the *Freedom*. It flung Tikaya into the bulkhead, her head cracking against the solid metal. Dazed, she was barely aware of sliding down the wall to the deck. The interior lighting went out, and blackness invaded the cabin.

Shouts erupted from elsewhere in the boat, but a loud snap echoed from the hull, drowning out the men's words. Tikaya had a vague sense that she needed to get up, to help somehow, but the boat continued to rock, as if they were in a storm on the surface, and she struggled to find her knees. Dampness covered her hand. Blood? She blinked and lifted it, as if she could see through the blackness to identify it. Wetness found her knees too.

"Not blood, you dolt—water." The ramifications washed over her. Any second, the rest of the hull might snap, or it'd collapse in on them, crushing them. "Rias, leak!"

Tikaya scrambled to her feet, blood surging through her veins and pushing away the fog in her head. For all she knew, Rias was already busy with a leak, or he was injured. Or dead. "No," she whispered and groped her way to the hatch. Maybe if it was just in that compartment, she could—

Something bumped against her torso. A hand?

Before she could identify it for certain, it gripped her and yanked her out of the cabin. Metal clanked, announcing the hatch being shut. A soft squeal sounded as the wheel was turned. A thunderous crack came from the other side of the hatch.

"You all right?" Rias asked, his voice brusque but concerned.

"Yes, but—"

He released her and pounded away, boots ringing on the metal decking. "I have to get us up," he called back, already in the navigation chamber.

In the utter darkness, Tikaya couldn't move as quickly, but she patted her way to the front. Heavy breathing came from a corner. Mee Nar.

"Should I close this door too?" Tikaya tapped the hatch leading to navigation.

"If anything besides the science station floods, it won't matter." From the sound of Rias's voice, he was sitting at the navigation chair. Not an iota of light seeped in from outside. He wouldn't be able to see the gauges, his instruments, or *anything*. "As it is, we're rising slowly.

I've pumped as much air into the ballast tanks as we have, but when there's water inside…"

"I get it," Tikaya said. Her ears popped. At least they *were* rising. For now. "Does the lighting being out mean the power source is dead?"

"Dead or disconnected. That was quite a jolt. Mee Nar, I've still got some steering capability. Can you let me know if any more of those explosives are dropping around us?"

A rapid chain of Nurian curse words flowed from Mee Nar's lips, punctuated by orders for Starcrest to shove his sword up his butt and laments for his choice to answer the door that morning.

"He says no," Tikaya said.

"Yes, I got the gist."

"Just doing my job as team linguist." Tikaya snapped her mouth shut. Her words were coming out almost as quickly as Mee Nar's. She probably sounded hysterical.

"I'll try to bring us up as far away from the Kyattese ship as possible," Rias said.

In the aftermath of the explosion, Tikaya couldn't imagine how he had any idea of which direction they were pointing.

"Did you get anything more out of the wreck before we left?" Rias asked quietly, as if he was afraid of the answer, afraid to find out that this had all been a waste of time.

"A chest, but I doubt we still have it. If we *do* have it, I doubt it's still shut with anything inside. I had the claw wrapped around a ring on one end." Tikaya imagined them pulling up an empty chest, its secrets spilled all over the ocean floor, the depths too great for them to descend to again. If the submarine was even salvageable after this.

Rias sighed.

Tikaya thought she could see his outline in the shadows. Yes, shadows. There was a hint of light coming from the viewport. Her ears popped again. "Are we close to the surface?"

"I'm guessing fifty meters."

"It must still be night," Tikaya said. Otherwise, the water would be brighter, even that deep.

"Yes."

Hard to believe they hadn't been underwater longer. A great weariness weighed down Tikaya's limbs, and she leaned against the hatchway. It seemed like they'd been down for days.

"I didn't see any weapons on the Kyattese ship," Rias announced a moment later, "but I suppose they could have more magical ordinance to throw at us. Tikaya can you man the controls? I need to see if the power supply is dead or can be brought back to life." He sighed again, the sigh of a man who doubted it mattered either way.

Tikaya caught his arm as he stood. "We're still *alive*. That's something to be thankful for."

"Yes." Rias hugged her, but pulled away too soon. "But we've gained nothing and lost a chance to do it again."

"You don't know that. We could fix—"

"I saw two of those spheres drop on the wreck as we were pulling away. It's gone."

"Oh." Tikaya stared at the deck. "Maybe we'll have managed to retain that chest, and it'll contain what we sought."

"Maybe." Rias didn't sound optimistic.

CHAPTER 20

THE *FREEDOM* BOBBED ON THE surface, the stars telling Tikaya that dawn wasn't that far off. Mee Nar hadn't said anything since they'd come up, but she imagined he was thinking of opening the exit hatch and swimming to shore. It might not be a bad idea. The Kyattese ship wasn't visible at the moment, but Mee Nar had nodded when she'd asked if it was out there. The dark sky and darker sea might hide the gray of the submarine for the moment, but it'd be easy to see once dawn came. They were about a mile out from the black cliffs and dead in the water unless Rias could get power flowing to the engine again. If the engine were the problem, she'd have faith that he could, but he wouldn't have any experience fixing Kyattese energy sources.

"I wonder if he'd mind if I swam out and took a look at that claw," Tikaya mused. She'd been musing upon the idea for a while, but hadn't gotten further than that. As long as she *didn't* go outside and check, she could hope they'd managed to pull up something. If she went out and found nothing there...

Rias appeared in the hatchway, holding a lantern turned to its lowest setting. "Something struck the power supply and there's a hole in the exterior. I could patch it, but somehow I doubt that would fix it." He shrugged.

"No," Tikaya agreed. "You'd need to Make a patch with your mind."

"If you have a technical manual that explains how to do that, I'll give it a try, but I'm guessing such things aren't taught in such a manner."

Mee Nar snorted.

"They're not," Tikaya said. "Are we dead in the water, then?"

"There's some energy stored in the battery. We may be able to make it to shore."

May be able to make it. That didn't sound promising. Where would they go that was safe anyway?

"I'm hoping the practitioners won't be able to track us as easily with the energy source inoperable," Rias said.

"They'll see us floating on the surface as soon as it gets light," Mee Nar pointed out.

"We'll leave soon," Rias said.

"Back to the cave?" Tikaya yawned. Back home to her bedroom sounded better. But would that ever be an option again? After she'd sabotaged a Kyattese ship and put her family in danger with her choices?

"We'll see." Rias eyed the sky outside. "Let's see if we pulled anything up first. It's doubtful the grasper kept its grip in the face of that explosion, but..."

"Yes, I was thinking about that too." Tikaya rose from her seat and swung her arms to encourage blood flow—and to wake herself up. "It was my project. I'll go check on it."

"I'll do it," Rias said.

"You better stay in here in case there are more mechanical problems. Besides you've done enough."

"I don't know why you two are arguing," Mee Nar muttered. "There are probably still sharks out there." He'd lost his hysterical edge and didn't seem to retain any of his animosity from earlier. He just sounded... defeated. Maybe he suspected he, too, would not be allowed to remain on the island—and with his family—because of his choice that night.

Tikaya hoped she didn't sound that way. Rias was watching her.

"What?" she asked.

"I want you to stay in here while I take a look," he said, his eyes intent, like he wanted to pass some secret message to her.

What couldn't he say out loud? There was little left that Mee Nar didn't know. Without waiting for her agreement, Rias tugged off his shirt and sandals, opened the upper hatch, and climbed out of the submarine.

"Are you sure he's entirely on your people's side?" Mee Nar asked.

"I'm entirely sure he's on *my* side," Tikaya said. "As for unswerving loyalty to groups of people en masse, I don't think he feels that toward any nation any more. Akahe knows, my people haven't welcomed him." She lowered her voice and added, "Idiots."

"Can you blame them? *My* people would have shot him full of arrows the moment he set foot on one of our docks."

"I doubt that," Tikaya said. "I think the Nurians are smart enough to see the value in a high-ranking officer who's forsaken his emperor."

"The Great Chief perhaps, but it'd only be luck if someone on the citizen protection force had that sort of foresight and didn't shoot him on sight."

The sound of water dripping interrupted Tikaya's response. Her first thought was of the sealed science station, that it might be leaking somehow, but then a soggy Rias dropped through the open hatchway. Wet hair plastered his brow, and his trousers clung to his legs. He was empty-handed.

Tikaya's hopes sank, but he immediately jogged into the rear, an intent expression on his face. Maybe he *had* found something.

"Need help?" Tikaya called.

Clunks and clanks answered her. A moment later, Rias reappeared, unwinding a coil of rope as he went. "Can you two turn the winch back there? This is heavy."

Without further explanation, he climbed back outside. A splash announced his descent into the water again. Tikaya waved Mee Nar to follow the rope to its source, but she paused to stick her head outside. Either the moon had set or clouds covered it, for there was little illumination. The only light came from the Kyattese ship, a mix of mundane firelight in lanterns and green-glowing Made lamps.

The craft didn't seem to have moved from the area over the wreck. Didn't they know they'd completed their mission? Maybe they were out there with spyglasses, searching for the submarine even now.

A clank sounded as something struck the hull. The rope had gone taut. Rias's head popped out of the water.

Curiosity hummed inside of Tikaya, but she dropped back below. If they had pulled up something heavy, it might take two people to operate that winch.

She joined Mee Nar, who was indeed straining to operate the hand-cranked machine. He shifted to the side, so she had room to grip the lever. A lantern on the floor cast his face in shadow and light, illuminating the sweat moistening his skin.

"Still regretting that you answered the door this morning?" Tikaya asked.

"Technically, I think that's *yesterday* morning, now," Mee Nar said. "And yes and no. The Kyattese won't be pleased if they learn I had a role in this, but we made it back up. If this boat starts to sink now, I can swim to shore. Having spent time in here, and taken a look at everything, I'm sure I could create detailed drawings should anything befall Starcrest before he can sketch the blueprints for me."

Tikaya supposed she couldn't be surprised that Mee Nar was more interested in relaying information to his people than finding out what they'd pulled from the wreck.

"I will also remember that throwing explosives into the water is a possible way to damage one of these boats," Mee Nar added.

"If you get lucky. We could have easily avoided them if my people hadn't known exactly where we needed to go down there."

"Yes, I know." Mee Nar paused to wipe his brow, and the effort required to move the lever doubled. "Imagining the empire with a fleet of these boats is terrifying. Especially after what he said about..."

"What?" Being back in the science station, Tikaya had missed quite a few conversations between the two men.

"These torpedoes of his. He said he's working on a clockwork mechanism that would cause them to explode a specific number of seconds after leaving their launch tubes. They travel at a specific knots-per-hour so he could gauge the distance to an enemy ship, so they'd explode precisely underneath it."

It chilled Tikaya to think of Rias designing such weapons. Given how easily the submarine could slip beneath the waves, why did it *need* weapons? For their purposes, it could simply evade those who might wish them ill intent. Though she didn't want to doubt Rias, or question his word that he'd broken ties with the empire, she couldn't keep away the niggling doubt that tugged at a sleeve in the back of her mind.

A clank sounded against the hull behind them.

"We're almost there," Rias said, lowering his head through the hatchway for a moment. "Keep pulling. Thank you."

Mee Nar grumbled and joined Tikaya at the lever again.

"An explosion underneath a ship is apparently even more powerful than one that strikes it," Mee Nar said. "Or so he explained to me. That explosion forms a sphere of gas, and the gas rises with such force that it hurls the ship into the air and breaks it in half."

"That's... disturbing."

"More so if you're an innocent Nurian sailor *on* that ship." Mee Nar gave her a significant look. "Or a Kyattese one."

"He's not going after my people," Tikaya said.

"Their successful resistance is the only blemish on his otherwise perfect naval record."

"He doesn't care about his record, and I don't care to discuss this further." Tikaya stared at the winch, avoiding eye contact with Mee Nar as she focused on turning the crank.

More scrapes and clunks sounded outside as something was dragged across the hull. The chest. It couldn't be anything else. And from the weight, it must still have something in it.

"You can stop pulling," Rias called.

He hopped inside again and lowered the chest with his bare hands, though he staggered under the weight before dropping it to the deck with a thump. "There. Much easier to move when you're not in the water or trying to clamber up the side of a submarine."

Given its weight, Tikaya was surprised the chest had fit through the hatchway, but it was only about two feet long and a foot-and-a-half wide. Maybe less once one removed all the grime crusted to it. Prying open the lid would be challenging.

"Too bad all the tools are in the flooded science cabin," Tikaya said.

"I'll handle it," Rias said. "Can you climb up top and keep an eye on the other ship?"

"What?" How could he think she didn't want to be here, helping him pry that lid open?

"I imagine they'll start looking for us as soon as they confirm that the wreck has been destroyed and that we're not down there."

"Mee Nar can keep watch."

"Mee Nar will be busy concentrating to see if any magical attacks are being readied," Rias said.

Mee Nar leaned against the hull, his arms crossed, and his eyebrows raised as they discussed him.

"Let's find a way to get the *Freedom* someplace safe, where we don't need to worry about the other ship," Tikaya said, "and then we can all open the chest together."

"When practitioners are involved, I don't believe there *are* any safe places to hide. At least on or around this island."

"*Rias*," Tikaya said, "I want to see what's in the box too." She knew she sounded whiney, but what was he *doing*? Her curiosity was as great as his. He had to know that.

"Yes, I understand, and I'll show you when it's open. I want to open it by myself, though, in case it's booby-trapped."

"Booby-trapped?"

"These are *my* ancestors we're dealing with," Rias said dryly.

Tikaya wasn't amused. If those amphoras were any indication, his ancestors had been too besotted to think of anything as clever as booby-trapping. "I'm sure seven hundred years at the bottom of the ocean will have eroded any security measures they might have employed."

"I don't want to risk having you harmed if something goes off while I'm opening it." Rias gripped one of the rings on the ends of the chest and started dragging it into the bowels of the submarine. "I've already endangered you enough tonight."

As Tikaya watched him go, it was all she could do not to stomp her foot like a petulant schoolgirl. She might have, but Mee Nar was gazing blandly in her direction. A hatch clanged shut. Rias sealing himself in to open that chest in private.

"Do you truly think he believes it's booby-trapped?" Mee Nar asked.

"It might be. Paranoia *does* seem to be bred into Turgonians."

"Or maybe he just wants to see what's inside before he shows it to you."

Tikaya glowered at him. "He'll show me."

"Perhaps."

"What's your agenda here, Mee Nar? I thought you were just along to get your government its precious submarine schematics, not try to start something between Rias and me."

Mee Nar held out his open hands. "I'm simply making observations. I believe he's fond of you, and vice versa, but in the end, he *is* still Turgonian. And you are not."

If Tikaya could melt stone—or Nurians—with her glower, she was sure its intensity would be turning Mee Nar into a puddle. She was tempted to stomp back to wherever Rias had secluded himself and bang on the hatch, demanding to be let in.

But... what if she did and he *didn't* let her in? Knowing the truth might sting more than having doubts.

"Aren't you supposed to be checking for Science work?" Tikaya asked, then climbed outside for her own appointed task. Keeping watch. She grumbled and hoped Rias couldn't read whatever he found and had to come out and beg for her help.

Tikaya sat cross-legged next to the open hatch, watching the Kyattese ship. It had left its spot over the wreck and was sailing back and forth in lines running parallel to the cliffs. Search pattern.

She was surprised the ship's practitioners hadn't tracked the submarine down yet, but supposed it was a big sea, and they might be looking under it instead of on top of it. Also, as Rias had mentioned, the energy source would have acted as a beacon to practitioners; without it, they were only three people amidst all the life in the nearby sea. Isolating the humanoid auras would take time. Though daylight would make the process much easier. She cast another uneasy glance toward the eastern sky. It seemed a smidgen lighter than it had when she first came outside.

"Tikaya?" Rias called up softly.

"Yes?"

"Why don't you come down for a minute? We have... something to discuss."

"That sounds ominous," Tikaya muttered to herself.

She climbed inside where Mee Nar and Rias waited. The chest wasn't in sight. Rias wasn't holding anything either.

"Well?" she asked.

"I opened it," Rias said.

Tikaya propped her hands on her hips. "And was it proliferated with booby traps?"

"Actually..." Rias lifted his palm to display a new gash. "Yes."

Tikaya dropped her arms. "Oh."

"There would have been more of them seven hundred years ago, but, as you said, water and time effectively disarmed most of them."

Booby traps. That meant there'd been something to protect.

"The chest was carved from granite," Rias said. "The rings on the sides too. Only the locking mechanism was made from iron—I'm guessing because it was missing. I believe there are bacteria in the sea that consume iron. Only the shell of half-petrified grime on the outside kept the lid from falling open as we rose. We're lucky the contents didn't fall out."

It was as if he was avoiding telling her what those contents were just to frustrate her. "Not to belittle your wound, but *what*—" Tikaya grabbed his arm, "—is inside?"

"Ah, yes, about that. Before I show you, I'm going to need a favor."

"A favor." Tikaya glanced at Mee Nar, wondering if he'd been privy to the chest's contents, but he merely shrugged. "Rias, you know I'll be happy to perform all sorts of favors, but later. I want to know if all this has been worth it."

"The favor needs to be done soon." Rias glanced toward the open hatchway and the fading stars above. "Now. I need you to go to the Kyattese ship and open negotiations with them. On my behalf."

"*Your* behalf?"

Rias took a deep breath. "On behalf of the Turgonian people."

Tikaya didn't know what to say. Had he truly found something that he couldn't share with her because he worried she'd be forced to choose her people over his? Over *him*? She opened her mouth to say that she'd never make that choice, but she closed it without uttering a word. Would that be the truth? What allegiance did she have to Turgonia? Absolutely none. She cared about him, yes, but enough to betray her people if it came to that? She'd gladly hand over the idiots out there on that ship, but what if the contents of this chest somehow threatened her entire nation?

"I see." Tikaya released her grip on Rias's arm. "What if they don't want to negotiate? What if they're more interested in capturing me and throwing me in the brig—or worse—because I've been your accomplice? A half hour ago, you were worried about me falling victim to a booby trap, but you're perfectly happy sending me over to a ship full of people who've been trying to kill me?"

"Not happy, no, but this is the only way."

Tikaya took a step back, putting distance between them. "Were you truly worried about booby traps or were you just determined to keep me from seeing what was inside before you did?" She didn't know why she was asking. She already knew the answer.

"Will you go over and act as intermediary for our negotiations?" Rias asked.

A part of her was tempted to tell him to send Mee Nar. He'd make a more believable third party anyway, but she couldn't stand the idea of completely stepping away from this. Besides, the *Kyattese* knew what this was all about; they wouldn't have been so desperate to blow up the wreck before Rias found it otherwise. If *he* wouldn't tell her, maybe they would.

With that thought, Tikaya's musings leaped off one rail and onto another. Was that exactly what Rias wanted? What if they'd pulled up a pile of junk, and he hoped that, in pretending they'd already discovered the big secret, the Kyattese themselves would reveal it to her? Now that she thought about it, the odds that they'd found, in their hasty rush, just the right piece of information down there were slim. Though, she argued with herself, Rias had known where the captain's cabin was. If any one spot on the ship were to hold a secret, it'd be that one. And that chest obviously had *something* in it.

There was no way to tell one way or the other for certain. And as long as she didn't know the truth, she couldn't give it away if some telepath invaded her mind to check for himself.

"I see," Tikaya said again, more to herself than Rias this time. "Are you going to turn on the lights and wave a flag so they'll come pick me up? I don't fancy another swim."

"Until negotiations are complete, it would behoove me to remain out of their reach. I have a collapsible dinghy that you can use to row out to them."

"Oh, fabulous." She imagined the other ship either shooting her with a harpoon as she approached or not picking her up at all, leaving her to float out to sea. "I'll have you know that my life has become incredibly fraught since I met you."

A hint of his old half-smile touched his face, though it had a self-deprecating edge. "I've heard that from people before."

Mee Nar snorted. "That I don't doubt."

"Come." Rias lifted a hand toward Tikaya. "We need to discuss my terms and what I can bring to bear if they're not willing to negotiate."

A mischievous—or perhaps wicked—glint entered Mee Nar's eyes. "I wouldn't mind seeing that ship-breaking-in-half explosion you mentioned earlier."

Tikaya ignored him and told Rias, "I can tell that negotiating on your behalf is going to be quite the experience for me."

"Fraught?" Rias asked.

"Undoubtedly."

CHAPTER 21

I F THERE WAS ANYTHING THAT could test a woman's love more than rowing a flimsy dinghy across choppy waters toward a cannon mounted in the stern of an enemy ship, Tikaya couldn't come up with it at the moment. A sailor in typical island garb, clam diggers and a loose hemp shirt that flapped in the breeze, stood behind that cannon with a lantern in hand, one that could be touched to the fuse to loose the deadly black ball. She imagined the man's contemplation. *Should I fire on this nettlesome woman now? Or wait until we've interrogated her for all she knows and then fire on her?*

Normally, Tikaya would chastise herself, proclaiming that Kyattese citizens were peaceful and would never contemplate such things, but whoever commanded this ship obviously followed a different philosophy than the majority of her people. Though the simple two-masted schooner had the design of a typical research vessel, the cannons were an atypical addition. If the craft held more of those explosives, the cannons were probably the most innocuous weapons aboard.

A man and woman in white robes came to stand beside the sailor. Though dawn brightened the horizon, and lanterns dotted the ship, shadows lingered on the deck and Tikaya couldn't make out facial features yet. A hood further guarded the woman's face, leaving only a hint of dark, wind-tangled hair.

"Greetings," Tikaya called when she was close enough to be heard. "May I have permission to come aboard?"

"Are you surrendering?" the man asked, his voice familiar.

Professor Yosis. Tikaya couldn't claim to be surprised, but she would have preferred enemies who didn't hold a personal grudge against

Rias—or her. She hoped Yosis was some underling, not the person in charge.

"Surrendering?" Tikaya continued to row as she spoke, not out of any real desire to hurry aboard, but because it'd be preferable to face people instead of the black mouth of that cannon. "I'm here to act as a third-party intermediary. Former Fleet Admiral Sashka Federias Starcrest wishes to open up negotiations on behalf of the Turgonian people."

"I thought he wasn't in a position to do that," Yosis said. "Didn't you *claim* he was exiled?"

"He claimed that to me, yes. I am merely relaying the information he gave me."

Rias had given her a great deal of leeway insofar as what claims she could make about him and the empire, giving her only, as he'd said, his terms and, "My trust that you'll handle the situation far more competently on your own than if I tried to instruct you." Nice of him to say that, but she couldn't help but feel she'd been given, as the old Turgonian expression went, enough rope to hang herself.

Yosis and the woman bent their heads together. Two other practitioners in white robes watched from the railing while sailors in island garb called to each other, preparing to steer the ship into shallow waters so they could set anchor. Someone had decided to stop searching, it seemed, to see what she had to say. Though the sky had lightened, Tikaya couldn't see any sign of the *Freedom*. Rias must have submerged again. She was on her own.

"May I come aboard?" Tikaya asked again. "He knows our people's long forgotten secret, and if we don't want a message going straight to the emperor, we need to deal with him."

A moment of silence passed, not shocked silence, Tikaya decided. Others on the ship were looking back and forth, as if wondering if anyone knew what she was talking about, but the shoulders of Yosis and his female comrade drooped. The woman pressed a hand to her forehead and muttered something. Yosis's answer was short and sharp, though the wind swept the words away before Tikaya could hear them.

"*We?*" Yosis asked. "You've been walking at his side and fighting us since you returned, and now you want to identify yourself as one of us?"

Not in the least, Tikaya thought. Out loud, she said, "You should have *told* me what was at stake from the beginning. This is... this could change everything." She shut her mouth and told herself not to rush things. They wouldn't likely blurt secrets across the open deck, and if she said the wrong thing and clued them in on the fact that she had nothing more concrete than hunches, this trip would have been for naught.

"When he so clearly had you in his pocket?" the woman asked, speaking for the first time. Her voice sounded familiar, but Tikaya couldn't place it. "Despite your old lover's stories, nobody knows for sure what happened during those months you were gone," the woman continued. "Many people believed—*believe* you've been brainwashed."

"I wouldn't do anything to put our people at risk," Tikaya said. "My entire family lives eight miles from the capital city. Do you think I want to help the Turgonians attack?"

"That's exactly what's going to happen now," Yosis grumbled, "thanks to you helping that murdering joratt."

So, whatever was down there would give the empire reason to attack? Tikaya thought of the skull in her room, and the arrowhead that had pierced it.

The white-robed woman put a hand on Yosis's arm. "Let's bring her on board and see what she has to say."

"You mean what she's being a joratt mouthpiece about."

Tikaya sighed. By now she'd reached the hull of the ship, and she bobbed in the water beneath the arguing practitioners. Maybe it'd been better when she hadn't been able to hear all the muttered snarls.

Yosis leaned over the railing and glared down at Tikaya. "If you want to be welcomed aboard, why don't you tell us where he is?"

"So you can hurl more explosives at him?" Tikaya asked. "No." As if she knew where Rias had gone, anyway. Not far with the limited energy in his battery. "You needn't welcome me. I'll settle for not being shot."

While Yosis stewed on that, the woman disappeared for a moment, then returned with a coil of rope.

She tossed the end down. "Tie up your dinghy and climb up."

Tikaya obeyed and soon found herself being escorted below decks. The woman had disappeared, leaving Yosis to prod Tikaya along. She wondered if she was about to find out who was captaining this ship. If so, was that person in charge of the entire mission? Was he or she the one who'd ordered the wreck destroyed, along with the explosion in the harbor? What if it was someone prominent amongst her people? The president, perhaps? Was it suspicious that he'd been unavailable ever since Tikaya had returned? Or what if her hypothesis about her family being strong-armed proved incorrect because one of them was involved here? Father or maybe Grandpa?

Sweat dampened Tikaya's palms as Yosis guided her down a narrow passage, ducking frequently to avoid low beams. He knocked on a polished koa door. Several seconds passed, and Tikaya found herself tracing patterns in the whorls of the rich wood with her eyes. Muffled voices came through the door, but she couldn't make out the words. Yosis huffed and shifted his weight, but he didn't raise his voice to call. Not-in-charge, his body language said. Tikaya nodded to herself. She was about to meet those who were. If they decided to let her in.

"Come," the call finally came.

Tikaya glanced at Yosis, and he jerked his chin for her to open the door. She licked her lips, turned the knob, and pushed. It wasn't a captain's cabin but a conference room. Or perhaps war room was the better term. Bathymetric maps scattered the surface of a table that occupied most of the floor space.

Two people sat in high-backed wooden chairs at the end. High Minister Jikaymar and the woman who'd stood beside Yosis at the railing. She'd lowered her hood, but it took Tikaya a moment to identify her, as they'd never spoken previously. High Minister Tosii, that was it. The woman who presided over the College of Practitioners and set policies and precedents for all things Science-related on the islands. Well, Tikaya thought, numb to learn she faced people who were effectively the president's left and right hands, Tosii certainly would be the one with the skill and power to craft those explosives or else she'd know exactly who to recruit to Make them. Though the rank of the people behind this was cause for concern—she wasn't dealing with some crazy fringe group of zealots here—she was relieved that none of her relatives seemed to be involved. At least not on this ship.

"Sit down, Tikaya." High Minister Jikaymar sighed and waved to a chair. Dark circles smudged his eyes.

Yosis started forward, but Jikaymar waved him back. "You have duties up top."

"Are we still looking for Starcrest, sir?" Yosis asked.

"Yes. No. I don't know." Jikaymar gave Tikaya a tired look. "Is there any chance that we'll find him?"

"He submerged as soon as I rowed away, so I suppose it depends on how well you can track him." Tikaya shrugged, as if it mattered little to her.

"Yes, that's worked so well." Tosii snorted and tugged a hairband off her wrist. She scraped her disheveled brown locks back into a tail. She and Jikaymar both looked like people who hadn't slept, maybe in several nights. "We thought we'd have no trouble finding his energy source, but it's too sophisticated. However did you get Iweue to work on that for him? You'd think she'd be the last one to help you with your new beau."

Tikaya must have been wearing a blank stare, for Tosii explained, "Her work is good, recognizable, and she weaved some sort of deflection field into the outer layer. I can sense that it's out there, but not where. We've almost hit rocks twice now as I tried to guide us toward it."

"I didn't know about that feature," Tikaya said. She'd have to give Iweue a hug next time they met.

Tosii's lips twisted down, her expression wry as she peered into Tikaya's eyes. "Yes, I see that."

A telepath. Not surprising. A good one too. Tikaya couldn't even feel the touch inside her mind, not like that clunky probing that Gali had done. She decided not to point out that the High Minister of the College of Practitioners probably shouldn't be rifling through people's minds unasked; after all, she was the one who had a hand in making such laws.

Tosii's expression grew even wryer, as if she were following right along with Tikaya's thoughts.

"You'll likely find it very difficult to find him then," Tikaya said aloud, for Jikaymar's sake. "He has the chest and little reason to linger around the wreck, not like before. Also, he has a Nurian warning him when the charges are coming."

"Does he now?" Tosii murmured.

"Chest?" Jikaymar frowned.

Uh oh, maybe that hadn't been the right thing to mention. If they knew for a fact that chests weren't involved, they'd know Rias had nothing that mattered. Aware of Tosii scrutinizing her, Tikaya thought of the skull and the arrowhead. That alone might be enough to rouse Turgonian suspicions and bring a fleet.

Tosii winced and stretched a hand out, laying it flat on the table. "It's not right that we should be blamed, or *punished*, for the choices our ancestors made seven hundred years ago."

"Do you truly think the empire will seek reprisal after all this time?" Tikaya asked.

"Of *course* they will," Jikaymar said. "During the war, they were busy with the Nurians, and they were fighting on multiple fronts. Now that they've signed an armistice with the Nurians..." Jikaymar shook his head. "However temporary that peace may be, it's got the president, *all* of us, concerned. And with reason. We've long feared that, with nothing else to distract them, they'd set their sights on Kyatt again."

"We fought them off before," Tikaya said, more to keep him talking than because she disagreed with his concern.

Jikaymar lifted his arms toward the ceiling. "At what cost? We *barely* fought them off, and that was when their forces were split. Now they could afford to send their entire fleet to our doorstep. And this would be just the excuse they'd need."

Tikaya wanted to say, "Yes, and what is that excuse exactly?" but they wouldn't be fooled by anything so simple. She groped for a better way to get them to admit it.

Tosii's eyes narrowed. Erg. Tikaya tried not to squirm.

"You don't know," Tosii said.

Jikaymar dropped his arms. "What?"

Tosii closed her eyes, lips flattening as she concentrated.

Tikaya tried to keep her out, but she couldn't even feel the woman's deft touch inside her mind.

Scant seconds passed before Tosii announced, "He didn't show you what was in the chest."

"I have hunches," Tikaya said. "There's a Turgonian woman's skull in my room with a Kyattese arrowhead in it. And we have other evidence that proves their lost colony ship sank down there. Not that they'd need evidence. They already want our islands. Any excuse..." Tikaya didn't know whether she was having an effect on them with her words or not, so she closed her mouth. Let them make the next move.

"So, they have a chest," Jikaymar told Tosii. "And she hasn't seen what's in it, but Starcrest has. Does she think they found anything or that he's just bluffing?"

"She doesn't know. She thinks it might be a bluff, but she's not sure." Tosii snorted. "Starcrest played that well."

"He's very smart," Tikaya said. "I wouldn't be surprised if he'd pieced everything together before we ever went down there and only sought some proof to send back to the emperor." She didn't truly believe Rias had meant, all along, to send anything back to the emperor, but she couldn't be entirely certain. He'd been harder than ever to read when he'd been briefing her on his terms.

"Yes, we all know he's 'very smart,'" Jikaymar said, imitating her voice when he said the last two words. "That's why we were so terribly tickled when you brought him here to nose around."

Tikaya bristled. She wanted to say that she hadn't forced him to come and it wasn't her fault, but... he truly was only here because of her. If all this ended up being detrimental to her people, to her family, it *would* be her fault.

"What *are* his terms?" Tosii asked.

For the first time, Tikaya felt like she might have a little power. At the least, they needed her to negotiate with Rias. "Tell me first what *really* happened back then. Until I know, I won't know who I'm negotiating for here."

"You'd *better* not be negotiating for the Turgonians," Jikaymar growled.

"I am negotiating for my and Rias's safety," Tikaya said. "You *have* been trying to kill us."

Tosii winced.

"We were trying to destroy the wreck before you got to it. If you'd stayed away, you never would have been harmed. Even Starcrest, we didn't want to kill him—Fircrest said that'd be a huge mistake—but he wouldn't stop with that sprite-licked underwater boat."

"Fircrest?" Tikaya didn't recognize the name.

"We've had to work day and night to create those abominable explosives," Tosii said, ignoring Tikaya's inquiry, "something sturdy and powerful enough to sink to the bottom of the ocean. We never would have—our people *don't* create weapons."

"Seven hundred years ago, someone created a bow and arrows and drove one into a Turgonian woman's skull," Tikaya said.

"If we share this story, you'll have to agree to *our* terms," Jikaymar said. "Or rather Starcrest will. Nothing spoken of here must make its way back to the Turgonians."

"I can't assure you of that, as he may already know the story. I'm the only one who's—" Tikaya decided the word 'clueless' spoke poorly of her and switched mid-sentence to, "—missing information. I can, however, give you my word that *I* won't share any of this with the Turgonians."

"You wouldn't have anyway. As if they'd listen to someone who played an instrumental role in their defeat during the war."

"Actually, they would," Tikaya said. "They respect enemies who challenge them." Well, Rias had anyway. Every other Turgonian she'd met, with the exception of Corporal Agarik, had wanted to take her face and grind it under his boot. Turgonians only seemed to respect those who challenged them with swords. "Either way, you have little to lose by telling me the truth."

"I doubt that." Jikaymar's eyes narrowed. "What is at stake if we *don't* cooperate? I can't believe the president wished to allow him to stay and build that monstrosity. We *know* Starcrest has built weapons into his craft."

Of its own accord, Tikaya's mind pulled up the memory of Mee Nar describing how the torpedoes could be made to detonate beneath a ship, resulting in the craft being hurled into the air with such force that it snapped in half like a reed toy.

Tosii sucked in a quick breath.

Tikaya thought to assure her that Rias would never do something like that, but she had no interest in assuaging the woman's concerns. Besides, if she was reading all of Tikaya's thoughts, Tikaya hardly needed to voice anything.

She watched Tosii for a further reaction, but the concern never left her face. Another Gali type perhaps, who thought Starcrest was brainwashing her, or at least using her to further his own goals, and those of the empire.

Tosii's lips stretched in what might have been a pitying smile.

"Where *is* the president?" Tikaya asked. "It seems he's of a different opinion of how Rias should be handled."

"He's an optimist," Jikaymar said. "If he wasn't, we already would have learned... Never mind."

Tikaya considered him through slitted eyes. "Does the president have something to do with why you didn't probe Rias's mind when you took him prisoner? And why you took that bracelet off him?"

Jikaymar's face twisted with disgust. "That had nothing to do with the president. Lord Fircrest, the Turgonian spy-cum-diplomat on the island, heard that Starcrest had been apprehended and came to my office and demanded to know what we planned to do with him. After being appalled that we'd put a lizard tracker on Starcrest—the man was actually stuttering—he informed us that the emperor would retaliate with great swiftness if he found out someone had been sifting through his former fleet admiral's thoughts. You don't reach that lofty a rank in the Turgonian military, he said, without becoming privy to numerous secrets that are worth killing over. I wasn't willing to risk any of my people to some imperial assassin."

"Knowing the empire," Tosii said, "the entire island might have been a target. Just to ensure those secrets were squashed."

Tikaya sank back in her chair. She hadn't known there was a Turgonian diplomat living in Kyatt, but she imagined he would have been following Rias's arrival closely. She doubted his warning had been hyperbole. The story of the tunnels alone, not to mention the powerful artifacts contained within, were secrets the empire would probably kill to keep undisclosed. She thought of the relic raiders who'd been dragged off to the Turgonian capital for who knew what fate. It was probably only Rias's protection that had kept her and Parkonis from being targeted. She shuddered.

"Fircrest said the smartest thing we could do to ensure our people's safety was to get Rias off our islands as quickly as possible." Jikaymar sighed ruefully at Tosii. "In hindsight, we should have *given* him a ship." He turned back to Tikaya. "As for the president, he's been busy of late. We've taken matters into our own hands."

Obviously. But that didn't mean... "You didn't do something to him, did you? To ensure he wouldn't return to the capital?"

"Don't be ridiculous. We're not criminals or scheming murderers who would—"

"You almost *did*." Tikaya pointed downward.

"It's not our fault you insisted on prying and got in—"

"Enough." Tosii flung a hand up.

"Tell me what you're defending," Tikaya said. "Let me be a part of the solution rather than an impediment. Regardless of what you think, I do have Rias's ear."

Jikaymar sat and fumed, but Tosii cupped her chin with her fingers. Considering the offer?

"It *is* part of her family's history," Tosii said. "She would have likely found out one day anyway."

Tikaya shifted in her chair. Just how many people in her family *knew*? Mother didn't, Tikaya was certain, but Father, yes, and Grandpa maybe. Her cousin, Elloil? Surely nobody would have included him on a sensitive matter. Despite her roaming thoughts, Tikaya clasped her hands in her lap and waited. If Tosii was thinking of sharing, there was no reason to say anything.

Before speaking, Tosii shared a long look with the still-fuming Jikaymar. There was nothing blatant about it, but it might have held a trust-me-I-know-what-I'm-doing undertone. Tikaya resolved not to take any offered information for fact.

"Our people left their ravaged homeland in the Southern Hemisphere hundreds of years ago," Tosii said, "and found their way here. It was not the first place they stopped. They were driven from mainland ports by people who feared they carried the plague. They sought uninhabited islands instead, but all the places they found had cities or at least tribes on them, and news of the devastation—and sickness—down south had spread even to these remote places. Again and again, they were driven away at spear point. When they finally found a promising island they thought uninhabited, the dense jungle interior turned out to house cannibals with sharpened teeth and necklaces made from the finger bones of their eaten enemies. Again our people were chased away."

Tikaya nodded, though she wanted to prod Tosii to move the story along. This part was in the history books. Though she supposed time wasn't a concern at this point, there was always the possibility that Rias would fear for her safety and make a move.

Tosii frowned at Tikaya. "Yes, the history books tell us all that, but what they don't dwell on is the fact that our people were hungry, sick, and extremely weary to the point of desperation. When they found these islands, which were full of animals to hunt, sea life to fish, and fruits and vegetables to gather, their hopes finally rose. With the warm tropical climate so different from the hot and cold extremes of the mainland they'd left behind, they believed they'd found paradise. The first island they explored, Nimu, was uninhabited and they believed they'd finally found a home. They started recuperating and building houses, but one day someone saw smoke arising from Muiele." Tosii waved to indicate their main island. Outside a porthole, the cliffs and beaches had grown visible as dawn's influence spread. "They'd avoided it because of the active volcano, and they hoped it was merely smoke from lava flows that they were seeing. They sent a team to investigate and found... another group of people in the process of building a town. At first, our ancestors thought they'd found more refuges from the desecrated continent, but these people had darker skin and hair coloring, and they spoke in an unfamiliar tongue that seemed to be an offshoot of Nurian."

"And did these early Turgonians arrive first?" Tikaya asked.

"It's impossible to say. We believe both groups arrived at approximately the same time."

Tosii rattled off the response quickly, and Jikaymar glanced at her. When he noticed Tikaya following the glance, he dropped his gaze to study the table.

"Though I usually decrypt documents rather than spoken words," Tikaya said, "even I can see that's code for, 'Yes, the Turgonians were here first.'"

"Believe what you wish," Tosii said. "Both groups could have *shared* the islands. With more than ten in the chain, there was plenty of room for the two peoples to grow and prosper."

"But the Turgonians weren't interested in sharing."

"No. They had only one ship in the harbor at the time, but they spoke of their colonizing mission, saying they'd soon be building more ships and going off to find the rest of their people to bring them back. Our ancestors tried to negotiate, but the Turgonians were intractable. They wouldn't share the islands." Tosii met Tikaya's eyes. "A linguist by the name of Jeo Komitopis was doing the translating."

Tikaya swallowed. She'd had a feeling some ancestor of hers would come into the story eventually.

"We can't know for certain what conversations went on all those years ago," Tosii said, "but a woman, Eolila Mokkos, kept a journal that has survived."

"Mokkos, as in some ancestor of the president's?"

"Yes. We also believe the Turgonians kept records." Tosii's gaze dropped to the deck, perhaps indicating the wreck and what they believed it held—*had* held. "Through Mrs. Mokkos's journal, we know that our ancestors decided they weren't leaving. Some felt we had to attack, to strike first and drive the Turgonians away. Others said they were tired of fighting and pointed out that they'd left their homeland to seek peace. Some noted how many weapons the Turgonians had brought with them and the way they practiced with swords in their daily lives. They pointed out that it'd be ludicrous to pick a fight with a warrior society. While all this discussion was going on, a small group of people decided to solve the problem on their own. A botanist had brought seeds and samples from home, wanting to bring some of their old life to their new habitat, and apparently there was also a sample of the organisms that caused the plague. The botanist had thought to study the species and find a cure. Regardless, this group of people took the sample, sneaked into the Turgonian town, and spread it around."

Tikaya shuddered. Even though she'd known something like this must have happened, it disturbed her anew to think that her people could have, in a calculating, premeditated manner, chosen murder. It was a strong word, but she couldn't bring herself to use a less condemning one.

"The Turgonians were decimated, but they were a hardy folk and more people survived than was expected. At that point, our ancestors believed they were forced to attack, to finish the job that an unauthorized few had started. If not... the Turgonians would have no doubt as to who'd caused all these deaths. So, our people charged in and attacked, using hunting bows and boar spears against swords and harpoon launchers. The Turgonians had superior weapons and training, but their numbers were few. Our people were winning, but a few Turgonians slipped away during the night with their most prized possessions, and, we assume, records of the events. They boarded their ship and used darkness to cover their escape. Almost."

"We didn't see what sank the ship," Tikaya said. "The wreck was as pristine as something that'd spent centuries at the bottom of the sea could be."

"Our journalist, Mrs. Mokkos, wasn't amongst the attackers and only recorded that our people destroyed it without warning, to ensure no reinforcements could be brought. They proceeded to kill everyone in the settlement as well. Many were against it, but their choice had been made for them. To let anyone survive would be to risk the annihilation of our people when word reached the remaining Turgonians. And those original colonists... if they hadn't survived, our entire people, our culture and all we've accomplished in science and the mental sciences would never have existed."

Justification, Tikaya thought. "History is full of atrocities, though I suppose it's different when it's your own people who committed them. Easier to lord over those warlike Nurians and Turgonians when we have the luxury *now* to live a peaceful lifestyle. We've done a good job of portraying a pure image to the world, haven't we?"

"It's not our image we're worried about," Jikaymar said. "The Turgonians already want our islands. This would give them an excuse to marshal their entire force and take them. No other country would come to our aid, not if it came out that the Turgonians were here first and we slew them to take the islands for ourselves." He gave Tosii an exasperated look, as if to say he'd known Tikaya wouldn't understand and ask why she'd bothered to share the story.

Tosii was gazing at Tikaya through hooded eyes. "It was a small group of people who made a decision the rest of the colonists had to live with. And which their descendants must, per force, live with also. According to Mrs. Mokkos, the rest of the colonists were outraged, but we know the names of those who participated in the group that sailed over to unleash the plague spores. Their descendants have extremely large, fertile parcels of land on the main island, close to the harbor."

Suggesting they'd been rewarded, not ostracized. And, from the way Tosii continued to stare at her, she must want Tikaya to think of her own family. "I assume the Komitopis who served as translator was also in this party," Tikaya said.

"He was."

That made Tikaya wonder if her father had been strong-armed at all. Had he chosen to go along with the high ministers, to ensure the family's secrets remained buried? "Well, I'd already learned about the adulteress in my bloodlines. Apparently we weren't all wholesome plantation workers after all."

Tosii blinked. Had she expected Tikaya to be more upset? To jump to join their side because of this revelation?

"The Turgonians already want me dead for my role in the war," Tikaya said. "What are they going to do? Kill me twice?"

Jikaymar frowned at Tosii. "This was a waste of time."

"Let's get back to discussing Rias and his terms," Tikaya said. "I doubt very much that he wants to see the Kyatt Islands ravaged or our people annihilated over something that happened seven centuries ago."

Jikaymar snorted. "Why not? He was the one who tried to make those things happen three years ago."

"All he wanted was an outpost here, for more convenient monitoring of the Nurians. As I understand it, he came here openly, hoping to negotiate for it. You must have been privy to that." Belatedly, she realized she had only Rias's word as to those events. She didn't doubt him, but if these two ministers hadn't been involved, they'd have no reason to believe it.

"Yes, he came," Jikaymar said, "and I said no. To give the Turgonians a base would have been, in the Nurians' eyes, to ally with the empire."

I? Jikaymar had been the one to veto the outpost? Had the president been consulted? Rias, she recalled, had never met the president. One of the first things he'd asked her, back when he'd been Prisoner Five, was if the president was a good man.

"In response," Jikaymar said, "they sent a fleet to utterly destroy us."

"By the emperor's orders, not Rias's," Tikaya said. "He respected us for fighting back. He even respected—" *me*, she thought, but changed it to, "—our cryptanalysts for deciphering their codes. He's an honorable man who appreciates an honorable battle. He refused to help the assassin the emperor sent to kill the president."

"The what?" Jikaymar looked at Tosii, but she only shrugged and said, "If that's true, that might explain why the president hasn't been as quick to see him as an enemy. Perhaps we should have..." She glanced at Tikaya and shut her mouth.

"You've mentioned his terms multiple times," Jikaymar told Tikaya. "What does he want? More specifically, what is it going to take to keep him silent on this matter?"

"He's not willing to remain silent," Tikaya said.

Jikaymar gave her the sort of look one gives to an ill-prepared squid dish with the rubbery texture of a bicycle tire. "That's your opening move? That's obviously going to be unacceptable to us."

"He believes that as long as he's the only one outside of your inner cadre to know this secret, his life will be at risk. At any point, someone may decide it's safer if he's simply not around to drop the coconuts."

"We're not assassins," Jikaymar said.

Tikaya intertwined her fingers on the table and gave him her best is-that-a-fact stare. Out loud, she said, "He's unwilling to risk that, given the events that have take place over the last couple of weeks. He proposes, instead, that the information be made publicly available to the entire world and—"

Jikaymar's sputtering interrupted her. Tosii dropped her forehead into her hand.

"In exchange," Tikaya continued, "Rias is willing to act as a military adviser should any nations sail into Kyattese waters with hostile intent."

"Oh, sure," Jikaymar said, "he's going to take our side against the Turgonians. You expect us to believe that? What reason does he have to defend the Kyatt Islands?"

"Me, you dolt." Tikaya caught herself rolling her eyes at him, but stopped. Negotiators probably weren't supposed to do such things. Before Jikaymar could deliver an insulting comment on the value of her worth, she added, "He proposed to me. And I would have accepted by now if you folks hadn't been so busy trying to blow us up."

For the first time in the meeting, neither Jikaymar nor Tosii could come up with a response. Tosii must not have been browsing in that particular pasture in Tikaya's mind, for she seemed even more shocked than Jikaymar.

"In addition to his council, Rias is willing to share the schematics for his submarine with our people." All right, he hadn't said that, but Tikaya believed he would if she negotiated for it. He was giving the plans to the *Nurians* after all. "And he will assist with building a small fleet of research submarines as well." Hm, maybe she should have checked with him on that one. How did marriage customs work in Turgonia? Did the bride give a gift to the husband's family or was it the other way around? The Kyattese used to have a bride price. Goats, pigs, and sometimes canoes, as she recalled. Rias could be the first one to offer a bride's father submarines.

"Research submarines?" Jikaymar asked.

"He's Turgonian. If the prototype is anything to go on, they'll have torpedoes and deployable mines. I'm sure these submarines could be invaluable in defending the islands, should that ever be necessary."

"That prototype has certainly vexed the rum out of our barrels," Tosii said. "Even with the Science, it's difficult to judge where it is when it's submerged. The Turgonians don't even study the mental sciences, so they'd be doubly clueless in finding a craft like that."

Though surprised by the support, Tikaya gave the other woman a quick nod.

Jikaymar rubbed his chin. "With underwater attack vessels—"

"Research submarines," Tikaya said.

"—available to protect against sailing fleets, I imagine we'd be able to fight off far greater forces. They'd learn to consider the Kyattese seas akin to a mine field."

"Undoubtedly," Tikaya said. "And Rias has quite the reputation in Turgonia. His people would think twice before launching an attack if they knew he was an honored and valued adviser to our government, an adviser who walks freely about the islands without being harassed by its citizens."

Tosii snorted. "Is that one of his terms?"

"No, that's *my* term." Tikaya didn't want her future... husband—she blushed at the thought—to be forced to wear ridiculous clam diggers and sun-colored floral shirts because he was worried he had to appear unthreatening here.

Shouts sounded on the deck above. A second later, knocks struck the door with enough force to rattle the planks. "High ministers?" came the accompanying shout.

"Yes, what?" Jikaymar called.

The door flew open, and an earnest cabin boy clutched his hat to his chest. "Pardon, sir, ma'am, but there's a ship. It's swung out of the shipping lane and is approaching our position. It's the *Eagle's Perch*."

It wasn't until Jikaymar and Tosii exchanged knowing glances that the significance of the name emerged from Tikaya's memory. "That's the president's ship, isn't it?"

"He did say he'd be returning this week," Jikaymar said.

"There's more, sir," the cabin boy said. "The black monster? It's on the surface and is approaching the *Perch*."

"What?" Jikaymar stood so quickly, he knocked his chair over.

Tosii stood as well, but ran straight past the cabin boy and out the door.

Jikaymar spun toward Tikaya. "Starcrest won't attack the president, will he?"

It took Tikaya a second to realize "black monster" had to be their name for the submarine. "No, of course not. He probably thinks he can get further circumventing you and approaching the president directly." Tikaya hoped that was all Rias had in mind. In addition to everything else, he might be worried about her at this point. She had been on the ship for some time. It wasn't surprising that he'd know who sailed around in the *Eagle's Perch*, but he didn't mean to force a resolution in a... martial manner, did he?

Jikaymar may have been thinking along the same path, for he grabbed her arm and jerked his head toward the door. "We're going up top."

Tikaya twisted free from his grip before they reached the stairs and jogged up of her own accord. She rushed to a railing that was already lined with people. The president's large catamaran could reputedly make great speed, but they had brought down its sails and it was gliding to a stop. The *Freedom*, its form indeed nearly black compared to the twin white hulls of the *Perch*, bobbed alongside it. It was close enough that Rias could have hopped out and climb aboard the president's ship.

Tikaya cleaned her spectacles and squinted. The hatch was open. Maybe Rias had *already* boarded. What was he up to? He'd given up his advantage by coming to the surface—Tosii or another practitioner could easily target the submarine now. Rias hadn't known if the president was aware of the assassination attempt he'd stopped or not, so he couldn't be certain he'd receive a friendly reception on the *Perch*. For all he knew, he'd be shot if he stepped aboard.

"What's he about?" Tikaya murmured.

Tosii walked up to stand at Jikaymar's elbow. She whispered something in his ear. Pointing out that the submarine was on the surface and therefore vulnerable? They wouldn't fire with the president's ship next to it. What if they missed? Of course, a weapon guided by the mental sciences might be trusted *not* to miss.

"Yosis, come here," Jikaymar barked.

Before the practitioner could obey, a young sailor scrambled down from the crow's nest, almost tripping over his bare feet as he ran up to Jikaymar. "Sir, we can't fire at the black monster. The president went *aboard*." His voice squeaked with excitement—or intense alarm—on the last word.

"What? What's he thinking?" Jikaymar flung out an arm. "Take us over there."

Tikaya blew out a slow breath.

"Did he go aboard of his own will?" Tosii asked.

The young sailor nodded. "The crew of the *Perch* was terribly concerned when the black monster popped up in front of them, and men were scurrying all about on deck, but the Scourge popped right out and started talking to folks. It wasn't long before the president himself came out. Don't know what they were telling each other, but he climbed overboard with one of his men and they disappeared inside."

Jikaymar's ship glided closer as the conversation progressed. They'd be alongside the *Perch* in a moment. Full daylight had come, so Tikaya could see the nervous expressions on the faces of the sailors pacing the *Perch's* deck. Watching the president disappear into the strange craft had to be nerve-wracking, especially for those who knew exactly who Rias was.

Everyone on both decks halted their pacing when a head rose from the *Freedom's* hatchway, and Tikaya imagined she heard collective exhales of relief. The president's short sandy hair was more gray than blond these days, but, with a clean-shaven face and a slender build, he appeared similar to the last time she had seen him. Rias climbed out behind him. They were still too far away for Tikaya to hear words spoken, but the president must have invited Rias aboard, for they clambered up onto the *Perch*. Leaving the *Freedom* unguarded? Mee Nar wasn't in sight, but he wouldn't know how to take the submarine under if someone tried to board it.

"Mister President," Jikaymar called.

The president squinted into the rising sun at them. "Yes, yes, come aboard, high ministers." He didn't sound that pleased with his right- and left-hand people. Good. "You too, Ms. Komitopis."

Hm, he didn't sound that pleased with *her* either.

CHAPTER 22

ONCE ABOARD THE *EAGLE'S PERCH,* Tikaya found herself sitting at a fancy full-slab wooden table with Rias to her left and the president to her right. Jikaymar, Tosii, and a couple of other officials that hadn't been introduced sat across from them. Rias had given Tikaya a reassuring pat on the shoulder before they sat down, whatever that meant. She wanted to tug him to the side and brief him on her discussion with the high ministers, but there'd been no opportunity.

Once everyone had settled into their seats, the president rested his hands on the table, fingers steepled, and met each person's eyes. "I understand there are no secrets left in this room."

Tikaya glanced at Rias, still wondering what he knew. His face gave away nothing, not even to her.

"And," the president went on after a glance at Tosii, "I understand we have an offer on the table."

The president was also, Tikaya recalled, a telepath. But Tosii had seemed as surprised as anyone at the appearance of the president's ship, so they couldn't have been in communication for long. A single hasty exchange perhaps?

"And that there's been a marriage proposal." The president didn't smile exactly, but the creases at the corners of his blue eyes deepened.

Several faces swung toward Tikaya, and she blushed. Rias, too, regarded her, as if to ask what had prompted her to include that tidbit in the negotiations.

"Yes." Tikaya cleared her throat and faced the president. "Is that pertinent to this discussion?"

The president spread his hands. "It may be. What Admiral Starcrest wishes to reveal to the world... Well, once the octopus is released from the trap, one does not shove it back in."

Tikaya kept herself from wincing at the mention of an octopus.

"Thus it is, with our... checkered history," the president went on. He liked to make those dramatic pauses, Tikaya noticed. Maybe he was simply guarding his words carefully before letting them fall. "Admiral Starcrest, on the other hand, can only prove his willingness to keep his word over time. In short, he is asking much from us with nothing tangible that can be given immediately, to ensure his future cooperation."

Tikaya leaned back in her chair. It sounded like the president wanted something physical that could be used to, essentially, blackmail Rias if he decided to wander off without following through on his promises.

"Were he married to a citizen and living on the islands, with a passel of children perhaps..." The president spread a palm toward the ceiling. "Many would see this as a sign that he'd be unlikely to betray us…or simply forget us, and return to the empire at some future point."

Rias's eyebrow twitched, and Tikaya guessed he might be thinking something like, "Oh, sure, *now* you want me to stay on your island." All he said was, "While it is my desire that this might come to pass in time, Ms. Komitopis has not given me an answer to what was not a particularly well-timed proposition. Apparently music and candles are preferred to..."

"Explosives detonating outside the window?" Tikaya suggested.

"Indeed."

Tikaya was about to tell him that she'd happily accept his proposition, for reasons that had nothing to do with an interracial marriage being convenient for the president, but Rias spoke first. "I am, however, a man of my word, Mr. President, as you can verify if you ask any of my old comrades or enemies. It sounds like Ms. Komitopis has delivered my offer. I stand behind it."

"I believe you to be an honorable man, Admiral, which is probably why—" he gave the high ministers a frank look, "—so many outer island problems have come up to delay my return to the capital since your arrival. But you have no old comrades or enemies here to vouch for you. I must consider this carefully before deciding. What you ask... could be the undoing of our entire nation." The president pushed his chair back. "We shall reconvene after I've contemplated this offer thoroughly."

"Mr. President," Tikaya said.

Rias touched her wrist and shook his head.

Tikaya hesitated, not certain if he knew what she had in mind, to tell everyone that she wished to accept his proposal. In case he did, she only said, "He does have an enemy here. Didn't you meet Mee Nar when you toured the submarine?"

Half-standing, half-sitting, the president frowned and looked back and forth between them. "No."

"He hid," Rias said dryly.

Uh oh. Tikaya had thought it'd be an innocuous question.

"I believe he still hopes he may continue on with his current job," Rias said, "something that might not happen if he enters the president's awareness."

"Mee Nar," the president said, as if trying to dredge the details of a familiar name from memory. "Is this the Nurian spy who lives near the Komitopis plantation?"

Tikaya almost laughed. How long had the government known of Mee Nar's secret occupation? Rias didn't seem surprised. Spying upon spies was probably commonplace in the empire.

"Yes, sir," Tikaya said.

"If he'll... come out of hiding, I will speak with him." The president rose from his chair. "My officers, come with me please."

"Shall we leave a guard for them?" Jikaymar asked.

The president considered the bank of windows overlooking the sea—the side of Rias's submarine was just visible outside—then eyed Tikaya and Rias in turn. "I think not." He walked out the door.

Tosii frowned at his back, but followed after with the others. Tikaya scratched her head. Was he offering them a chance to escape if they wished it? Or leaving them with the possibility of escape to see if they could be trusted by *not* taking it?

"As much as I'd love for you to accept my marriage offer," Rias said, pulling her attention away from the windows, "I don't want it to be out of some political motivation."

"It wouldn't be. I would have said yes already if people hadn't been hurling explosives at us. And if the submarine hadn't sprung a leak. And if you hadn't turned annoyingly secretive over that chest." Reminded of the chest, Tikaya added, "Care to tell me what's in it yet?"

Rias glanced at the door. "Not yet."

"And you don't care to accept my marriage-proposal acceptance, either?"

Rias smiled sadly. "Not like this."

"Marriage proposals don't have to be perfect, you know. My first one involved drinking and vomiting."

"On your part or his?" Rias asked.

"His. I understand he was nervous so he fortified himself beforehand."

"And you accepted anyway?"

"Yes."

"Even with—was the vomiting a part of the evening or did it come the morning after?"

"Let's just say that I retired that pair of shoes after that dinner," Tikaya said.

"Given these revelations, I'm feeling even more stung that you hesitated at my offer."

"Only because of extenuating events." Tikaya grasped his hand. "You don't have to tell the president, but I accept now."

"No vomiting required?"

"None at all."

"I always suspected that scrub-brush-headed boy lacked class," Rias said.

"His name is Parkonis." It was the first time Tikaya could remember him insulting anyone, and she didn't believe for a second that he'd forgotten Parkonis's name. She supposed she could forgive him the flaw; after all, she'd have less than savory things to say about his former wife if she ever strolled onto the waterfront. Still, she couldn't resist teasing him. "How much class did you display when proposing to your first wife?"

"Well. I didn't vomit."

"But you drank?"

"Copious amounts. Any man will tell you that legions of enemy troops are less intimidating to face than a woman." Rias leaned closer and smiled. "In the empire, kissing is customary to seal a marriage proposal."

Tikaya returned his smile, taking a moment to admire his strong jaw, the old scars that somehow added to his handsomeness instead of detracting from it, and those dark brown eyes with their flecks of gold—and mostly the way those eyes gazed back at her with love. The proposal might not have gone quite how she'd imagined, but he was here and he'd denied any interest in returning to Turgonia. "An imperial custom that doesn't involve bloodshed?"

"Yes, it's one of two or three that fall into that category." Rias leaned closer, his lips parted, his—

The door opened.

Rias drew away, and Tikaya sighed. All the mischievous sprites on the island were conspiring to keep them apart. This time, only Tosii, the president, and Mee Nar entered the room.

"We accept the premise of your proposal," the president said as soon as everyone sat down, "but require modification of the final details."

"Such as?" Rias asked.

"We need time to prepare before this information is released into the world. These submarines, for example, must be built, and we'll need to increase our readiness in military matters. We'll also need to see that you're still around and committed to the continuing safety of the Kyatt Islands, or at least some of its residents."

The president glanced at Tikaya, and she remembered his comment about a passel of children. Though she was getting all that she'd wanted—a place for Rias on her island and a chance to have a life, even a family, with him—this new twist did disturb her, the suggestion that their choices going forward might not be entirely a matter of free will. Rias's profile was toward her, and she watched him, wondering if he had similar thoughts.

"In theory, a time delay would not matter to me," Rias said, "but as long as I am the only Turgonian with this knowledge, I will be a target for your people." The president shook his head and opened his mouth, but Rias interrupted him. "You can attempt to promise me otherwise, but it's clear that you don't have full control over all of your people. Even those you work closely with. Also, you are an elected official whose term is up in two years. There is no guarantee you will be reelected for another term."

"I understand your objections," the president said, "and have anticipated them. I propose that you send the information to one or more trusted colleagues or family members you have in the empire, with instructions not to open the sealed information for a certain period of time. Upon the date specified, your acquaintance would be free to deliver the message to your emperor. I suppose it's too much to hope that *he* won't be reelected for a second term." The corner of the president's mouth twitched.

The negotiations had been flowing along in Kyattese, and, thus far, Rias had seemed to follow every word, but at this joke, he gave Tikaya a curious translate-please look.

"I believe the president is hoping your emperor might be somehow replaced in the near future. Lifelong reigns are tedious for those who don't care for a particular ruler."

"Ah." Rias faced the president again. "Assassinations aren't terribly common in Turgonia. It's considered a cowardly way to get rid of a man, though I suppose you could hope for him to fall in a war."

"Or trip and hit his head in the bathtub," Tosii muttered to herself. "Fatally."

"The emperor is fairly young," Rias said, "and his heir is only a year old, so you'll pardon me if I don't share your hope for his demise. His passing would cause internal strife, and my people would only lose in that matter."

"But the rest of the world would enjoy peace while it lasted," the president said.

"Or take advantage of the turmoil," Rias said. "If I were to agree to write the letters you suggested, what do-not-open-until date would you require?"

The president straightened, a back-to-business firmness steeling his jaw. "You can pick the exact date, but we want twenty years."

"Twenty years?" Tikaya asked at the same time as Rias and in the same startled tone.

The president frowned at her. Right, she was probably supposed to be on the Kyattese side of the negotiations. He was probably asking for a high number, so he could afford to settle at a lower one.

"Too long," Rias said. "I'm not a young man and the trusted confidants that come to mind were my superiors when I was coming up through the ranks. I shouldn't wish them to pass on before they can deliver the letters."

"You are welcome to send the news to more than one person. I am the one taking the largest risk here." The president spread his arms, palms up. "I have only your word that you'll send the letters with instructions for a post-dated delivery, and I can only hope that the people you choose will deserve your trust and not open the envelopes prematurely. I would... not be able to live with myself if the decisions I made today resulted in imperial warships filling the harbor before the year was out."

"Five years," Rias said. "That is enough time to build the submarines that have been promised."

"Fifteen years. Our volcanoes don't ooze metal ore. We must import the raw materials and we'll need to upgrade our manufacturing facilities. Military issues aside, we'll want to build larger underwater boats than the one you've shown me, thus to house teams of scientists on extended voyages. There are a great number of wrecks in the world, and this offers a fascinating opportunity for exploration and study."

Though Tikaya knew he was bargaining for more time, she smiled at the way the president's eyes lit up as he spoke of exploration. He'd been a history professor at the Polytechnic before running for political office, and he doubtlessly did find the idea of undersea research intriguing.

"All you wish can be done in five years, but I'll agree to ten if you accept that I will not divulge the names or locations of the persons I'll entrust with these letters. Though I find the idea of a Kyattese assassin unlikely, I would not wish to tempt anyone."

"I will agree to these terms so long as you show me the content of the letters before you send them."

It sounded like a formality. For whatever reason, he seemed inclined to trust Rias. Perhaps, down in the *Freedom*, they'd discussed the imperial assassin that had once tried to find passage to the president's doorstep via Rias's flagship. Or perhaps the president had already known about that. Rias had once said he'd sent a message of warning, though who knew if letters from enemy admirals were placed on the president's desk?

"I accept." Rias stood and lifted a hand.

The president nodded solemnly at him. "I suggest, then, that we leave these waters to the surfers. We can formalize the agreement tonight after dinner. My staff will prepare a hearty sampling of local dishes, certain to satisfy even a Turgonian appetite."

Hand still poised in the air, Rias gave Tikaya another questioning look. Recalling that Turgonians often sealed deals orally, with nothing more than a hand clasp, she said, "Papers will be written up, and both parties will have to sign them. There'll be multiple papers with multiple pages that require multiple signatures. Make sure to eat up at dinner. You'll need your strength to get through it."

Rias lowered his hand. "I see."

The president gave Tikaya a wry look, but made a gesture of dismissal for everyone. He escorted Tikaya and Rias to the railing where the *Freedom* was tied. Mee Nar waited nearby, having apparently been, as Tikaya suggested, consulted in regard to Rias's character. Speaking of wry expressions...

"Coming?" Rias asked him.

"I've had enough of that deathtrap." Mee Nar waved a dismissive hand. "The captain of this ship has offered me a ride back to the harbor. Where I should apparently start looking for a new job."

Tikaya paused. "You'll stay here even with everybody knowing about...?"

Mee Nar twitched a shoulder. "I've grown somewhat fond of my wife. And the weather is most agreeable."

"See?" Rias nudged Tikaya. "Your climate is more of a draw than you realize."

"Apparently so."

Tikaya caught sight of Yosis glowering from the deck of the other ship, but nobody objected when she and Rias climbed down onto the hull of the submarine. He untied the line docking them to the larger craft, and they dropped into the interior. Despite the peaceful conclusion to the negotiations, Tikaya's shoulders didn't lose their tense hunch until Rias sat in his chair at the navigation console and began pulling the *Freedom* away from the *Perch*—and the vessel with those explosives.

She sank down in the seat beside Rias. "I'm glad we were able to reach an arrangement that didn't involve bloodshed. Though I'm sorry you were, ah, I hope you won't feel unpleasantly pressured over the president's suggestion of marriage and, er, passels of children."

Rias rotated toward her in his seat, a serene expression on his face.

"Personally, I find big families overrated," Tikaya said. "I should think two children would be a nice, manageable number, but only if you have notions of fatherhood." It would be difficult to stomach if he didn't, but they'd never spoken of it. Rather, they'd spoken of going off in the submarine and exploring together. That might prove difficult with babes along.

Rias was still facing her, his expression calm, almost bland. Or maybe... expectant?

"What?" Tikaya asked.

He smiled slightly. Waiting.

Erg, was she supposed to be figuring something out? Oh, had he...? Tikaya squinted at him. "You didn't by chance manipulate the president into thinking he wants you to have a tie to the islands, did you?"

Finally, Rias chuckled. "Your people haven't been that welcoming thus far. I thought it might take something on the order of a presidential mandate to gain me acceptance, or at least the right to walk and breathe without fruit being pelted at me." He touched his jaw, and Tikaya feared that had actually happened.

"So, when we were arguing about marriage... Were you *really* arguing with me or was that for show?"

"Well, I wouldn't want *you* to feel pressured about that, but, yes, I did assume we were being monitored when we were alone in there. One way or another."

Tikaya leaned back in her seat. "Huh."

"I hope that vague grunt denotes approval."

"It does. And also that I was thinking that if our children are as sly as you, they're going to be challenging to raise."

"Perhaps you and my mother can exchange letters," Rias said, facing the controls again.

"I wonder if she'd send advice, or warnings." She waved to a lever he was gripping. "Back to the harbor?"

"Hm. Not quite yet, I think." Rias nudged a control. The lighting dimmed as the submarine dipped below the surface, and water covered the porthole. He took them down ten feet or so, then leveled the craft.

"Don't you need to find a safe harbor for conducting repairs?"

"Yes, but I had something else in mind first." Rias draped his arm over the back of his chair. "This is the first time we've been alone together, somewhere that nobody can interrupt us."

"Oh?" Tikaya bit back a smile and strove for an expression of innocence instead. "Did you have... something in mind?"

"Yes, my lady." Rias surged to his feet and swooped her up into his arms. "I did."

"You did? Whatever is it? I require details." Tikaya looped her arms around his neck.

Rias ducked and slid sideways through the hatchway so her legs wouldn't bump the frame. "It's been irking me to no end that my *helper* is the only one who's entertained a woman on *my* bed." He ducked through a second hatchway, this time into the sleeping cabin.

"That does seem terribly unfair."

"I'm glad you agree." He bent his head and kissed her jaw, then her neck.

Tikaya would have happily given into the delightful sensations and crawled into the bed with him, but she caught sight of that chest. It sat in the corner by the door, grime still crusted to the outside, though enough had been cleared away from the lid area to reveal handsome hand-carved stone features. "*Rias*. You still haven't told me what was actually in there."

"Hm?" he asked, lips moving down to her collarbone. He set her on the bed.

Tikaya promptly squirmed out of his grasp. "I *have* to know. Was the captain's log in there? A detailed explanation of the events that befell the colony? Protected and preserved in a waterproof scroll case sealed with beeswax?" Tikaya almost laughed at herself. As if the captain could have guessed that his words would spend centuries on the bottom of the ocean. "Or some other treasure of historical significance?"

Rias sighed. "I suppose it depends on how you define treasure." He lay propped on his elbow on the bed.

Tikaya wasn't sure if the chest would be locked again, but when she tried the lid, it opened. It was heavy, though, and took two hands to lift. She found herself staring at—

"Gold coins?" Her shoulders sagged. "That's it? That's all there is in here?" She raked through the mound. "They're not even an interesting collection; just plain old coins stamped from a seven-hundred-year-old Nurian mint."

Rias's laughter echoed from the walls of the small cabin. "You're the only woman I've ever met who would be disappointed by finding a fortune in gold."

Tikaya curled her lip at the coins. She'd seen dozens of similar ones in the past. They weren't rare or collectible, and were simply worth their weight in gold. A fortune, perhaps, but nothing historically intriguing. "I should have taken one of the amphoras."

"The chest is nice," Rias said. "Hand-carved by a master mason, unless I miss my guess. Perhaps if we clean it up further, the carvings will have some historical value."

"I suppose." Tikaya let the lid drop. "So, all that time, you didn't know anything at all in regard to the secrets of those old colonies."

"Nothing but guesses."

"I'll have to tell you the story, so you can relay it properly."

"It was nice of you to get the information, but..." Rias patted the bed. "Why don't we save story hour for later?"

Tikaya climbed in beside him. "If you insist."

EPILOGUE

TIKAYA SEARCHED THE GROWING CROWD of friends, colleagues, and relatives as she plucked at a seashell bracelet dangling from her wrist. She kept hoping to see her father. She didn't expect Grandpa—he'd probably die before he called Rias anything other than an ugly joratt, and her a fool for marrying one—but she'd hoped... She *wanted* to see Father there. She shouldn't, after all he'd done to try and get rid of Rias, but if he came to the wedding, it might mean that he regretted those choices, and regretted letting himself be strong-armed into making them. Or at least it might mean that he could accept that Rias would be a part of the family.

She sighed and leaned against a post supporting a flower-bedecked bamboo bower. Inside awaited a simple table supporting an old carved wooden bowl. It overflowed with stuffed dates, coconut candy, and other sweets designed to entice Akahe to visit and perhaps bless the wedding. Of course, it held at least two times the normal amount of sweets—dates had spilled out of the bowl onto the lace doily beneath it. Mother must think much more than the usual bribe would be required to get a blessing for *this* pairing.

"What's taking so long?" Tikaya glanced at the house and toyed with the bracelet again. Her mother had given it to her when she'd been putting on her dress. Generations old, it had apparently been worn by many Komitopis women on their wedding days. Sensing a touch of the Science, Tikaya had asked what sort of properties it was imbued with, but her mother had simply smiled. Knowing her, it probably encouraged fertility.

"Last I heard, your mother and aunts are fiddling with Rias's wardrobe, trying to make him look unthreatening and unmilitary." Elloil was lounging against a post on the other side of the bower and eyeing the sweets.

"Not one of your floral shirts, I hope." Tikaya thought Rias looked quite dashing in a Turgonian uniform—it suited him far more than island clothing—but she supposed not everyone there would appreciate seeing him so garbed.

"Nah." Ell was wearing a chaste cream-colored shirt and forest green trousers. He almost looked respectable, though his yellow and orange sandals, replete with blue tassels, rebelled against the sedateness of the rest of the outfit. "Though, on my last trip through the house, I did hear someone musing about a vine crown woven with flowers."

Tikaya groaned. "I hope you're teasing me."

"Would I do that?"

"Yes."

Ell grinned.

Tikaya touched his arm. "Listen, I want you to know... I appreciate the help you gave Rias—and me—these last few weeks." She especially appreciated it, given that she'd been suspecting him of being the spy in the house. His eagerness to please and help out hadn't faded of late, and she'd finally decided he'd just been following them around because he was, much like all those young Turgonians, a touch enamored with Rias.

"You're welcome." Ell said it solemnly and seriously, but the grin soon returned, and he winked. "It's been enjoyable *not* being the biggest ham-head in the family of late."

"Out of curiosity, why did you follow me to the Polytechnic that night and claim my mother sent you?" Tikaya wriggled her eyebrows to let him know she'd found out Mother had made no such request.

"You had that knapsack with you. I thought you might be running away from home to go with Rias. Forever."

"Oh. I don't think they call it 'running away' if you're over thirty."

Ell shrugged. "I was going to offer to come along. They have surfing in Turgonia, don't they? Anyway, I didn't realize you were just meeting Rias to do unspeakable things together in the reading chairs in the library."

Tikaya decided to smile rather than wince in embarrassment, though the gesture faded as she searched again for Father amongst the seventy or eighty people chatting while they browsed the mile-long buffet table. Mother and her chosen kitchen helpers had smothered it with platters that were sending sumptuous scents into the air, and few guests were straying far.

Someone cleared his throat nearby. "Tikaya?"

She turned, thinking her father had joined them, but it was her brother. "Oh, hello, Ky." He'd dressed up and looked like he meant to stay. That was something. Nothing he'd said thus far led her to believe he was excited about having a Turgonian in the family.

"Give us a moment, Ell, will you?" Ky asked.

"Sure." Ell offered Tikaya a you'll-get-through-this pat and strolled toward the buffet table, his sandals slapping against his heels, the tassels dancing with each step.

Ky stuck his hands in his pockets. "Mother said to tell you we'll be ready to start soon. I guess they're almost done dressing your... I don't know what to call him."

Rias, Tikaya thought, but she imagined it'd be some time before her brother would deign to speak to Rias, much less call him by his first name. "My husband?" she suggested.

Ky grimaced. "I suppose. I had a chat with Father about... things. I hope Starcrest's name will be as much of an umbrella as the president seems to think it will. And that he's truly here for innocuous reasons. I don't trust—nobody's been in his head, have they? We don't have any way of knowing... not really... that he's not still the emperor's man."

"Ky..." Tikaya tried not to sound weary, but it was hard. This should be a happy day, she reminded herself; it wasn't the time to start another fight. "If he were the emperor's man, do you think he'd be bothering with Kyatt? Yes, the empire would like a base here, but they'd like to take over the whole world, too, I gather. Rias was too talented of a naval commander to be relegated to a spy position. If he were working for the empire, he'd be back out at sea, in charge of a fleet."

"Huh." Ky scratched his jaw.

Tikaya arched an eyebrow. Had that argument swayed him? She should have tried it earlier. Maybe it would work on Father too.

"About your chats with Father," she said, "did he say if he was coming today?"

Ky shrugged. "I'm not sure."

That sounded like a no. "Did he... Do you know if the pumping house was truly an accident or...? Well, I guess he was the one around the homestead, trying to thwart me and get rid of Rias."

"I gathered he was a victim at the pumping house and that the incident was meant to insure his compliance. After that... he was only trying to protect the family. And you."

Tikaya wished Father could have come and told her that himself, instead of telling her brother. But then she hadn't gone to talk to him in private either. Maybe she should have. "It's good that Rias isn't the sort to hold a grudge."

"I guess," Ky said neutrally.

Something bumped into Tikaya's ankle, startling her. She looked down to find some sort of clockwork bamboo toy rolling around with a large jar secured horizontally to its back. Butterflies flapped about inside the glass. A hand crank and staging chamber allowed one to put in new specimens without losing those already inside. Before she could puzzle out more details, laughter reached her ears, and Lonaeo bounced over to her with a net in his hands.

"Where did you get that, Lonaeo?" Ky pointed at the ambulatory jar wagon.

Tikaya could guess, but she held her tongue.

"Uncle Rias!" Lonaeo announced and plucked up the jar—it detached from the carrier wagon. "Do you want to see my butterflies? Here's a green swallowtail and a spotted moon, a dark cerulean, a..."

Ky didn't manage to utter anything as this list went on, but his mouth silently formed the word, "*Uncle?*" over and over again.

"We're going to build a habitat in my room with food and water so I can keep the butterflies and draw them and study them," Lonaeo finished.

Ky shook his head and walked away, mouth still stuck on that one displeasing word. Lonaeo shrugged and headed to the buffet table to impress the other adults with his finds.

"He's built toys for a number of the kids," Ell said, returning with a drink in his hand.

"He's got a knack for knowing exactly who he has to sway to his side to win a battle." Tikaya wondered if Rias had figured out yet that Lonaeo was Grandpa's favorite grandchild, or if that was simply a coincidence. They might not have enticed the old grump into coming to the wedding, but maybe he'd eventually join them at family dinners again.

"Kids are easy to win over," Ell said.

Tikaya gave her cousin a frank stare. "Didn't he win *you* over with the promise of surfboard designs?"

"Oh, yes, and I forgot to ask you. Rias said, if it was all right with you, you two would invest in my business, enough to help me open a big shop and stock some initial inventory."

"Invest? But we don't have any—"

"Why didn't you *tell* me you pulled a chest full of gold off the bottom of the ocean?" Ell asked.

"Oh, that." Tikaya supposed they had funds to invest with after all. "The coins weren't historically significant, so I forgot about them."

"You forgot. About a chest of gold. You're a strange woman, 'Kaya."

"I prefer to think of her as unique," came Rias's voice from behind them. "Extraordinary. Sui generis."

"Careful," Tikaya said, turning around. "The Kyattese love for vocabulary words might be rubbing off on..." She forgot her words when she got a good look at him.

Mother must have brought in a tailor, for Rias finally wore clothing that fit him and there wasn't an obnoxious pattern or color in sight. The creamy vest and trousers and white button-down shirt accented his olive skin, broad shoulders, and powerful form. He'd trimmed his thick black hair and shaved the goatee, leaving an admirable view of his strong jaw. Tikaya wasn't certain even the most sedate plantation suit would hide the fact that Rias was a physically imposing man, but she'd have been disappointed if Mother had succeeded in making him look like a farmer or an academic. Or getting him to put flowers in his hair.

"You're missing the banana yellow shirt, aren't you?" Rias asked after she'd looked him up and down a few times.

"Oddly not." Tikaya grinned and resisted the urge to fling her arms—and maybe her legs—around him. Too many relatives were gazing on, ready to cast judgment, no matter what agreements had been reached with the president. She limited herself to gripping his hands. "You look wonderful."

"Thank you. You also look lovely." He nodded to her white, satiny dress and touched a lock of the hair that she'd let Mother talk her into wearing unbraided. The loose blonde strands dangled to her hips. "Though I am partial to your usual ensemble," he added.

"A hemp dress?"

"One blotted with ink stains and draped in cobwebs and dust acquired while rooting around in attics, archives, and library wings that have been closed for repairs."

"I'm sure I can get this one dirty somehow tonight."

Ell groaned. "All right, nobody wants to hear mushy pillow talk between my cousin and the Black Scourge of the Seas. Look, Yolo is taking the pig off the spit. It's time to get this shindig started." With that, he sauntered away.

"Your mother said the ceremony would begin soon." Rias held up a pen. "Should I be concerned that she gave me this and said I'd need it?"

Before Tikaya could explain the implement, Mother and one of Tikaya's uncles strolled past, Mother with a plate of fig cookies to add to the bowl for Akahe, and her uncle with two chairs, which he sat down beneath the bower, side-by-side in front of the table. He rested two stacks of documents next to the overflowing bowl of sweets. Tikaya rubbed her face as Mother balanced as many cookies as she could manage on the already huge mound.

"I shouldn't have mentioned that you're an atheist," Tikaya said. "Now she's doubly concerned that Akahe won't bless us."

"Is that a concern of yours?" Rias asked, probably wondering if they'd need to have the what-religion-do-we-raise-the-children-in discussion soon.

"No. Don't tell Mother, but I'm not that interested in religions that aren't at least a thousand years old."

"Good." Rias eyed the stack of papers on the table.

Tikaya was about to explain them when she caught sight of Iweue and Dean Teailat strolling toward the buffet table. She'd already run into the dean that morning—after a quick congratulations, he'd reminded her that he hadn't leaned on the police for her sake so she could run off and get randy with a Turgonian; he expected her back at work in the morning—but this was her first time seeing Iweue. Though she wore a formal dress and sandals, she still managed to look quite bookish with her spectacles on the bridge of her nose and a pencil tucked behind one ear—Tikaya suspected the latter was an accidental rather than intentional ornamentation. She hadn't been certain about inviting Iweue, given her relationship to Parkonis, but she and Rias owed the woman for that energy source. She'd thought Iweue might like a chance to meet the legendary fleet admiral she'd only read about thus far. Tikaya waved for Iweue to join them.

"Good afternoon, Tikaya," Iweue said, then offered Rias a shy smile. "Admiral Starcrest."

"Just Rias, ma'am."

Tikaya didn't think they'd met in person and was about to introduce Iweue when Rias gave her a deep warrior-caste bow. Judging by the degree of inclination, Tikaya figured he knew whom he was addressing. Iweue had apparently read enough books involving Turgonians to recognize the respect that the deep bow indicated, for she flushed and her shy smile spread wider.

"Your energy source proved invaluable to us," Rias said. "The *Freedom* needs repairs, but when she's ready, she'll be at your disposal for a journey wherever you wish to go."

"That sounds wonderful, thank you."

Poor Parkonis wouldn't be happy when he learned that Rias had won over both his ex-fiancée and his mother.

"I'll bother you for more details later," Iweue said. "I know you have a lot of paperwork to do today." She winked at Tikaya before heading over to join the other guests.

"Paperwork?" Rias asked mildly, eyeing the stacks of documents again.

"Yes. Ah, what are Turgonian weddings like these days?" She hadn't spent much time studying wedding customs that weren't described in interesting dead languages.

"The bride and groom make promises to each other and kiss in front of witnesses, then the man carries the woman over the threshold and into the bridal cabin, suite, cave or other bed-containing shelter where they... make things official. No witnesses required for that part."

"It's done similarly here, except the promises aren't delivered orally." Tikaya pointed to his pen and the stacks of papers. "There are contracts to sign."

Rias's eyebrows rose. "Contracts?"

"Come, I'll show you." Tikaya led the way into the bower. "That's your stack, so you sit there. And I sit here. When we're all done, the priestess will notarize them, we'll kiss, the audience will cheer, and they'll drink and dance the night away while we're busy making things, as you say, official."

"Your holy person notarizes documents. Sounds like an enlightened religion." Rias eased into the chair, careful not to bump the table with his long legs—he was probably worried the precariously balanced sweets would tumble to the earth.

"Almost everybody in a position of authority can notarize documents here, even the clerks at the adult novelties store. Welcome to the Kyatt Islands."

Rias leafed through the first few papers in the prodigious stack. "It looks like there's something to sign on every page. During these Kyattese weddings, is it typical for the consummation of the marriage to occur on the same night that the festivities start?"

"Not *early* in the night, but eventually." Tikaya decided not to mention the essay portions she'd heard about. "Divorce is frowned upon, so we Kyattese like to make sure young people have time to think things through before they consummate anything."

"I better get started then." Rias removed the cap from his pen and studied the first page. "This probably goes more quickly for people who grew up reading the language."

"I'm not sure how closely the documents get read, regardless." Tikaya patted about, searching for a pen of her own.

One appeared in the air beside her. She lifted a hand, intending to thank Mother, Ell, or whoever was providing it, but found herself looking into her father's eyes. He wore his dark gray dressed-for-the-symphony suit, the only non-plantation clothing he had, and his short hair was damp and freshly combed, his chin shaved clean of stubble. He gave Rias a flat look. It wasn't friendly, but it wasn't antagonistic either. Tikaya swallowed. It was a start.

"Make sure he signs page eighteen," Father said. "That gold won't last forever."

Tikaya smiled and accepted the pen. "I will. Thank you."

While Rias flipped through the pages, no doubt wishing to check what eighteen contained, Tikaya glanced about, searching for Mother, certain she'd had a hand in Father's appearance. She was carrying yet another tray out to the table, though, and seemed startled when she spotted him. With his pen and message delivered, he walked over to join her.

"I must vow to practice my bow and spear skills, thus to ensure I can always deliver a boar to your spit?" Rias asked, summarizing the page's contents.

"My society wishes to ensure its mothers and children are well cared for. Given your physical prowess in other areas, I expect only the finest boars." Tikaya winked.

"Yes, ma'am. I'll do my best."

Tikaya glanced over her shoulder and caught Mother giving Father a hug. "I wonder what made him decide to come," she mused.

Rias said nothing, keeping his head bent over the pages and scribbling initials and signatures in the appropriate spots. Tikaya remembered the look Father had given him.

"You didn't have anything to do with it, did you?"

"I might have spoken to him this morning," Rias said.

"And he *listened*?" Tikaya imagined Rias in there, hands clasped behind his back, sturdily taking the brunt of her father's ire. "Without calling you any derogatory names?"

"Well, he listened. I told him I wanted to see you happy, and that it'd please you to have him here."

"That worked?" She was sure her mother would have already tried that argument, though maybe it meant more coming from the enemy camp.

"I also promised to install the shock absorbers on his runabout," Rias said. "That may have been the tipping point."

Laughing, Tikaya bounced off her chair and wrapped her arms around him. "Thank you. I love you."

He returned the embrace, dropping his chin onto her shoulder to murmur, "Just remember that feeling when the first boar I bring home is scrawny and emaciated."

Before Tikaya could say she doubted he'd be anything less than a superb hunter, Mother's voice interrupted. "Now, now, dear, you know the rules. No physical affection is permitted until *after* both parties have signed the contract."

"Yes, do get back to work, please," Rias said as Tikaya huffed and returned to her chair. "I want to see what sorts of tasks *you're* signing up for over there."

"Hm." Tikaya decided not to mention the last quarter of the contract which contained instructional information on satisfactorily fulfilling bedroom duties. Waiting until marriage to have sex had fallen out of favor in recent generations, but the contract had originally been devised to assist young couples who might lack experience in that area. More entertaining, she decided, to let Rias find that section on his own. If nothing else, it ought to amuse him how thorough her people were with labels and diagrams.

"What're *they* doing here?" Ell asked.

On the road at the edge of the palm tree copse, several elegant runabouts were gliding to a stop. Aides and white-robed men and women stepped out, followed by the president and four high minsters, including Jikaymar and Tosii.

"It seems they've come to ensure the event goes as planned," Tikaya said.

"Not exactly." Rias lifted a hand toward the president and wriggled the pen. "I invited them."

"You, what? *All* of them?"

"My side of the guest list looked a tad sparse." His smile was on the sly side. Sparse, indeed. He might have denied an interest in politicking once, but Tikaya had a feeling he'd be one of the most popular men on the island in five years.

Shrieks of laughter sounded as Lonaeo raced past the bower, chasing after his self-propelled butterfly wagon. Tikaya lifted an eyebrow at Rias. He gazed back blandly.

Five years? It might only take one.

THE END

Also by the Author

Encrypted
Enigma (an interlude between books 1 and 2)
Decrypted (thanks for reading!)

THE EMPEROR'S EDGE UNIVERSE

<u>NOVELS</u>
The Emperor's Edge, Book 1
Dark Currents, Book 2
Deadly Games, Book 3
Conspiracy, Book 4
Blood and Betrayal, Book 5
Beneath the Surface (a novella, but really Book 5.5)
Book 6 (Forged in Blood), coming in 2013

<u>SHORT STORIES</u>
Ice Cracker II (and other short stories)
The Assassin's Curse
Shadows over Innocence (a Sicarius background story)

THE FLASH GOLD CHRONICLES
Flash Gold
Hunted
Peacemaker

THE GOBLIN BROTHERS ADVENTURES

Printed in Great Britain
by Amazon